MW00387491

All Rights Reserved
Copyright © 2013 by Zoe Reed

ISBN-13: 978-1490595177
ISBN-10: 1490595171

www.facebook.com/Author.ZoeReed

Acknowledgements

As always, I owe an enormous deal of thanks to Nicholaus Williams, who's always so quick, diligent, and thorough in the work he does for me that publishing would seem an almost impossible task without him. I must also give a grateful shout out to my mother, Jenny, and her wonderful wife, Lisa, for always giving their most thoughtful input to my late-night questions of "how does this sound" or "what do you think of that". Publishing is never a one-man job, and I wouldn't have been able to do it without you guys.

Phantoms of
the Otherworld

Contents

Preface

Greg sat on the park bench in his black suit and tie and stared out over the dark river in Portland, Oregon. The moonlight glittered silver and white over the small ridges of the current, and the breeze carried the sweet smell of the water to his nose. His mouth turned up in a sad, reminiscent smile as he remembered all the fond memories of his mother bringing he and his siblings here when they were young. Every Saturday they packed a picnic basket of fruit, cheese, and a loaf of bread. Half the loaf always went to the hungry ducks, which, after weeks of visits, grew comfortable enough to eat from their hands. He wiped a tear from his cheek. Having just left his mother's funeral, this was where he wanted her memory to lie.

Standing up, Greg grabbed the lotus flowers and small urn from off the bench next to him and walked to the canal's edge. He and each of his siblings had been given a bit of his mother's ashes to either keep or rest in a place of fondness. Reaching the stone lining of the water, he knelt and unscrewed the vine-patterned lid, taking a last, long look at the stars reflected on the glassy garnish of the channel. He slowly cascaded the water with the ashes before laying the lilies on the surface and saying a last goodbye.

A small breeze picked up as he rose, and even through his thick overcoat the hairs on his arms and neck stood on end. At first he thought it was the breeze, but he was used to the cold. It was something else. He felt like he was being watched. He twisted to squint into the darkness, and after a minute of staring the feeling of paranoia subsided, and he shook off the chill.

With a final look across the water, Greg turned and started his walk home. Or was he going home? Going home to be alone. Granted, it was getting late, but home was the last place he wanted to be. The nearest bar was a bit farther of a walk than his house, but it was one he could tough out. While he meandered he hummed a sad tune to himself, giving small smiles to the few passersby. A couple blocks later he waited for a taxi to pass before crossing the street, and then headed toward the bar at the end of the road.

Except for the lights outside the bar and the dim lamps that seemed to randomly litter the way, it was dark. Perhaps the darkest street he'd strolled yet. He laughed while, as he strode toward the bar, he could see a couple of drunkards goofing off outside, making fools of themselves for the attention of a girl that leaned against the wall. After a few more steps he recognized one of them as an old family friend.

Greg was about to holler his friend's name when he stopped walking and turned his head. Down the alley to his left he could hear crying. It sounded like a woman.

"Hello?" The feeling of paranoia returned, his hairs again standing on end, but he told himself to man up. This girl could be hurt. "Hello," he called again, greeted still by the quiet sobbing.

Pulling out his cell phone, he used it to illuminate the way into the dark alley. He was about halfway through when he could see a small woman leaned against the front of a large trash bin. Her knees were pulled up to her chest and she had her arms wrapped around them, sobbing with her head down.

"Hey, are you okay?" He continued forward cautiously until he was standing directly in front of her. The small, pale, blonde looked up at him with bright, tear-filled blue eyes. "Are you hurt?" He knelt beside her and waited patiently for her to answer. Through the stench of the garbage he could smell what he assumed was her – a sweet, vanilla aroma that flooded his senses, and in any other situation he might've made an attempt at flirting.

"No," she answered in a soft voice, barely audible.

"What's your name?"

The woman looked up at him shyly, boring into his eyes before she answered, "Cynthia."

He carefully held out his hand for her to take, and then helped lift her off the ground. "Well, Cynthia, let's get you out of here?"

She nodded and let him lead her toward the entrance of the alley. They were about twenty feet from the street when a man stepped in front of them, blocking their exit. Greg hesitated for a split second before confidently leading Cynthia forward.

"Excuse me sir." He stared at the ground and tried to politely side-step the man, who moved again into his path.

Greg looked up into the man's eyes. He wasn't tall, about the same height as Greg, who was only five foot nine himself. Nor was he muscular. But his dark eyes stood out against his pale skin, and conveyed a cold emptiness that sent a shiver down Greg's spine. He felt Cynthia's grip tighten on his arm, and assuming she was afraid he tried to sidestep the man again. He soon realized Cynthia wasn't clutching him for comfort. She was making sure he didn't go anywhere, holding him in place, and she held onto him with an almost supernatural strength. His heart skipped, and an overwhelming knot of fear settled in his gut. He frantically shook his arm free of the girl, and took a step backward while his eyes darted from side to side, deciding which way he'd have the biggest chance of escaping if he needed to bolt.

Cynthia greeted the man with a smile, and took stride beside him as they advanced on Greg, pushing him farther and farther into the alley. As he realized his only escape route was blocked, his mind started racing. His brothers, his sister, his father, would he never see them again? The newspapers. His mind flashed to the local paper. Over the past few weeks there had been a spike in the number of kidnappings, and not just women – men, some of them large men. His back hit a wall as he reached the end of the alley, and the two continued to close in on him. Both Cynthia and the man smiled evil grins, sharp, bright white teeth glowing in the dark night. Against the cold air he felt something hot run down his leg, and seconds later the stench of urine reached his nose.

"Coward." The frightening man's deep, ringing voice cut through the silence as he chuckled.

Greg tried to think of anything else but this. To turn his mind somewhere happy, somewhere he could escape to, but it returned to the newspaper. How many people had been reported missing? Eleven, and not a single body or survivor had been found. He closed his eyes and felt a cold hand press hard against his mouth, stopping him if he tried to scream. Eleven people had been taken, and he would be the twelfth.

1

Crouched as low to the ground as I could get in the Dolan's wheat field, I held my breath against the cold night and pricked my wolf ears forward. No more than thirty feet in front of me I could hear the tiniest crackling of semi-frozen twigs in rhythm with a slow stride. With minimal progression I crawled a few paces, using the weight of my body to muffle any crackling sounds I may have made with my own paws. The rustling was getting closer. Luckily what little breeze that blew wasn't coming from behind me. I was hunkered downwind, and my scent wasn't going anywhere near my target. Not only was the wind on my side, but I also had the advantage of camouflage – my golden brown fur matched perfectly with the wheat.

Just a little closer... I urged my mark to take the last few steps that would bring it in striking distance. *Finally.* Teeth flashed in a wolfish grin as my back and shoulders tensed, paws digging into the dirt, preparing for the pounce. The rustling stopped, as if detecting my presence. Releasing all the tension in my muscles I leapt, the white wolf noticing me a second too late. I crashed down on its back, sending us tumbling through the field. I had the upper hand in catching it off guard, but because the wolf was smaller and had so much more experience it was able to wriggle out of my grasp and knock me off my clumsy feet, pinning me to the ground.

A big smile reached Luna's hazel eyes, as she remained champion. I gave a defeated sigh and rolled out from under her hold. I understood now why Camille had so many tiny scars on her arms. While Luna and I had only been play fighting and romping around for less than a minute, I could already feel the slight sting of a few bite marks on my limbs. I instinctively ran my tongue down one front leg, too busy cleaning my little wounds to notice Luna, who came running at me, lightheartedly but roughly head-butting me and sending me rolling in the opposite direction. I heard the crashing of her paws disappearing across the field and swiftly got up to bound after her.

Upon bursting out of the wheat field I could see the blur of white sprinting ahead of me. I was closer than I thought. I jammed my paws harder into the ground, pushing forward with more powerful strides to try and catch up. It wasn't long until I nearly did, and with one last strike I crouched and sprung into the air, flying at the white wolf. But the second I jumped the wolf hit the brakes, and I went soaring over Luna's head only to hit the ground ahead of her, spiraling repeatedly head over heels. Once I finished wheeling across the dirt and came to a stop Luna pranced over, jumping and nipping at me gloatingly. The smaller wolf stopped when I growled at her, and a blink later took off, leaving me to chase once again. It required all my strength to catch up, but instead of pouncing when I did I just ran at my companion's side.

It didn't take long until we were in our own field of grape vines, and a minute later we sauntered onto the front porch, gulping frosty air into our burning lungs. I casually trotted to the clothes I had folded and laid on the deck and which now, as I touched them with my nose, I could feel were as freezing as the air.

Luna had promptly Changed back, and was already pulling on her own icy clothes. "Got to love winter, huh?"

I huffed my sarcastic agreement and then Phased. Without my thick fur to keep me warm I could already feel the cold seeping to my bones, and pulling on frigid clothes didn't help one bit.

"You're really getting good," Luna praised excitedly as I followed her into the kitchen of her house.

"Eh," I shook my head humbly. "You're still the champ. I can't even keep you on the ground long enough to pin you."

"Hey, Camille," Luna greeted her twin sister, who was rummaging through the refrigerator, as she sat at the table and shrugged with equal modesty. "Yeah, but I didn't even hear you coming. Once you get better at your pinning technique, you'll be unstoppable!"

"Where'd you guys go?" Camille sat down at the table with us, directing her question more at Luna than at me.

I avoided making eye contact with her, knowing she probably wouldn't look at me anyway, and instead glanced at the smaller of the twins. It had been two months since I'd been Changed, and Camille still hadn't forgiven me for having to break up with her. I understood that it had to have been painful for her, and assumed that maybe she was afraid of it happening again. While I was willing to wait the rest of my long life for her to forgive me, I'd been hoping I wouldn't have to.

Over the past months it was Camille who'd been teaching me how to control my Changes. Even though we'd slowly been recuperating our relationship to friendship, it was still awkward between us. I could admit it was due in large part to my mood swings and angry outbursts. Being a werewolf made all my emotions and instincts more acute, and while I learned how to control them I was prone to frustration tantrums. Unfortunately for Camille and I's relationship, it was almost always her who was at the receiving end of my fits.

I tried to hide a frown as I remembered one of my worst spells. I'd learned to Phase when I wanted to, but couldn't stop it when I didn't want to. Camille had been trying to get me close to the edge when I lost control of myself. Because she thought I had more restraint than I really did, she didn't back up in time, and I bit her on the hand. I'd let go as quickly as I could when I realized how out of line I'd been, but the damage was done, and she'd needed stitches. I'd almost died of guilt, and wanted so badly for her to bite back sometime, or at the very least get mad. But she'd just shrugged it off and said we'd try again in a few days.

My eyes led me to the pink scar on the back of Camille's hand. Even though it was a couple weeks ago, the mark still appeared fresh. Or maybe it was my mind playing tricks on me, amping up the damage so I'd have a reasonable symbol of my guilt. Her hand disappeared under the table, and I looked up to see that she'd caught me staring at it. I stiffly cleared my throat and stood to get a glass of water.

"You really should've come this time, Cami." Luna was still talking about our night as I sat back down. "Kyla's getting really good. I bet she could hold her own even against you."

Camille let the corner of her mouth turn up halfway in praise, and I realized it had been an entire two months since I'd seen a real smile, one that spread beyond those perfect pink lips to her dark brown eyes.

"I think you can go home in a couple days," she told me. That perked me up immediately, and couldn't help but grin. "You have to make sure you run at least every other day, but your uncontrolled Changes are happening less often. I think you're ready."

My joy disappeared as more guilt raided my emotional privacy. The night a deranged mutt named Jonathan had kidnapped me, he'd forged a note from me to my parents, telling them I'd run away. I'd passed by my house on runs, snuck close to catch a fleeting glimpse of a family member, but they hadn't seen me. I hadn't spoken to them or left any clues as to where I was, and this whole time I'd been not even ten minutes away. After months of no contact, knowing the trouble I'd get in for leaving and how much of a struggle it would be to be back home, the idea made me antsy as hell.

Both Camille and Luna were looking at me concernedly, as my anxiety must have been etched on my face. "I'm just nervous. I know I'll be in a lot of trouble." In my apprehension I busily fidgeted with my fingers.

"Maybe, but I know they'll be really happy that you're okay," Camille offered reassuringly.

"And they'll be even happier you're okay so they can kill you themselves," Luna nodded her agreement, trying in her own sarcastic way to make me feel better.

"Oh, that's something to look forward to, thanks," I laughed, rolling my eyes.

Luna shrugged indifferently and got up to stretch. "I'm going to bed. Night ladies."

Both Camille and I said 'goodnight,' and then sat there in a moment of semi-awkward silence. We both stood at the same time, chuckling nervously as the tension thickened. To avoid even more strain, I motioned toward the door for her to leave first, and then followed her into the living room. While she sat on the couch and flipped through television channels I walked to the large bookshelf on the far side of the room. The whole time I'd lived with Camille's family, I hadn't even noticed the books until now.

Nearly all of them were old, and I took in a deep breath of the rich, musty smell they gave off. Running my finger along the spines, I silently mouthed the titles until I reached one that spurred my interest. *The Underworld Omnibus.* I pulled the large volume from the shelf, and as I opened the cover I plopped down onto the couch. Camille's body tensed when I landed closer than I'd expected to her, and after an embarrassed and apologetic smile I scooted a couple inches over.

It took a moment for me to recover from pulling myself away because it made me realize how much I missed being close to her, and pushing back the deep sense of longing rising in me, I flipped through the first couple pages. Each of the leathery pieces of paper was thick, and if not for the yellowing crisp of old age they'd have been strong and flexible. Going through the table of contents, I read what seemed to be a categorized list. *Deities, page 5. Demons, page 98.* I continued reading until a section caught my eye. *The Undead, page 387.* Turning to page 387, I skimmed through until I found what I was looking for. Vampires. I'd heard about vampires in stories and movies, but I never thought they could be real. Of course, a few months ago I wouldn't have thought werewolves existed either.

"Camille?" I waited for her to raise her eyebrows questioningly. "Are vampires real too?"

"Mhm," she mumbled the affirmative, and with a click she flipped to the next channel.

I looked over the picture of the vampire in the book, and studied what seemed to be an exaggerated drawing. The humanly creature was wearing ancient, tattered formal wear. Two large, pointed wings stemmed farther than both arm-spans from each side of its back, and it smiled so that its sharp fangs flashed menacingly. "Have you ever met one?"

"No," she answered, and I could see her give a concealed glance my direction. "Why?"

"I was just wondering. They're in this book." I held up the text so Camille could see the picture. "Are we really mortal enemies with them?"

She chuckled, shaking her head. "No, but we're not best of friends either. I'd say it's more of a," she paused thoughtfully, "You do your thing and I'll do mine, and we'll try not to cross paths kind of a relationship."

"Oh." I yawned and closed the book. Phasing seemed to take more energy out of me when it was cold out. "Well, goodnight. We'll practice Changing more tomorrow?"

Camille nodded and said 'goodnight,' and I trudged up the stairs to her bedroom. Since I'd been staying here Camille had given up her room for me and moved in with Luna. I felt bad for having kicked her out, but even though I missed her, I preferred it to the tension between us. Closing the door behind me, I started stripping my clothing, then stopped to look at myself in the mirror. I slowly gazed down my torso to the scar under my left breast, and twisted to look at the same one on my back. I don't know where the bullet had gone after Jonathan shot me, but when I was bitten the werewolf gene left me with a nice blemish to remind me of the pain. Holding up my hand, I studied the two small, round scars on my palm, then flipped my hand to look at the matching two on the other side. They weren't very big, but I did wish Luna had bitten me in a more inconspicuous place. I rarely wore gloves, and so the bite-marks would be ever-present and visible.

After pulling on my pajamas I lay down on the bed and buried my face in the pillows and sheets, inhaling as deeply as I could. Camille's scent was long gone from the covers, but it didn't stop me from trying. With a gloomy sigh I grabbed the extra pillow and set it beside me, wrapping my arm around it and trying to trick myself into believing there was a warm body with me. That Camille was there with me.

During the day, with all the distractions and people around, I could push the memories out of my mind. But in the dark I relived the nightmare of when Luna and I had been kidnapped, the night that ruined everything. Even after I'd fall asleep the demons would find me. A couple times right after the event Luna or Camille had come into the room, disturbed from sleep by my yelling or knocking things off the bedside table. The severity and frequency of the terrors lessened every day, but if it wasn't those that kept me up, it was Camille.

The first couple weeks as her scent faded from the bed, it got harder and harder to fall asleep, and now that it was gone it was almost impossible. I could no longer fool myself into believing I wasn't alone. Adjusting to being a werewolf wasn't easy, and even though I had enthusiastic help, I was completely and utterly alone. Luna was the only member of the Zade family who wasn't at all tense around me because of what happened with Camille. The others tried not to let it show since I didn't really have a choice in the matter, but I could feel it, there was soreness toward me for hurting her. The only time I felt like I might actually belong in this world was on a run, which was strange to me seeing as it was the wolf's fault I was in this situation in the first place.

Eventually I managed to drift off, and woke the next morning with the pillow in the same place under my arm. I could hear Camille's parents downstairs, talking in the kitchen, and the savory scent of bacon wafted up to me. The only thing that got me to slide out of bed and make my way down the stairs was the promise of food; otherwise I would have been too tired to move. When I got to the kitchen, an equally pleasing smell rivaled the aroma of bacon – coffee. I grinned as I grabbed a cup and sat down at the table.

"Good morning, Kyla," Camille's mom greeted me while Camille's dad smiled his hello.

"Morning, Rachel. Good morning, Adrian." I took a sip of my coffee and then pushed it forward so I could lay my head on the wooden surface under my cup.

Adrian sat down across from me, propping his head up with his arm. "Didn't sleep too well?" Lifting my head, I shook it, and he nodded in understanding. "Me either. Are you and Camille working more today on controlling your Changes?"

"Yeah, I think so," I affirmed, taking another sip of coffee. "It's just so hard, and she's being so patient."

Rachel set a plate in front of both Adrian and I, and then scooped mounds of bacon and eggs onto each. "From what Luna describes, you're adjusting very well. Don't be too hard on yourself."

I smiled my thanks and began to shovel down food. I had my dish nearly cleaned when Luna and Camille walked in and sat on either side of me, both of their groggy eyes only half open. I sat there silently while they ate, eyes darting from Camille to anywhere else in the room.

"I can't wait until you can go home and come back to school." Luna paused from eating just long enough to look up at me. "Math sucks without you."

"You're still bringing me homework," I reminded her sourly. "It's like I haven't missed a day."

Niko walked in then, and ruffled my hair before grabbing a plate and saying good morning.

"Morning Niko," I greeted him, smoothing my hair back into place.

"Don't bother." He came to sit down at the table and ruffled my hair again. "You've got bed head anyway."

I gave him a light-hearted glare while he started to scarf down his food, and fixed my hair regardless. Niko had always been somewhat wary of me, but since I'd been Changed and living at their house he'd become more comfortable with me, and now he treated me like he did Camille and Luna. Sometimes, usually when Camille was around, he toned down the playfulness our relationship had gained. I'd even caught her scowling at him for it a couple times. It seemed this morning, however, he was in too good a mood to care.

I laid my head back down on the table until I had to lift it to say goodbye as everyone left for school, after which I laid it back down for another five minutes. The house grew strangely quiet while no one was there. Of course Adrian worked from home, and Rachel didn't work at all, but they were off doing their own thing, and I was left in the kitchen with the penetrating silence. Sighing, I pulled myself off the table and back up the stairs to Camille's room. I threw open my math book and started on the homework Luna had brought home for me last week. I wasn't even sure if my teachers would accept the work when I eventually went back, but at least I was learning, and wouldn't be too far behind when I did.

Writing down the first problem, I read the directions. *Solve the complex equation.* I set up the equation by carefully reading the directions in the textbook, and then stared at it, confused. 'i' is the square root of negative 1? I thought there was no such thing. I read the example from the book, and copied the steps to solve the problem before checking the answer in the back. Wrong. I huffed as I erased my work, and read the directions again before starting over. Again I solved the equation and checked the back of the book. Still wrong.

I growled at my book and shut it, frustrated and not in the mood to feel like a failure today. I needed to be back in class, back with my family, back with Camille. Everything was mixed up and today was already going badly. *Typical Monday*. The itching started in my fingers while my frustration grew, so I stood up from the desk and took a deep breath, shaking my hand to try and rid it of the feeling. It took a minute, but after a few tapering inhales the itching subsided, and I grinned triumphantly. I'd stopped the Change. But my grin faded as I remembered it wasn't the first time, and I'd only been slightly upset. I couldn't *really* stop a Change.

With a groan of defeat I turned on the radio and lay down on the bed. The strumming of the guitar made me miss my own instrument. I hadn't been able to go to my house and get it because it was too risky, so during the hardest period of my life I'd been without my favorite and most relaxing hobby. Nor had I been able to go anywhere public for the past two months. Or talk to anyone about my problems. It was mostly Camille I needed to talk about, but I especially couldn't confide in any one of *her* family members.

The prickling started to return as a heavy bit of cabin fever made me grow restless. Standing up again, I slammed my hand down on the 'off' button of the radio. I couldn't do a damned thing without getting that aggravating itch. I stomped irately down the stairs and out the front door. I needed some fresh air.

"Hey, Kyla." Adrian looked up from under the hood of his SUV, and waved when he saw me come out.

I couldn't help but smile at the sight of his dirt-streaked face, and I was relieved when it abated the tingling. Dirty really didn't suit him. "What are you doing?"

"This hunk of junk won't run, and I'm trying to figure out why." He turned to lean against the front while I poked a curious head over the engine.

"I didn't know you knew anything about cars," I said as I mindlessly reached out to wiggle a random hose, lured by the idea of a distraction.

"I don't," he admitted, laughing embarrassedly. "Well, not much anyway, but I got this manual and I figured now's a good time to learn."

He raised the thick book about cars in his hands, and then held it out to me. "Want to help?"

I nodded, grateful for something to do, and took the book to read some instructions. "It won't start?" Adrian shook his head. I 'hm-ed' and flipped through the pages. "Does it want to start?"

He leaned his elbows casually over the edge of the open front end, still looking like he was trying to figure it out. "Yeah, it tries to start, but won't."

"So it's not the battery," I read aloud while skimming through to the next page.

Adrian moved to glance over my shoulder. "Where on earth did you read that?"

"There," I flipped back and pointed, giggling at his shock. "And you have gas in it right?"

"Yes, there's gas in it," he chuckled sarcastically.

I continued to scan the pages. *Fuel pump.* That sounds important. I read the next section and then showed Adrian the page. "Sound familiar?"

"The fuel pump, huh?" he asked, looking over the engine of the car. "Where's that at?"

Shifting to the back of the book, I looked over a diagram of a similar SUV, staring hard until I saw it. "Oh." I stood over the vehicle and searched around before pointing to the part. "That's it, right there."

He squinted, pulling himself farther over the edge. "That little thing?" he asked, motioning to it.

I shrugged obscurely, "Looks like it."

Shaking his head in disbelief, Adrian shut the hood. "Whatever you say, chief. I'll have to wait for Niko to get home so I can take his jeep and pick up a new one." I nodded my understanding and handed him back the manual. "How's your homework going?"

My face twisted with disgust. "It's hard. I was going to wait for Luna to get home and help me."

"Cars may not be my thing, but math I can do," he laughed, and waved for me to follow him back into the house. "Why don't you bring it down and I'll see if I can help."

Smiling my thanks, I ran up the stairs to grab my homework, and then met Adrian at the kitchen table. He helped me for hours until everyone finally returned home from school, and studying with him made me realize where Camille got her patience. I grew frustrated and had wanted to give up multiple times, but Adrian sat calmly and explained it to me until I understood it. I had only a few problems left of the whole week's assignment when Camille and Luna walked into the kitchen. I waited for them both to get something to eat before asking if it was time for my control practice. Camille nodded, and I followed her to the backyard. While I stood facing her, Luna sat and leaned against the house. Over the past months while Camille had been helping me, Luna watched carefully and acted only when she was needed – usually when I lost my temper.

"How do you want to do it today?" Camille asked, shoving her hands in her pockets and scanning the ground while she waited for me to answer. She rarely even looked me in the eyes when she was talking to me.

"I don't know." I thought about it. "I guess I'll start to Change and then try to stop it?"

"Okay," she said, absentmindedly kicking at the gravel beneath her feet. After a few seconds she added, "Can you do it with distractions?"

I had already started building the itching in my fingers and toes. Confused, I widened my curious eyes at her. "Distractions?"

"Yeah. It's not always going to be nice and peaceful like this when you need to stop a Change." She started walking in deliberate circles around me.

"Okay. What kind of distractions?" The sensation spread to my limbs, and I could feel it getting nearer to my core.

"Let me know when you're on the edge." She continued her circles, ignoring me all except for the fact that she was maneuvering around me.

"I am." The itching turned to tingling, and I clenched my fists to try and slow it. Camille moved to stand right in front of me, and without warning slapped me hard across the cheek. I couldn't help but laugh at how startled I was by it. I should have expected it – it wasn't the first time. "You really like slapping me, don't you?"

"Why?" she asked, her dark brown eyes finally meeting my own. Despite the teasing tone of her voice, I could see by the pain in her eyes that she really didn't like it. "Does it make you mad?"

"Maybe a little," I admitted, already wincing as I braced myself for another smack. It came seconds later.

Even though I was expecting it, trying to focus on stopping the Change *and* subside the slight rage that rose with each slap was hard to do. I couldn't completely get rid of it, but I was at least getting it under control.

I stood stiff, hands clenched at my sides and waiting for another one when Camille moved behind me. She pressed on the back of my leg, causing my knee to buckle and me to crumble to the ground. I stood back up only to find her waiting for it. She pushed on my other leg, and it sent me falling back down. I growled in frustration, grimacing as the tingling became unbearable again.

"Come on, Kyla, you can stop it," she encouraged, still waiting behind me. I stayed kneeling on the ground, trying to recover before I could get back up only to be knocked down again. Instead of waiting she strolled to my side and knelt with me. "You're never going home if you can't control it."

I knew she was only saying it to get a rise out of me, to give me something to fight against, but it still made me furious. I turned my head to glare at her, and she only looked back with a blank apathy. I was about to stand back up when she pushed me sideways, all the way over, and stepped back. Tumbling to the ground I rolled, and sprang up snarling. I clenched my teeth. I was so close to Phasing that even the smallest thing would set me off. Taking slow, deep breaths, I tried to calm myself, fearing another outburst that might lead to stitches.

"Stop the Change, Kyla!" Camille commanded, purposefully yelling to try and distract me. Luna stood up, ready to intervene if needed.

A combination of the burning in my limbs and the frustration she was causing made my temper flare. I lost it. "I didn't ask for this shit, Camille! Just give me a goddamned second!" The moment I shouted the words, I wished I hadn't. Camille flinched and stared at the ground, clearly too hurt or shocked to try and hide it. The guilt did the trick. The tingling in my body rapidly subsided, but I didn't care. I would have rather lost control than ever yell at her like that. Than ever make her think I didn't want this. "I didn't mean that."

"You're right, you didn't ask for it." She shook her head, glancing up to meet my eyes for a split second before looking away again. "I've forgotten how hard it is. You and Luna should run." With that she turned and walked back into the house.

I stood there frozen, eyes darting from the door to Luna. Luna did the same, unsure of what to say. "Luna, I'm sorry. You know I don't wish for one second that you hadn't Changed me, right?"

"I know." She shrugged nonchalantly, seemingly unmoved by my blow. "But I'm not the one you need to apologize to."

I nodded in agreement and started toward the house. I found Camille in the kitchen, along with Niko and her mom, rummaging through a cupboard. When I walked in Niko looked at me, and Rachel avoided eye contact at all costs. I knew they'd heard me yell, and because they knew I came in to apologize they gradually cleared out to leave me alone with Camille.

"Cami?" I spoke softly, taking a couple steps forward into the kitchen. I saw her shoulders rise with a deep breath before she turned from the cupboard and took a seat at the table. I sat across from her, staring at the surface in shame. "I'm sorry."

I looked up to her face and expected to see some anger, but there wasn't the slightest bit of it, none whatsoever. Instead, she'd plastered on an expressionless appearance, skillfully hiding her emotions. If I didn't know her so well I'd have missed the small amount of agony that managed to expose itself in her eyes. It had been obvious to me these past months that she felt guilty I was here. That she thought it was her fault I got dragged into this life.

"I didn't mean to yell at you like that," I told her sincerely. "I didn't mean any of it, and I'm really sorry."

She managed a small smile, almost as fake as the apathy on her face. "It's okay. Don't worry about it."

"No, it's not okay." I wanted so badly to reach out and touch her hand, to show her how truly sorry I was. "I made it seem like I don't want to be a werewolf, but that's not true. I don't regret that Luna Changed me." Camille's eyebrows furrowed for a brief second before she dropped the seemingly confused expression. "It's just, sometimes this isn't as fun for me as it is for you."

"I don't like doing this to you, Kyla," she said despairingly. "Hurting you isn't fun for me," and when she spoke that time, that's when I could hear how she truly felt. The pain was heartbreaking, and no matter how hard I tried I just couldn't keep from wounding her. "I don't want you to fail. I want you to go home as much as you do."

She wasn't looking at me, but I still had to glance away so she wouldn't see how much that stung. "That's not what I meant," I whispered disappointedly.

I knew I deserved that and more for the ways I'd been treating her, but she'd taken what I said the wrong way. I gave her a few seconds to think about how I really meant it. After that I knew she understood, because the corner of her mouth turned up apologetically. She didn't say anything though, and it made me wonder if she'd meant what she said anyway. That she really did want me to go home so she wouldn't have to see me so much. That thought hurt even more, but I decided to let it go. Maybe because I didn't want to hear that pain in her voice anymore, or maybe because I just didn't really want to know if it was true.

"If it's any consolation," I started, changing the subject back to my own apology. "Feeling guilty about yelling at you stopped the Change."

"Glad I could help." Camille gave the tiniest huff of sympathetic laughter, and a wave of relief washed over me that at least she didn't sound cheerless anymore. "Do me a favor though, and let's not make it a habit."

"I can't make any promises, but I'll do my best," I told her honestly. "Can I really go home soon?"

"Yeah, but remember to Change as often as you can," she said, her voice growing serious. "Just call here and one of us will go with you."

I nodded. I knew I had to Change often, and I also knew I shouldn't go running alone. Not because I was in danger, but because I was still so new to it. If my instincts took over someone could get hurt.

We sat there for a minute in silence, me thinking about what to say and Camille glancing around uncomfortably. I'd wanted so badly to make amends with her so we could fix our relationship, but I never got her alone. Now might be my only chance. I watched her for a second, waiting until I could catch her darting eyes. Then her stare met mine, and our gazes lingered long enough for me to open my mouth, preparing to start the difficult conversation. She must have read my mind though, because the second I opened my mouth she stood awkwardly.

"I, um," she hesitated, tapping her fingers thoughtfully against the surface of the table, and once more refusing to look right at me, and that agony was once more reinstated in her tone. "I still have homework."

Before she could dart out of the kitchen, Luna came in impatiently with her hands on her hips. "Can we go now? It's starting to get really cold and the sun's going down soon." I glimpsed the time on the clock – it was already five. I got up to follow Luna out, but she stood there watching Camille. "Are you going to come?"

Camille looked thoughtfully from Luna to me, and, especially because she'd just avoided my attempt at talking about us, I expected her to decline. To my surprise, and much to my joy, she nodded and moved to go with us. The only other time she'd gone running with us was the first time I Phased. Even though I usually tried to give her space and time to forgive me, I was excited for her to see how far I'd come.

Stepping onto the porch, each of us stripped and then Phased. Being the last to finish, I looked around for where Camille and Luna had gone, and found them play fighting on the side of the house. Once they saw that I was ready to go, the two wolves took off across the farm, and I gladly followed. It felt so good to Change after having to stop it, and it felt even better to be on good enough terms with Camille for her to go running with us. It was a start at repairing our relationship, even if she wouldn't really talk to me, and it filled me with hope that soon we'd be back to the way we were. Running also gave me an excuse to be close to her, and I ran as close to her side as I could, my tongue hanging happily out of my mouth. Soon.

"Hey, Kyla, wake up." Camille lightly shook me by the shoulder. "Are you ready to go home?"

I groaned and sat up lazily, shielding my eyes from the light pouring through the open window until Camille graciously pulled the shades halfway shut. I would finally be going home today, and I had never been more nervous for anything in my life. I'd been up almost all night fretting over it, running through every 'what if' I could think of, and it seemed that I'd only just fallen asleep minutes ago.

After stretching I got out of bed and looked around the room. Since I'd been here I'd mostly been sharing clothes with Camille and Luna, and because I didn't go anywhere in human form my requirement for a variety of options was limited. What few items I owned personally lay scattered around the room. A pair of jeans draped across the desk chair. A couple wrinkled t-shirts and undergarments thrown into the corner.

While I walked around and shoved my stuff into my backpack, Camille took my jacket off the nightstand and sat on the bed, anxiously wringing the article in her hands. "Are you sure you're ready?"

I took a last glance around the room, and then pulled on the jacket Camille handed me. If I didn't know any better, I'd say it kind of sounded like she didn't want me to leave, and hearing that tone from her was starting to give me second thoughts. Not only was I unsure of if I was ready or not, but I feared that if I wasn't living at the Zade house our relationship would dwindle to nothing.

"No," I admitted, plopping down beside her. "But my family needs to know I'm okay."

She nodded in hesitant agreement, and we sat there for a minute in silence before Niko yelled up at us to hurry because they had to leave for school. I stood and studied Camille's face, as she hadn't yet gotten up. She was worried, that much was obvious, but there was something more. Reluctance? Before I got a chance to ask about it she stood and walked to the door, making her usual exit before I could have a real conversation with her.

I followed her out, and we both hopped into the jeep with Niko and Luna. Before Niko drove off I took a final gander at the large house I'd spent the last two months in. The old porch swing on the side of the wooden deck, the creaky screen door that was almost always open and was releasing light out into the dim morning, straight down to the fading white exterior paint that desperately needed a new coat. Even if I didn't feel completely at home here, I'd grown to love it all.

On the drive to my house nobody spoke. All of us hardly breathed. I had no idea how my family would react to me coming home. If they'd be happy, or sad, or furious. Or even want me back at all. I could only imagine the pain that I'd caused, and while I hadn't written the runaway note in the first place, I *had* chosen to stay at Camille's all this time.

Niko stopped the car at the end of my long driveway, and we all sat for another minute before any of us spoke. During the silence I studied each of my comrades. I could hear every one of their hearts racing along with my own, each of them nervous for me. I'd expected as much from Camille and Luna, but I was pleasantly surprised that Niko was bothered to see me go. He was always the first to fight and the last to show he had any emotions. If he hadn't grown so playful with me over the past eight weeks I'd have thought for the rest of my life that he simply didn't like me.

"Are you sure you don't want me to go with you?" Camille warily looked past me to the house at the end of the small road.

"I should do this on my own." I followed her gaze and suddenly felt sick. I was scared. Regardless of whether or not I had parents and siblings of my own, Camille's family were all I'd known lately, and I didn't understand why this felt like goodbye. Would my real family even want me back?

Not knowing what else to say, I smiled my goodbye and opened the car door. After closing it behind me I stood and stared at the house for a good three minutes before taking a step forward. Then I heard the jeep sluggishly pull away behind me, and I continued to walk up the driveway. It was slow going. My nerves threatened to buckle my knees beneath me. The house seemed to grow substantially larger every step I took. The gray-stone exterior had never seemed so frighteningly dark, and the white trim never so blindingly bright.

From the front I could see a light on upstairs, and the kitchen light from downstairs, but other than that the house was black. Finally, I reached the porch, from where I could hear someone in the kitchen doing dishes. My knees shook more and more violently the closer I got to the front door, until eventually I stood directly in front of it, feeling lightheaded. I turned the handle and walked in, cautiously and quietly making my way to the kitchen.

I stopped in the doorway. My mom stood there, still in her purple, cloud-patterned silk pajamas. Her back was turned at the sink and she hadn't heard me walk in. "Mom." I barely got the words out. She froze for a moment as if hearing a ghost, and then shook her head in disbelief and returned to the dishes. I took a couple steps forward and mustered the courage to speak louder. "Mom."

Haltingly, my mother looked over her shoulder, and seeing me standing there instantly turned, staring. I felt tears stinging my eyes, mirroring the water welling up in hers. "Hi, Mom." I managed a small, nervous smile.

My mom looked exhausted and hopeless. Her normally brilliant blue eyes were dim and empty, surrounded by deep age lines and dark circles. It was like she hadn't slept a single minute the whole time I was gone.

"Kyla?" Her voice broke into a near sob as she took a few unsteady steps forward and covered her mouth with her hand. "Is it really you?"

When I nodded she rushed forth and pulled me into her arms. I dropped my backpack to the floor and wrapped my own arms around her waist, taking in a deep breath. The wonderfully comforting smell that flooded my nose caused tears to stream freely down my cheeks. Not only did my mom look tired beyond belief, she felt frail. She'd always been a thin woman, but she'd lost a lot of weight, and she felt fragile in my strong embrace. She pulled away to look at me, mouth opening and closing in a speechless stupor. Her fingertips hovered over my face, like she was afraid to touch me and find I was only an apparition. A few seconds later she gently touched my forehead, then my cheekbones, she pushed my hair behind my ears, and traced my jawline.

"Are you–where–you look so healthy. You're not hurt? Oh my God, we thought we'd never see you again." Her voice broke again into heavy sobs, and she pulled me into another tight clutch.

"I'm okay, Mom. I'm okay," I assured her, patiently letting her hug me for as long as she needed to.

Pulling away promptly, she looked at me again, and this time she seemed angry. "Where the hell have you been? Do you know how worried we've been?" Guess she hadn't forgotten I'd run away in the first place.

I stared at the floor, my face burning bright red, embarrassed and unsure of what to say. I could never answer the question truthfully. "I'm sorry. I'm back now."

I heard footsteps from behind me, and seconds later the scent of my oldest brother, Jeremy, reached my nose. I turned to look at him and grinned. "Hey, J."

"Holy-" His jaw dropped, eyes wide with confusion and disbelief. After a minute of staring he grinned, grabbed me in his arms, and lifted me two feet into the air, spinning me around happily. Setting me back down on the ground, he stepped back and looked at me concernedly. "Are you back? You're not going anywhere right?"

"No," I shook my head, laughing for lack of a better reaction. "I'm not going anywhere."

Jeremy directed me to the island in the middle of the kitchen, and we sat down beside each other. While I was greeting him my mom had picked up the phone and called my dad.

Hanging up, she turned and studied me for a moment, still unsure of whether I was really there or not. Or maybe she was unsure of whether or not to be pissed. "Your father and uncle were in town running errands. They're coming home now. Are you hungry? How about a sandwich?"

I nodded and smiled my thanks. While I ate I could feel all eyes on me, watching and studying, as if waiting for me to disappear. My other brother, Scott, had come down in the middle of my meal and greeted me much the same as Jeremy had, and again I reassured him that I wouldn't be leaving. I repeated the process a third time when my dad and uncle arrived home. Despite the fact that I was still incredibly apprehensive, I was glad to be back. I knew I'd missed my family, but I hadn't realized just how much until we were all together.

Granted, it was strange. Every one of them looked as tired as my mother had, filling me with guilt at the fact that my disappearance had such an impact on them. Depressing as it might have been to think about, I somewhat expected them to be on with their lives. So we didn't speak much for lack of anything to say, but their eyes never left me.

After my mom had finished feeding me all I could eat, she suggested I go and get settled back into my room. Unsure of whether they'd be comfortable with me out of their sights, but in desperate need of a break from their gawking, I gladly made my way upstairs. My room was just as I'd left it, although it had been cleaned – the dirty clothes I'd left on the floor were washed and put back in the drawers, and the bed was made.

I sat on the fluffy orange comforter and looked around the long-empty room. It felt weird. I'd grown so accustom to the smells and sounds of Camille's house that it had become comfortable, and even though I was back home, I didn't feel like I belonged here either. Already I felt trapped. The wolf inside me wanted out. I lied back on the bed and put my hands behind my head, staring up at the ceiling. The kitchen was right under my bedroom, and I could hear my mom and dad below me talking.

"I'm glad she's back too, Eric, but it's not okay. She's a seventeen-year-old girl who was gone for two months without giving us a clue about where she was." My mom sounded upset, confused. "There need to be consequences. I don't know how to deal with this."

"We'll get her a psychologist. Doesn't the high school have counselors for this kind of thing?" I sighed at my dad's question. Seeing a psychologist was the last thing I needed.

"Is that enough? How do we know she won't take off again? We don't even know why she left in the first place. I thought she was happy." I heard my mom start crying, and I was flooded with more remorse. I wanted to hug her, tell her that I was happy, that I'd never been happier. But I couldn't, they could never know what happened.

"You're right, we don't know if she'll leave. So we need to do our best to be understanding." I heard the scraping of a stool against the floor as my dad stood up. "Come on, let's go talk to her."

I waited patiently on the bed until my parents knocked gently on the door. They both walked in, and while I sat up and leaned against the headboard they took a seat at the edge of the mattress.

"Kyla, we need to talk," my dad said in the softest voice he could produce. His thinning black hair had started showing strands of gray, and the wrinkles in his forehead had deepened. If I hadn't been keeping track of time, I'd have thought I was gone for years. I nodded knowingly. "Were you," he paused, like he wasn't sure how to say what he wanted. "Did someone force you to leave?" He meant was I kidnapped. I wanted to nod. The grievous look on his face made me want so badly to tell them the truth, and it was like they already knew, because even though Jonathan had left that note, they still asked. But I shook my head instead.

"You left on your own?" he clarified, and this time, though it panged me to do it, I nodded. "Me and your mother were worried sick about you. We thought–" He paused, shut his eyes tight, and swallowed. "We thought you were dead. Don't you *ever* put us through anything like that ever again." I stared at my knees and nodded once more, feeling too guilty to look them in the eyes. Then, to my surprise, he leaned forward and hugged me again, "We're glad you're back though, and safe."

My mom nodded her agreement. "We'd like nothing more than for everything to go back to normal. But you do understand that there are repercussions to what you did?" Again I nodded, still without making eye contact. "You'll return to school tomorrow. You're grounded for pretty much the rest of your life, so you'll come straight home after your classes. No cell phone, no computer, and we're going to talk to the high school about you seeing a psychologist."

After a moment of silence I glanced up to meet my parents' gazes. I didn't like the punishment I was receiving, but I'd take it for the hell I put them through. "Okay. That's fair."

Both of them sat there uneasily. "Kyla," my dad said, and his eyes grew sad, disappointed. "Where were you?"

My breath caught in my throat, creating a lump the size of a bowling ball. I knew the question would come, but I didn't think answering it would be so hard. I closed my eyes, forcefully sucking a breath past the knot. "I was safe."

Discontent and a bit of anger at my lack of response flashed across my father's face, but he caught himself and said, "Well, when you're ready to talk, we're here."

I half-smiled my thanks for them not making it harder on me than it already was, and they reluctantly left me alone to have some time to myself. At least I'd gone for a run the night before. If I hadn't all this tension would have left me itching for a Phase. A tiny glimmer from next to the desk caught my eye. My guitar. I grinned as I reached over and picked it up, lightly picking at the strings. It was out of tune, most likely because Scott had been messing with it. He had a habit of trying to teach himself new hobbies, and multiple times before he'd used my guitar for practice.

Bending my head closer to the instrument, I strummed at it while turning the tuning pegs. *There we go,* I grinned again and started playing. It felt so good to play. It gave me something to focus on, something to clear my mind of everything I had to deal with and fake. Running was a nice time waster, but playing was an escape. One I'd been missing and desperately needing. I played for the rest of the day, breaking to eat and take a nap, until my parents came up to say goodnight and, I assumed, make sure I was still there, and eventually I fell asleep.

***

"They seriously made you talk to the cops?" Camille asked in shock as we walked down the hall toward our lockers. Luna had taken stride beside us as Camille said that, and her eyes widened with similar surprise.

"Yeah," I sighed. "We had to let them know I turned up so they could stop searching. They asked me so many questions." We reached the lockers and I opened mine to switch out some books. "I kept having to say that I ran away and wasn't kidnapped. The police looked furious. My parents looked mortified." Then I added sarcastically, "It was great fun."

"And they're really making you go to the school psychologist?" Luna asked as her and Camille leaned against the wall next to me.

I nodded and shut my own locker, leaning my head against it with a disapproving frown. "Yup. Every Monday, Wednesday and Friday. I have to go right now, actually."

Luna took her back off the wall so Camille could get to her locker, and moved to stand in front of me. "How is it being home?"

"It's a little weird. I really ruined their trust in me." I watched them both nod in understanding.

"What about Changing?" Camille shut her locker and rested her shoulder against it, turning to face me.

This was only the third day I'd been gone, but I felt like the space was doing Camille and I good. She was talking with me a little more easily, and starting to make regular, if brief, eye contact.

"Yesterday was tough, and today's been even harder," I admitted as we began to push our way through the crowded halls toward the counselor's office. "And I don't have a phone to call you guys when I need to run. Can we plan a meeting time? Every night if it's not too much."

Luna smiled and nodded. "Yeah, definitely. One of us can always be there. How about twelve, every night?"

We reached the front office, and I turned before opening the door. "Sounds good, thanks. I'm going to be late for my appointment. I'll see you tonight."

Luna and Camille said 'bye,' and then I opened the door to the main office and walked nervously to the front desk. The secretary looked up at me, impatiently smacking her gum and tapping her pencil, waiting for me to speak. "Hi, um, I'm supposed to meet with Mrs. Hunter."

"Kayla?" The secretary popped a bubble and raised an eyebrow at me, and I had to refrain from rolling my eyes that she'd pronounced my name wrong. I nodded, not bothering to correct her. "She's waiting for you. That's her office right there." She pointed to a door behind the large desk she was at and to the left.

I told her 'thanks' and made my way to the room. When I reached the office door I knocked and heard a 'come in' from the other side.

Timidly, I stepped in, carefully and lightly closing the heavy door behind me, too anxious to make any noise with it.

"You must be Kyla?" Mrs. Hunter looked up from some papers she'd been shuffling through with a big, friendly smile on her face.

I was surprised at how young she was. When I thought of a school psychologist I pictured some old lady with white hair, wrinkled skin, and glasses hanging on a colorful chain around her neck. Nor did I expect someone attractive, but I was clearly mistaken. Dark brown eyes glittered amiably underneath her black-rimmed glasses, and although the young woman was a bit shorter than me, she had a splendidly full, curvy figure. At that reflection I cursed the wolf hormones raging through me. I wasn't in any way attracted to the woman, but I couldn't keep from noticing.

I quickly dismissed my thoughts, and the nervousness started to grow. What was I supposed to do with a counselor? Instead of saying anything, I nodded hesitantly.

The woman walked over and stuck out her hand for me to shake, causing me to jump at the movement. *Jesus, calm down. She's not going to attack you.* While she made every word and smile exaggeratedly friendly, her movements were slow and careful, purposefully avoiding being intimidating. "I'm Mrs. Hunter, but please, call me Amber."

I squeamishly took the woman's hand and gave a small, shy smile. "Nice to meet you."

"Please, have a seat." Amber motioned to a pair of chairs in the far corner of the small room. I sat in one while she sat in the other. "Have you ever spoken with a psychologist before?"

"No." I felt small in the large armchair. It was soft, and I sank right in, feeling engulfed by it.

Mrs. Hunter smiled comfortingly. "The most important thing for you to know is that anything said in here is strictly between you and I, unless you or someone else is in danger. Then I'm required by law to say something." I nodded awkwardly, unsure of what was supposed to come next. "So," Amber started expectantly, but stopped after the word.

"So," I repeated, still unsure. *Mrs. Hunter. Amber.* I tested the words in my mind. I felt uncomfortable with calling an authoritative figure by her first name, but that's what I'd been told to do. I decided I'd try to avoid calling her anything. "What happens now?"

"I'm here to listen. Anything you want to talk about, or just to say out loud, I'm all ears." Amber leaned back in her chair to get comfortable, and waited patiently for me to say something.

I was shocked at the informal tone with which our meeting had started. I'd been half-expecting to have to lie down on a couch in a cold room, and answer questions while Mrs. Hunter took notes on a yellow legal pad. Now I just sat in the big leather armchair, stiffly glancing around the room. Even though the office was small and decorated quite sophisticatedly, it was homey and warm. The walls were a light cream and trimmed in a dark, rich brown – a color I noticed matched Amber's eyes and the chairs we sat in.

"And if I don't have anything to say?" I asked curiously, testing the criterion of my visits.

"I can wait until you do."

It was silent for little a while after that. I could feel Mrs. Hunter's eyes on me, and I occasionally met them with my own. But every time, when I remembered I had nothing to say, I smiled nervously and rapidly looked away. I read each of the few credential plaques hanging on the wall. There were three. One was from a university, and the other two from organizations I'd never heard of. I studied all of the photographs placed around the room. Amber wasn't in any of them alone. Out of the six pictures I noticed two were pictures with friends, three were of a small poodle dog, and one was of Mrs. Hunter and a man. I glanced to her left hand. Yep, a nice-sized diamond-ring. Safe to assume the man was her husband.

Before long I sat there twiddling my thumbs, and soon after I resorted to shaking my leg and tapping my foot on the floor. It didn't take long before the silence started to gnaw away at me. I looked at the clock. It had only been fifteen minutes. Too bad it felt like an hour.

"What college did you go graduate from?" I asked, crossing my legs and sitting straighter in the chair.

Amber smiled, obviously also glad that the silence had been broken, whether or not we were talking about me. "UCLA, it's down south, in Los Angeles. I graduated about six years ago."

"How come you're working in a small town like this?"

She chuckled to herself. "I grew up here. I tried the city life while in college, and it didn't suit me too well. Have you lived in the city?"

"No," I shook my head. "I moved here from Texas a few months ago."

"Why'd you move here of all places?"

I glanced around tensely. Something about the way Mrs. Hunter spoke was encouraging. Perhaps it was the nice tone of her voice, or the fact that she made just the right amount of eye contact. Whatever it was, there was also the fact that I'd always been talkative, and I worried that if we kept speaking I'd accidentally say too much. "My uncle lives here," I told her cautiously.

"Walters," Amber said my last name aloud. "Rob Walters is your uncle?"

"That's him," I nodded matter-of-factly.

"And how do you like it here?"

I exaggeratedly closed my mouth, slinking down in the chair and wishing things would keep from getting awkward. I felt bad, like I was being rude, but I was afraid. I couldn't let the conversation carry on further.

"I'll take that as a no," Amber whispered, more to herself.

I shook my head, "I like it."

I feared the question I thought was coming. Then why did you leave? I braced myself for the guilt that would flood with the inquiry. I wanted so badly for someone who wasn't a werewolf to understand, to tell me that I was right for not going home, right for not putting my family in danger.

I assumed the fear I felt deep down showed in my eyes, because Amber changed the subject. "What kind of stuff are you interested in?"

I sighed with relief. "Like, hobbies?" A nod. "I play guitar." I glanced at the clock, and Amber followed my gaze. It had been thirty minutes.

"I think you did well for your first time." Mrs. Hunter smiled and stood up.

After saying bye I left to go home. For the week after that I snuck out of my window and ran with Camille and Luna every night. Sometimes it was just Luna, and other times it was just Camille. My meetings with Mrs. Hunter continued much the same as they had the first day. We made small talk and got to know the basics about each other. I found out her husband's name was Rick, and he worked as a car salesman in San Joaquin. They met at UCLA, and Rick fell in love with the simple lifestyle of living in a small town. The small black dog in the photos was Pluto. They wanted kids in the future, but for now Pluto was enough work. I let Mrs. Hunter know certain irrelevant details, like my birthday and random things about my family, but any time I felt we were getting too close to talking about what happened to me I shut down until the subject was changed.

A week after I'd been home I sat in film studies, exhausted from the lack of sleep. We were watching an old black and white film I couldn't even remember the name of. It just played in the background as I lay with my head on the desk, trying to tune it out so I could fall asleep. The night before I'd been caught for the first time sneaking back in from a run with Luna, and now, not being able to fall asleep, I had nothing to do but think about it. I'd left my window open and climbed the tree outside of it as a ladder to get back through. I'd been so tired from that particular run that I didn't notice my father sitting there in the dark, waiting for me to return.

He flipped on the lights once I closed the window, and the second he did I could see the fury etched on his face. He'd yelled and yelled about rules and dangers and not knowing if I'd ever be coming home. I told him I'd only gone for a walk, but that wasn't specific enough. Or he didn't believe me. Either way he continued to yell. I tried not to hold it against him. I could only imagine how hard it had to be to think that at any time they'd never see me again. And of course I felt guilty about defying them, but I didn't have a choice. Without sneaking out and Changing I'd be putting them all in danger.

The sudden silence broke through my thoughts. The period was almost over, and the teacher had just turned off the movie and flipped the lights back on. Out of the corner of my eye I could see Camille stealthily looking back at me, so I swiveled my head toward her to let her know she'd been caught. She instantly turned around and ran a hand through her hair, pretending like she hadn't been looking at me, and I wondered how long she'd been watching me for.

Finally the bell rang, and Camille took stride beside me as we left the room. "Luna told me your dad caught you sneaking out."

I sighed deeply and simply nodded. I'd been so upset about it that it only added to my difficulty sleeping. I hadn't gotten a wink all night. For the whole day I'd been tired and grumpy, and talking about it was the last thing I wanted to do.

"Well, are you okay?" she pressed, the concern in her voice apparent even though I wasn't looking at her.

I waited until we reached our lockers to answer, at which point I turned and leaned my back against them. I tried not to get grumpy at her, it wasn't her fault, but my nerves were shot, and my emotions already at extremes. I couldn't keep my voice from sounding short and agitated. "Yeah, I'm fine."

Camille studied my face for a moment before opening her locker and whispering to herself, "You don't sound fine."

I sighed again, but this time it was a harsh, aggravated huff of breath. I was already almost too frustrated to function, and the sarcasm behind her tone put an aching pain in my chest. "Okay, no, I'm not fine. I'm tired and pissed. I can't sleep. I get yelled at for things that I have no choice but to do. My parents have no faith in me." I swallowed past the growing lump of despair in my throat. "Do you know how hard it is to see the disappointment on their faces every time they think I fuck up? It's hard, Camille, and no one can understand that. Not even you." I stood there for a second, too blinded by emotions and exhaustion to see the look on her face, but I was glad I couldn't see it. I knew it only would have made me feel worse.

Without saying goodbye or going to my locker I started down the hall. I wanted desperately to leave, to be alone, but I had to go see Mrs. Hunter. Fine, I'd go see her. And I did, and practically stormed into the counselor's small office.

"You want to know an intimate detail about me?" I stood in front of Amber's desk, the woman now looking up at me, clearly startled by the volume of my voice. "Did you know I was seeing someone? After I moved here. Not for long, but God, was I in love. Still am too, and no matter what I do it never gets easier. I have nothing left to give and I can't do a damned thing right by anybody." The second I finished my short rant I couldn't stop a single tear from falling down my cheek, and my face flushed red. I hadn't meant for Mrs. Hunter to ever hear any of that. I'd never wanted the woman to have the privilege of real knowledge about me, but now that I'd let it out, even though I was embarrassed and on the verge of a breakdown, it felt good.

Amber stood up and, with eyes full of concern, ushered me to the armchairs. "I didn't know you were seeing someone. What happened with him?" she asked as she sat down across from me.

"Her," I corrected simply and honestly, too tired to worry about making up a lie.

"Oh, I'm sorry, I shouldn't have assumed." If she was surprised she didn't show it, instead she kept the look of concern and focus on me. "So, you're gay?"

"No." The defensive tone with which I said the negation was my first instinct, but I quickly realized I didn't need to be defensive. She wasn't judging me. "Well, I mean, yeah, I guess."

Amber nodded, a comforting nod meant to encourage the ease with which I was talking to her. "Do your parents know?"

I shook my head, sniffling to clear the water from my sinuses. "But that's not the point."

"What is the point?"

"The point *is*," I took in a deep breath, holding back the fresh tears that stung my eyes, "The point is that if I had her back then all of this wouldn't be so hopeless, because if she forgave me I'd have one less thing to feel so damn guilty about. Because with her, I could deal with being a disappointment to everyone else."

Amber was silent for a few moments while she thought about which part of my confession to comment on. She still looked concerned for me, but there was also a certain curiosity she couldn't hide. "What does she have to forgive you for?"

I stared into the counselor's eyes, delving as deep as I could to measure the amount of trustworthiness in them. Again I took a deep breath. I'd already said so much. Why not get it off my chest? Give me one less thing to keep to myself. "For breaking her heart. For breaking up with her and crushing the happiness out of her, and you want to know the worst part? I can see it. Every time I look into her eyes I can see the pain I caused. The pain she has to put up with every day, and it kills me."

Amber let another moment of sympathetic silence pass by. "How come you broke up with her?"

"But that's the thing!" I nearly shouted, and I watched her jump from the unexpected noise. "I said the words, but I didn't really break up with her. I never wanted to, never in a million years would have even thought about it, but he made me do it, and she hasn't forgiven me for having to."

"He made you do it? Like an authority figure?" I didn't like the tone Amber's voice took on. A protective tone, like she thought someone had threatened me. That was the exact truth, but she could never know that.

I bit my lip, instantly regretting how far I'd let my confession go. "Yeah, sure, something like that."

Amber picked up on the ambiguity I was trying to enforce, and enforced her own sense of authority. "Kyla, I realize this is hard for you to talk about. But no one hurt you, did they?"

Yes! He hurt me in too many ways to count! He took everything! He – no, stop. It didn't happen. "No, no one hurt me."

I waited for Amber to say something, but she just nodded, seemingly satisfied with my answer. I could see the wheels turning in the counselor's mind. There was something she wanted to know, but even after how much I'd just opened up it was clear she didn't know how far she could push it.

"Is that why you left?" The counselor's voice was soft, inquiring but far from forceful.

I couldn't stop the tears from flowing now. I was embarrassed to be telling all this to someone I barely knew, and even more embarrassed that now I was crying about it. But wasn't this the release I needed? "I never left."

"Isn't that why you're here?" she started, her voice confused. "I thought you ran away from home?"

"I didn't run away," I said briskly, and a little bit too abrasively. I instantly turned the corners of my mouth up in an apologetic smile. "Just stayed away." I could feel myself getting tired, exhausted of talking, but I still had about fifteen minutes left of my session. Fifteen minutes until I could go home and catch up on much needed sleep.

"Can I ask you something else, Kyla?"

I shrugged. "Might as well."

"Your parents mentioned some dogs." The volume with which Amber spoke dropped, like she knew she was treading on thin ice and any second it would fall apart.

My heart started pounding. Dogs could mean anything, and I prayed she didn't mean werewolves. "What dogs?"

"Your uncle's dogs."

"Blue and Brandy," I whispered, every bit of that frightful night flashing before my eyes and causing me to cringe. Before Jonathan took me, he'd poisoned my uncle's two Gordon Setters. It was unnecessary and cruel, and even now it made me sick. Then my head shot up, and I stood as I realized what she might be implying. "I didn't kill those dogs!"

"I didn't say you did," Amber said softly, trying to calm me. "But you know you can tell me who did."

I glared. I didn't like that she even knew they'd been killed on purpose. "It doesn't matter who did."

"I know you're scared, Kyla, but–"

"Scared? I'm not scared of anything!" I fumed. This woman had no right to keep bringing up what happened that night. I'd been working so hard on fitting into my new life and forgetting about it, the last thing I needed was to be vividly reminded. I was tired, running on too little sleep for so much emotion, and the defensive itching started in my fingertips. *Shit.* "I have to go."

"Kyla, please, we can talk about something else." Amber stood, and carefully tried to stop me as I made my way to the door.

Taking a deep breath to try and calm myself, I turned. "Look, I'm sorry I yelled, but you really don't understand. I *need* to leave." I could see my counselor's face riddled with confusion, but I didn't wait for an answer. Instead, I flew out the door.

Mrs. Hunter would probably label me bipolar. Throwing fits, apologizing, and then storming out. To my surprise, I didn't care one bit. I guess I *was* glad that I was able to get everything off my chest. I did feel slightly bad for using Mrs. Hunter and then leaving her without any real answers, but it didn't matter. I deserved a break. Deserved to do at least one thing the way I wanted. Besides, today was already going so horribly, I couldn't imagine how it could get any worse.

"Abby!"

Abby immediately recognized the shouting voice as her friend Madelyn's, and stopped and turned, waiting for her to catch up. Their classes for the day had just finished, and she'd been hoping to get back to her dorm room for some peace and quiet. As a telepath, not only was the school day mentally stimulating, it was exhausting, and the thing she looked forward to most every day was getting back to her room where she could put in her headphones and enjoy the serenity of her own mind.

"God, I've been looking for you everywhere!" Madelyn's bright blue eyes glittered with excitement, and her black ponytail bobbed as she grabbed Abby's arm and started pulling her in the opposite direction she wanted to go.

Abby tried to pick her friends thoughts to see what she was so gleeful about, but there was so much going on in that erratic teenage head that she couldn't figure it out. She settled for giving her friend an exaggerated eyebrow raise.

"Stephen Harding just told me that he's going to ask you out." The accomplished grin on Madelyn's face made Abby cringe. She'd begged her friend about a million times to stop trying to instigate relationships for her, but every time she did Madelyn's selective hearing kicked in. "You don't look happy about it."

"Where on earth would you get the idea that I wanted to date Stephen Harding?" Abby sat down on a bench in the cold, stone courtyard, pushed her dirty blonde hair behind her shoulders and zipped her jacket up.

Aw man, I forgot my jacket in class. Abby held back a laugh as Madelyn watched and remembered she'd left her own jacket, rubbing her arms for warmth. "Why *wouldn't* you want to date him? He's tall, dark, and handsome. And kind of smart." Madelyn put emphasis on the 'kind of' part, like that was a good thing. "And didn't you hook up with him at The Orchid?"

"Whoa, whoa, whoa," Abby shook her head, emphatically waving her hands in front of her to assert that she hadn't. "There's a *huge* difference between hooking up and dancing. Dancing doesn't imply or ensure that I'm going to date him – ever."

You're so picky. Her friend sighed as she mentally complained. "What's wrong with him? You always find an excuse."

"He's a pig," Abby said simply, remembering the night she'd danced with him.

They'd all gone to The Orchid, a club that wasn't concerned with age and the place most of the kids from her school went whenever they left campus. After the hundredth time of him asking her to dance she finally gave in and said yes. It didn't take long until she'd recalled why she didn't want to in the first place. Abby knew she was attractive, and being a telepath she'd grown accustomed to hearing the kind of thoughts that passed through most men's heads. The music at The Orchid was always too loud for her to hear anyone's thoughts, but Stephen's hands were just as relentless as she imagined his mind to be. She wasn't opposed to slapping a guy, but if she didn't have to she liked to avoid making a scene. That night she'd simply walked away, but she didn't know where he would get the idea that she liked him, and was even a little offended by it.

Abby studied her friend, as she seemed to contemplate Abby's claim. *Oh well, maybe he'd like to go out with me sometime...*

"Abby Johnson, please report to Miss Reins' room. Abby Johnson to Miss Reins' room."

Abby withheld a sigh of relief at the announcement from the loudspeaker. Standing up she turned to her friend, who was still daydreaming about Stephen. "You're too good for him, Maddie. You know, I think Alex kind of likes you. He's a nice guy."

She'd heard Alex thinking about Madelyn during English class multiple times. He wasn't what Maddie would consider 'popular', but Abby liked him. She laughed when Madelyn made an apathetic face, and said 'bye' before heading off toward Miss Reins' room. It was all the way on the other side of the campus, but since school had ended it was starting to empty, and she didn't have to push through crowds of students to get there.

Abby walked across the large courtyard, her feet crunching over the fresh snow, before passing under a tall stone archway and pushing through the double doors of the main hall. Going so quickly from the cold air into the warm building, her nose and ears started to burn, so she unzipped and removed her jacket. The main hall was an enormous two-story entranceway that stemmed off into corridors lined with classrooms. She walked across the worn slate floors and to the beginning of the stairs. She smiled at a student from one of her classes as she reached the top, and then took a right down one of the long halls. Despite the school's updated plumbing and electric lighting, its high, tapestry-decorated stone walls still gave off a sense of antiquity. Her footsteps echoed as she walked down the corridor, and finally reaching the fifth room on the right she pushed open the large wooden door.

"Abby." The teacher was removing papers from each of the desks when she looked up to greet Abby with a smile.

"Lahni," Abby smiled back as she walked to the front of the long room and sat at the edge of the older woman's desk.

"How was your day?" Miss Reins continued to add to the stack of papers in her arms as she started to go through a typical greeting with Abby.

"It was good, just a normal, boring day. Senioritis is already kicking in." Abby listened hard to Lahni's thoughts, and even though she could tell that the woman was terribly uneasy, all she got were the names of the students whose papers she was picking up. Years of practice, and maybe a little bit of magic, had made Lahni an expert at omitting the things she didn't want Abby to hear. "What's wrong?"

Lahni picked up the last assignment, made her way to the other side of her desk, set the papers on the corner of it, and sat down in her chair. *Vampires.* The thought immediately got Abby worrying.

"You've heard about the kidnappings?" Lahni asked, and Abby nodded. "They're getting closer and closer to the school."

"But no students have been taken, right?" she questioned, pulling from her memory the various news articles she'd read about all the missing persons.

"No, but," Lahni's bright green eyes gained a reminiscent glaze as parts of her visions came back. Her thoughts were scattered as several images and thoughts clouded her mind. There was too much for Abby to focus on.

"You've seen something?" Abby had gotten drifts of the psychic teacher's visions before, and while she could never make out what they were or what they meant, they were easily distinguishable from conscious thought.

"Yes, but not much." Lahni was trying hard to organize her vision into manageable facts, but was having a difficult time of it. Her eyebrows furrowed with concentration, and she took deep, calming breaths. "There's a vampire, and a werewolf. Both allies. The wolf is in danger." Abby was about to ask who the wolf was when Lahni answered her question. "I don't know who the wolf is. There's just the silhouette, and dark, frightened eyes."

"There are a few werewolves at this school. You don't have anything else to go off of?" Abby thought of the werewolves she knew of. The American Pack lived nearby and three of the young ones went to school with her, but if she was going to help keep an eye on them then she needed to know which one to watch. Lahni shook her head 'no,' and Abby sighed. "And I don't trust vampires either."

"Yes, well, if you can succeed in keeping this thing under wraps, it would secure your place on the board. The Supernatural Council could greatly benefit from your ability." The teacher leaned back in her seat, the images of each of the board members flowing through her mind one by one.

"That's if I wanted a seat on the board. My abilities would be better utilized in the field." Abby set her face sternly. She'd had this conversation before, with multiple people, and they all treated her the same way. Like a kid who didn't and wouldn't know what was best until she grew up. But she'd been in the minds of adults since she was young, and she knew better than most of them how the world worked. They were all just being stubborn. If she defied her father, the leader of the Supernatural Council, then she was an irresponsible child. If she succumbed to his wishes, she was a closed-minded robot.

"Your father–"

"My father," Abby interrupted, "Is a lazy old warlock who runs his sect with outdated politics. He hasn't cared for innovation since he was voted in as Director." Lahni constructed her face to disagree, but she let her thoughts slip to slight concurrence. "I'll play soldier, you know as well as I do where my loyalties lie, but I won't participate on the council."

Lahni nodded. "I know, but I have to try with you sometimes. Your father's orders." She winked.

Out of all the board members, Abby had the most respect for Lahni. She'd never treated Abby like she was incapable or juvenile, and whenever she unfairly fell into the habit of partiality against her father's diplomacy, Lahni carefully reminded her who was in charge.

"Is there anything else I need to know?" Abby stood up and pulled her jacket back on.

"Something big is coming, Abby. I don't know what it is, but I can feel it. Just be careful." Even if Abby couldn't feel the fear from the older woman, she could've seen it on her face. What few age lines she had deepened with worry, and the corners of her mouth turned down in a frown.

"You know I'm always careful." Abby smiled at the woman and turned to leave.

She was off to complete step one. Find whichever werewolf it would be her job to protect.

4

"Camille, where are you going?" Luna looked up from her dinner at the kitchen table as I passed by the doorway, snapping her fingers to emphasize that she wanted my attention.

I stopped and backtracked into the kitchen as I finished pulling on my jacket. "You know where I'm going."

She patted the spot at the table next to her while shaking her head, and waited for me to sit down. "Do you really think Kyla's going to be pleased when she finds out you've been spying on her *every* night until we run?"

"I'm not spying on her," I growled defensively, but I lowered my head in embarrassment. I'd told Luna I was going a few times, but I didn't know she was aware I went every night.

"Then what *are* you doing?" She raised an eyebrow expectantly. "We wouldn't have let her go home is she wasn't ready, and we're running every night. Even I'm starting to get too tired to Change easily. She doesn't need a babysitter."

"I know she's ready. I just get this bad feeling sometimes." I tugged at my jacket, anxiously zipping and unzipping it. "I'd never be able to forgive myself if something happened."

"You're so weird," Luna laughed, but when she realized I wasn't smiling she studied me. "You're really that worried?" When I nodded, she stood and walked to the hallway, coming back in a minute later with another coat. "Here, take a thicker jacket, it's really cold out."

I smiled my thanks and replaced the jacket I was wearing with the bigger one Luna gave me. I then grabbed the keys off the counter and hopped into the Jeep, making my way to Kyla's house. I *wasn't* spying on her, but I wasn't exactly keeping an eye on her solely for *her* benefit. Everything in the house – the couch, the stairs, the car I was sitting in, and worst of all my own bed – everything smelled like Kyla. Everything reminded me of the fact that she'd broken up with me. It was bad enough I had to put aside the heartbreak and help her adjust. Now that she wasn't around all I had to do was wallow in what I didn't have. I just figured I might as well keep an eye on the real thing instead of brooding.

I could see Kyla's driveway coming up on the road, so I turned off the headlights and pulled onto the dirt shoulder to park the car. As I got out, I was glad Luna had given me a thicker jacket. Even though it was only six o'clock it was already dark, and every breath I let out created a thick fog in the frosty air. Zipping the coat a little bit more, I started my walk up the long driveway to Kyla's house.

When I was about two hundred feet from the house I watched the leaves on the trees to figure out which way the wind was blowing. North. The best place for me to stay so Kyla wouldn't catch my scent was behind the house. I slunk into the trees to my left and slowly made a circle to the back. Once I got there I took a few steps farther into the orchard, far enough that if someone came out they wouldn't see me, but close enough that I could hear a lot of what was going on in the house – the distant clatter of dishes in the sink, the mumbling chatter from someone watching TV.

Hearing that the house was quiet and safe, I sat and leaned my back against one of the small trees. Taking in a deep breath of the oranges that surrounded me I remembered the first time I'd ever seen Kyla. I'd been on a run passing through these fields when her sweet scent carried to my nose. Ever since that night I'd been in love with the girl, and now that same scent only haunted me.

I pushed away the memory and closed my eyes, laying my head back against the trunk. Every night that I'd been coming to Kyla's house this was mostly what I did for five hours. Sit where I knew I wouldn't be seen and take a small nap until it was time for either Luna or I to run with her. My sleeping patterns had been so screwed up lately anyway that I welcomed the few hours I got to rest.

A while later my head jerked forward, pulled out of sleep by some new sounds. I checked my cell phone and then put it back in my pocket. 8:30. I was surprised I'd dozed off so easily. I stood up and listened hard for the sounds that had woken me. Two sets of footsteps. I lifted my nose to the air. Kyla and Jeremy. As swiftly and silently as I could, I followed the pair, making sure to stay in the cover of the trees. Kyla and Jeremy had gone into the barn, so I took a couple strides forward in order to hear better. I could sense the horses growing extremely restless with Kyla's presence, and Jeremy didn't sound too happy either.

"Kyla, you might have only been caught once, but I know you've been sneaking out every night."

"You've been spying on me?" Kyla sounded frustrated, and I instantly felt guilty that she was being confronted about it. That must have been what she was talking about earlier when she said that not even I could understand. She'd been right. I could never understand what it was like to hide a secret like this from family.

"No, but I've been checking in on you, every night while you're *not* in bed. Where do you go?"

"I don't go anywhere."

"Do you have any idea how much it hurts Mom and Dad when you act like this? How much it hurts me? I'm your brother, I thought you could talk to me about anything."

Even though Kyla's voice sounded agitated, I could hear the despair mixed in. She knew exactly how much it hurt, but thanks to me she didn't have a choice. "I can talk to you, but not about this. This you would never understand."

"You've changed, Kyla. Ever since you met Camille."

"This is not Camille's fault!" The sudden way that Kyla yelled made even me flinch. Over the past month she'd yelled a lot, but it was always *at* me, never defending me, and I couldn't help but be somewhat surprised.

"It's drugs isn't it? I think you'd be surprised how much I can understand what you're going through." Jeremy tried a different, more sympathetic tactic, but to no avail.

"You don't know the first thing about what I'm going through!" I could hear Kyla getting more and more upset, and I took a couple steps forward, feeling in my gut that things were about to take a turn for the worst.

"You're not going out any more," Jeremy said with resolve, voice starting to grow angrier and louder with Kyla's defiance. "I won't let you sneak out. I won't let you hurt Mom and Dad anymore."

"Goddammit, Jeremy, just get out of the way! You don't get it!" I took a few more steps forward. I knew what was coming. I knew how tired Kyla was, and how hard Changes were for her to control. "Let go of me! Just let go!" I pressed on, worried that if Jeremy was trying to restrain Kyla then he was putting himself in a dangerous position. "Jeremy, get away from me. Please!" The second I heard those words I started sprinting toward the door of the barn. There was no way Kyla would be able to stop the Change, and this was the exact reason I'd been so worried about her going home.

I reached the entrance of the barn right as the huge, honey-colored wolf burst out of Kyla's skin. I could see Jeremy's terrified and utterly confused face, his eyes wide with horror as he was flung away from her. The wolf crouched, preparing to pounce, and I ran as fast as I could to reach them. And I did. Just as the wolf leapt I threw myself into it, knocking it against the side of a horse stall before it could take a swipe at Jeremy. The wolf sprung off the ground, furious at being hit and ready to snap at me, but I stood my ground between it and Jeremy, peering hard into its eyes, daring it to try something again. A few seconds passed while Kyla and I stood in a stare-down, and then her eyes grew wide and filled with water. Tears. The anger was subsiding, and she'd realized what she'd almost done.

My expression softened with sympathy. "Kyla," I reached out to touch the large canine, but it backed up, letting out a strange, sob-like whimper, and then took off, darting out the door.

I stared after Kyla for a few seconds before Jeremy started to panic. "What the fuck was that?" He tried to bolt, but I grabbed the back of his jacket and held him in place so he couldn't leave.

"You should sit down," I told him calmly as he continued to struggle against my grasp.

"Yeah right!" he yelled sarcastically and pulled his arms out of his jacket, running toward the door. I threw it to the ground, swiftly caught up, and wrapped both my arms around him tightly. I let him squirm and fight against me until he realized that while he was bigger, I was stronger, and eventually he grew too tired to keep struggling. "Okay, I'll sit," he growled angrily, plopping down and leaning his back against the stables.

"You promise you won't try and leave?" I stood between him and the door nervously until he looked up, eyes full of contempt, and nodded. I sat beside him and waited until I heard his breathing start to slow, and his heartbeat returned to as close to normal as it would. "At least she's not on drugs."

Jeremy glared at me, and in the most hateful voice he could've managed he muttered, "You did this to her, didn't you?"

I pushed back the shame that pitched through my stomach, making me queasy. He was looking at me like I was a monster, like *I'd* killed Kyla. "Does it matter?" Then I couldn't help but grow annoyed that I was being *blamed*, like it was a bad thing. He couldn't understand that she would have died otherwise. "Unless you can accept this, I'm all she has."

"Accept this? I don't even know what *this* is!" He ran his hands through his short brown hair, ending at the back and leaving his arms there, covering his slowly shaking head like he was shielding it from a harsh blow.

"You know what it is," I said softly as I tried to be comforting, but all I could think about was that I wanted to get to Kyla, who was probably having the biggest meltdown of her life.

Jeremy stood, causing me to scramble up thinking that he was about to leave. "This isn't real. I'm dreaming. I'm having a really, really bad nightmare." He stuck his arm out toward me. "Pinch me." I shrugged as I grabbed his skin between my fingers, pinching as hard as I could and holding back a smirk as he yelped and shook it out. "Not that hard!" Then he started panicking again, taking in fast, shallow breaths. "I need to sit down."

I let him sit for a minute before I began to grow impatient. "She's still your sister. She's the same old Kyla, and you have no idea how hard it's been for her. That's why she sneaks out every night. So something like this doesn't happen and none of you get hurt. She knows how much it hurts you guys, and it kills her, but she'd rather feel like a huge screw-up than put any of you in danger."

"Jesus," he said without so much as looking at me, and his face was hard to read as he simply nodded while he digested everything. The next time he looked at me, his green eyes were wide. "Was she with you this *whole* time?"

I glanced away, not sure if he'd be furious, though my silence was enough of an answer. I let him sit there a bit more before I decided we'd been there too long. "Do you love your sister?"

He squinted up at me, clearly somewhat irritated by the question as he tried to figure out why I'd even need to ask. "Of course I do."

"Well, then I know you're the only one who could make her feel better right now." I let it sink in, and then motioned for him to get up, which he did, and tugged his coat back on before following me.

"You know where she is?" he asked curiously as he followed me to the car.

"I really hope she's at my house," I told him, but the truth was, I didn't know. Kyla could have been fifteen miles away by now.

"Can you do that too? And your family, can they?" As we reached the car Jeremy climbed in and pulled on his seatbelt, and I pretended not to hear his questions. Better to leave something like that to the imagination. He seemed to be taking everything pretty well, but I didn't trust him like I did Kyla.

I drove as fast as I could back to my house, and neither of us said another word on the way there. I could tell Jeremy was still frightened and, I assumed, entirely nervous. Even though I turned on the heat he shivered violently the entire ride, and I hoped he wasn't going into shock. I sped into the driveway and pulled the jeep as close to the porch as I could get it. I jumped out, unworried with whether or not Jeremy was following closely enough. I was too concerned about Kyla.

"Please tell me she's here," I begged Luna, who was waiting on the porch swing.

"She's in your room. Here." Luna nodded and tossed me the blanket she was holding. The confusion and concern on her face was apparent, but she had sense enough to wait until the right time to ask.

I smiled my relief and thanks, and then turned to Jeremy. "This is my sister, Luna. Wait with her for a few minutes." I didn't wait for him to answer or protest.

I threw open the screen door and practically sprinted up the stairs. My bedroom door was closed, and I knocked lightly before easing it open. I closed it behind me and hesitated turning around, unsure of the state Kyla would be in. It was about as bad as I expected. She was still naked, sitting on the floor and leaning against the side of my bed. Her head was laid on arms folded across her knees, shoulders shaking violently as she sobbed.

Before taking any steps forward I unfolded the blanket, then I draped it over her and sat on the floor next to her. I had no idea what to say – she hadn't even acknowledged me or lifted her head from her arms. Asking if she was okay would be stupid, because clearly she wasn't. I couldn't say I understood, or that everything was fine. Nothing fit the situation. Instead of saying anything I wrapped my arms around her shoulders and pulled her into my body, squeezing her as tightly and comfortingly as I could. It seemed to help a little; Kyla pulled the blanket more firmly around herself and buried her face in my neck.

Ten minutes later she finally stopped sobbing so fiercely, and let out a short, embarrassed laugh when she noticed my shirt was soaked and snotted on.

"Hey." I held back a chuckle at her embarrassment, and rubbed her back through the blanket, smiling warmly.

"How's Jeremy?" she asked through sniffles and sharp, whimpering breaths.

"He's okay," I told her, my hand still hovering over her back, unsure of the kind of comfort I could offer without bringing her into another embrace. "I brought him to see you."

Kyla threw her arms around me, pulling me into a tenacious hug as she broke into tears again. "I almost killed my own brother, Camille. How did you know? He could've–thank you."

I hugged back for a moment before clearing my throat uncomfortably at the fact that Kyla's bare body was now practically intertwined with my own. She smiled apologetically and let go, pulling the blanket around herself once more.

"I need help." Kyla wiped her tears off on the blanket and stared at the floor. "I can't stay here. I'm unstable. Dangerous. I need help."

I put my hand on her shoulder, and even though she couldn't see it, I nodded. She was right. I'd done all I could do, but it wasn't enough. She needed more. "I know. I'll talk to my dad. Just promise me in the meantime you won't go anywhere. Promise me you won't run off?"

Kyla's gaze remained locked on the floor as she woefully agreed, "I promise."

"Okay good," I patted her on the back and then stood, offering my hand to help her up. "Do you want to see your brother?"

"Yeah, but I need to get dressed." When Kyla stood I could see how shaken she really was. Her knees wobbled and her whole body quivered, much like Jeremy's had earlier.

"You going to be okay?" I asked, putting my hand under her elbow for support. I wanted to pull her back into my arms, to hold her until she was truly okay.

"I'll get there eventually." She managed to muster a small smile.

"You can borrow some clothes. You know where to find them." With that I reluctantly left her alone in my room.

After I closed the door behind me, I took a deep breath. I knew there was only one thing that could really help Kyla, but she had just returned home. I didn't want to pull her away so soon. I trotted down the stairs and back onto the porch where Luna and Jeremy were sitting silently, an obvious apprehension between them. Luna's eyes filled with relief when she saw me open the screen door.

"Hey, can you take Jeremy upstairs to see Kyla?" I asked her.

She made an irked, reluctant face at me, but complied. I smiled my thanks and went looking for my dad, who I thought I'd seen out of the corner of my eye sitting at the kitchen table. Sure enough, when I backtracked to the kitchen he was there waiting for me.

"How's she doing?" he asked as he looked up from a large novel he'd been reading.

He pulled a chair out for me to sit down. I gladly did, and laid my head on the table in exhaustion. "She stopped crying, but she's not good, Dad. We never should have brought her into this."

"I know you don't really believe that." My dad dog-eared the page he was on and closed his book, then turned his eyes on me sympathetically.

I could feel myself starting to break down. I wished Kyla had never broken up with me. Wished Jonathan hadn't tried to kill her so she didn't have to go through all this. Wished she wanted me back and we could just run away, leave for years until we'd had time to grow sick of each other. "I never wanted her to be in this much pain. I can't stand it."

My dad studied my face while I spoke, his concern clear as he couldn't hide the fact that he hated seeing me upset. "You want help from the Pack?" I simply nodded. "Kyla's okay with going to Oregon?" He sounded surprised.

"I didn't tell her yet, but she knows she can't stay here, around her family." I tiredly propped my head in my hand.

"What about you?" he asked expectantly, although he already knew the answer.

"I can't let her go alone." I met his eyes with my own, trying to judge how he felt about it, but aside from the obvious worry, it was hard to tell.

He nodded and continued to watch me for another minute. I glanced up when Luna came into the kitchen and lifted herself up onto the counter, and then looked back at the table while my father sat thoughtfully.

My dad stood and rubbed his forehead anxiously. "I'll go call Eli."

I nodded, and for a while just sat there. When I finally felt Luna's eyes on me I looked over to meet her gaze. "What?"

"Sorry I doubted you." She jumped off the counter and sat down in a chair next to me. "You know Kyla better than anyone, and if you thought something was wrong I should've trusted you." I smiled to let her know her apology was accepted. "But, if you knew she wasn't ready, why'd you let her go home?"

"She needed to see them," I shrugged. "By keeping her here I felt just like him, like I was kidnapping her."

"I guess," Luna said, and then a spark of curiosity lit her eyes. "Is it really like what they say?" I raised an eyebrow at her, not really sure what she meant. "You know what I'm talking about. You're in her blood now. Do you really feel like you guys are more connected?"

"Luna, will you keep it down?" I whispered angrily, putting my finger over my mouth in a shushing motion. I looked around to make sure that, even though no one was in the room with us, no one had heard. It really wasn't my family I was worried about hearing, they already knew. It was Kyla.

"Sorry," she said, imitating my panicked gaze and then furrowing her eyebrows in confusion. "Why don't you just tell her it wasn't me?"

I thought about it. We'd never actually told Kyla anything. She'd just assumed it was Luna that bit her. But I *didn't* want Kyla to know. I wasn't exactly sure why. It just didn't feel right. "Because if she decides she hates being a werewolf I'd rather she blame you."

"Gee, thanks," Luna rolled her eyes sarcastically. "But is that how you knew? Do you think she can feel it too?"

"Yeah, I guess so," I shrugged. "Any time I was near her I started getting this tight feeling in my chest, you know? A different kind than the heartbreak feeling. I knew it was coming from her, that I was feeling what she did." I pulled at my lip thoughtfully. "If she does feel it, she probably doesn't realize it. She still thinks it was you, so she wouldn't think anything of it."

Luna nodded understandingly, a fascinated glow prevailing in her eyes. A moment later the glow faded, and she glanced toward the kitchen door. "Dad's calling the Alpha," she started, and her big hazel eyes grew sad, her mouth turned down in a frown. "Are you leaving too?" I nodded without looking at her. The last thing I needed was to feel guilty about leaving with Kyla. "You're still in love with her."

I sniffled past the stabbing pain that statement brought, that the word 'love' brought, and wiped at the stubborn tear that fell down my cheek. "I always will be, whether she wants me or not. There isn't a thing I wouldn't give to help her get through this."

Luna slowly shook her head in awe. "I can't imagine caring about someone as much as you do about her. Even after everything." Her mouth turned up in a smirk as she teased, "It's borderline masochistic."

"Yeah, well, you're still young and stupid," I countered, chuckling when Luna punched me in the shoulder.

"I'm the older twin, doofwad," she laughed, and then sighed. "I'm going to miss my running partners."

"You could always run up and visit us," I grinned deviously, knowing how long that would take.

"Run clear up to Oregon?" she asked, eyes wide with disbelief when I nodded. "Screw that. I won't miss you that much."

I couldn't hold back the laughter as I stood up and hugged Luna around her shoulders. When I let her go and glanced toward the door, I grew suddenly nervous. "I have to go talk to Kyla." Even though Kyla knew she needed more help than I could give her, I wasn't sure how she'd react to having to move to another state, and I greatly feared having to be the bearer of bad news.

I walked to the door, and before leaving to talk to Kyla I looked back at my sister and smiled that same, evil grin. "And by the way, we both know you're going to miss me that much eventually."

5

"Kyla," Jeremy sighed from his seat at my kitchen table. "I can't let you do this."

Kyla glanced up from the note she was writing, and from where I was sitting on the counter a few feet away I could see the pain on her face. She had to leave again, and that heartbreaking agony was entirely my fault. She didn't answer Jeremy, and instead looked back down at the paper beneath her. The pen in her hand was shaking visibly when she started writing with it again, and if that wasn't enough to make me feel even worse, a moment later a teardrop slipped off her cheek and onto the fresh ink.

She carefully wiped the smudge with the sleeve of her jacket, and after scribbling one more thing she carried the letter to me. "Can you make sure I didn't say too much?" She refused to look me in the eyes, so when she passed the piece of paper to me I set my hand on hers. I wanted to be more comforting, to wipe the tears from her eyes or pull her into a hug, but I could tell Jeremy was watching, and there was a feeling of scrutiny in his gaze.

When I nodded Kyla pulled her hand away from mine, and then returned to her seat so I could read the note:

Mom and Dad,

I wish I could tell you through this letter how sorry I am for doing this to you again, but I know it won't be enough. I've had to go away. I know you don't understand, and I wish I could explain it all to you, but I can't. You'll have to trust that, just like last time, I'm safe, and though you might not believe it, you're safe now too.

Please don't try to find me. I promise that one day I'll come back, and when the time comes maybe I'll be able to tell you everything and it will make it all okay. I hope you'll be able to forgive. Don't forget me. I'll be thinking of you every day. I love you.

Kyla

I swallowed past the miserable lump in my throat and forced myself off the counter. "It's good," I told Kyla as I set the note in front of Jeremy, and he instantly put it into his pocket without looking at it. I hated it, using the word 'good' to describe the letter, but I didn't know what else to call it. Her parents wouldn't be satisfied, and they probably would try to look for her. The only thing that mattered was that Kyla felt satisfied.

"They're probably freaking out already," Jeremy whispered, staring hard at the top of the table, like if he looked anywhere else, especially at Kyla, he might break down.

"You should get back," I agreed.

Slowly, his eyes wandered toward my face, and after a composing pause he nodded and stood. He took in a deep breath and trudged across the table to Kyla, waiting patiently for her to work up the nerve to say something to him. Eventually she stood, unable to meet his gaze, and wrapped her arms around his waist. The moment his arms encompassed her shoulders they both sniffled, and I had to purse my lips to keep from frowning, because that frown would've been the start of my own tears.

"Promise you'll come back," Jeremy begged, comfortingly burying his face in Kyla's hair.

"*I promise.*" *I could see her nod, and her arms tightened around him.* "*I love you, J.*"

"*You too,*" *he squeezed her again before pulling away and studying her face one last time. Then he turned around to face me, and once he was sure Kyla couldn't see him anymore a tear cascaded down his cheek.* "*Take good care of her,*" *he told me, giving the tiniest of parting smiles.*

"*Of course,*" *I assured him, gently and briefly putting my hand on his shoulder.*

Jeremy strode out the front door, and Kyla took a few steps toward it, as though she wanted to follow him. I immediately paced to her side and, despite the fact that being close to her brought me so much pain lately, I wrapped an arm around shoulders.

"*It's for the best,*" *she said, staring after the entrance of the house.* "*I know it.*" *But she sounded like she was having a hard time entirely convincing herself.*

"*That doesn't mean it can't hurt,*" *I told her.*

In response Kyla sniffled once more and wiped at her eyes. "*I'm just,*" *she paused to look at me briefly with those watery green eyes,* "*I'm going to go lie down.*" *Maybe it was kind of selfish of me, but as I nodded and watched her disappear up the stairs, I hoped she wouldn't hate me for this some day.*

***

"Hey, don't fall asleep on me." I finally woke up in the passenger seat and gave Kyla a flick on the earlobe, holding back a laugh as it jolted her from her thoughts.

"Don't worry, I'm awake," she chuckled reassuringly after blinking away her surprise.

I was bewildered this morning with how much Kyla's mood seemed to have shifted since the night before. Of course she wasn't overjoyed about having to leave, but I think the biggest help was that she felt some sense of closure because of the note she'd written. We both knew the consequences of her leaving again, and even though she'd promised, part of me wondered if after this she'd ever want to go back home. After only two months of her first absence she'd been terrified of returning, and there was the possibility that training with the Pack could take much longer. But she didn't seem to want to think about what this decision meant for the future – she knew she needed help now.

I assumed part of her being so okay with all of this was because she wasn't going alone. When Kyla arrived at my house early that morning to find me loading the jeep with a few boxes of my own clothes, she was clearly shocked. After that shock had subsided she seemed genuinely excited that I was going, which didn't do much to enlighten my confusion on her feelings for me.

Occasionally she seemed comfortable with me, so much sometimes that it killed me, and I shied away from her. It was those times she grew frustrated. She didn't show it, she was good at hiding it, but I could feel it, and I didn't understand. After all, it was her who'd broken up with me, and I could never come to terms with it if I felt like there was hope. Sometimes I thought it might just be easier if she really did hate me for bringing her into this life.

"Do you want to switch?" I stretched my arms as far out in front of me as I could and yawned.

She squinted at the GPS that hung in the windshield. "No, you already drove for like seven hours, and we're almost there." We'd left at six in the morning, and I'd driven until one o'clock when we stopped for lunch. It was now six-thirty in the afternoon, and Kyla was about to exit the highway. "How was your nap?"

"Refreshing." My stomach burned with hunger as it let out a loud growl. "I'm starving."

Kyla vigorously nodded her head in agreement. "Ever since Luna Changed me, I eat so much. I'm surprised I haven't gained a million pounds."

I turned my head toward the window so Kyla wouldn't see me wince. Every time she mentioned Luna Changing her it caused a flurry of pain and unease. I knew I should probably tell her that it wasn't Luna who'd bitten her, but I couldn't bring myself to do it. I was afraid of her knowing the truth. Afraid she'd think I'd done it for selfish reasons, to force her to stick around even after she'd broken up with me.

I cleared my throat and then chuckled nervously to fill the awkward silence I'd created. "Yeah, well, werewolf metabolism. One of my favorite perks."

A shiver traveled down my spine. Whether it was the tangible tension between Kyla and I or the fact that the cold air was seeping through a small tear in the roof of the soft-top jeep, I wasn't sure, but I turned up the heat and leaned my head against the window for the remainder of the drive. As I stared out into the forest that lined the empty road we were on, I was starting to get a little jubilant. When I'd lived in Oregon, years before moving to California, my favorite thing had been the striking density of the woods that surrounded the area. Especially now in the winter, when most of the evergreen trees were covered in snow, the forest was thick and spectacular, and the deep layer of frost that blanketed the seemingly unending wilderness provided a comforting sense of mystery and refuge.

"It's beautiful," Kyla said softly, as she must have noticed my gaze.

"Yeah." I couldn't help but grin, suddenly growing impatient to be out of the car. "I can't wait to run in it."

She slowed the jeep and turned right onto a familiar, smaller gravel road. "Looks like you won't have to wait much longer." No longer needing the GPS, she took it from the windshield and stowed it in the glove box.

We were on the small road for a good eight minutes before it stemmed off to an even smaller, unpaved driveway. I nearly bounced in my seat when the house at the end corner of it came into view. The massive two-story home was entirely made of gray stone with large, clear windows dotting the outside. The setting sun glimmered through the only opening of trees around the house, illuminating the frosted stone and acting as a spotlight on our magnificent fortress.

I pointed to a paved clearing beside the house where a couple other cars were parked, letting Kyla know to pull in there. Niko hadn't been too bummed about letting us take his jeep seeing as he'd been looking to get a new vehicle for a while. I waited borderline impatiently for Kyla to drive up next to the other cars, and the second she shifted into park I jumped out and took a huge breath of the crisp air. There was something about snow that made everything fresh and new. Pure. It cleansed the world of everything dark and dirty, leaving only the fresh scent of unpolluted air and frozen forest.

I started toward the front door of the house, but stopped when I felt something was missing. I turned and laughed when I realized it was Kyla. "Don't worry, you'll get the chance to explore," I assured the girl, who was slowly twirling and staring with awe in every direction into the forest.

She gave an apologetic smile for getting sidetracked, and followed me up the short stone steps to the large wooden door. "Should we knock?"

"No," I answered as I twisted the handle and slowly pushed open the door. "We're family." The warm air and fragrance of familiar werewolves flooded my nostrils as we walked in. We strode along the dark wood floor farther into the grand entranceway, which was lined on either side by stairs, straining our ears for the sound of anyone in the house. "Hello! Eli?"

A door opened from the second floor, and light footsteps thudded down the hall until a head peeked over the balcony. "Camille!" The slightly younger girl's bright brown eyes filled with excitement, and her black hair flowed behind her as she sprinted down the stairs. "My dad told me you were coming!" Even though she was a good four inches shorter than me, she almost managed to knock me over when she wrapped her arms around my neck in a fierce hug.

After spinning the girl around in an embrace I set her back down and grinned. "Don't act too disappointed to see me," I teased, and then watched as her eyes fixed curiously on Kyla. "Lacey, this is Kyla. Kyla, Lacey."

"Oh," Lacey drawled mischievously. "Dad said you had a new girlfriend."

"Uh, no," I barely managed to choke as both Kyla and I's faces flushed bright red, and I uncomfortably cleared my throat. "Is your dad home?"

Lacey tensed the bottom of her lip down in an apologetic wince. "Yeah, he's around here somewhere. I'll take you guys to the kitchen and then see if I can find him for you." She turned and led us under the left staircase and through a large set of double doors on the left. "Kyla, are you going to school with us now?" Kyla nodded. "What grade are you?"

"I'm a junior," she answered, and sat in a stool next to me at the dining room side of the bar that separated the kitchen from the dining room. "What about you?"

"Sophomore. I bet you guys are starving." Lacey opened the enormous refrigerator and began to pull out large bags of deli meat and cheese slices, throwing them onto the bar top. Then, mumbling to herself about food groups, she grabbed a large box of assorted berries and set it next to the meat and cheese. "I'll go find my dad. Be back in a minute."

I watched my enthusiastic friend skip out of the kitchen, and out of the corner of my eye I saw Kyla start to reach into the box of berries. I slapped her on the back of the hand, laughing in amusement at the startled glare she gave me. "I'd wait. Alpha always eats first, as long as he's coming to join us we should make sure he's already eaten."

"Oh." Kyla pulled her hand away, and her stomach growled angrily at nearly having food.

I was just as famished, and with all the savory food sitting there in front of us I couldn't deny that it was dreadfully tempting not to wait.

Luckily, Eli didn't keep us waiting for too long – he and Lacey entered the kitchen a couple minutes later.

"Camille." He grinned happily as he gave me a gentle hug. I didn't know what it was about Eli, but he seemed to have gotten younger since I'd seen him a few months before. His mahogany hair seemed to have lost some of its gray, and his hazel eyes shone brighter than ever. It had to be the season, I always remembered him being especially fond of winter. "And Kyla, it's good to see you again." Eli extended his hand, offering it to Kyla to shake.

For some reason, though I'd never known Kyla to be uncomfortable at being touched, she cringed at the movement, and I couldn't help but wonder what had changed. Maybe being bitten had made her more sensitive to it. After releasing Kyla's hand, Eli then leaned against the kitchen counter next to his daughter.

I exaggeratedly glanced from him to the food. "Have you eaten?"

His face filled with surprise as he noticed for the first time all the food in front of us. "Oh yes, yes of course. Please, dig in." I nodded the 'okay' to Kyla, and we began to scarf down our much-awaited dinner. He gave us a few minutes to slow down on eating, and then started the conversation again. "How was the drive up here?"

My mouth was full of food, so I nodded at Kyla to answer for me. "It wasn't bad," she told him. "It's a beautiful drive."

Eli's eyes lit up knowingly. "You'll find that Oregon is a beautiful place. Have you guys seen the school yet?" When both of us shook our heads he got up and walked to the far end of the kitchen counter, where there was a small stack of papers. After grabbing the stack he returned to his spot near us. "I've enrolled both of you. You'll have different classes than you did in California, and it might be hard catching up with the curriculum, but you'll only be graded for the work here on out. Nearly all of the students, including Lacey, live at the campus on the weekdays. Is it safe to assume that's okay with the two of you?"

I gulped down my food and looked to Kyla to see if she was okay with it, and receiving a slight nod I smiled at Eli. "That's fine."

"The weekends," he started thoughtfully, and popped a berry into his mouth. "I'm guessing all your belongings will be in your rooms, it's not at all uncommon for students to stay on the weekends either. Most of them are from out of state." He waited for each of us to nod again in acknowledgement, and then shuffled through the papers in front of him and pulled out two pink and two white sheets. "These pink ones are your schedules, and the white ones here are your dorm room numbers and rules. The key is attached." He pointed to the keys that were taped to each of the white sheets of paper. "I couldn't get you guys neighboring rooms, but they're only one floor apart."

Kyla pulled her key out from under the tape and looked at it happily. "Thank you, Eli."

"Sure," he said, waving it off like it was no big deal. "It's not a problem. Lacey, help me put this food away." Noticing that Kyla and I had stopped eating, he stood and started to put the items back into the refrigerator. "Now, Kyla," he started when he was satisfied, grabbing two bottles of water out before he closed it and handing them to Kyla and I. Then he grabbed a manila envelope off the counter and brought it over. "The way everything played out with your family, I had to secure you new identification – for safety reasons."

"Okay," Kyla said unsurely, and then for clarification asked, "Identification?"

Eli nodded, opening the manila envelope and dumping its contents onto the top of the bar. "Yes, new drivers license, birth certificate, social security card, and passport."

"Oh," Kyla said slowly, picking up her new drivers license to look at it. "Kyla Zade."

I'd lifted the bottle of water to my lips to take a sip, but when Kyla read the name on her license it went down the wrong pipe, and now I was coughing violently. I put the bottle down, patting my chest to try and stop myself from choking. It was bad enough I'd come all the way here with Kyla after she'd broken up with me, but now she'd been given my last name. The torture would never end.

"You okay?" Eli asked, when after thirty seconds I was still struggling to compose myself. He watched me for a few moments more after I nodded, just to make sure, and then addressed Kyla again. "The most important thing for you out here is your training. I'd like you to come here Saturday, Sunday, Tuesday, and Thursday, and train with Wesley, and every other night you'll run. Whether it's here or in the woods near the school is up to you, though if it's near the school I'd like you to take someone else along."

While Eli explained to Kyla the terms of her being here and the importance of all her training, I took the time to study the kitchen. It was rather large, and everything had been redone since I'd lived here years before. Next to the enormous, new steel refrigerator was a separate, matching freezer. Lining the wall next to the two was a dark granite counter that wrapped around to the adjacent wall, where there was a deep sink underneath a large window to the forest outside. In the wall opposite the refrigerator, beside the bar we were sitting at, there was a large walk-in pantry, which with the door open I could see was filled with all kinds of canned and boxed foods.

"You ready to go?" Lacey asked as Kyla and Eli's conversation ended, and she stood to put on the coat she'd been holding in her lap. I nodded while both Kyla and I grabbed our papers, and stood up to follow her out of the kitchen. "I'll lead and you guys can follow me in your car. Sound good?"

"When did you get your license?" I asked, eyes brightening with excitement. Lacey had been dying to drive since she was old enough to know what a car was.

"The very day after I turned sixteen, in June." Lacey grinned and pushed open the front door of the house, pulling her jacket tighter when the cold air hit her skin.

Reaching the vehicles, Lacey opened the door to a bright red coupe and laughed at me, because I was gawking. "He did *not* get that for you," I sputtered in disbelief.

She shrugged indifferently, but couldn't stop a proud smile from widening her mouth ear to ear. "You know my dad. He can't resist getting his little angel what she wants." She winked playfully before sliding into the driver's seat and closing the door.

I pulled out of the driveway and followed behind Lacey. From Eli's house, and on roads much like the thickly forested one we'd taken to get to his house in the first place, it was about a twenty-minute drive to the school. Lacey teased along the way by speeding up to lose us, and then slowing down to irritating speeds. It was all fun and games until I mockingly tailgated closely enough for her to become worried about her precious car, at which point she evened out our pace to the speed limit. I'd never been to the Tollbridge Private Academy, and upon arriving at the campus I'd have thought it was a small college. We drove past a large park into a small complex of six five-story buildings arranged in a circle, with small parking lots in between each one. At the center of the circle between all the dorms was a two-story building, where on the first floor and through a large window I could see a bunch of students lounging around.

"Is this the kind of private school where you have to wear uniforms?" Kyla kept turning her head to look in all directions out the windows.

I thought back to the times Lacey had described the school to me. "No. I remember the day Lacey almost died of excitement because uniforms got voted out."

"How long have you known her?" Kyla twisted in her seat to lean her back against the window, and her green eyes scanned me curiously.

"Forever," I answered honestly, instantly regretting it by the disappointed look on Kyla's face. "We haven't actually seen each other in years, but we'd email or talk on the phone every once in a while."

"You never mentioned her." The crestfallen look on Kyla's face deepened, flushing me with a flurry of guilt. *I didn't have time to tell you much before you broke up with me,* I thought defensively, and had to turn away from Kyla's gaze at the stab of pain it put in my chest.

"I'm sorry. It really never crossed my mind." We pulled into a couple of empty parking spots near one of the far buildings, and I avoided eye contact with Kyla at all costs. I could feel that she was still watching me disappointedly.

"It would just be nice to know who the Alpha's family is, don't you think?" She shrugged apathetically to play it off, but it was obvious she was still bothered.

I sighed silently as she and I got out of the car, not really sure how to deal with my confusion when it came to where we stood. Instead of coming up with a response at all I handed her one of the boxes she'd packed of her stuff, picking up her remaining box and duffel bag myself. "I'll come back down for my stuff," I told her after receiving a questioning glance.

When we met Lacey on the curb in front of our building I handed her Kyla's duffel bag, and we followed her inside to the elevator. The dormitory buildings were built much like a hotel. The entrance opened up into a lobby, where a staff member manned the front desk checking ID cards. The aroma of various types of food floated down the hall across from the opening of the elevator, and I assumed there was a cafeteria somewhere on the first floor.

"What's your room number, Kyla?" The doors of the elevator closed, and Lacey waited patiently for Kyla to reach into her pocket for the piece of paper with her information on it.

"Um, three fifty one," Kyla answered.

Lacey pushed the button for the third floor, and we stood in silence until it dinged and the doors opened. The hall the elevator opened up to was brightly lit and lined with numbered doors, a few of which were open.

"The halls are co-ed, but boys and girls have separate bathrooms." As we walked toward the end of the hall, Lacey pointed to a miniature foyer with a single swinging door at the end. "That's the girl's bathroom, showers and toilets of course. Did you guys bring shower sandals? Because you're going to want them."

Both Kyla and I shook our heads as we stopped in front of a door numbered three fifty one. "That's okay, we'll go into town tomorrow and get you guys some. Key?" Lacey held out her hand while Kyla pulled the key out of her pocket and handed it over.

Before we walked into the now open room, I briefly caught the eye of a girl stepping out of her own room at the end of the hall, and then I disappeared into Kyla's dorm. A desk sat near the far wall of the carpeted room, while on one of the adjacent walls was a tall dresser and armoire. I dropped the box I was holding onto the bed on the opposite side of the room as the dresser, and sat down next to it.

"You guys just moving in?" The girl I had seen moments before knocked on the doorframe and poked her head in. She smiled when she recognized the youngest of us. "Hey, Lacey. Friends of yours?"

Lacey grinned and skipped to the door, pulling her in excitedly. The girl was average height, maybe an inch shorter than Kyla. Her dirty blonde hair was pulled back into a ponytail, and under her bright hazel eyes light freckles dotted her tanned cheeks.

"That's Camille, and this is Kyla," Lacey introduced. "Guys, this is Abby."

"Nice to meet you." I reached out from my spot on the bed and shook the girl's hand, then watched as she shook Kyla's.

I probably wasn't meant to notice, but I saw Abby give Kyla a discreet up-down as they greeted each other. It was subtle, and maybe even unintentional, but I didn't like it, and I couldn't stop a fit of jealousy from raging in the pit of my stomach. The last thing I needed was for Kyla to find someone new while I was still trying to help her adjust. As she let go of Kyla's hand, Abby's eyes met mine, and she cleared her throat uncomfortably. I looked away instantly, somewhat ashamed. I didn't think I'd made my unease that obvious, guess I'd have to hide it better.

"Well, I should let you guys unpack." Abby started for the door, somewhat awkwardly at me having caught her gander.

"Hey, wait, are you busy? Why don't you help Kyla out so me and Camille can go get her stuff?" Lacey suggested, and before Abby could give an answer, she was pulling me out of the room.

I did my best to hide my aggravation from Lacey as we got back on the elevator, but I couldn't keep from letting out an exasperated sigh. Lacey glanced over at me with a curious squint, but quickly shrugged it off when I gave no explanation. I was being ridiculous. I couldn't be jealous after hardly one minute with the girl, and it was no longer my place to be defensive over Kyla.

I was, however, curious. "What's the scoop on Abby?"

Lacey opened her mouth to answer, but then stopped as a smirk tugged at her lips. "What's the scoop on you and Kyla?" We stepped off the elevator and made our way through the lobby.

"What?" I asked as I pushed open the front door and held it for Lacey, who smiled thankfully.

Then she rolled her eyes. "You know what I'm talking about. I might be young, but I'm not stupid. You could cut that tension with a knife."

Even though the mention of my relationship caused a slight pang in my chest, I shouldn't have been surprised – Lacey had already said that Eli mentioned Kyla to her. "We were together, but she broke up with me."

"Then why is she a werewolf?" Her face scrunched with confusion.

"Your dad didn't explain anything to you?" I asked, wishing he had so I wouldn't have to talk about it. She shook her head. "One of the mutts that was creating problems for everyone tried to kill her. I couldn't let her die like that."

Lacey tsk-ed sympathetically, "And now you're here trying to help her?" I nodded solemnly and pulled my belongings out of the jeep. "That's rough."

I shrugged, and remained silent for the next minute while we re-turned to the building carrying a couple boxes. I hadn't thought much about it until now, but it *was* rough. When I'd talked to Luna about coming to Oregon with Kyla, I'd downplayed the weight of the situation. But as I said goodbye to Lacey and sat on the bed of my single-student room, I'd never felt so lonely.

The room was uniform and cold, and while I still cared for Kyla, and Lacey was a good friend to me, they were all I had. I didn't know or really care much about anyone else. Without unpacking, I stripped and put on my pajamas, set my schedule on the desk near the wall, and lay down to go to sleep. I would have fallen asleep quickly if not for the noise that came with student dorms. The sound of my new peers in neighboring rooms thickened the silence of my own. It boxed me in, in my own silent prison.

6

"When did you get in?" Abby asked me as she unfolded the sheets that had come with the room and stretched them over my bed.

"About an hour ago. We had dinner at a friend's house first." I looked up from the box I was unpacking and studied the girl who'd kindly stayed to help me.

Abby was certainly attractive. Not in the same provocative way Camille was, but in her own simplistically pretty sort of way. At about the same height as me she was rather thin, which made her curvy attributes surprising. The smooth appearance of her tanned, freckled cheeks gave her a lively complexion, emphasizing how attractive she was by making her seem energetic and fun. *Damn these werewolf hormones.*

I saw Abby smile out of the corner of my eye, and raised a curious eyebrow at her. "What are you laughing about?"

"Oh, nothing. I was just thinking about something." It was obvious that she tried to force the smirk from her face as she answered, but I let it rest at that. "Can I ask you something?" I nodded. "Are you seeing Camille?"

My jaw dropped as I struggled for a response. It wasn't that the question was out of line. I'd been talking with my new friend for nearly fifteen minutes now, certainly long enough for the topic to come up. I just didn't know how Abby had gotten the idea about Camille and I. "How–what makes you ask?"

She chuckled and sat cross-legged on the freshly made bed. "Honestly?" she asked, to which I nodded again, almost impatiently. "The same way I know you're a werewolf."

That particular word coming from Abby's mouth made my heart speed up, and not in a good way. How did she know I was a werewolf? And did that make her a threat? I took a deep breath, if I let thoughts like that continue it wouldn't be long until the itching began in my fingertips. I knew how the Pack dealt with threats, but I certainly wasn't fond of entertaining the violent idea.

"Whoa, calm down there jumpy. I didn't mean to freak you out." Abby unfolded her legs and scooted to the edge of the bed with urgency. "I'm not normal either." I took another deep, calming breath, and questioningly held my hands out in front of me to request an explanation. "Telepath. I can read minds," she said, tapping her index finger against her temple.

I slowly nodded as I let the information sink in, and once it did my face flushed redder than it ever had. I had definitely been checking her out a minute ago. "Oh God, did you hear?"

Abby grinned, clearly unworried about putting my embarrassment to rest. "That you think I'm attractive?" I covered my face ashamedly. "Don't worry about it. I've heard much worse."

By that grin you didn't seem to mind it, I thought. I just couldn't stop it, and I'd certainly underestimated the amount I could blush. The corner of Abby's mouth turned up amusedly, but she seemed to ignore the thought so as not to embarrass me further.

"So, you and Camille?" she repeated her question expectantly.

"Oh, uh," I pulled the chair out from the desk, and sat in it facing her. "It's really complicated." I expected to end the discussion on the topic there, but Abby waited patiently for further explanation. "I guess I kind of screwed up, and she hasn't forgiven me yet. At this rate I don't know if she ever will. So, I don't really know where her and I stand right now."

"Did you cheat on her or something?" she asked, clearly not at all shy about the things she said.

"You're blunt," I couldn't help but laugh in amusement as I pointed it out. Abby just shrugged, either unable to come up with a defense or not really caring to, but I wasn't interested in supplying the detailed answer to the question, so I said, "No, it wasn't anything like that." Then I repeated my first answer. "It's complicated." I wasn't sure exactly how Abby's mind reading ability worked, but if she could read the flashes of explanation that involuntarily ran through my thoughts, then she would probably get the gist of it.

I gave her a few seconds to pick my brain, and she seemed to understand a little better, because she nodded. "I'm sorry to hear it." She pursed her lips sympathetically and, now that I was no longer freaked out, resumed her comfortable position in the middle of the bed.

"You don't seem too uncomfortable with it, um, the topic, I mean. Are you?" I couldn't decide on the best way to end the inquiry, but Abby knew what I was asking.

"I'm not anything," she answered with a nonchalant shrug. "When you're in peoples' heads as much as I am you kind of forget certain preferences. Like gender." I nodded in understanding while Abby took a good look around the room. "A single dorm, huh?" she mused. "I guess that's what you get when the Pack pays your tuition."

"What?" I asked, confused. "I thought all the rooms were singles."

She shook her head. "Nope, most the students have roommates. The single rooms are for those of us who care to pay the extra price for it. I certainly wish I had my own room."

"Oh." I suddenly felt guilty that Eli was not only paying for my tuition, but also for me to have my own room.

I understood that he was worried about me being put with a human and having to Change all the time. That would get terribly suspicious. I just couldn't help but worry that I was starting to become a burden to the Pack. He could have easily put me with Camille. Though that would have been a bit of an uncomfortable living situation. Abby could undoubtedly hear while I contemplated all the information, and she gave an affectionate smile as if to say she understood how I felt.

"How much do you know?" I asked curiously, leaving my reflections behind to engage her in a conversation.

She looked to the ceiling in deep thought. "A lot. Actually, a lot of the students at this school aren't normal. The area is sort of a gathering place for the different races of supernaturals. I don't know how that was decided, but it's true. I don't know, I know plenty of things," she said, growing shyly modest.

"Yeah, the whole mind reading thing doesn't really seem fair," I laughed, but I was struggling to keep my thoughts from going anywhere I didn't want Abby to hear, and I found myself wondering if she knew that.

She must've known it, because she gave a sly smile. "I usually do my best to stay out of people's heads, but I can't exactly turn it off, and sometimes it's too hard to resist." I felt my face flush again, and Abby's eyes glimmered with a witty remark, but instead of saying whatever she wanted to she pulled out her cell phone and gawked at the time. "Oh, crap, I got to go. My friends go to this club called The Orchid every Friday night, and I'm supposed to go today. You're welcome to join, if you're interested."

I considered the offer for a moment, and as much as I'd have liked to go, I was exhausted. "Thanks, but maybe next time." I ushered her to the door, and before closing it gave a grateful smile. "And thanks for helping me unpack a bit."

"Yeah, sure." Abby waved goodbye and started heading down the hall toward the elevator, calling over her shoulder, "I'll see you around."

I let out a sigh as I closed the door and turned to stare at the empty room. I was definitely going to have to go into town and buy some posters to decorate the bare walls. After I threw on my pajamas and turned out the lights, I climbed into bed. I would have gone to see how Camille was settling in, but I couldn't remember what room she was in. I figured it was for the best anyway. While I'd been ecstatic and grateful that she'd come to Oregon with me, I couldn't help but feel like she was slightly resentful of it. After all, I *had* pulled her away from her family and home.

I took in a deep breath of the bed I was lying in. The thing I'd missed most in the two weeks I'd been home was having Camille's scent around random areas of the house. Now that I was in my own private dorm, her scent was nowhere to be found. This place was unfamiliar, stressful, and nerve-wracking, and if I hadn't been so tired from driving all day I never would have been able to fall asleep.

***

I groaned as I picked my head up off the bar in Eli's kitchen. It was quite early Saturday morning, and when he meant I'd be training every Saturday, he wasn't kidding. I didn't even get a couple days to adjust. Camille had gotten a wake up call from Lacey at seven that morning saying Eli wanted us there early, and breakfast would be provided. So, despite the ungodly hour for a weekend, I did my duties and sat with a fresh cup of coffee.

"Next time you can take the jeep on your own and I'll sleep in," Camille whined next to me as she lay her head down.

Lacey skipped into the kitchen all too cheerfully, black hair wet from a shower. "My dad's almost done getting ready. He'll be down in a few minutes." How she was so happy to be awake, I would never know. Lacey looked down, startled as her stomach growled, and giggled. "Good thing, too. That bacon smells good, David."

We all looked over at the young werewolf who'd been cooking for the last forty-five minutes, mercilessly overwhelming my starving stomach with the savory aroma of bacon and eggs. I'd met the large, black-haired, blue-eyed Beta wolf back in California when they came to help with the mutt situation. I'd never gotten the chance to put a personality to the rough exterior, but now I was growing aggravated at the twinkling of laughter in his eyes as he teasingly stirred the bacon to release more of that delicious smell into the air.

"Are you training with us, Lacey?" Without lifting her head, Camille turned it to the side to look up at the joyful girl.

"Pfft." Lacey waved her hand at us sarcastically. "I don't need training. I'm the best damn werewolf in this town."

"Except for that exceptionally large head of yours." Eli walked into the kitchen and thumped his daughter playfully on the head. "Is the food done?" David nodded as he removed the large pans from the stove and dumped the bacon and eggs into separate bowls. Eli stepped out of the kitchen and yelled so that anyone in the rest of the house could hear, "Food's ready!"

David handed Lacey the enormous bowl of eggs, the bowl of bacon to Camille and two plates piled with toast to me. We all walked past the bar and into the dining room, and set the food in the middle of the table before taking our seats around it. I watched as four other men came in and sat around the table. I'd smelled the various scents of werewolves in the house, but the whole time I'd been here I hadn't heard or seen a sign of anyone else being around. Probably because they were all getting the sleep I wished I could have. One of them I also knew from California. A tall, lanky, beachy looking blond named Will. A smile tugged at my lips as I remembered the crush Luna had developed on him, and I found myself wondering if they'd talked recently.

Once everyone was seated around the table, Eli was the first to dig in. He stacked his plate with food, and I followed suit in that everyone else was waiting until he'd eaten. I couldn't say I understood the incorporation of the wolf custom into our almost human lives, but the importance of the show of respect was obvious, and so I waited patiently along with everyone else while the Alpha ate. Everyone talked noisily to distract their hungry stomachs from watching Eli, because once he'd finished his first round of food it was David's turn. As the Beta, he came just behind Eli in importance, which meant he also got to eat before the rest of us.

"Kyla, you've met Will right?" Lacey was sitting across the table from me and pointed to Will, who was next to her.

I nodded and waved at him. He smiled back, and then I motioned to the others. "But I haven't met everyone else."

Lacey's face brightened with excitement that she'd get to do some introductions, and she pointed to another man on her other side. He was an older guy, although with the slow aging of werewolves it was hard for me to pinpoint his exact age. His short, sandy brown hair was dusted with gray, and his green eyes shone bright under his dark eyebrows. "This is Richard, he's Will's dad, and this is Nathan. He goes to school with us, he's a junior like you." She pointed to a boy who was sitting next to Camille at the end of the table.

Nathan stood shorter than Lacey, but he was incredibly burley. His dark hair was buzzed short, and his eyes were a matching dark brown. Even though I noticed him walk in, he hadn't really caught my attention, and I realized he hadn't said much of anything since we sat down.

"And I'm Wesley." The last remaining werewolf enthusiastically stood, and mopped his straight brown hair off his forehead before he reached across the table to shake hands with me.

"Nice to meet you." I held back a giggle as I took his hand, slightly put off by his fervor. His teethed flashed in the biggest, most charming grin I'd ever seen, the excitement extending to his big gray eyes.

Before I realized it the clanking of forks against plates grew louder. David had finished eating, and so everyone else had begun to pile mounds of food onto their plates. I grabbed the bowl of eggs that Camille was passing to me and dumped some onto my dish. The house grew strangely silent as each of us starving werewolves filled our empty stomachs. I was sure there was nothing special about the food David had made, but I was so hungry it was already one of the best meals I'd ever had.

I could have eaten more, but as I went back for another round there was no food left, so I settled for more conversation. "Where's Julian?" I asked as I noticed the absence of the one other werewolf I'd met in California.

"On a much deserved vacation," Eli answered after taking a sip of his coffee. "He's visiting family in Arizona for a few months."

I nodded in understanding and agreement. If anybody deserved a vacation, it was Julian – nothing like a few days of torture to get you some sympathy and a Pack-paid trip. It made me wonder how Eli managed to house multiple werewolves and pay for Camille's, Lacey's, and my tuition at the same time, and decided I'd ask Camille about it later on. Now that the food was gone and everyone had scraped their plates clean, there was no reason for anyone to hang around. I sat patiently with Camille while everyone dumped their dishes in the sink and dispersed to do their own thing.

"Ready to start training?" Wesley asked from the gap between the bar and kitchen, and then motioned for us to go with him.

I got up and followed him to the rear of the house, closely trailed by a tired and still grumbling Camille. Shortly after we started I grew surprised at how long we'd been walking. While the house *did* look big, from the front it didn't look *this* big. We walked down a long, rounded hall until we reached the back of the house, and Wesley led us onto a patio. The patio, much to my pleasure, was indoors, with walls made completely of glass so as to give the feel of being outside without letting in the cold. The floors were a shiny white marble that reflected the sun at us, both warming and lighting the bright room at the same time.

"Are we going to Phase in here?" I asked, warily looking at the glass walls, which would be a hazard to a bunch of large, rambunctious wolves.

Wes simply shook his head, a mischievous smirk turning up the corner of his mouth. "This is where we'll be doing yoga."

My jaw dropped, and Camille shared an equal reaction as she scoffed, "Yoga?"

"Yes, Camille, yoga," Wes replied sarcastically, but still he received skeptical glances from both of us. "Okay, stand on one foot," he instructed, and I watched curiously as Camille did what she was told. "Now fold your arms across your chest."

Once Camille did so he gave her a second to steady her balance, and then lightly tapped her on the shoulder. I held back a laugh as Camille stumbled, having to stand normally so she wouldn't fall over. However, Wes had made his point. He'd barely touched her, and if she'd had better balance she wouldn't have been affected by it.

"Controlling your Phases isn't just about emotional control. You need to know, intimately, your body's limits. You need to be able to control things like your breathing." When he saw both our eyes glaze in disinterest, he added, "You'll find exercises like this help your fighting, too." We still just stared at him blankly, so he stopped trying to convince us. "Okay, well, you're doing this regardless, so sit."

"Yes, Master Wesley," Camille said tauntingly, and put her palms together and bowed, causing me to burst into laughter.

Wesley glowered at both of us, but lowered himself to the floor and waited patiently for us to follow his lead. Once we'd sat across from him he crossed his legs pretzel-style, and motioned for us to do the same. "Put your hands on your knees, and make sure your back is straight. That means no slouching, Kyla." I sighed and twisted my tired body until I relaxed enough to maintain good posture. "When you take in a breath through your nose, you don't want to use your nostrils. You use the back of your mouth, like this." The light hissing sound of air going through Wesley's throat sounded uncomfortable, and I couldn't figure out what he meant. It took a few tries, but after finally replicating the sound, I understood. "Good," he praised happily. "Now close your eyes and breathe just like that, but don't let your shoulders or chest move. You want your ribs to expand out, not up."

Wesley closed his eyes and started breathing. Curious as to whether Camille was doing it or not I glanced over, only to find her looking at me with the same puzzled expression that I had. I held back a giggle and shrugged, closing my eyes to do what I was supposed to. After about three minutes of sitting there and just breathing, I began to grow restless. My mind wandered, and I put off the urge to shake my leg or tap my fingers. Eventually I opened one eye to see what the other two were doing, and, finding that they were still focused, I sighed silently and continued the exercise.

Forcing myself to relax, I was finally able to keep my mind at ease. I concentrated on the smells that whipped through my nose with every breath. The subtle sounds of chirping birds from outside the thin glass walls. Camille's slow, steady breathing next to me. Now that I thought about it, we were sitting rather close. Even though our folded knees weren't touching, I was close enough to feel the heat that emanated from her warm body. It made the restlessness return. I desperately wanted to be closer. The only sign she'd given to let me know she even still cared about me was coming to Oregon, and even though that was a big statement, it wasn't affectionate. Or intimate.

"Kyla, focus on your breathing," Wes warned without opening his eyes.

I hadn't realized I'd started breathing faster, but I instantly tried to regain my inward balance. Only, I couldn't. Not with that tiny inch of space between Camille and I. It embodied the terrifying distance I felt her forcing between us, mocking the fact that she could live without me, and it was driving me crazy. So I twisted my body, pretending to stretch as I discreetly scooted that inch closer so our knees would touch. I rapidly closed my eyes to act like I hadn't noticed, but I knew the action had caused her to look over. I could feel her watching me. Studying. And I prayed she wouldn't pull away.

Much to my content, she didn't move, and moments later I felt that heavy gaze removed from me. I let the corner of my mouth turn up in relief as the heat from Camille's body flowed freely to mine, filling my very core with the calming, satiating energy I needed to achieve perfect composure. For the next five minutes that's how we sat, breathing deeply, in and out, at such a similar and steady pace I felt we could be one person. It was comfortable, as though now that I was touching her, I was where I belonged. Camille was home.

After a while Wes stirred and stood, motioning us to our feet so he could show us the next exercise. The following few hours consisted of us doing various poses and exercises meant to increase our connection with our own bodies, and I was feeling the connection all right. Even if we were only doing yoga for hours, I never would have thought it could make me sore.

"Just thirty more seconds," Wes announced as we stood in a one legged pose. I sighed with relief, my leg was shaking and I couldn't hold myself up for much longer. A few moments later he set his other foot on the ground and gave a content grin. "Nicely done. You girls hungry?"

Both of us nodded vigorously, and he chuckled as he led us out the glass door in the side of the room to the limitless backyard. We walked around the side of the house until we were hidden from everything but the forest. There were no windows on the exterior of this side, and no sign of the driveway. No sign of anyone but us. There was, however, a two foot, camouflaged, watertight box against the wall. Wesley lifted open the lid and swiftly removed his jacket and shirt, casually throwing them into it.

"We're Changing? I thought we were going to eat?" I asked in shock, averting my eyes as Wes continued to strip.

"We're doing both," he answered, a smug smile parting his lips when my confusion deepened. "You're going to catch your meal. I need to see how you're doing in wolf form, and this gives me a good opportunity." He finished piling his clothes into the box, and took a few steps away from Camille and I. "Woo, it's nippy isn't it? Make sure you close the lid before you Phase."

Without giving us a chance to ask questions or protest, Wes Phased, and an enormous multicolored wolf took his place. His tongue lolled out happily, and I could see the grin flash in his gray eyes before he bound-ed off into the forest, leaving us on our own as his color-specked fur disappeared in the woods.

"But I've never hunted before!" I called after the retreating wolf, which undoubtedly heard me but paid no mind.

I looked worriedly to Camille, who just chuckled and shrugged. "Don't look at me. I've been dying to run since we got here." I watched nervously as she shrugged off her jacket. "You're going to do fine. Luna always bragged about how good you were getting. Hunting is just like sneaking up on her."

I sighed in defeat, and copied Camille in taking off my jacket and throwing it into the box. She was the first to finish undressing, and Changed as I threw my last article of clothing away with the rest of them. I closed the lid quickly while jumping from foot to bare foot, trying to keep the snow from making them too cold. I pushed away the shivers growing in my spine and focused on the start of the itching in my limbs.

The itching rapidly grew to tingling, and I embraced the last moment of cold against my skin before I felt the pain like my body was being ripped to shreds. After the short flash was gone, I stretched my giant wolf paws in front of me and shook out my golden fur. Camille was right about the pain of Phasing getting easier. I'd almost passed out from it the first time. I wasn't sure whether it was hurting less or I was just getting used to it, but either way, it came and went more fleetingly every time.

I looked up to see my dark brown companion rolling playfully in the snow, kicking it in all directions with her paws and scooping it with her mouth to throw it into the air. I crouched and dug my toes into the snow, watching closely for the perfect time to pounce. It was easy enough since she wasn't paying any attention to me. I scooted forward a couple inches, and once she was rolling on her back I bolted toward the wolf, eventually plowing into the side of her. The dark wolf let out a growl of surprise, but swiftly rolled onto its feet and lowered its front paws playfully. She sprang, and thinking that she intended to land right on top of me, I ducked. Camille landed behind me, but instead of turning to pounce again she took off into the forest. I followed, and soon realized we were tracking Wesley's trail.

It led us about a mile deep into the forest, where we spotted him hunched low to the ground. Thinking he hadn't noticed us I crouched, about to show him just how good at sneaking I was, but I'd gotten too far ahead of myself. He glanced back at us, ears low to his head, and lifted his nose to the air, signaling us to sniff. I immediately recognized the scent as prey, though I was uncertain of what kind. It was something big judging by the strength of the smell. Deer, bison, hell, I wouldn't put it past a werewolf Wes's size to see a bear as a suitable meal.

With my belly to the ground, I crawled alongside Camille to where Wes was crouched behind a small bush. I lifted myself up just enough to see what he was watching – a deer, and a big one at that. My eyes met Wesley's, and he nodded his head in the direction of the animal, telling me to go for it. I almost whined with fear as I shook my own head, refusing to go, but when he nudged me with his snout it was clear he'd made up his mind.

I sighed and peeked around the bush for the best way to sneak up on the animal. It was standing behind a tall collection of shrubs, only the top of its head bobbing up as it took breaks from feeding on something under the snow. Fortunately the forest was thick, leaving plenty of places for me to hide. Even more fortunately, the deer didn't have antlers. Otherwise I would have flat out refused. I didn't know the first thing about hunting. Yeah, I'd snuck up on Luna plenty of times, but I didn't know how well deer could see or smell. Or even where I was supposed to jump, or push, or bite. As I crept my way closer and closer while hiding behind trees and bushes, I knew I didn't have the slightest clue.

Eventually I was hunched behind a large tree about thirty feet from my target, and ironically, *I* was terrified. I'd gotten as far as I could without it becoming aware of me, and from here on out I wasn't sure how to proceed. I carefully studied the deer, and while it was tall, it looked thin and feeble. I decided I'd run for it and then pounce on its back, hopefully buckling it to the ground. It worked every time I did it to Luna. Without another thought, I sprinted straight for it.

It immediately took off in the opposite direction, but I already had my momentum built and easily caught up. Finally, with a last push off the ground and jaws wide open, I sprang to land a bite wherever I could, managing to get a hold of the deer's flank. Instantly after, I felt a sharp pain shoot through me as one of its hooves caught me in the shoulder, causing me to yelp loudly and release my grip. I tried to maintain my balance and continue chasing the freed animal, but the injury in my limb caused me to stumble, and I rolled across the snow before coming to a halt on my side.

Camille was the first to reach me, and she nudged me worriedly as I lie there, willing the stabbing away. I growled in aggravation, in too much pain to be touched, but she nudged me again. When I still refused to get up, she took the scruff of my neck in her teeth, and pulled me off the ground so I would stand. As she studied the hurt front limb I realized she was checking to make sure it wasn't broken. To appease her I stood on all fours, and even though the shooting pain wasn't subsiding, I was able to put weight on it, thankfully signaling my shoulder was only bruised.

I took a few difficult strides to play off the pain I really felt, trying to tell myself that my ego was hurt more than my shoulder. Did a deer seriously just kick me? Wesley watched the spectacle silently with a mixture of concern and amusement in his eyes, and I could tell he was deciding what to do. I lowered my head at him and let out a whimper, letting him know I was done for the day. Thankfully he seemed okay with that, and we made our way slowly but surely back to the house.

"Kyla, you took that hit like a pro!" Wes praised happily as he pulled his clothes back on.

"Gee, thanks," I mumbled unenthusiastically. I was struggling to pull my clothes on since the jabbing pain returned every time I moved my arm.

Camille must have noticed each time I winced, because she grabbed my coat out of the box and held it up behind me. I let her help as I pushed each of my arms through, and she delicately slid it over my shoulders. Then I felt a gentle tug on my uninjured arm to turn me around, and even though it wasn't necessary, she began to zip my jacket for me.

"Thanks," I murmured, with difficulty since my breath hitched at how close she was. My grateful eyes met hers as she finished sliding the zipper up, and, as if suddenly growing shy, she gave a timid smile and backed away. "So, lunch?" I asked Wes, trying to get my mind off the wanton longing Camille had put in my chest.

Wes started to lead the way back into the house, glancing behind at us as he walked. "I guess I'll make something. I owe you that much," he winked apologetically at me. "Why don't you guys hang out in the living room? I'll call you when it's done."

Both of us nodded, and once we made our way into the house we parted with Wes and walked to the living room. I was expecting it to be a large, dark, old-fashioned room lined with bookshelves and globes. Instead, it was rather light and modern. A large television was mounted on the farthest of the white walls in front of a long, black leather couch, and in one corner sat a beautiful, antique-looking grand piano. Aside from those it was a rather empty room. A few decorative paintings hung on the walls, and a black shag rug took up the large space from the door to the back of the couch. It made me wonder what other rooms were in the house and how they were decorated.

"Do you want to watch TV?" Camille asked as she pointed to the large couch.

I shook my head and continued glancing around the room. "The house is a lot bigger than it looks, huh?" I looked to Camille, who nodded. "Want to give me a tour?"

She gave a consenting shrug. "A lot's changed since the last time I was here, but we can explore together."

I nodded my approval, following her out of the living room and farther down the hall away from the kitchen. I soon discovered that the house was built in a sort of circle, each of the rooms arranged around the grand entranceway.

"Bathroom." Camille flicked on the light of a small bathroom, and then turned it back off before I got a chance to go in because there was nothing out of the ordinary.

The next room we ended up in was a small library. Each of the four walls was lined from floor to ceiling with books. There was a single break in the bookshelves on one side of the room to make a spot for a large brick fireplace, above which there was an old painting of someone I assumed was an important family member. The dark, oriental carpet matched perfectly with the large chandelier that hung high on the ceiling, illuminating the room in a bright glow. Five leather armchairs were arranged in a circle at the center of the small library, set around a low, dark wood coffee table. I took a deep, satisfying breath. The whole room smelled like that one book I'd discovered at Camille's house – old, textured, and rich.

Suddenly the light dimmed and then brightened back to normal, and I passed a startled look to Camille, who laughed as she pushed down on the light switch once more. "Mood lighting."

I beamed as the chandelier dimmed, and a small amount of light was cast around the room, playing off the dark wood and textured ceiling like sparkles. It was magical, and I wouldn't have minded lying comfortably in front of the fireplace to relax in here for hours.

"Ready?" Camille interrupted, and motioned for me to follow her to the next room. As we continued through the house, she pointed to an open door without stopping, "We already saw the glass room."

Eventually we reached a closed door farther down the hall, and Camille stopped before turning the handle. I watched silently as for the next few seconds she stood paralyzed, staring at the door like she was afraid of what was behind it. Then she sighed, pushed it open, and stepped into the room. I was surprised at where we were. The entire back wall of the room was a window, letting in a flow of natural light. Aside from the glass room, this had to be the brightest in the house. The walls were a luminous white, and, just like the glass room, the floors were a pure, brilliant marble. Near the sidewall was a simple wooden chair sitting in front of a painting easel. Next to those was a white metal cabinet, which had been painted and covered with beautiful vine like designs of all different colors. I assumed inside the cabinet were various painting supplies like brushes, oils and canvases. Marvelous paintings of different people, objects and animals hung on and leaned against every inch of wall. Now that I looked more closely at the white floor, it was spotted all over with accidental drips of color. As I did with the library, I inhaled, and the wonderful smell of oil paint and fabric flooded my nostrils.

"This room hasn't changed a bit," Camille whispered, quiet enough that it was barely audible even to me.

"What is this place?" I asked as I took my time walking around the room, studying every painting closely.

"The studio." Camille gave a small, wistful smile. "Lacey's mom was an artist. When I lived here Lacey and I used to spend all day this room, lying in the sun and watching her mom paint. She painted us a lot, and taught us all about art." Camille pointed to a messy looking canvas leaned against the wall next to her. "Let us finger paint sometimes too."

There was no way I could have missed the sadly reminiscent tone Camille's voice had taken on. "What happened to her?"

She strode beside me and ran her fingers gently down a painting that hung on the wall in front of us. "There's no bigger accomplishment for some mutts than killing an Alpha. When you can't get the Alpha, his mate is the next best thing."

"Oh," was all I could think to say, but then I remembered that Camille's family had moved away because her dad grew worried about them. "Is that why you left?"

She nodded. "My dad used to be Beta, like David is now. He never minded until he saw how far mutts were willing to go. It was the hardest thing he ever had to do, leaving his best friend after his wife just died. I threw a fit, too. Lacey needed me, and my dad was taking us away."

"How long ago was that?" I asked as I realized I had no idea when exactly Camille had moved to California.

"Not too long. I was nine, so, nine years ago." Camille moved a painting so she could sit and lean her back against the wall, and then cleared a space next to her for me. "She was the first one I told that I was gay. Lacey's mom, I mean. She was like a favorite aunt. I could always talk to her about anything. She was going to help me tell my parents about the whole thing too. That was only a few days before…"

"I'm sorry," I sighed sympathetically, and rested my hand on Camille's knee in an attempt to be comforting. "Is it weird being back?"

Camille's eyes wandered cautiously to my hand, and then back up as she shrugged. "It's actually really nice being back. I like California, don't get me wrong, but this place has always been home." Those dark brown eyes ambled to my hand again, and this time she pulled her knees up to her chest, my hand slipping off as she did.

I tried not to let my disappointment show as I continued the conversation. "How'd you realize so young that you liked girls?" I felt strange talking to Camille about this since our relationship was on such delicate ground, but at the same time I hoped it would open her up to forgiving me and letting things go back to normal.

The sadness disappeared from Camille's eyes, and she grinned. "That was actually Lacey's doing. She used to try so hard to get me to kiss the boys from town, because she'd had her first kiss before I did. She thought I never wanted to because I didn't know how, so one time she offered to show me." My jaw dropped as I pictured Camille kissing Lacey, and realizing the look on my face Camille burst into laughter, shaking her head and waving her hands in front of her for emphasis. "No, no, we didn't actually. Lacey's the straightest person I know, I *think* she was just kidding. But I did realize that I would have rather kissed her than any of the boys from around here."

"That's because you've always had a secret crush on me," Lacey teased as she appeared in the doorway. Her eyes dimmed for a few moments as she looked around the memory-filled room, but she quickly pushed it away and turned her glance cheerfully back to Camille and I. "Wesley's looking for you, he says lunch is ready."

Starving and excited to eat, I stood, but Camille stopped me before I could leave the room with Lacey. "How's your shoulder?"

"It still hurts," I said, turning back and watching curiously on as she drew closer. "Now it's only throbbing."

"Let me see." Without further comment she carefully stretched my shirt back from my shoulder to study the bruise, wincing when she saw it. "That looks pretty bad." She gently laid her hand across the wound. "And it's really warm."

I knew it was warm and that's why it was throbbing so painfully, although I would swear Camille's hand was hotter than my bruise was, but her touch made my heart skip. It had been so long since she voluntarily got anywhere near me. Moments before this she'd even shrugged off my attempt at comforting affection. I couldn't help but wonder where the sudden complacency had come from. I met her eyes with my own, preparing something to say or ask, but she looked away and hastily replaced my shirt to my shoulder, her cheeks flushing red like she'd been caught with her hand in the cookie jar.

"We'll get you some ice while we eat," she said as she turned and left for the kitchen, as usual avoiding the one topic I wanted to bring up.

I stood there bewildered, and stared after her for a few moments. So she would touch me as long as I pretended not to notice? I didn't understand it, and the touch only left me craving more. She was punishing me. That had to be it. She was trying to play games with my head so I'd feel the way she had. It was cruel, and confusing. Either that, or she just couldn't make up her mind. In any case, I'd try not to care. She was talking to me, laughing with me, touching me. At that moment, I couldn't have asked for more.

7

"Don't forget that homework tonight is questions twenty through fifty on page four-oh-three. Also, questions one through fifty on page four-sixteen." I watched my new math teacher, Mr. Werner, write our homework assignment on the white board as the students began to file out of the room. "Miss Zade, can I see you up front?" I continued toward the exit, unaccustomed yet to being called anything but Walters. "Miss Zade," he repeated.

Finally realizing that the teacher was talking to me, I redirected my route from the door to the front desk and sighed, not just because I was overly ready for lunch, but also because of the already excessive homework load. That's what I got for enrolling in a private school. My teacher was fairly young, and while I'd already heard plenty of the girls in the class talk about how attractive he was, I didn't think he was anything special – brown hair, brown eyes, and a generic face that easily blended him into a crowd.

"You know there's a test coming up at the end of the week?" Mr. Werner sat on the edge of his desk and twirled his pen in his fingers. I nodded. "Since this is your first day, if you need it, I'm willing to give you an extra week to prepare."

"Oh, that's okay." I smiled appreciatively, but shook my head. "I was taking advanced algebra at my last school. We weren't to this topic yet, but I can catch up by the end of the week."

"Okay, great," he said, seemingly impressed that I didn't want the extra time anyway, and set his pen down behind him. "If you need any help don't hesitate to ask me or any of the other students."

Unsure of what else to say, I smiled again, said 'thanks,' and left. The old halls of the school were crowded with students and a few teachers, going every direction to enjoy their hour of lunch. I didn't know where Camille was, and since I didn't have a cell phone to call and find out I decided one of the courtyards I'd passed outside would be a good place to eat. I made my way through the long halls, down the stairs of the entranceway, and out the doors. The cold air instantly sent a shiver down the back of my neck, but I was pleased at how refreshing it was. The school somewhat overcompensated on heating, especially since there were so many students per classroom, and it easily grew hot and stuffy.

One of the largest courtyards sat in the center of the school, and was spotted with quite a few stone lunch tables and benches. Because it was so cold not many students braved being outdoors, and I didn't have trouble finding an empty place to sit. Luckily, small awnings overhead protected the tables from being frosted with snow, so I didn't have to worry about sitting in it or brushing it off. I sat down and pulled from my backpack the five slices of leftover pizza Eli was generous enough to send me home with the night before. Cold pizza wasn't my ideal meal, but as per usual, I was too hungry to care.

"Aren't you cold out here?" I had three pieces gone by the time Abby's backpack hit the surface of the table with a loud thud, and she plopped down in the seat across from me.

"Hey, Abby." I smiled in greeting, partly because of the girl's contagious grin, and also because I wouldn't have to eat alone.

At my hello she gave a shocked but approving nod. "You remembered my name."

"Why wouldn't I?" I asked with a chuckle.

"I don't know." She chewed the inside of her cheek for a thoughtful moment. "I figured you'd be meeting so many new people you'd just forget."

"You know how to make an impression," I told her.

She raised an eyebrow at me, the smirk on her face gaining a playful tilt. "Good or bad?"

I squinted at her teasingly as I thought about it, though I'm sure the amused smile I had was just as coy as hers. "Verdict's still out. I'll let you know."

"You're the choosy type, huh?" she giggled, clearly amused at the banter. "I guess I'll just have to step up my game."

"You're doing alright so far," I said reassuringly, not wanting her to think I was a grouch who didn't want any friends.

At that she smiled, watching me curiously for a few silent seconds. That's when I realized the banter of the whole conversation had contained a wildly flirtatious tone. Abby didn't seem to mind, but I looked away, suddenly uncomfortable seeing as I wasn't quite sure how I should feel about it. Now I didn't know what to say. Couldn't think of anything to say when I wasn't sure if it would come out right. When that playfulness had been so easy.

Abby seemed to read my thoughts, because she changed the subject instantly. "So, you're not freezing out here?"

I shook my head. "A hundred and two degree temperature sort of makes you cherish the cold."

Her hazel eyes widened with intrigue. "Is that really how hot you guys are?"

I laughed and shrugged off my jacket – talking about heat was making me realize how readily my body had adjusted to the weather. "Just like a wolf. I got really curious one time and I used a thermometer to check."

"That much body heat sounds pretty good right about now." Abby finally pulled a brown paper bag from her backpack, and then rubbed her arms furiously for warmth.

"Oh, here," I said, pushing my jacket in her direction. "I don't need it."

She smiled her thanks, chuckling while she pulled it on over her own. "You guys do get hot. Your jacket's still really warm."

"Told you," I said knowingly. "What brings you to this neck of the woods?"

"I was on my way indoors, where it's not an icebox, to eat lunch with some friends when I saw you sitting over here," she answered while pulling a sandwich and chips out of the paper bag. "I had to see for myself if you were lost or just crazy."

"Maybe a little of both," I admitted with an embarrassed giggle. "You don't have to keep me company if your friends are waiting for you."

She waved a carefree hand at me. "Don't worry about it, they'll survive. How are you settling in?"

I shoved the last bite of pizza into my mouth and used the few seconds before I swallowed to think of an answer, even though she could hear it anyway. "Not too bad. The people are nice and everything, but it doesn't seem like there's too much to do around here."

"There's really not," Abby laughed in agreement. "Everyone goes to The Orchid, it's this pretty decent sized club that's about a ten minute drive from here. Have you been yet?" I shook my head. "My friends go almost every other day. You could come with us this week, if you want. On Wednesday?"

"You guys stay out late on weeknights?" I asked, genuinely surprised when Abby nodded. I'd expected the school to enforce a curfew. "Um, I can't on Wednesday. I have to run. I'm on sort of a strict schedule." I rubbed my neck nervously when Abby's eyes narrowed thoughtfully, as she no doubt had to pick my thoughts to completely understand what I meant by run.

"Is that a Pack werewolf thing?" she asked when she figured it out. "Having a strict running schedule?"

"No," I said, continuing to look around nervously, knowing I'd have to explain. "It's more of a recently bitten werewolf thing."

"Really?" She didn't try to hide the shock from her face. "How'd you end up with the Pack? I thought only mutts bit people."

"Long story short," I started, still figuring out the best and shortest way to explain my situation, and doing my best to keep certain thoughts at bay. "Camille and I were together. I almost died. Her sister bit me to save my life. I almost attacked my brother on accident, and now I'm here so the Pack can help me control my Changes."

"Wow. You almost died, huh? Freak accident?" Abby leaned forward, her curiosity almost too much for her to handle.

"Murder," I said simply, not wanting the conversation to carry on further, but it was too late to stop the memories of that night from resurfacing. The pain Jonathan had caused. The fear.

Abby cleared her throat uncomfortably, her mouth turned down in an apologetic frown and her cheeks gaining an embarrassed tint of red for having brought it up. "Oh, Kyla, I'm so sorry."

The way she avoided eye contact I knew she'd heard that one thing I didn't want anyone to know. "You weren't supposed to know that. Camille doesn't even know." I rubbed my temples as though it would physically help to push away the memory. "I just want to forget about it."

"Okay, okay. I'm sorry. If you ever want to talk-" Abby stopped short as her gaze was pulled behind me.

I knew exactly who it was by the familiar scent that wafted to my nose seconds before Camille sat down. "There you are. You really need a cell phone. I'll talk to my dad about that," she babbled as she took a seat, and I watched her gaze wander anxiously toward Abby. A slight scowl seemed to crease her eyebrows when she noticed Abby was wearing my jacket.

I gave a distracted chuckle, more than a little thankful for the subject change. "I was thinking I need one too, but make sure it's nothing fancy."

She nodded, and I could feel the tension in the awkward silence that ensued. It was clearly a discomfort between my two companions – both of their eyes drifted to the other repeatedly for only a brief moment until they'd look away. I just couldn't understand why.

"Either of you know where Misses Nix's room is?" I threw the question out there when the silence became too much to handle, but as I glanced from Camille to Abby and realized both of them were reluctant to answer, I regretted hinting I needed someone to take me.

"You should take her," Camille told Abby as she stood up to leave, and started mumbling as she walked away, "I have stuff I need to do anyway."

I watched her retreat, utterly bewildered by her behavior. As Abby and I left the table for my next class, I found myself terribly curious what exactly was going on in that incredibly stubborn head of Camille's.

"You're not going to ask me?" Abby said expectantly.

My eyebrows furrowed in confusion, and then I remembered that she could hear my thoughts. "Oh, uh, no. As much as I'd like to know, that's not fair to you. I'm not going to use you like that."

"Wow," was all Abby said until she received a questioning look in return. "Most people would jump at the chance to know what others are thinking, whether it's using me or not," she explained. "That says a lot about you."

I chuckled in disagreement with her regard for my character. "I'm not all that great."

"I beg to differ." She shrugged and smiled, a smile that made me blush just slightly, and that I couldn't stop from contagiously tugging at my own lips. She was definitely straightforward, which after so much confusion with Camille was a bit of a nice change. "Okay, you're busy on Wednesday. What about Thursday?"

"Thursday, I can do. What time do you usually go?" I asked as I followed her through a separate entrance of the same building my last class was in.

"Eight o'clock. I'll come by your room and we can drive together?" Abby stopped in front of a room and turned to face me as she leaned her back against the wall. I nodded and followed her gaze to a clock on the opposite side. "Lunch went by quick! This is your class here," she said, pointing to the door next to us. Then she dropped her backpack so she could shrug out of my jacket and hand it back to me. "Thanks for that. My next class is on the other side of the school, so I got to get going. I'll catch you later."

I waved goodbye and leaned near the door while I waited for my next class to start, smiling at the fact that I'd made a new friend. I liked Abby, she was easy to talk to and seemed like a lot of fun. Not to mention her infectious smile, which I could never help but reciprocate. When it came down to it, a new friend was a good distraction from all the tension and indecisiveness between Camille and I.

***

The sudden knocking from my door startled me out of my concentration. I'd been studying for my math test the next day for the past two hours, and hadn't been expecting Abby for another fifteen minutes. I rubbed my tired eyes, grateful for a distraction and a well-deserved break.

"Hey, come on in," I greeted Abby happily, leaving the door open so she could follow me in. "I just have to put some stuff away real quick."

I shoved my textbooks into my backpack, and then while I pulled on my jacket looked around for my shoes. Unable to find them, I sat down on the desk chair to think about the last place I'd put them, until Abby tapped my shoulder and held the shoes up to me.

"They were behind the door." She handed them over and then sat patiently on the bed while I slipped them on. "You play the guitar?" she asked excitedly, eyeing the instrument I had leaned against the foot of the bed.

"Yeah, I play a little bit," I admitted, shyly avoiding eye contact.

She picked it up and ran her hand gently down the strings. "Will you play something for me?"

My cheeks flushed red and I buried my face in my hands, peeking out from between my fingers. "Don't make me. I'm too scared."

"Oh come on, don't be shy." She tried to encourage me to get over my nerves, but I stubbornly shook my head. "Fine, but you owe me one. Promise? I'll know if you're lying." After the last statement she teasingly stuck her tongue out.

"I promise," I laughed, and made a crossing motion over my heart. She studied me thoughtfully for a few moments before nodding in approval, and then motioned for me to follow her out the door. "Where is this place exactly?"

"It's in town. Well, closer to town. It's one of those places that are on the side of a stretch of highway. The kind that normally look a little bit dicey, but I promise The Orchid is a lot of fun." Abby seemed genuinely excited about going to the club, which succeeded in getting me excited too. As we entered the elevator, she leaned against the wall and examined me again, eyes scanning me like she wasn't aware she was doing it. I wasn't uncomfortable with being watched, but something about the way she did it made me self-conscious.

"What?" I asked, and once again my face started to color. She pulled her bottom lip between her teeth, giving a timid smile, and just shook her head. "You know, it's not entirely fair that you can hear my thoughts, but won't tell me what you're thinking."

"Trust me, it's not always a gift," she chuckled, glancing around the elevator in obvious hopes I would forget about it, but I just raised an eyebrow expectantly until she sighed in defeat. "I was just thinking that the song you have stuck in your head is one of my favorites, and you have a beautiful voice."

I'd hardly even realized I had a song stuck in my head, but now that she mentioned it, I'd been singing it to myself all day. "You can tell how good my voice is from my thoughts?"

"Yeah, no matter how it sounds to you it comes out in your natural voice." Abby snorted to herself, clearly holding back maniacal laughter. "For example, last month Mr. Carson, my history teacher, kept belting Broadway songs in his head. Believe me when I say you'll wish death on the world if you ever hear him sing anything out loud."

I hadn't met Mr. Carson, but the thought of any teacher singing classic show tunes caused me to burst into laughter. Even as we stepped off the elevator I received strange looks from a couple of girls getting on because I was still giggling. I followed Abby out into one of the side parking lots and to a dark blue sedan. The interior smelled mostly of the sweet perfume I noticed Abby often wore, along with a mixture of the lavender freshener hanging in the window and various smoking products. I inhaled sharply as I recognized one of the scents as an illegal variety, and squinted suspiciously at Abby.

"Not me," she assured with a chuckle as she started the car and pulled out of the parking space. "My freeloader brother was back a couple days ago and treated his friends to a night on the town. It doesn't really smell that bad, does it?"

"Just try not to get pulled over," I teased, reaching behind me to pull on my seatbelt. "So, what's your story?"

"My story?" Abby asked, seemingly surprised by the question. "Um, parents are divorced, lived here my whole life. That's about it."

"And that's what makes you Abby?" I laughed, cocking my head disapprovingly and making it clear I wasn't satisfied with that answer. "You don't talk about yourself much do you?"

"Not really," she said honestly, still sounding reluctant. "Most people ask those kinds of questions just to be nice. They don't really care about the answer."

"I care," I told her confidently, and for added reassurance I gave a toothy grin when she cast me a wary glance. I wasn't the kind of person who asked questions when I didn't really care to hear the answer, and I definitely liked knowing basic stuff about the people I hung out with. Noticing that Abby didn't know where to start, I tried to find a good place for her to begin. "Where does the whole mind-reading thing come from?"

She turned off the road we were on and onto a long stretch of highway that was thickly lined with trees. "My mom can do it actually, and my dad is a warlock. Strangely though, my brother doesn't have any gifts, I think it's a bit hard on him."

"You mean your dad does magic?" I asked curiously, to which she nodded. "Does he teach you anything?"

She shook her head apathetically. "If only we were that close. He's too busy for me. He has books though. I used to look through them when I was younger, taught myself a few things."

"What does he do that keeps him so busy?"

"Oh, we're here," Abby said jovially, and pulled off the road toward a brightly lit building in a section of cut out trees.

I knew she'd heard the question, but figured if she hadn't answered it was because she didn't want to. Instead of pushing the topic I got out of the car and followed her back to the front of the tall brick building, where I stood in awe of the enormous neon sign. Bright red letters read 'The Orchid,' and were finished with a massive white flower. Muffled rumbling of loud music pierced the silent night, and through the brick walls the stench of hot bodies, smoke, and booze seeped into the cold air. Mixed in with the scent of The Orchid, however, there was something else. A smell I didn't recognize but that made every hair on my arms and neck stand on end.

"Do you smell that?" First it was the sweet aroma of vanilla, then the retched stench of decaying flesh. It smelt like death. Death and vanilla, one in the same. It made my eyes burn and my mouth water, each desperately trying to wash away the filth.

Abby furrowed her eyebrows curiously while she deliberately breathed in the night air. Unable to smell what I did, she shook her head. "No, but should we go inside?"

I cast a last, searching glance around the outside of the building before nodding and following her through the red, metal double-doors. It certainly wasn't what I'd expected. I was finding most things in my new home were a lot bigger than they looked from the outside. A stage on the far side of the club sustained an excessive turntable, manned by a single DJ in the center. Directly in front of the stage was where everyone was dancing, probably because that was where the music was loudest.

Farther toward the center of the club and just in front of us were scattered tables where the less rowdy could enjoy the music with a drink they got at the bar, which jutted from the wall on the other side of them. On both sides of the long bar was more seating and a couple of large booths set against the walls. I squinted against the multiple strobe and neon lights that illuminated the scene before me, and a solid light from above caught my eye. I hadn't noticed the second floor until now. It was sectioned off by glass walls and was lit normally, even if rather dimly, and from below I could see more seating and a few pool tables. I found myself wondering if it was quieter upstairs, since the loud music was already ringing in my sensitive ears.

"Do you want a drink?" Abby asked, bringing her lips close to my ear and pointing to the bar. My mouth hung open in a silent 'um' as I tensed awkwardly, and thought about how to best decline an alcoholic beverage. Even though I couldn't hear Abby laugh, her lips curled into a smile. "Let me rephrase that, would you like a soda?"

Letting out an embarrassed giggle, I nodded and followed her to the bar. I watched as she skillfully acquired the busy bartender's attention and ordered two drinks, which she paid for with a bill that seemed to appear from thin air. I took the drink she handed me and sat down across from her at the nearest empty table.

"What do you think?" She didn't have to shout quite as loud as before, but I still wondered how I was able to hear or think at all.

I took a sip of my soda and glanced around the booming club. "I can't. Maybe you could let me know?"

She leaned forward halfway through like she couldn't hear me very well, and then smirked amusedly while shaking her head. "I can hardly hear your voice, let alone your thoughts."

I nodded thoughtfully. That was the trick? Blaring music and my mind was once again my own. I watched curiously as a girl about our age hugged Abby's shoulders from behind, and her along with two others greeted us with smiles. Abby introduced the three as Maddie, Tory, and Hannah, and I waited patiently while she made small talk with them. I didn't mind, I found it interesting the way Abby talked with them. It was different from the way she talked to me, like even though it was easy to listen she had to force herself to be interested or say anything back.

I sipped my soda and used the opportunity to study Abby in the privacy of my own mind. Though she was clearly attractive, I didn't consider myself to be extremely captivated by her. But then again, I refused to think about it when she could hear, and so I hadn't yet come to a conclusion. The other thing that had kept me from thinking too much about it was Camille, because I still wasn't sure where we stood. Lately, however, I'd felt myself growing restless, especially where romance was concerned – I still blamed it on the wolf. Now my curious eyes kept leading me back to Abby's smile. Perfect pearly-whites beamed through her grin, and dimples creased her soft, freckled cheeks.

One of the girls, who I tried to remember as either Hannah or Maddie, cheerfully said something about college boys, and waved bye to Abby before pulling the other two away. Abby returned her attention to me and laughed, "They like trying to get the college boys to buy them drinks."

"Do you drink?" I asked immediately. I hadn't really meant to ask, as I figured it wasn't an important question and since I already felt I'd given the impression I was picky about friends, but it slipped.

Abby just shook her head, unconcerned with how direct the question was. "Not usually. It's already hard to tune out people's thoughts, it's worse when I'm under the influence. What about you?"

I shrugged and finished off my drink. "I've never tried it, but I'm already having trouble controlling my Changes, I don't see how alcohol would help."

Nodding in understanding, Abby looked around as if searching for something to say. "Do you want to dance?"

"Dance?" I repeated, and thoughtfully glanced toward the crowd of people in front of the stage before agreeing.

I followed her out into the middle of the large group and couldn't help but be a little nervous. I'd danced with an ex-boyfriend a few times, but never with a girl, and I wondered if we were supposed to move in that same, suggestive way. Was that what Abby had even meant in the first place? She looked unsure too as she stood in front of me, shyly starting to sway her hips in rhythm with the music. I knew it was up to me to raise the comfort bar, and so I began to do the same, gradually and hesitantly. After a song or two I grew more at ease, and my movements became more emphasized and fluid. Then I noticed that Abby's hands had settled on my hips, and we'd gotten informally close. Maybe that's what made me feel more confident. I didn't know what I thought about her proximity to me. Couldn't think period with the pounding of the bass in my ears.

I didn't want to pull away because I worried that she might find it insulting. But watching her hips sway and feeling the way her hands guided my own planted an inkling of lust deep within me. It was the wolf's influence over me, and it was strong. Even stronger, however, was Camille's influence over me. Though what I was forced to do hurt Camille, it hadn't been sincere. There was that part of me that still felt attached to her, even if I was confused about what she wanted. That confusion was powerful enough to keep me from taking it further with Abby. It conquered the wolf and gave me the sense to turn around. Because even if I was still dancing, not being able to see the skill with which Abby moved allowed me to push away the bawdy thoughts that would've eventually surfaced, and I thanked my lucky stars the music was too loud for her to hear my internal argument.

After some time I was able to view my dancing with her as a strictly friendly gesture. The lack of distance from us and everyone else made it feel like we weren't dancing just the two of us, and most the time I couldn't even tell if it was her against me or somebody else. That's how it was for quite a while, until both of us were too hot and too tired to continue, at which point Abby took my hand and led me back to the bar area.

"Do you want to go or hang out a bit longer?" She pulled out her cell phone and held it up so I could see the time.

11:15, we'd been dancing a lot longer than I thought. It wasn't too late into the evening, but I did have a test in the morning, so I pointed to the door. "We can go." I followed her out into the night and to the side of the building where we'd parked, and every hair on my body pricked up before I even registered that I could smell that horrid stench again. "God, tell me you can smell that now. Hey, wait…" There was something familiar in the air. I let go of the handle to the car door I was about to open and walked toward the fragrance, which was coming from the woods behind the building.

I heard Abby's footsteps close behind me, but I was too preoccupied with my nose in the air to explain. It was the scent of a werewolf, one I knew. What was his name? Nathan. As I got nearer the forest and farther from the club the music started to fade, and I could hear the sounds of scuffling, and the breaking of branches and leaves. It sounded like a struggle. I took off sprinting into the woods, and was about a hundred feet in when I finally spotted Nathan, naked and leaned against a tree. Much to my confusion he was alone, and while there was the tiniest lingering of the horrible smell, it was nearly gone, and the only one that remained was his.

"Nathan?" I called, rushing toward him and catching his waist as he almost dropped to the snow.

"We need... to leave..." A tiny wave of relief turned up his lips when I reached him, but he was heavily out of breath, and his eyes were dark and wild.

I wrapped one of his arms around my shoulders to help him up. "What happened?"

As I started leading the battered werewolf back toward the parking lot, Abby, who looked terribly uncomfortable at his lack of clothing, lifted his other arm over her own shoulders and helped me support him. Nathan just shook his head, too exhausted and still breathing too heavily to explain. I worriedly looked him over, but while he appeared to be a little bruised in areas there were no cuts or serious injuries.

Despite his rather healthy state, his face was colorless with fear, and he was shaking violently, though I didn't know if he was going to go into shock or was just really cold. Either way, I let Abby fully support him while I pulled off my jacket and laid it across his broad shoulders. We opened the back door of the car and he climbed in, collapsing over the seat where he mumbled something about getting him to Eli, and then seemed to pass out.

I slid into the passenger seat while Abby hurriedly started the engine and pulled out of the lot. "Do you know where the Pack house is?" I asked, to which she nodded. "Could you hear what he was thinking? Do you know what happened?"

Abby's eyes had grown wide, mirroring the fear in Nathan's, and her mouth set in a tense line. It was obvious there was far too much going on in her head to form a complete, explanatory sentence, so she mumbled one word before turning her eyes back on the road and speeding up. "Vampires."

My eyebrows furrowed in utter bemusement. Vampires what? Was Nathan fighting with them? Maybe that's what that horrible smell was. I glanced over my shoulder to the boy in the back seat. His chest rose and fell rapidly with his breathing, but I couldn't tell if he was passed out or not because his hands cupped his face protectively. As I took my eyes off of him a frustrated growl escaped from deep in my chest.

I thought Oregon was going to be safe. We could run here and rarely have to worry about other mutts. I thought there would be no more danger. Clearly something tried to hurt Nathan. What would stop it from trying to hurt me? Or even worse, Camille? Out of the corner of my eye I saw Abby's head turn so she could look at me. When I met her gaze I expected her to mutter some friendly reassurances that we weren't in danger. Instead, the girl's eyes dropped uncomfortably, the corners of her mouth sunk in a frown.

For the rest of the record short ride to the house I focused on Nathan's breathing in the back seat, making sure it never stopped. Abby's car skidded to a halt at the front of the house, and we hurriedly removed Nathan from the back seat to carry him in.

"Hello!" I shouted frantically, and we set Nathan on the short couch between the stairs of the grand entranceway.

I was surprised to see Camille run down the stairs with Lacey. Probably just as surprised as Camille looked to see Abby. Lacey stopped when she saw Nathan lying on the couch, covered only by my small jacket, and ran back up to grab a blanket.

"What the hell happened?" Camille asked worriedly, catching the linen Lacey threw over the balcony and wrapping it around him.

"I was attacked, near The Orchid." Nathan sat up. His breathing was returning to normal, but he sounded exhausted, still almost too tired to speak. "I was out for a run and two vampires attacked me. Where's Eli?"

"Everyone's out. It's just me and Camille." Lacey settled on the couch next to him and rubbed his back tenderly. "How'd you fight them off?"

He covered his face, but not before I could see the blood drain from it again. "I couldn't. They could have killed me in an instant if they wanted." I was waiting for somebody to ask why they hadn't killed him, but we all stayed silent until he continued. "It was like they were trying to catch me."

Each of us looked completely dumfounded, and even more so at a loss for words. Camille's expression was the first to turn to anger, her protective nature flaring. "We need to go back and investigate. Maybe the vampires will still be around. Abby, you drove right? You can go home now."

"I'm going with you." Even though Abby said it somewhat quietly, there was an edge and command in her tone.

"That's not a good idea." Camille appeared to remain calm, but it was obvious by the firm set of her mouth that she was already growing impatient.

Still, Abby just stood her ground. "I wasn't asking."

"You don't belong here." The finality rang in Camille's voice as she turned for the door. I had to agree with her, this could be dangerous for Abby, and there was no reason to get her involved if she didn't need to be.

I was decided, and about to follow Camille to the door when Abby took a step forward. "The Supernatural Council says I do."

That didn't mean much of anything to me, but Camille froze in her tracks, every muscle in her body tense while she turned around to face Abby. "What's your last name?"

"Johnson."

Apparently the name registered, and Camille took a deep breath, speaking through clenched teeth. "You are going to tell me everything you know. *Now.*"

Confusion deepened, twisting my haggard brain painfully as I watched the spectacle. I half expected Abby to buckle in fear under Camille's intense and angry glare and bolt out the door, especially since Camille hovered a few inches taller than her.

Instead, Abby shoved her hands in her pockets and gave a defeated sigh. "In the past few months there have been increased vampire attacks in the area, but they've never been so close to the school. There's a teacher, a psychic. She told me that we have a vampire ally, but a werewolf is in danger. I'm under my father's orders to protect that werewolf."

"Clearly you didn't do a very good job," Camille spat, pointing at Nathan. I didn't understand the sudden hostility, I felt like it was about more than just Nathan. I'd only ever seen Camille so protective when it came to me, and I couldn't help but feel like she was angry that Abby and I had been together that night.

Abby's face set in a bitter scowl that was enough to make me cringe. "There's a whole lot of you, and only one of me. I can't protect you all at the same time."

"Oh yeah, and I'm sure you were doing a whole lot of protecting at The Orchid." As Camille said that her nostrils flared, and I knew she could smell me on Abby. "We're not your responsibility, and we don't need protection, but a little heads up would have been nice." Camille's voice was getting louder, and Abby's face twisted with anger for a brief second before going blank.

"But you're not my responsibility," she smirked.

The cold calm of Abby's exterior set Camille off. She yelled, and as she took an angry step forward I tensed, preparing to stop fists from flying. "What's your fucking problem?"

"My problem!" Abby shouted back, and took a step forward to meet Camille's aggressive advance. "What's *your* problem? The second I walk in here you can't stand me. Why don't *you* tell *me* what the fucking problem is."

"Shut up! Both of you just shut up!" I had never yelled so loud in my life, and from the shocked looks on both Abby and Camille's faces, they didn't think I could raise my voice so much either. Nor had I ever been so confused. How did the conversation spiral out of control so quickly? It didn't matter what anybody's problem was, we all had a common enemy, and we had to figure it out before someone else got hurt. "Now sit."

Both Camille and Abby did as they were commanded, sitting on the floor with their backs against the couch, and out of the corner of my eye I could see Lacey holding back amused laughter. Abby opened her mouth as she turned her head to glare at Camille, as if Camille had continued the argument in her mind so only Abby would hear.

"Camille, knock it off," I growled, making my aggravation clear by pointing a scolding finger at her. "Would one of you mind telling me what's going on?" Neither of them looked up from the same spot on the floor, so I sighed impatiently. "Okay, Abby. Explain."

Abby's eyes met mine, then immediately returned to the floor, and it was clear she was ashamed at how she'd acted. "My dad is the director of The Supernatural Council, I'm just a foot soldier. We don't know what the vampires want, and we didn't think anyone would be in trouble so soon." At the end of her explanation she looked at Camille, as if to explain and apologize.

"The Supernatural Council?" I folded my arms across my chest, not ready to let either of them off the hook just yet.

"A group of other supernaturals that monitor the goings on of our world," Lacey answered, stepping forward. "They do their own thing keeping other beings under control and out of the public eye, like the police. We don't associate with them often."

"Except for when one of us is in danger," Camille added quietly.

I held back a smirk as I thought about how cute Camille was when she was pouting. Then realizing that Abby could hear the totally out of place thought, I cleared my throat awkwardly. "But nobody knows anything about what's going on?"

"No, not yet," Abby admitted, giving a despondent sigh.

"Can I get some water?" Nathan asked, timidly interrupting, and Lacey nodded and left to the kitchen.

"Nathan, did they say anything useful?" I asked.

He closed his eyes thoughtfully for a few moments, and then shook his head. "No, they didn't really say anything at all." Lacey came back with a glass of water, and he smiled appreciatively before gulping it down. "Only one vampire is an even match for a werewolf. There were two, and they knew what they were doing. If they didn't smell so god-awful they would've caught me completely off guard."

Abby stood up, impatiently fiddling with the car keys in her jacket pocket. "I should go. My father needs to know what's happened."

I glanced around to see if anyone else had something to say before Abby left, or if perhaps Camille wanted to get into another shouting match. When no one looked concerned I nodded. "I'll walk you out." As I turned to take Abby back out to her car I saw Camille's head shoot up, and I knew she was staring after us.

When we reached Abby's sedan, and before getting in, she turned to face me and leaned back against the door. "Look, I'm really sorry about that."

"I always knew Camille had a temper, but I didn't expect *you* to have such a short fuse," I teased, garnering a small laugh from her. "Why didn't you tell me about this Supernatural Council stuff?" I asked, nervously putting my hands in my pockets. I couldn't help but feel like people kept leaving me out of things, not telling me stuff I felt like I should know. I was a part of this world now, and it was hard enough adjusting to it without having secrets kept from me.

Abby shrugged, and gave an apologetic half-smile to my thoughts. "I was under strict orders to keep this under control. That means not sending the werewolves into a panic." I just nodded, not really sure what to say. "I'll see you at school tomorrow?"

It was a question, unsure and timid. I assumed it was code for making sure I wasn't upset about her fight with Camille. "Yeah, I'll see you tomorrow. Drive safe."

I watched as Abby's car disappeared in the trees before turning and going back into the house. Everyone had dispersed, and through the silence I could hear someone moving around in the kitchen. It was Camille, various kitchen utensils and ingredients spread out on the counter.

"Hey," I said softly as I sat down on a stool at the bar. Camille looked up to give me an apprehensive greeting-nod, looking entirely unhappy, and maybe even mildly pissed. "Where's Nathan?"

"Lacey took him up to his room so he can get some sleep," she answered flatly, measuring some salt and putting it into a bowl in front of her. "She'll talk to Eli when he gets home and let him know what happened."

I nodded understandingly, and it was followed by a minute of tense silence. The way Camille was acting, I felt like I'd been caught doing something wrong. Even though my time with Abby had been innocent, and Camille was so unclear on where she and I stood that it was as though we weren't even together, I still felt like I had to explain myself. "We were just hanging out, you know."

It was silent for another minute, and I wasn't sure if Camille understood what I'd meant by 'we'. "Okay," she said shortly.

I sighed, wondering what I could do to get her attention. What I could do to get her to forgive me. Wouldn't the prospect of another girl in my life be enough for her to give me some sign, even if it was just telling me to wait for her to heal? "You know how sorry I am, right?" Then I added in the sincerest voice I could, "I'm so sorry."

She went frigid, and without glancing up or even moving replied just as tersely as before, "Okay."

"Camille, what do you want from me?" I asked desperately. A painful spur lodged in my chest at her emotional distance, but I couldn't go any longer being so confused all the time. She obviously didn't want an apology, but I didn't know what else to give.

"Just," she started angrily, and paused. Then, turning to face me, whispered in a voice as desperate as mine, "Please, just stop."

"Stop?" I repeated. Even though I was somewhat bewildered, my heart dropped. The finality in her voice sounded like an end.

"Yes," she said in exasperation. "Stop trying to make it okay. Okay? You can't just," she paused again, whether from anger or anguish I couldn't be sure, but her eyes welled with tears like this was hard for her to say. "You can't make me feel better about it."

I felt a pained wetness set in my own sinuses, but I forced it back. I don't know if I was trying to maintain some dignity, or if I just didn't want Camille to know how much that hurt, but I definitely didn't want her to see me cry. "Ever?" This was it. It was over.

Her deep brown eyes met mine for a brief moment before turning to the floor. "Probably not," she said, so soft it was barely audible.

"Well," I paused, composing myself because I felt a lump forming in my throat. She would never forgive me for giving in to that crazed werewolf's demands, for breaking her heart even though I never meant it. I knew how she would have responded to him, even if her family were being threatened. She would've told him to go to hell. I'd been scared and alone, a human incapable of defending myself, but it wasn't enough of an excuse for her. She expected the same courage from me, and I'd let her down.

There was so much pain in my chest that I wanted to yell. I wanted to break down and shake her and beg to know why she couldn't let it go. But she'd asked me to stop trying to make it okay. Even more than I wanted her to forgive me, I wanted to stop hurting her. "Can't we be friends?" I finally asked in complete defeat. I was giving in, because even though I wanted so much more than that from her, I'd take it if it were all she'd give me. I'd take it because she said 'probably' and not 'definitely.'

"I'm trying, Kyla," she breathed, holding out her hands like she was begging me to make it easier on her. But I didn't know how to make it easier on either of us. "I'm trying really hard. I just need time, okay? I need you to stop trying to bring it up."

"You *never* want to talk about it?" I asked, praying that if I agreed to this then she'd eventually forgive me and bring it up on her own. She shook her head. "Okay," I said, still trying to convince myself I'd comply with whatever she wanted, because she knew better than anyone what she needed, even if what she needed wasn't me. "What are you making?" I asked, swallowing past the despairing lump that finally lodged in my throat and taking a deep breath past the icy brokenness in my chest.

She turned to glance over all the ingredients before looking me in the eyes and trying to give a smile. "Cookies."

"You do realize it's almost midnight?" I said, trying to make my tone light even though it hardly sounded anything but heartbroken.

At my doleful expression she watched me for a second, scanning my face with a searching concern. Then she gave an indifferent shrug, her voice as playfully sarcastic as our moods would allow. "I do what I want."

"Can I help?" Even if being with Camille right now was agonizing, at least setting my mind to something would keep me from thinking too much about it. Being alone would hurt even worse.

With a nod from Camille I began to help pass and pour ingredients. Even though it was somewhat silent, it felt almost like old times, minus the heartbreak. She seemed less tense, and we worked together fairly easily and comfortably. Sometimes I felt I knew what she was thinking, I could sense the ingredients she wanted me to pass her. Could feel her smile thanks. It was like the first time we'd done yoga with Wesley. When our knees finally touched and I felt connected. Something bonded us deeper than words or thoughts. Or even love. For some reason the word 'blood' came to mind. Our connection ran deep as blood.

Abby stood at the wooden door of her father's office Friday afternoon, highly reluctant to knock. The Supernatural Council had set up a place in a business complex under the guise of a law firm. It wasn't too far of a stretch, as Abby could vaguely picture a couple of the members that she knew had gone to law school. Her reluctance to knock wasn't due to the fact that she didn't like her father. On the contrary, she loved him, even if she didn't agree with his politics. He also loved her, and she knew it, though years of being a busy man with little time to practice being an actual dad had left him with a failure to express those kind of emotions. The reluctance stemmed from the fact that even though they loved each other, they fought. Constantly.

Her dad was a large, rather muscular man, and it was from him she got her bright hazel eyes. His hair was jet black, and matched the color of his favorite business suit perfectly. Abby never understood why he dressed so formally to the office when all the other board members, while they didn't come in ratty clothes, dressed fairly comfortably. His looks didn't make her nervous, and she was never intimidated by her father's magic or the power she could feel emanating from him. However, she did find the numerous occult artifacts that hung on the walls and sat on the shelves to be a bit creepy.

Abby lightly knocked on the door before pushing her way inside. When she entered her father was intently staring at his computer screen, and held up his index finger to tell her to wait one second. She sat slouched in the armchair across from his desk until he swiveled his chair in her direction and removed his attention from the computer.

"Abby," he smiled, the extent of his affection. "How was school?"

She shrugged apathetically. "It was good. But I've needed to talk to you since last night. Something happened near The Orchid." No need to waste time with small talk, it would only lead to meaningless conversation and awkward pauses.

"Go on." He leaned back in his chair to get more comfortable while he listened.

"One of the Pack werewolves was out for a run last night. He ended up near The Orchid and was attacked by two vampires. Well, kind of attacked. He said they tried to catch him. Luckily, we found him and he walked away with only a few bruises." Abby waited patiently while he digested the information, but one of his thoughts caught her attention. "We *need* to keep the werewolves posted on any new information. It would be irresponsible to keep them out of the loop."

His face crinkled into a scowl. He knew Abby couldn't help hearing his thoughts, but he still despised it. She figured that was the reason her parents had gotten divorced. Her mom was a telepath too, and her dad hated it. "No. They're animals, Abby, irrational and violent. The last thing we need is to worry about what actions the Pack might take."

Abby sighed, her sense of urgency instantly turning to pure aggravation. They couldn't have a single conversation without arguing about something like this. Oh well, why change the habit now? "You've been the director for almost thirty years now. How are you so blind to the things that have changed? The werewolves aren't savage, and they have a new Alpha."

"I don't care who their Alpha is. They refuse to cooperate with this council, and so separation is what they'll get." His face was getting red, as Abby had clearly offended him.

"They refuse to cooperate because you treat them like expendable errand boys. They're human too, just like you and me." She glared at him. If not for years of arguments numbing her to his temper, she'd be slinking back in fear of the large man.

She could see he wasn't going to change his mind. He had no reason to listen to an immature high school student. With an overly exaggerated sigh she turned and walked out of the room.

"You're not to involve them, Abby," her father growled after her.

She just waved an irritated hand at him and closed the door behind her, taking deep breaths to slow her temper. Most people complimented her on her countenance and thought she was the sweetest person they'd ever met, until they saw what a short fuse she had, courtesy of her dad.

"I thought I heard yelling." A short, light-brown haired woman smiled at Abby fondly, her grin lighting up her dark blue eyes.

"Hey, Mom." Abby smiled back and followed her mom to the front of the office.

The woman sat in a chair at the reception counter and turned to Abby, who'd settled on the edge of the desk. "What could you two possibly be fighting about now?"

"He's a stubborn asshole," Abby sighed, and picked up a rubber band to busy her hands with something.

Her mom held back a smirk as she gave Abby a stern look and a warning. "Language." If she could read her mom's mind though, she was sure her mother would have agreed. "Want to elaborate?"

She sighed, this time more in a calming manner than out of frustration. "He doesn't think we should keep the werewolves involved with new information, and I think they really need to be involved. It's not fair if one of them is in danger and they don't have all the information we do."

Her mother gave a small, knowing smile. "You hate getting involved with your father's politics, why so concerned with who's kept up to speed?"

"Just because. They could be helpful," Abby lied, not doing a good job of holding back a smirk, as she knew that though her mom couldn't read her thoughts, she could read her expression.

Her mom laughed at her reluctance. "You're not going to tell me are you?"

Abby shook her head, glad that her mom couldn't read her mind. That was one of the reasons they were so close. They were both telepathic, but couldn't hear each other. She'd always been told it was like trying to communicate on walkie-talkies when you're both pushing down the talk button, nothing would get through.

"No, I should get going." Abby hopped off the desk and shot the rubber band across the room. "I would avoid him for a while though. He's probably still pissed off."

"Noted." Her mom laughed as she hugged her goodbye. "Oh, Lahni stopped in and wanted to talk to you before you leave. She's in her office. I think she had another vision."

Abby smiled thankfully and took off down the hall toward Lahni's office. It was a lot smaller than her father's, but Lahni took the care to make it comfortable. The door was open when Abby got there, and Lahni was waiting for her at the desk.

"Hey, Lahni," she greeted the woman. "My mom said you were looking for me?"

"I was, yes. I had another vision today." Lahni folded her hands in her lap as she sat back in her chair.

"And?" Abby questioned, as usual all she could see from the psychic's mind was a muddled mess of images that made no sense to her.

"You know, the usual. Just a bunch of pictures and words." Lahni leaned forward, her voice growing more serious. "There was a phrase that very much stuck out to me though. It slays the beast within."

"It slays the beast within," Abby repeated, thinking hard about what it could mean. "The beast, a werewolf?" Lahni nodded. "Something will kill a werewolf. What will? Vampires?"

"I'm not sure," Lahni admitted. "But there's something else. Everything is in multiples of three. Three pairs of eyes. Three times that phrase was repeated." She waited to see if Abby would catch on to what she was hinting at. "Three werewolves…"

Abby's eyebrows furrowed bitterly. "Three? They want three wolves." She was already having a hard time grasping the concept of a vampire trying to catch a werewolf, and now they wanted three? "We just need to figure out which ones they want right?"

Lahni nodded her agreement. "I suppose. I'd assume they'd go for the weakest three. Though I don't know any of the werewolves like you do."

The weakest three. Abby's heart dropped. Kyla was the newest werewolf, and therefore would be one of the weakest. "Yeah, I think I know who they'd go after. They already gave one away by attacking last night. Nathan was his name. There's Kyla, she's the newest, and so she's not as experienced. Same with Lacey, she's the youngest, and the smallest." Abby began to pace at the edge of the desk. "I need to let them know, we need to warn them."

Lahni's face wrinkled in concern. "The yelling was muffled through the walls, but it did sound like your father told you not to involve them."

"They're already involved, Lahni. You can't really expect me not to tell them." Abby raised an eyebrow in sarcastic challenge, making an attempt to lighten the tone of her statement.

"I don't expect you to. So I know nothing about it." Lahni winked and let out a nervous chuckle.

Abby grinned and winked back. "Nothing about what?"

After saying goodbye to Lahni and her mother, Abby rushed to her car to get back to the school. She knew Kyla went out for runs about every other night. It was already getting dark, but she hoped Kyla hadn't left just yet. She also hoped that Kyla, or any of the other were-wolves for that matter, never went running alone.

Abby shivered as she sat down in the cold driver's seat of her car and cranked up the heat. For the first few minutes of the drive she might as well have had the air conditioning on. From The Council's office it took about fifteen minutes for her to get back to the school while driving as fast as she could without risking a speeding ticket. That was the last thing she needed to argue with her father about. She hastily parked and made her way up the elevator and down the hall to Kyla's dorm room, knocking as urgently as she could without sounding rude.

"Good, you're here." She couldn't hold back a grin as Kyla opened the door.

"Yeah, I was just about to go for a run. Is something wrong?" Kyla opened the door a little wider, motioning for Abby to come in and then closed it behind them.

Abby took a seat in the chair at Kyla's desk while Kyla sat and dangled her legs over the side of the bed. "I just came from my father's office. We found out some news about the vampire attacks." Kyla's head cocked curiously, but she waited silently for Abby to continue. "The psychic kept hearing the phrase, 'it slays the beast within.' I don't know why they were trying to catch Nathan, but he probably wouldn't have been alive for long if they had, and he wasn't the only werewolf the vampires want. They want three."

"Three?" Abby didn't have to read Kyla's mind to hear the concern in her voice. "You guys don't know which three?"

"No," Abby shook her head. "But, if you were trying to catch werewolves, you'd probably go for the weakest ones, right?"

She sat silently while Kyla thought about each of the Pack werewolves, her mind coming to conclusions about which three were the weakest, herself being one of them. "So, Nathan, me, and?"

"Lacey?"

"Oh," Kyla said slowly, and nodded in agreement. "What now?"

Abby shrugged. "Well, you should probably let the rest of the Pack know, and unless you're here, the three of you probably shouldn't go out alone. I figure me or Camille could always be with you, and some of the others could be with Lacey and Nathan?"

God I'm sick of this shit. Abby cringed at the first hint of frustration from the werewolf, and feeling bad that Kyla would have to be babysat, she tried to lighten the mood. "Don't worry. We'll make it fun. It'll hardly be like anything is different."

Kyla sighed and gave an uneasily forced smile. "I guess. What happens if I'm with you and we get attacked?"

She smiled at the fact that Kyla's dark green eyes were full of concern for her safety. "Hey, I may not be the tallest, strongest looking person, but I can hold my own."

Kyla laughed lightheartedly as she stood up to usher Abby toward the door, and glared teasingly. "I won't believe it until I see it."

"Watch yourself, or you'll find out the hard way," Abby challenged playfully as she walked to the door. She was about to leave, but something was keeping her in place, and Kyla looked at her expectantly, patiently waiting for her to say whatever she was about to. "Would you want to have dinner with me?" Abby instantly regretted the question. It was completely out of context, but her mouth formed the words before her brain could stop her.

"Like a date?" Kyla's eyes inadvertently darted around the room, and Abby felt guilty for putting her on the spot. She could hear that the girl's first instinct was to say no, but while she was obviously hesitant, she wasn't entirely unwilling.

"Or not, we could just go to dinner. Or lunch, if that would be better," Abby said hastily, trying to ease Kyla's feelings about it.

Kyla's mind was racing too fast for Abby to really pick up on what she thought, but after a few seconds of contemplation she laughed. "Sure, we could go to dinner. Um, but, just dinner?"

Abby nodded and smiled reassuringly. "Not a date, just dinner. Monday night, I'll get you at five."

As Abby said goodbye, she couldn't deny that having a date declined was a bit stinging to her ego, but she knew that while Kyla obviously found her attractive, the girl still had feelings for Camille. She didn't know exactly how deep those feelings went, as Kyla clearly tried not to think about it whenever they were together. Either way, she couldn't say she expected anything more or less from an entirely young friendship. Dinner was a start.

9

"What the?" I rubbed my eyes tiredly as I got out of bed and looked out the window.

I thought the campus seemed unusually loud for a Sunday morning, and now I could see why. The round street in the center of all the dormitory buildings had been closed off, and was now filled with various booths of all kinds of bright colors. The booths stretched father than I could see, and I assumed it spread all the way to the actual school campus – some kind of fair maybe. I hurriedly ran a brush through my unruly blonde hair, and pulled on my clothes and shoes. I was halfway out the door when a small box on the desk caught my eye, and I mentally scolded myself for almost forgetting. Last week I'd called my dad and asked him to add a cell phone to our plan for Kyla, and I'd just gotten it in the mail yesterday. As fast as I could I tore open the box, shoved in the battery, and called my own phone so I would have the new number. Then I bolted out the door.

Everything seemed like a race with Kyla lately. I was always in a hurry to be the first one to her dorm in the morning. I had to get there before Abby did so we wouldn't have to vie for the girl's affection. It was probably torture, trying so hard to spend so much time with Kyla, the one person I wanted and the one person who didn't want me. I don't know why tried so hard to convince myself it was better than not seeing her at all. Maybe it's because I didn't really have a choice in the matter. Finally reaching her room, I knocked on the door, sighing with relief when I heard mumbling from inside.

Kyla opened up, looking so tired that she had to lean on the handle for support, and blinked hard when she saw me. "Are you insane? Why are you awake?"

I laughed and followed her back into the room, closing the door behind me. "There's a fair or something today. Did you hear anything about it?"

"No," she said groggily, but she peered outside anyway, and her eyes widened a bit in excitement. "Looks like fun though."

I lay back on her bed and stared at the ceiling while she changed out of her pajamas, trying not to torture myself by sneaking a peek. "By the way, before we left yesterday, Wesley told me that he was going to be busy today. He said we should go by for training sometime tonight."

"Good, that means I can come back and take a nap," Kyla said, already grinning at the idea.

I sat up, watching her patiently as she tied her shoelaces. Then, remembering the extra cell phone in my pocket, I pulled it out and handed it to her. "From my dad. I already put the number in my phone."

"Oh." She took the phone, looking it over happily before shoving it into her pocket. "I'll have to call and say thanks. You ready to go?"

I nodded and followed her all the way out of the building. We stopped at a little ticket booth that said 'Fair For Charity', and as I bought multiple tickets for Kyla and I, I thought about how vague that sounded. Throughout the morning a few times we played the game where you try to knock down a stack of bottles with a baseball. Neither of us was able to win a single thing until finally Kyla played the game where you try to throw a ping-pong ball into a cup with water and a goldfish in it. What did she win for accomplishing the amazing feat? A goldfish. Which she happily gave away to the first small kid she saw.

Neither of us talked much. Lately I'd been finding it hard to find anything to say. Every time we had a conversation she tried to say something about breaking up with me, but I didn't want to hear it. There was never passion or determination in her eyes when she was about to bring it up, only sadness and hesitation. Apologizing to me wouldn't take away the hurt. Nor would it make it easier for us to be friends. However, when I told her how I really felt the other night, she seemed to have taken my words to heart. She hadn't seemed about to bring it up since.

During the times the heartbreak-pain wasn't overwhelming I was happy just being able to hang out with Kyla. When she'd broken up with me she'd implied that it was because she realized she wasn't really into girls. But I got the feeling there was more than a friendly connection between her and Abby. If she was just confused, spending time with her could be my way of convincing her I was the right choice all along.

"You hungry?" I asked as Kyla threw her last basketball toward the far away hoop. My stomach had been rumbling for the past half hour, but it had just gotten strong enough to do something about.

Her smile widened ear to ear at the mention of food. "Always."

I glanced around at the various booths to see which had the biggest meals. Most of them were small lemonade stands, or were serving cheesecake and ice cream. Finally I spotted a stand with hotdogs, and eagerly led Kyla over to it. After ordering a few each we sat down at a little picnic table to eat, or more accurately wolf down, our food. I took the opportunity to carefully study each of the booths that hadn't caught my eye in the first place. There was one with an artist who would draw you in a caricature, and a couple from organizations handing out free items.

"Have you ever been to a fortune teller?" I asked, my eyes now glued to the booth across from us.

Kyla glanced over her shoulder to where I was looking. "No, but we should go do it."

I nodded in agreement, and after we polished off our hotdogs we made our way to the fortuneteller's booth. The psychic was an older woman. Her shoulder length, graying hair accentuated her ambiguous green eyes. When she noticed we were making our way to her she gave a friendly smile, and then sat us in a pair of chairs across a small table from her own.

"How are you ladies doing?" she asked, and both Kyla and I went with the flow of the formal greeting, answering with 'fine, and you?'. Aside from that she didn't waste time getting into what she was there to do. "Would you like your palms read, or a tarot card reading?"

I looked over at Kyla questioningly, but she didn't seem sure either, so I shrugged. "I've never had my palm read."

"Ah, good, good. Go ahead and lay your hands on the table for me, palm side up." The woman waited patiently for me to do so, and then gently took my left hand in her own. "So warm, and soft too. You're a sensitive one, huh?" I heard Kyla laugh as she mumbled 'marshmallow,' an inside joke her and Luna had about just how sensitive I was, and I gave her a playful glare. The psychic then ran her finger along the topmost line of my hand. "This one is your heart line. It starts here, under your index finger, which tells me you like security in your relationships. The line is deep, like your emotions. It's also long, and straight. While you handle your emotions fairly well, you have a tendency to be jealous."

I blushed at the reminder of what had happened at Eli's a couple days ago, and passed a stealthy glance over at Kyla to see if she was thinking the same thing. I could agree I was a jealous person. That was why I'd yelled at Abby, because I hated seeing Kyla with another girl. Even though she'd said they were just hanging out, Abby's scent was all over her that night. I couldn't be sure exactly how Kyla felt about Abby, but I could see the way Abby looked at her, and it made me fume.

The psychic finished going through the other various lines on my hand, and then asked Kyla to put her hands on the table. "Interesting," the woman mumbled to herself as she grabbed Kyla's hand.

"What's interesting?" Kyla asked, but the psychic ignored the question and began running her fingers along the creases of Kyla's hands.

I zoned out for most of Kyla's reading while I surveyed the rest of the area we were in. So many people crowded the booths and food stands that there was no way all of them were from our school alone. This had to be a countywide fair. As I scanned the grounds, a familiar tuft of dirty blonde hair not far off caught my eye, and my gaze met Abby's. I didn't know if the girl had been staring at me or we'd caught each other's eye at the same time, but now I just kept looking, as did she.

I felt a fair amount of competition from her since we were chasing after the same girl, and Abby had the upper hand seeing as Kyla broke up with me in the first place. Regardless, I was no longer mad about our exchange at Eli's a few days earlier, nor did it appear Abby was upset. The other girl wasn't glaring. Her eyes weren't hard or stern, or hateful. They were considerably thoughtful and soft, and maybe even a bit confused. It made my own eyebrows furrow in confusion. Abby had every reason to glare at me – our competition over Kyla, or the fact that I'd insulted her and yelled at her being just two of the reasons. Instead, she turned up the corner of her mouth in a small smile and walked away.

"Your life line," I turned my attention back to the woman who was pointing to the third of the deep lines on Kyla's hand. "It is very short, and deep. The depth indicates vitality. You're healthy, but the shortness of it indicates an early death." She ran a single finger down the line. "A death already past." I leaned forward curiously as the woman's eyes grew terribly thoughtful, and she poked at the teeth-mark scars on Kyla's hand. "Not cold-skinned at all, and you have a heartbeat." The woman leaned forward a bit too, whispering to us ominously. "Werewolf?" Both Kyla and I's jaws dropped simultaneously, and the woman let out an amused laugh, her voice growing informal. "I'm Lahni, the psychic of The Supernatural Board."

"Oh," Kyla let out a sigh of relief. "Abby mentioned you."

"Did she?" Lahni's smile grew fond at the mention of Abby's name. "Well, I'm glad to hear she's been doing her job." I held back a scoff. Sure Abby was doing her job, if taking Kyla out to The Orchid was protecting the werewolves. Then I self-consciously took a gander around, wondering if Abby was around where she could have heard the thought. I didn't feel even a little comfortable with her being around where she could hear thoughts I didn't want her to, I couldn't imagine how Kyla put up with it.

"What was so interesting before?" Kyla asked, making a deliberate glance down at her hand.

"Oh." Lahni stuck her index finger in the air out of recollection, and instantly reached out to grab one of my hands and one of Kyla's. The woman pressed the palm of my hand to Kyla's, and the unexpectedness of it made my heart skip and my breathing stop. "Can you feel it?" Yeah, I could feel it all right. I could feel all the blood rushing to my cheeks, and I was too afraid to look over and see Kyla's reaction. "The heat, the energy, the connection. It's unlike anything I've ever seen." She pointed to me, and then to Kyla. "You are the essence of her. The life force is one." As rapidly as Lahni had grabbed our hands she dropped them, moving off the topic as if we'd brought up the weather. "Miss Zade, do you believe in destiny?"

I cleared my throat, desperately trying to get the blood to fade from my cheeks so I wouldn't appear flustered, and Lahni seemed to smile knowingly at my efforts. "I think you make your own."

The psychic rested her chin in her hand, and the intensity of her gaze made me want to fidget uncomfortably. "Can you fly?"

"What?" I held back a laugh at the absurdity of the question, but the woman just sat there, waiting for an answer. "No."

"So you can't defy gravity?" Lahni asked, to which I shook my head. "Destiny is like gravity, Miss Zade."

I didn't understand. If this was a metaphor, it was terribly confusing. "I need a pair of wings?"

A smirk turned up Lahni's lips as she passed the briefest glances to Kyla, it was so concise that if I blinked I would have missed it, and then she winked at me. "You've already got them." Just like our previous conversation, the topic ended there, and Lahni stood. "That's going to be three tickets each."

"Um," I stammered, still thrown off, and awkwardly dug through my pocket for our last tickets. "Here, thanks."

"What was that all about?" Kyla whispered as we walked away, that way the woman wouldn't hear.

I raised an eyebrow sarcastically. "Destiny is gravity, Kyla. Haven't you heard?"

She giggled and playfully pushed my shoulder. "No, I mean about the palm-connection thing. Do you know what she was talking about?"

My heart skipped at the residual warmth of Kyla's hand against my shoulder. Anytime she touched me I came undone. Then I grew nervous at her question. I knew exactly what that was about. Apparently the fact that *I* was the one who'd bitten Kyla was clear to everyone but Kyla. If she couldn't figure it out on her own, what was the point in telling her?

Aware that the silence between us was growing in length, I shrugged. "I haven't got a clue."

Kyla muttered something like 'oh' under her breath, and we walked the rest of the way back to her dorm in silence. I couldn't help but wonder if she was even slightly suspicious. No one had ever flat out told her that Luna was the one who'd done it, she'd always just assumed. Was she catching on that she shouldn't always assume? Not only were we all vague about the topic, but Luna was also significantly smaller than me. The bite marks on Kyla's hand were more wide-set than what Luna's jaw would have done. What would I say if Kyla did figure it out? What would my excuse be for not correcting her in the first place?

"Are you okay?" she asked, stopping in front of her door and turning to me. I simply nodded. "Okay. I'm going to take a nap since you woke me up super early. You'll come get me for training?"

My phone started buzzing in my pocket, and as I nodded again I pulled it out to look at who was calling. "Of course I'll come get you. Have a good nap." I waved goodbye and started back toward the elevator as I put the phone up to my ear. "Hey, Lacey."

"Hey, you're going home today, right?"

"Yeah, in a couple hours. Why?" I stepped onto the elevator and pushed the number for one floor below Kyla's. A guy stepped on after me and looked me up and down, grinning at me sheepishly, and I was glad I was on the phone so he wouldn't talk to me.

Lacey sighed with relief. "Thank God. I've been stuck here at school and I desperately need a run. Since this whole 'slaying the beast' thing my dad doesn't even want me driving home alone. I have to catch a ride with you guys."

I was standing in the middle of the elevator, and I could feel the boy leaning against the wall behind me, staring. With an annoyed sigh and an exaggerated roll of my eyes, I turned and rested against the sidewall so he couldn't study my backside. If only Kyla gave me the same treatment. "Yeah, okay. I'm not doing anything for a little bit if you want to come over and keep me company. Kyla's taking a nap." Luckily the elevator arrived at my floor, and I got off and walked to my room right near the doors.

"That sounds good. I'll see you in a few." After that Lacey hung up.

While I sat on my bed waiting for the younger girl to arrive I started regretting asking her over. Not because I didn't want to spend time with her, but as I rested there in the silent room I began to get tired. A nap would have been fantastic right about now, and a nap with Kyla would have been even better.

A couple hours later we were all sitting in the jeep, driving to Eli's for training. Kyla had been unusually silent ever since we picked her up from her room, and the fretfulness of her mood had caused Lacey and I to remain quiet as well. We'd been in the car for ten minutes before she finally spoke.

"I figured it out," she mumbled, so softly I almost didn't hear.

Even though it was soft, the unexpected sound startled me in the silence of the jeep. "Figured what out?"

She hadn't looked at me the first time she spoke. She didn't look at me now either. "It was you."

"What was me?" I asked as I took a deep breath to calm my nerves, but it didn't help. She'd been studying the scars on her hand since we left the dorms. I knew what she was talking about.

She shoved her bitten hand within inches of my face, forcing me to look at the tooth marks. "This was you. You did this."

I flinched, not only at her sudden movements, but also the anger dripping from her voice. "Kyla, I'm sorry," I apologized, hoping that was all she wanted to hear, praying I hadn't severely messed up by not telling her.

"Sorry for what? Sorry you bit me? *You* bit me!" she shouted the last part, adding nearly far to much emphasis on 'you'.

"You're in trouble now," Lacey scoffed from the back seat.

"Shut up, Lacey," both Kyla and I growled in unison. I felt bad for yelling at the girl, but this wasn't funny. Kyla was clearly upset.

"You bit me and all this time you let me believe it was Luna." I couldn't bring myself to look her in the eyes. I didn't have to in order to know that she was glaring at me, yelling through clenched teeth.

"I didn't think it was important," I said quietly, a whispered lie that was nearly inaudible through the furious rasp of Kyla's breathing.

Even from separate seats I could practically feel the heat rush to her head as her anger peaked. "Oh really, Camille, really? It's not important, but you'll lie to me about it? I'm not stupid, Camille. Even the psychic knew it! She said something about it, but when I ask you, do you tell me the truth? No, Camille, you lied to me! It's bad enough you just let me believe something different, but then you lie. You flat out fucking lie." Kyla's voice broke at the end as she held back tears, of fury or of hurt I couldn't be sure, but the way she repeatedly said my name made me weak with guilt.

I didn't know what to say. I was frozen solid, my stomach cold and queasy, lungs incapable of forcing out any air to speak.

"Why?" Kyla whispered, sniffling as she tried to blink the water away.

Because I need you, every second of every day, and I don't want you to know it. "What difference would it have made?" I asked sadly. "It doesn't matter." It wouldn't have helped her adjust. It wouldn't have brought her back to me.

This time, when Kyla sniffled, she had to wipe off a tear. "It matters to me," she said, wiping her cheek once more, green eyes filled with misery rather than anger.

"I didn't want you to hate me," I told her honestly, hoping that if she knew it was because of my own fears it would make her feel better.

She was silent for a few moments, watching me until I found the courage to make eye contact with her again. "You're stupid."

In such a serious moment, the insult was so immature that I couldn't help but laugh. "I'm stupid?" Kyla nodded, letting a tiny smirk defile her teary scowl. "What are you, five?"

She laughed, but it was broken halfway through as she finally let out a sob, and then she shrugged. "You're not off the hook. I'm still pissed."

"Wow," Lacey scoffed bitterly, and crossed her arms over her chest to show she was still upset she'd been yelled at. "You guys are the epitome of bipolar drama queens."

"Sorry, Lacey," I apologized, and turned up the house's driveway.

Kyla nodded her head in agreement. "Yeah, me too."

"Good," she said with a playful glare. "Apology accepted."

As we got out of the car I realized the house's small lot was nearly empty, one of the missing cars being Wesley's. It made me wonder what we'd be doing if he really wasn't home. The three of us marched into the quiet house, light footsteps almost echoing in the emptiness, and glancing around curiously when Will peered over the balcony.

"Hey, everyone's out," he told us. "Wes said just to go for a run or something."

"Where is everybody?" Lacey asked, and waved for him to come down.

"Most of them went to meet with The Supernatural Council. I think they're trying to convince the director to let us in on information without owing anything in return." He finally made his way down the stairs, casually shoving his hands into his pockets when he reached us.

We all stood there nodding in understanding for a minute until Lacey piped up excitedly. "Let's go for a run already! Will, do you want to come?"

He shrugged, indecisive until we started making our way to the back of the house, at which point he caught up. Once we got outside a draft seeped through my jacket, causing me to shiver and pull it tighter around my shoulders. Tonight had to be the coldest night since Kyla and I had arrived, and when we reached the watertight box I was reluctant to remove my warm layers. Being so eager to Change, Lacey was the first to shrug out of her clothing, and soon Will and then Kyla mustered the courage. With a hesitant sigh I finally gave in and Phased with the rest of them.

I gave a deliberate puff to watch my breath fog the freezing air. At least my fur kept me warmer than my clothes did, and I stretched my front limbs to circulate the heat of my blood. Will was lying down, patiently waiting for us to be ready to run, Kyla was playfully crunching the hard-packed snow beneath her paws, and Lacey was prancing around in circles, bowing, and then prancing some more in impatient excitement. I dug my paws into the ground, visibly preparing to take off while Lacey stopped and tensed, ready to give chase. Both Kyla and Will's heads turned toward me, watching carefully for the moment when I'd let loose, which I wasted no time in doing. In a split second I released the energy building in my limbs and flew past Lacey, who immediately began chasing after me.

The one thing I'd forgotten about Lacey was that, while she was the smallest of us, she was fast, and she easily caught up and passed me. I followed her through the trees, which were thick enough to slow us down, two pairs of thudding paws close behind me. One of them was getting closer, and I promptly learned it was Will, his long limbs carrying him so far with each stride that soon he passed even Lacey. I let out a wolfish chuckle as I realized that for the past minute Kyla had been nipping at my heels, trying to slow me down. I playfully kicked out my back legs, feeling one of them graze her teeth as she tried to grab it and pull me down. She missed, but so as not to discourage her I slowed enough to run at her side.

Every icy breath I took in through my mouth burned down my throat, filling my lungs with a penetrating energy I only ever felt while in wolf form. It was powerful and exhilarating, and I found myself wanting to go faster. Not far off in the distance I could hear the soft sound of slow-running water. I nudged Kyla and nodded in the direction of the stream, speeding up in attempt to get her to race. There was a flash of mischief in her eyes as she got ahead of me with an unexpected burst of speed, and I grinned and sped up to pass her. I was almost there, and could have outdistanced her before we reached the water, but in the twinkling of an eye everything disappeared from sight.

I hit the ground hard and let out a startled yelp. Was I in a hole? It was about a foot deeper than I was tall while on my back legs, and was only wide enough for me to curl up in a ball, definitely not wide enough for me to crouch low and get adequate strength to jump out. As I stood there was a sharp pain in my flank. I'd fallen hard, but not hard enough to give a pricking sensation, and now that I was standing my leg started to throb where I'd felt the pain.

I pressed myself against the wall of the hole and twisted my head at an uncomfortable angle to search the center of the ground. I stared hard until a slight glimmer caught my eye. Something sharp and shiny. A needle, and not a very small one, stuck out of the dirt straight up. That must have been what I'd fallen on. And the throbbing in my leg? My heart dropped. Poison. Why else would there be a carefully dug hole in the middle of the forest?

Kyla's head appeared over the top, and she worriedly whined down at me. I stood on my back legs, put my paws against the dirt, and stretched as far as I could. She was able to bend over enough for us to touch noses, but if they were going to help me out I'd need to jump as high as I could. The pulsating in my leg was spreading fast, it had already reached my torso, and my limb was starting to lose feeling.

My heartbeat sped, a sudden fear making it feel as though it would pump right out of my chest. Still standing on just my back legs, I bent them low to the ground and hopped, to my embarrassment much like a kangaroo. I nearly lost my footing as I discovered the hard way that I no longer had control over the muscles in my leg. Not only that, my head was starting to get woozy.

I bent low again, knowing this had to be successful or I wouldn't have the strength to try again. With all the power I could get out of one leg, I jumped. This time it was high enough, and I felt Kyla's jaws clamp down on the ruff of my neck. I scratched against the dirt to try and help her pull me out, Will and Lacey were nudging at my sides to help too, and a moment later half my body was recovered. But now both my back legs had lost all feeling, and they dragged against the side of the hole, catching against the uneven dirt and a couple out-hanging roots.

Kyla's grip on my neck tightened, and I tried to let out a pained yelp as one of her teeth broke skin, but my voice was gone. If I didn't feel so paralyzed I'd be panicking. With a last, hard heave Kyla dragged me out of the hole. I tried to stand, but every one of my limbs gave out beneath me, and I fell helplessly to the snow. I could hardly think anymore, my mind was slowed and my vision was going. I couldn't even feel it when Kyla prodded at me concernedly. Was I going to die?

I desperately wanted to nudge her in return, tell the girl I loved her, but I couldn't even move. She bumped me again with her nose, harder this time. When I continued to just lie there, eyes open but unresponsive, she let out a scared bark, a harsh, awkward sound for a wolf. Or maybe that was just because I could barely hear. I shut my eyes hard, the only motion I could perform, and tried to blink away the dark tunnels that were closing in on me. This was it. I took a last, deep breath of that beautiful, intoxicating scent that was Kyla's, and then gave in to the darkness.

10

"Will, hurry! Help me get her inside where it's warm." I tugged my shirt on as speedily as I could, paying no regard to my shoes or a jacket.

Will dressed just as incompletely in the rush, and grabbed the back half of the dark brown wolf while I took a hold of the front. I never realized before now just how big and heavy we were while in wolf form. We carried Camille into the glass room and set her gently on the floor. I looked up, and was about to bark at Lacey to call her dad when I saw that she'd already pulled out her cell phone.

"Goddammit," she growled when it rang to voicemail. "Dad, it's an emergency. Call me back ASAP." She dialed again, and I held my breath while it rang. "Dad! Thank God. Something's wrong with Camille. There was a hole in the woods and she fell in. I don't know what happened, she just passed out."

I collapsed onto the floor beside the large wolf, running my hand repeatedly through its fur. Its ribs rose and fell consistently, its mouth hanging open while a rasping noise escaped with each slow, labored breath. I lowered my head to the wolf's side and closed my eyes, listening intently to the sluggishly rhythmic heartbeat. It was almost like Camille was sleeping.

"Yes, she's breathing." Lacey paused while her dad spoke. "Kyla, is her pulse fading?" I listened for half a minute and then shook my head. "No, it's not." Another pause. "Okay, bye." Lacey threw her hands to her head, taking in deep breaths while she tried to calm herself. "He said it sounds like she was poisoned, but if her heartbeat isn't slowing and she's still breathing then hopefully she's just knocked out. He's coming home right now."

I nodded and continued stroking the wolf's fur for lack of any better outlet for my worry. We sat there in silence for a few minutes, hearing nothing but the sound of Camille's breathing.

"It's strange," Will whispered from his seat against the wall, and both Lacey and I looked over at him for explanation. "She's still in wolf form. Usually when we're really unconscious, or dead, we change back, but she hasn't."

Up until this point I'd been too worried to realize it, but Will was right. So what did that mean? Was Camille different, or was this some kind of special poison? She shouldn't have even been poisoned in the first place, and that caused a sudden fit of rage to spring from the depths of me. I stood to pace, every second growing more and more furious.

"What are you doing?" Lacey had sat down next to Camille, and she glanced up at me from her spot on the floor, watching me worriedly.

"We know who did this," I growled. "Vampires. I'm going to kill them. I'm going to find them and kill them."

I made a move for the door, but in one swift motion Will got in front of me. "That's not the safest decision."

I knew he was right, but only rage fueled me now, blind, protective rage. "Move. They poisoned her and now they're going to pay."

Lacey scrambled up and over to Will's side to help block the exit. "Kyla, how are you going to find them?" There was silence as I thought about it, but she answered before I could come up with any ideas. "You're not. You need to stay here."

"I'm *going* to find them," I repeated, growing frustrated that they wouldn't let me go. I tried to squeeze between them, but they stood tight. "Move!" I pushed harder this time, and then let out a furious snarl when they continued to hold their ground. Leading with my shoulder I tried to rush past them, but Will had had enough. He wrapped his arms around my waist and carried me like a fit-throwing child back toward the middle of the room. "Let me go! I have to find them! What if she dies?" I yelled frantically as I squirmed in his grasp, trying desperately to kick out of it, but he was too strong for me. Fury gave way to panic and I stopped struggling, and when he let me go I collapsed to the ground with tears stinging my eyes. "What if she dies?"

Lacey knelt beside me and wrapped a warm arm around my shoulders, squeezing me gently. "She's not going to die. She'll be okay."

I sighed and made my way to the unconscious wolf, where I buried my face in the soft brown fur on its ribs, letting it soak up a couple of my silent tears. I felt so helpless. If Camille was being attacked by anything, I could help. I could fight. But poison, there was nothing I could do about that. So I lay there, completely oblivious to everything but her heartbeat and scent. Minutes later, after what seemed like an eternity, we could hear the distant sound of the front door opening.

It wasn't long after that that Eli came running in, followed closely by the others. "Still no changes?" He eyed me, and then looked to Lacey, who was shaking her head. "That's a good sign. She's still in wolf form," he mused, curiously studying the motionless figure on the floor before stepping forward. "Let's carry her into the library."

Eli and Will carefully picked Camille up and hauled her into the room next door, where they set her on the carpet in front of the fireplace. We all followed them in and stood around, watching nervously while Eli stooped beside her.

He placed his hand on the wolf's chest, and then ran it through the fur around its neck. "She doesn't feel too hot, and she doesn't seem to be in any kind of pain." He continued to study her intently for the next couples minutes until he sighed and straightened. "Will, take Wesley and David back out to the hole. See if you can find anything useful. Everyone else, give us some space. All we can do is wait."

I watched as everyone but Eli and Lacey filed out. I knew he'd said 'everyone,' but there was no way I was leaving, not when Camille could be in danger. Once out of the public eye, Eli collapsed into an armchair at the center of the room, rubbing his eyes tiredly. Wondering if he knew I was still standing there, I timidly cleared my throat to let him know, but he made no startled move to regain his aura of authority.

"Do you know what it is?" Lacey asked, taking her time to light the fireplace and then sitting in a chair next to her father's.

I remained standing at the side of the room, visible but not engaging. The ways I could act around the Alpha were still unclear to me, and with Camille not able to help, I wanted to be as unobtrusive as possible.

Eli sighed heavily, dropping his hand from his face. "No human poison would keep her in wolf form. This is supernatural, it has to be."

Lacey pulled at her lip thoughtfully for a few moments before asking, "The vampires are messing with magic?"

"There's no other explanation." Eli nodded, his sad eyes falling on the wolf, and I could guess what he was thinking. That Camille shouldn't be here. Shouldn't be back in Oregon where she was in danger. "I just hope this isn't permanent."

Permanent? The word caught my attention, and I instinctively strode to the unconscious wolf to sit on the floor nearby, as if my presence would have some beneficial effect. "She could stay like this?"

"I don't know," he admitted quietly. "Anything is possible at this point."

I looked worriedly at Camille, and then lay down to face the fireplace with my head resting on the side of the wolf's stomach. I knew Eli and Lacey were watching me, but I didn't care. It comforted me being able to hear Camille's heartbeat, to feel her chest rise and fall. The heat of the fire warmed my face, spreading throughout my entire body to fill me with serenity. Of course I was worried for Camille, but somehow I knew everything would be all right. I could feel it. As I lay so close to her heart, I could feel that familiar energy flowing through me. A lively, healthy energy that was bright as ever.

"Kyla." I was being nudged, and opened my eyes to see Lacey holding a cup of coffee. "Kyla, it's morning, wake up."

"I fell asleep?" I groggily pushed myself off the still unmoving Camille and rubbed my eyes, the cold of the fireless morning making me shiver.

She nodded and handed me the hot mug. "Yeah, you slept there all night."

"Thanks." I sipped on the strong coffee and visually examined the wolf. Still no changes. Camille was knocked out in the same position, looking like she was sleeping. "Did they find anything?"

Lacey pointed to a pile of cluttered books on the table in the middle of the room. "They were up all night trying to figure it out. They've got a couple theories, some involve her waking up pretty soon, some not for a few days." She squatted next to me and gently ran her fingers through Camille's fur. "You should eat though. We have to leave for school soon."

I inspected Camille, and knew there was nothing that could pull me away until she was awake. The thought of her regaining consciousness with nobody around to comfort or take care of her was troubling. "I'm not going, she needs me here."

"I figured you'd say that," she chuckled knowingly and straightened up. "I'd stay too if I didn't have my dad giving me no other choice but to go."

"I'll let you know if anything happens," I assured her, and then smiled goodbye as she turned to leave the room.

I sat there for another minute, sipping my coffee and trying to figure out something to keep me occupied while I watched over Camille. I eyed a box of matches near the side of the fireplace and moved closer to start a flame. The comfortable warmth of it immediately filled the room, making me sleepy even though I'd just awoken. I pushed myself off the floor and sat in one of the chairs around the cluttered coffee table. The house was completely silent except for the crackling of the embers, and I rested for a good fifteen minutes in the seat until I finished my drink, thinking about how time went painfully slow when I wasn't sleeping or doing something engaging. I looked searchingly around the bright room, taking in every detail when my eyes fell on a book I hadn't yet noticed sitting on the mantel of the fireplace. I tiptoed over to it, afraid to make any noise in the silence of the house, stepped deliberately over the wolf, and grabbed the volume, taking it back to my seat.

It was probably the oldest thing I'd ever seen. So old that it wasn't bound with glue and a cardboard spine like all the other books in the library. Its browning, cloth-like pages were loosely set in a worn leather cover. The antiquity of it left it flimsy to hold, like it would collapse under the gentlest touch. Etched into the dark leather cover were the title 'Leu Garoul' and the head of a wolf. The title of the book was intriguing in itself. I'd heard of the term 'loup garou' to mean werewolf, and it sounded very much like Leu Garoul.

I opened the book with interest, but much to my disappointment the entirety of it was written in a foreign language. Despite not being able to read it, each severely faded word and every picture was hand-inked in the most beautiful penmanship I'd ever seen. As I slowly flipped through the pages, taking in the artistic design, it made me slightly ashamed of my own sloppier handwriting.

Delicate footsteps sounded at the door of the library, and I looked up to see Wesley taking a seat next to me. "Leu Garoul." He titled his head toward the book in my lap.

"Werewolf?" I asked as I closed and reexamined the cover of the text. He nodded while I opened it back up and ran a hand over the elegant writing. "What language is it?"

"Old French," he said, leaning forward to double check the writing. "Old, old French," he clarified with a chuckle.

"Oh." As I studied the book some more I realized the author hadn't signed it. "Who wrote it?"

"The very first Alpha, Bastien Moreau. There are a lot more of us now than there were back then. We didn't need American Packs, or English Packs, or Russian Packs. In the 9th century, I think around eight hundred-fifty, Bastien traveled all over seeking out mutts, gathering information on their different experiences, finding out what was normal for a werewolf." Wesley delicately removed the book from my lap and laid it in his own, running a gentle hand over the cover of our legacy. "Bastien's father was a werewolf, so he was taught from the start how to control his Changes and desires as best as they knew how. Most of the mutts he found were living in chaos, slaves to instinct, running from the law. Wolves need a leader to survive, so he stepped in and, with the mutts that were willing, created the first pack."

"What's all this writing about?" I glanced at Camille to make sure she was still doing okay before curiously turning in my chair to face Wesley.

"These are his findings, the structure of a pack, ways to turn a person, safest times and methods to hunt. Of course, a lot's changed since then, but this was the start of everything we are." Wesley stood from his chair, carefully replacing the book on top of the fireplace before sitting back down.

"Can you read it?" I asked as I watched him, and then when he raised an eyebrow I added, "The writing, the old, old French."

He chuckled and shook his head. "Hardly, it's pretty different from modern French. A few of the things I can get the gist of though, and it helps that Bastien was a decent artist." I nodded understandingly, but I could feel Wesley's eyes on me as I returned my attention to the fire. "How are you dealing?" he asked eventually.

"Dealing?" My eyebrows furrowed at his choice of words.

"Yeah, dealing." He nodded. "Being turned isn't an easy thing. I mean, are you okay? You're not troubled, or unhappy, or angry?"

"Oh, no," I said instantly, my first defensive reaction to his question, and then took a minute to think about it. "I mean, it's definitely not easy, but I haven't really had time to be resentful for it. I was a pretty mad yesterday when I found out it was really Camille that bit me."

"Camille bit you?" The sudden excitement that brightened Wes' expression as I nodded startled me. "That's brilliant."

"It's brilliant?" I asked, and the obvious confusion on my face made him smile amusedly.

"Yeah, because of the kind of relationship you and her have," he paused and eyed me carefully for a second before correcting himself. "Or, had."

Nobody ever really talked about it, but I should have assumed everyone knew about Camille and I. In spite of the painful reminder that Camille might never want to be with me again, he'd officially piqued my curiosity. "What do you mean?"

"Well, you know it's not entirely normal for werewolves to fall in love with humans?" he asked. I knew it wasn't common, but he'd said 'normal'. I squinted, cocking my head unsurely to urge him on. "It would be like a dog falling in love with a monkey. Call it a biological safety net, but usually something prevents it so neither turns into prey." The corners of Wes' mouth turned up in a smirk, and he glanced over at the unconscious wolf. "Camille's a bit of a freak."

I chuckled a little, and then chewed the inside of my cheek thoughtfully. "What about when it's not love?" I asked, knowing werewolf and human relations weren't strictly emotional.

"Fine, you caught a hole in my metaphor," he laughed, rolling his eyes. "Anyway, my point is, usually when someone gets bitten it's on accident. It's rare for a bitten werewolf to even maintain a relationship with their maker, let alone have a relationship like the one you and Camille did. In theory you could make that bond so strong your souls practically become one. You could feel the other's pain from clear across the globe, or know instinctively what the other's thinking without saying it, feed off of each others' energy."

I knew what he meant immediately. The electric current whenever her and I were touching or working closely, or how I could feel deep down that she'd wake up all right. I just wished the bond was strong enough that I could tell why she was having such a hard time forgiving me. "But what about when that relationship isn't there anymore?" I asked him, and I could tell he knew what I meant by the somewhat un-comfortable way his eyes darted from me to Camille.

"I don't know," he shrugged honestly. "There isn't much data on it. Most of what I'm telling you is little more than speculation. To most of us it's a rumor."

I nodded understandingly. Rumor it might be, but it already felt more real to me than a simple rumor. "How do you know so much?"

Wesley chuckled like it was an inside joke, and shrugged. "I'm old-er than I look, and I've done my research."

"Yeah, I can never tell how old you guys really are." I studied the seemingly early-twenty year old's features thoughtfully for a few mo-ments. "How old are you?"

"Forty-four," he answered with a smirk. "I was bitten when I was twenty."

"You were bitten?" I asked, horribly masking the shock from my voice. "I assumed most Pack wolves are born."

"Most are," he agreed. "But Eli's a merciful man, and luckily for me a good judge of character."

"How's that?"

"The reason a lot of mutts kill people is because they don't know Changes can be controlled. They figure it's like the legends or Holly-wood – getting bit means Changing on a full moon and not being able to control it at all. That's what I first thought when I got bit, and I hated it." Wesley stared toward the fire as his eyes gained a reminiscent de-tachment. "Without guidance, everything from the pain of it straight down to the instincts feels like a curse."

Knowing that someone I knew had to go through a Change alone caused me to frown. I'd have *never* gotten through the adjustment if it weren't for Camille and Luna. "Did you kill people?"

He nodded slowly. "A couple. I was living in Chicago, Phasing in alleys and back roads. When people feel they're being stalked by some-thing they can't see their first instinct is to run, which makes not chas-ing impossible. I was drawing a lot of unwanted attention. Eli had been watching me for some time, deciding if I should be taken out or if I was worth saving. When they brought me back here about fifteen years ago, Eli and Camille's father taught me everything they knew."

"Wow." I shook my head in disbelief. "I never realized how easy I have it."

Wesley smiled knowingly, brightening the somber mood with his signature grin. "It's never easy, especially since you're so young, but you couldn't have picked a better family than Camille's."

"I can definitely agree with that," I smiled my consent, turning a fond eye toward the wolf.

He glanced down at his wristwatch and then stood with a sigh. "I've got to go to school."

"School?" I laughed. "Aren't you a bit old for that?"

"You're never to old to learn." He winked playfully, and with a friendly wave left me alone in the silent library.

As I sank back into my chair and gazed at Camille, a deep sense of longing pulled at my heart. I missed her. Not just because she'd been unconscious, but I missed the way we used to be. The way she reciprocated my smile when we looked at each other, how easily she made me laugh, and above all the way she felt. It had been three months since everything had gone to hell. I knew she wanted me to leave it alone, but shouldn't she have been able to forgive me by now? Maybe it was really all an excuse because she just didn't love me anymore. Maybe it was time I started to come to terms with the idea that she'd never want me back. I exhaled despairingly and stood up to make my way to the large wolf. Eventually I'd be able to come to terms with seeing Camille as a friend, even if it would take a while. I lay back down next to her and rested my head on the wolf's side. It didn't take long for the crackling and warmth of the fire to lull me to sleep.

What seemed like minutes later the dropping of my head woke me. I groaned sleepily and folded my arms to support my cheek, which was now between Camille's naked, curled-up human body. *That* jolted me awake, and I awkwardly scurried away so she wouldn't get the wrong idea. When I regained enough composure to look back at her I realized I didn't need to worry, because while the girl was no longer in wolf form, she was still unconscious. Taking a calming breath, I pushed myself off the floor and stretched. Hopefully Camille Phasing back to normal meant the poison was wearing off, and soon she'd wake up. Deciding she needed to be covered with a blanket, I strode down the hall and to the living room to grab the one I remembered was draped over the couch. On the way back I glanced at the clock hanging on the wall of the library, and almost on command my stomach growled. It was already three in the afternoon. I'd slept a lot longer than I'd meant to, so long that Lacey would probably be back from school soon.

After draping the blanket over Camille, I sluggishly made my way into the kitchen. There was nothing of interest in the pantry or the refrigerator. I wasn't half the chef Camille was. That, and I was feeling too lazy to really make something just for myself. Finally, I spotted an individual sized pizza in the freezer, and stuck it in the microwave for a few minutes before striding back to the library to sit and eat.

"How's she–" Lacey walked in a bit later and stopped, staring when she caught sight of the blanket-covered Camille. "She's human again," she observed happily. "Has she woken up yet?"

I shook my head and swallowed the last bite of pizza. "No, but hopefully the poison is wearing off and she will soon."

Lacey plopped down in the chair next to me with a heavy sigh. "You know, the vampires have a hang out in the city. My dad doesn't want to go, he says it'll start trouble, but I don't doubt that someone there knows what's going on."

"Nobody told me that," I growled in frustration. "What have we been sitting around here for?"

"I think we should go too, especially since things are getting this extreme." She pointed to Camille and then clenched her fist in her lap. "I mean, traps on Pack territory? That's fucking absurd. We need to send the message that we won't take it lying down."

I stared into the fire, which over the last few hours had dwindled to glowing embers, while I thought about our options. We could always go on our own, but that would be dangerous. Not to mention we'd be disobeying Alpha's orders, which, as I understood it, was the ultimate no-no. "Maybe you can talk to your dad again?" I offered, trying to mind my place as best as possible. "The way I see it, we don't have many other options."

Lacey nodded her agreement. "I'll try to convince him it'll be a calm, peaceful visit. Hopefully we could go tonight."

I nodded in return, and we sat there for the next few minutes in silence. I hated what had happened to Camille, and it drove me crazy that there wasn't much we could do. The last time we sat around waiting for the enemy to make a move I'd nearly ended up dead. I wasn't up for that again, and was pretty sure the others weren't either.

After a few minutes Camille started coughing, making both Lacey and I jump as it broke the silence. "Water." The request was barely audible, and I glanced at Lacey to see if I wasn't imagining it.

"I'll get it," she said, and hurriedly left for the kitchen.

I knelt beside Camille to make sure she was really waking up. The coughing had subsided, and while she was now motionless, her eyes were open. "Camille? How you feeling?"

"Cold, and like someone filled me with concrete." She blinked a couple times and then strained to roll herself onto her back. Her voice was harsh and quiet, as though every word was difficult to get out. "I can't really move, could you help me into a chair?"

"Sure," I nodded, scooted my arms underneath her body and stood, easily lifting the girl with me. As a human I never would have been able to pick her up like that, but now it was hardly difficult. I couldn't deny it felt good to have her in my arms, and I was reluctant to put her down.

When we reached the chairs I set her into one, and after pulling the blanket tighter around her shoulders I fell into an adjacent seat. Lacey returned with the water and set it in Camille's hand, and while Camille seemed able to grip the cup easily enough, she could only lift it halfway before she dropped her arm back down, letting out a tired groan. I reached over, carefully taking the cup from her to lift it to her lips. She smiled her thanks, and sipped on the fluid for almost a minute before pulling her head away.

"Hey, she's awake! And human!" David said excitedly, coming into the room and standing in front of us to study Camille. "How you doing?"

She tried lifting her arm as high as she could to display her weakness. This time she got it about shoulder height before her strength was gone and it fell back down. "Weak. How long was I out for?"

"Less than a day," David reassured her. "Now that you're awake your metabolism will speed up and the poison should wear off faster."

"Yeah, I can feel my strength coming back a little bit," Camille told him, and then rubbed her stomach as it growled hungrily. "I'm starving."

"What are you in the mood for?" David asked while I put one of Camille's arms around my shoulders to help walk her to the kitchen.

Every movement was sluggish, and when she talked it was even worse, like her energy could only be exerted in one task at a time. "Spaghetti."

"Spaghetti it is then," David laughed, and went ahead of us to the kitchen.

When we finally got there he had already pulled out the ingredients and started boiling water. I helped set Camille on a stool at the bar and took a seat between her and Lacey. Camille consistently stared at the countertop tiredly while Lacey and I sat in silence, watching David toss noodles into the boiling water. The sauce smelled good, and even though I'd eaten not too long ago my stomach rumbled at the aroma.

I was debating whether or not I was hungry enough to eat again when I glanced up and caught Camille's eye. She was watching me closely, an old, familiar and thoughtful look on her face. It reminded me of how she used to look at me before I broke her heart. Before I got a chance to get confused by it or to give her a consenting smile, the vibrating of my phone in my pocket startled me out of it. "Oh crap," I mumbled when I read the text. It was Abby, checking if we were still going to dinner.

I began to walk out of the kitchen to call her and explain that I couldn't make it when Camille stopped me. "What's wrong?"

I shook my head, silently scolding myself for forgetting. "I was supposed to hang out with Abby tonight, but I'm just going to call her and cancel."

"Oh," Camille said softly, and there was a flash of angry frustration in her eyes as she looked toward the floor. "You should still go," she told me calmly.

"What?" Now I was confused. It didn't take a genius to see Camille didn't really like Abby. I'd have never expected her to actually insist that I go.

"It seems like you were here all night worrying about me," she said with an indifferent shrug. "You could use a break."

"Are you sure?" I checked the time on my cell phone. It was only four. I had plenty of time to get back to the school and probably even to take a shower.

When she nodded I just stood there awkwardly, trying to figure out the best way to say bye. I felt like I should hug her. Or give some show of affection after what she'd been through and how she'd been looking at me, but none of it seemed appropriate, and now she didn't seem to want it.

"I'll see you later then," I said, unsurely turning for the kitchen door. "Feel better, okay?"

Camille simply gave a small wave in return. I still felt guilty for leaving her right after she'd woken up, but I'd already told Abby we could meet. As I left, I told myself that Camille was healthy enough to not need me, and for the most part she seemed okay with me leaving. More than that, it appeared she wanted me to leave. It felt like a long shot, but maybe Abby could help me start to see Camille as Camille wanted to be seen – as a friend.

He could see the address of the warehouse even through the hundreds of feet of darkness, and by the dim light over the single metal door he could make out the two vampires guarding it. A lot of asking around and a few hundred dollars lost on bribing had gotten him two things – this address and the name of a vampire. A vampire named Benjamin, who would either accept him or see through his bullshit and kill him. If his heart was beating, he imagined it'd be pounding right out of his chest, and while hundreds of years of practice let him wear a cool, calm expression, he was nervous.

As he neared the three hundred foot mark he could see the two guards stop talking to each other and tense up, catching sight of him nearing. Each moved a pale hand to a weapon on their belts – weapons all of them knew would do no good. He continued his silent walk toward the warehouse, footsteps treading almost print-free through the snow, carefully watching the guards' every movement, ready to run should they choose to attack.

He reached the two hundred foot mark, and then at one hundred feet one of the guards stepped forward, crossing his arms over his chest with an intimidating scowl. "Stop there. You've got about ten seconds to speak your intentions or leave."

"The name's Rook." He stopped and let his arms rest at his sides. "I'm here to see Benjamin."

The guard scoffed, relaxing at Rook's seemingly peaceful demeanor but returning his hand to the weapon at his hip. "Benjamin didn't mention it, you'd be wise to turn away."

"He doesn't know I'm coming," Rook admitted, and while he spoke he slowly reached into his pocket, holding up his other hand to show he meant no harm. "But surely you'll find my visit beneficial." When he finished, he tossed the shiny red stone he'd pulled out of his pocket to the guard. It was a rare occult stone, one it had taken him a lot of time to find and even more money to buy, but it was guaranteed to get him in.

The guard studied the mineral for a moment before stepping back and whispering to the other man, who after shrugging disappeared into the building. Rook stood there for a couple minutes, hands in his pockets while he waited under the intense stare of the guard. Finally, the door opened, and after a brief exchange between the two men Rook was ushered inside. One of them led the way through the building while the other remained at the door, watching after them.

He could feel the eyes of the dozen other vampires on him, looking up from their tasks or poker games and staring while he passed. About twenty army-style cots lined a far wall, letting him know not every vampire was present. It wasn't too large of a number, but it made for more than he'd expected. A quiet whimpering caught his attention, and he looked to his other side where a human girl was tied, no doubt for a snack. Rook held back a grimace at the sight. Sure he fed off of humans every once in a while. Every vampire had to drain lifeblood once a year to maintain immortality. But keeping them like that was cruel and unnecessary. These vampires had less regard for life than he'd hoped.

As they continued to the back of the warehouse, where a set of stairs led up to an overseeing office, Rook caught sight of what he'd come to find out. A manmade wall sectioned off a smaller part of the building. Over the top where it didn't quite reach the ceiling he could see a dark light. If the color black could shine, it would illuminate the room like that light did. He couldn't even look at it directly because the darkness of it was so blindingly bright. Whatever evil was behind that wall didn't want to be seen, and the overwhelming blackness drained the vitality of his already absent soul. Clearly supernatural, the immorality of it made him shiver. He didn't know what it was, but it was something big. The something he'd been hearing about, and knew he had to stop.

They eventually reached the stairs, and the guard let him walk up on his own. When he reached the top he knocked politely, and hearing an answer from within he opened the door and stepped inside. A tall, young looking man was standing beside the door, staring out the window that overlooked the warehouse below. Rook had heard of Benjamin before, the young vampire was notorious for getting into trouble and causing conflict with other supernatural races. From this, he'd imagined someone unsophisticated and rebellious looking. He was proved wrong when the clean dressed, bright blue-eyed, sandy brown haired Benjamin turned to greet him.

"Benjamin." The vampire held out his hand and introduced himself.

"Rook." He took the man's hand and shook it, then took a seat at the desk where he was ushered while Benjamin walked around and sat at the other side of it.

Rook's eye wandered to the empty mirror behind Benjamin. It had been some four hundred years or more since he'd seen his reflection. If his hair were just an inch shorter he probably would have forgotten its rich brown color. He'd long forgotten the color of his own eyes, though the color brown seemed to revive a certain familiarity.

Benjamin picked the red stone up off the desk and turned it over in his hands, studying it for a few minutes before tossing it from one hand to the other as he leaned back to finally address Rook. "So, what can I do for you, Rook?"

"Frankly?" Rook started, leaning forward slightly in his seat, as if telling a secret. "I've heard you got something big. I want in."

Rook refrained from clenching his jaw in disdain as Benjamin let out a scoffing chuckle. "Why would I let you in? I don't know you, and I certainly don't trust you."

"That's why," he stated simply, pointing to the stone that Benjamin laid softly on the desk. "You know the value of that stone."

"Yes, but it's of no use to me," Benjamin shrugged flatly.

"It wasn't meant to be. It's an example." Rook paused and waited for some sign of curiosity from Benjamin, which came in the form of a raised eyebrow. "I acquired that stone with a snap of my fingers. What occult items you need, I'll get. Definitely at more convenience than whatever route you've been taking now."

Benjamin nodded slowly as he thought about what Rook had said. It wasn't hard to see that he was interested. "And what do you want in return?"

Rook shrugged nonchalantly. "Let me help, let me see this through to the end, and I want what everyone else down there is getting, a piece of whatever you're supplying when it's finished."

"You don't even know what *that* is. What makes you think it's worth it?" Benjamin asked, a suspicious scowl hardening his face.

The intimidating look didn't faze Rook, and he let out a convincingly friendly laugh. "You've got a reputation, Benjamin. I've gathered enough faith from that to want in on this."

"Uh huh." Benjamin nodded slowly again, his lips moved as he bit at them thoughtfully. A minute passed, and Rook sat there calmly and patiently before Benjamin picked up the stone once more. "Alright, leave a number with the guard. I'll call you when I need something. You want this back?"

Rook glanced at the magical stone Benjamin was holding out to him, and stood while he shook his head. "Keep it." With that, he shook the man's hand and left back down the stairs.

On his way down he tried to catch a glimpse over the manmade wall, but it was too tall for him to see down. This meeting had gone better than he'd hoped it would, but these vampires were on high alert. It wouldn't be easy to figure out what was going on, and he'd have to be more careful than ever so that no one would discover his intentions. But if what he'd been hearing about was true, he couldn't let them go through it. Couldn't let the evil be woken.

I finished throwing on the shirt I'd finally decided on wearing the second I heard the knock come from my dorm room door – five minutes early. So far Abby had been early to everything we'd done together, even if I was just down the hall, and I was starting to get the feeling that she was never late. I smoothed the wrinkles along my torso and then opened the door with a grin. Abby's smile widened in acknowledgement, and I watched her eyes look me up and down approvingly.

"Do you need more time?" she asked, waiting outside as I turned to grab my cellphone off the desk.

I shook my head and stepped out of the room, closing the door behind me. "Nope, I'm ready." With a smile Abby turned to lead us to the elevator, and I waited until the doors closed before my curiosity got the best of me. "Where are we going?"

"Nowhere too exciting," she answered with a chuckle, clearly amused I'd waited so long to ask when she'd already heard me think the question. "Just a little Italian place in town." She said nowhere exciting, but the smirk on her face and the nicer than casual way she was dressed gave me the impression it was somewhere a little more exciting than she made it out to be.

The elevator doors opened to the first floor, and we stepped off and started toward the exit. As we made our way to the main doors of the building I wondered if I'd told Abby about the poison yet. The way her head shot in my direction at the thought gave me the answer.

"What happened?" she asked worriedly as we veered left toward the parking lot and to her car.

"The vampires are getting more aggressive," I answered, opening the passenger side door to get in the blue sedan. "We were out for a run on Pack territory, and Camille fell into a hole." As I explained I twisted to pull on my seatbelt. "There was a poisoned needle in the trap, she was knocked out all day."

"Goddammit," Abby muttered in frustration, and then began to talk quietly to herself. "If they want the weakest three, why would they be setting up random traps on Pack territory? It doesn't make any sense." I shrugged, not really sure either. "Your Alpha was at the Council office yesterday." I 'mhm-ed' knowingly, waiting for her to continue. Since the Pack had gotten home from meeting with the council I'd been too preoccupied with Camille to ask how it'd gone. Now that Abby was bringing it up I hoped there was good news, but she instantly shot that idea down. "Don't get excited. My dad's an asshole, and I'm embarrassed to say he turned them down."

I sighed. I wanted to agree with her about the asshole part, but seeing as it was still her father, I didn't want to offend her. "We'll have to take care of it on our own then. I'm just getting so worried." Again I thought back to the last time we'd waited for an enemy to make the first move, and I saw Abby look at me concernedly. As usual I pushed away the thoughts and tried to think of something to change the subject. "Anyway, let's forget all this vampire stuff. I could use a relaxing dinner."

Abby smiled in agreement, but I could still see the tint of worry in her eyes. I could imagine what she was thinking. You shouldn't keep it bottled up, you should talk to someone about it, all the worried things I purposefully wouldn't tell myself because I didn't want to think about it.

"You like Italian food right?" Abby asked, seeming as ready to change the subject as I was.

I grinned and nodded, the thought of food making my stomach growl. "I love Italian food."

"Good!" she exclaimed excitedly. "You're going to love this place then. It's a little hole in the wall restaurant, but their food is to die for."

"I can't wait," I chuckled at her excitement and looked out the window at our surroundings.

We'd gotten on a small highway, and a little distance ahead of us I could see we'd soon be entering the city. Now that I thought about it though, it looked more like a town than a city. There were lights, but definitely not big city glamour. There was little enough glow from the town that I could still see plenty of stars, but enough light that I didn't feel like we were still in the middle of the forest. Remembering a minute later that Abby could hear my thoughts, I figured I might as well make conversation instead of giving the girl a monologue about the area.

"Tell me more about you," I invited. "How'd you get into all this supernatural business?"

She shrugged just like she had the first time I asked her to talk about herself, but she made an honest effort this time. "Well, you know my dad is high up in the Council, and my mom is into it too. I pretty much grew up around it. They started training me in self-defense when I was really young, then when I was old enough to get involved I got simple assignments dealing with more peaceful supernaturals, mostly psychics."

"What about now? What kind of stuff did you do before you got to babysit me?" I asked playfully, trying to encourage her to keep speaking. I constantly got the feeling she was more of a listener.

She chuckled and shook her head reassuringly. "Trust me, I don't mind babysitting. You could always pay me for it though." I laughed, but didn't say anything as I checked our surroundings again and waited for her to answer my question. We were in town now, and Abby was about to make a left turn down a decent sized street. "Mostly investigative stuff, like checking in on those supernaturals we know to be troublemakers. Sometimes bringing someone in for questioning or follow-ing up on leads about those troublemakers."

"Sounds like a pretty interesting job," I mused, glancing out the window at the restaurant as Abby pulled her car into its small parking lot.

"Yeah, it's okay, I guess," she answered as we both got out of the vehicle.

Once we walked in the front entrance of the small and nearly empty restaurant, the host waved for us to follow without asking how many we wanted a table for. We went with him to the back of the restaurant and to a small, two-person table, where we sat and received our menus. There was a couple at another two-person table about twenty feet away, and a small family on the opposite side of the venue. Apart from them and a pair at the bar, the rest of the place was empty.

"So," Abby started as the host walked away and left us to peruse the menus. "I never asked you about your accent."

I blushed slightly, seeing as it had been so long since anyone brought up my accent that I'd begun to forget I even had it. "Texas, I lived there before I moved to California," I told her, absentmindedly glancing around the venue. "But I guess this is home now." I didn't know how long I'd be in Oregon, but so as not to get my hopes up I told myself I'd be here for a long time.

"Don't sound too excited," Abby said sarcastically, and I gave an apologetic smile. "Oregon's not so bad, and with all the supernaturals around life can't get too boring."

"No kidding," I chuckled, thinking about how I'd hardly just moved here and there was already danger to worry about. "Ah, the supernatural lifestyle."

Before Abby could respond the waitress came by to take our drink orders, and right after she left Abby turned her eyes back on me to con-tinue our conversation. "I know it's got to be hard being so far away from family and stuff, but how do you like being a werewolf?"

I shrugged, not bothering to premeditate my answer. "It's not so bad. I'm stronger and faster, have better hearing and smell. There're definitely perks. The hardest thing is just learning to control it. I'm still working on it." I finished my answer with a shrug and let my mind wander as I let Abby think about what to say next. When she nodded thoughtfully I began to notice how, aside from a little nicer than usual, she was dressed.

The top half of her hair was pulled back while the bottom half fell casually over her shoulders. As usual she'd done her make up, but now she wore some eyeliner, which made her cheerfully bright hazel eyes stand out more than they normally did. I couldn't see the pants she was wearing, but she had on a sleeveless white blouse. My first thought was about how cute I thought the shirt was, my second was about how low-cut it was. The deep v-line neck of the shirt led my eyes from Abby's delicate shoulders to the smooth flesh of her collarbone, and then downward, where the shirt dipped so low it teased by just covering the top of her ample – Abby cleared her throat, stopping my thoughts in their tracks and causing my cheeks to immediately flare at being caught.

I covered my face with my hands out of embarrassment so she wouldn't see how red it could get. "Oh my God, get out of my head."

As I peered out of the space between my fingers I could see that Abby was clearly amused. "I didn't have to read your thoughts for that one," she giggled. "Your eyes said it all."

Since she didn't seem offended, I was able to laugh at myself. A moment later, after I'd willed the blood out of my cheeks, though I was still embarrassed, I pulled my hands away from my face. "I'm so sorry," I apologized, to which she shrugged as if to say 'no big deal'. "If that was me I'd walk around all bundled up so I wouldn't have to hear people thinking about stuff like that."

"I'm used to it," she told me with another shrug, and then, looking up from the tablecloth at me, added with a smirk, "And I don't really mind when it's you."

At first I didn't know what to say. I'd never had a girl so openly flirt with me. Even Camille had been so much subtler. As I realized, however, that I liked the fact that Abby was so straightforward, I couldn't help but let a small smile crease my lips. At my smile, the curve in Abby's lips widened, as she seemed pleased with my acceptance of it.

Still, I didn't know how to respond, so instead I asked, "Do you like being able to hear people's thoughts all the time?"

She gave a prompt shake of her head like she didn't even have to think about the answer. "Honestly, I really wish there was an 'off' button. Especially at school or other places when I'm surrounded by a lot of people all day. It's a huge headache."

"I can see how it would be," I agreed, and then looked up as the waitress came back to take our food order. After we both ordered she walked away, and I returned my attention to the girl in front of me. "Sometimes I really wish I could hear people's thoughts though. Especially like you, when you know what I'm thinking but I can't tell what you are." I gave a fake glare at Abby, who just laughed at me.

"I'm pretty open about what I'm thinking," she told me matter-of-factly, a statement that I really couldn't argue with. *That's a nice change from Camille*, I thought. I'd practically had to pry to get Camille to even acknowledge me the other day. Catching where my thoughts were going, and not wanting Abby to hear about it, I pushed the ideas away. "You don't have to try so hard, you know," Abby said as her smile faded, and she busily took a sip of her soda.

"Try so hard to what?" I asked, unsure of what she meant.

"Not to think about Camille." She took another sip of her drink, and then picked at a piece of bread she'd taken from the basket at the center of the table. "You could even talk to me about it. It doesn't seem like you really talk to anyone else."

"Are you sure you'd want me to talk to you about it?" I asked timidly. I was pretty sure how Abby felt about me, and about Camille, and I didn't think it was something she'd want to hear.

She shrugged. "If it's on your mind, it's on your mind. Besides, it would help me get a better idea of what my chances are with you." She paused as if waiting for me to say something about it, but I didn't know what say. I didn't even know myself what her chances were with me, so after a few seconds of silence she continued so as to give me something to talk about. "Why don't you think she's open with you?"

I sighed. The first thing that came to mind was everything Camille hadn't told me. "Did you know she let me believe all this time it was her twin sister that bit me?" I said hastily, finding I was a little more eager to talk about it than I realized. "But it was actually her. She'd been lying to me this whole time." Abby tensed down the side of her lip in a wince, but waited for me to continue. "And after he made me break up with her I thought she just needed some time to get over it and forgive me, but I'm starting to think she's just using it as an excuse not to be with me." I paused, seeing if Abby wanted to get a word in, but when she didn't say anything I pressed on, "My whole life changed because of that one night. He hurt me, and she doesn't even seem to care about how that night affected me – aside from making sure I'm not dangerous and not going to bite anyone. Maybe that's what frustrates me the most. She's so busy being awkward with me that she hasn't tried to find out about anything that happened."

"So," Abby started and paused thoughtfully. By the way her eyes darted quickly from mine to the tabletop it was obvious she wasn't entirely comfortable with the subject, but I was thankful she was making an effort. "You think she's being selfish?"

"Yes!" I said, glad that she understood. Before talking about it with her I hadn't even really summarized my own feelings about it. "I know she got hurt that night, and I feel really, really bad about it, but I got hurt too." Again memories from the night I was kidnapped broke through, and it took all the power I had to push them away.

"Kyla," Abby started unsurely, and I nodded, encouraging her on. "I know you told me you don't want to talk about that, but you really should talk about what he did to you, even if it's not to me, even if it's with Camille."

"I don't want Camille to ever know," I said, almost panicking, as if Abby would say something to her. "I just... don't." My voice trailed off as I fought to push away the thoughts that she'd brought back once more, and my breath caught in my throat. "I just can't think about it."

"Okay, I can let it go," she reassured me gently, and then trying to change the mood of our dinner she switched subjects. "There's a talent show in a couple weeks, at The Orchid."

"Oh yeah?" I let go of the memories and put on a smile, thinking I'd get to see a talent in Abby that I hadn't yet discovered. "Are you performing?"

"No," she said hesitantly, and then added quietly, "Don't kick my ass, but I signed you up."

"What?" I asked in shock, I couldn't have heard right. I'd never been in a talent show. I didn't even consider myself to have any talents. "To do what?"

"To sing and play guitar, of course," she told me, giggling to herself, probably at how wide my eyes had grown with surprise. "A good friend of mine said the show was desperate for more acts, so I told her I knew someone." I sighed, already nervous about having to perform in a talent show. "If you really don't want to do it I'll tell her you can't."

I sighed again, this time more exaggeratedly, but I smiled to let Abby know I wasn't really annoyed. "Fine, I'll do it, but you owe me big time!"

"Anything you want! You're the best." She grinned a happy, thankful smile, and then rubbed her hands together gleefully as the waitress brought out our food. "This looks so good."

My stomach growled in response as the scent of the meal reached my nose. "It smells good too." As the waitress left we both dug in, and with the first bite I found Abby had been right about it being delicious. "Wow, it's amazing." She smiled her thanks and continued to chew. "How'd you find this place?"

"I was feeling especially overwhelmed from everybody's thoughts one day at school. It was around finals last year so everyone was stressed out and putting me in a bad mood. I just started driving around the city for some time to myself, and I stumbled on this place," she told me with a grin. "I haven't been here in a while though."

I nodded and continued to eat as I thought about what else to talk about. Then, remembering that Abby was a senior, I wondered about her life after high school. "What about college? Are you starting to apply yet?" We talked for the rest of dinner about what little plans she had for the future and other random topics that came up.

As I slid into the passenger seat to start our way back to school, I groaned happily and patted my stomach. "I'm so full!" I looked over at Abby who, as she was putting on her seatbelt, nodded happily. "You didn't have to pay for me though." I wasn't just saying that because I didn't like people paying for me all the time. It was bad enough the Pack was covering my tuition. Since Abby had paid for dinner, it felt more like a date than we'd agreed on.

She must have heard my thoughts, because as she backed out of the parking spot and pulled onto the street, she glanced from the road to me. "Let me ask you something. If this *was* a date, which it wasn't, but if it was, would you still have wanted to pay for yourself?"

I raised an eyebrow at the girl next to me, wondering what she was trying to get at. "Probably, yeah."

"Okay then," she started thoughtfully, and then added with a teasing chuckle, "This was like a date, because I don't think anything would have been different. It played out exactly like a date would."

"Hey, that's not fair!" I exclaimed, and pushed her shoulder sportily. "You can't change the terms at the end of the date."

"So it was a date?" she asked, grinning as I threw up my hands in exasperation.

"No," I told her, still giggling. "That's not what we agreed on. It's only a date if both people are thinking it's a date during it."

She sat there silently, in deep thought for a few moments before she chuckled. "I'm pretty sure I heard you think about it."

"Liar!" I buried my face in my hands as I shook my head, keeping my laughter on the inside. "Anyway," I started, deliberately changing the subject. "Are you going to help run the talent show?"

"No," she said, flipping on the switch for her high-beam lights and turning on her windshield wipers as bright flurries of snow blurred the already dark highway. "I'm actually going to be pretty late to the show that night, if I make it at all. I'll try my best to get there in time for your performance."

My jaw dropped in disbelief that Abby had signed me up for an event that she might not even make it to herself. "Oh, you're in big trouble. If this was a date you so wouldn't be getting a second one," I teased, and crossed my arms over my chest defiantly when she made a pouting face at me.

She exaggerated her disappointment for a brief second before her mouth turned up in another grin. "Actually, I owe you big time. You have to let me buy you dinner again."

"You just don't give up do you?" I laughed, and the bright lights of the school caught my attention as it came into view through the snow.

"Not when I know what I want," she told me as she parked the car next to our dorm building and opened the door to get out.

Even if Abby was uncommonly persistent, it was flattering, and I couldn't say I particularly minded it. As I opened my own door to get out I saw Abby smirk, and knowing my thoughts had been heard I pointed an accusing finger at the girl. "Don't let that go to your head."

She shrugged apathetically as she led me into the warm air of the building. "It might."

By the time I'd gotten back to my room I was pleased with how much I learned about Abby that night. The girl was attractive, funny, smart, and I could talk to her easily enough. But there was still something missing. I certainly liked her on a physical level – the wolf constantly reminded me of that. It was the passionately emotional bond that was missing. Something like that blood deep connection I still felt with Camille, even though things were weird between us. I could try to feel that with Abby, but I didn't know if I could ever really feel it as deeply with anyone but Camille.

13

I sat at the bar in the kitchen of the Pack house staring at the refrigerator across from me. I'd been conscious for a couple hours now and my strength had almost fully returned, no doubt thanks to the massive meal David had prepared. Even though my strength had been restored I was still tired, and hadn't felt like moving when he and Lacey left the kitchen. Lacey mentioned wanting to talk to Eli about going to a bar in town that was apparently a common spot for vampires. While she'd gone to convince him I sat patiently at the island, ready to go if he'd decided for it.

After about fifteen more minutes of staring around blankly, Lacey finally came in and sat next to me. "How you feeling?"

"Anxious," I told her with a sigh. Why was it that the werewolves were always the ones getting kidnapped? "What did Eli say?"

"He okayed it," she said with a victorious but somewhat somber smile. "He's sending me with David and Wesley, and you if you're up for it."

I nodded and stood, unhurriedly, lest my legs give out beneath me. When I felt confident on my feet I straightened up and stretched. "I'm ready. Let's see what we can find out."

I followed Lacey out of the kitchen and into the grand entranceway, where we waited a minute for David and Wesley to meet us. We all went in the same car together – I assumed it was Wesley's since he was the one who drove, and I sat with Lacey in the back seat. As I sat there quietly I stared out the window, watching each of the snow-covered trees fly by. My strength had improved, but I couldn't say the same for my mood.

Eventually, through the near silence as Wes and David argued softly in the front seat about core exercises, Lacey elbowed me gently. "Hey."

It was a careful, questioning 'hey', as if she was trying to ask what I was thinking. Instead of answering, I just gave a small smile and turned back toward the window. But she knew me better than that. Though, I supposed anyone could've figured out what was on my mind.

"You know," she started, waiting until I turned to look at her again. "She didn't leave the library the whole time you were unconscious."

I took in a painful breath. It should have meant something that Kyla stayed by my side, but what was it supposed to mean? I was all Kyla had out here in Oregon. She had to act like she cared. I couldn't let myself get my hopes up too much, not if I wanted to keep my sanity. "Yeah, but she chose where she wanted to be tonight."

Lacey shrugged and turned to look out her own window. Before she did I caught a discontented frown on her face like she disagreed, but I must have been successful in giving off the vibe that I didn't want to talk about it. The rest of the car ride was noiseless until we reached town and got to a part where the city was a bit denser than the rest. The buildings were crowded close together on either side of the street, and many of them were worn down and dim. The street itself was dark, and the beams of the car seemed to be the only thing that cast any light. After a few blocks on the road Wes turned into a parking lot with a single streetlamp in the center of it. He parked closest to the light in the near empty lot and shut down the car, peering through the windshield at the gloomy building in front of us.

"This looks like it," he said, and after glancing around the outside of the vehicle to make sure our surroundings were safe he opened the door. As he did an immediate rush of stench filled the car. "This is definitely it."

I followed suit and opened my door with the rest of them. The stench was overwhelming. It was a mixture of different body odors and the heavy scent of decay and vanilla, an odd and disgusting combination. The scent was clearly coming from the brown brick building in front of us, and though the door to the inside was closed, it was still strong. The windows of the two-story bar were blacked out, and the only thing that lit them up was a neon beer sign hanging in one window on the far left side of the building.

After a moment of letting our noses adjust David led us forward toward the main entrance. As he pulled open the heavy wood door and we each stepped in, what little chatter there had been ceased. Every pair of dark eyes watched us carefully as we made our way to a small booth near the door. I slid in next to Lacey, nervously glancing around at the eyes still on us. It was too dark in the bar for me to tell for sure by looks who was a vampire and who wasn't, and the rancid smell was definitely too overwhelming to pinpoint anyone in particular. There was a group of two men and a woman sitting a couple booths away from us, a pair of guys were playing billiards at the other end of the bar, two girls and two guys sat in stools at the bar top nearest us, and a single man occupied a stool at the far corner of the counter.

It took a good minute after we sat down for the eyes to gradually move focus away from us, and when the watchful customers finally stopped staring and the chatter returned to normal the bartender cautiously made his way to the table. "Look guys, I don't want any trouble, okay? And if you're going to start some, then I want you to leave."

David shook his head, his voice soft and reassuring. "No trouble friend, you have my word."

By the way the horrid stench of vampire increased as the bartender stood at the table, I knew he was one, though he seemed to be attempting the utmost civility toward us. One thing I knew about vampires was that they never aged, once bitten they were frozen in time. Judging by the bartender's looks he was turned later in life, probably in his early fifties. His hair was white and thinning, and his dark blue eyes were cold and emotionless.

"Your kind don't just come to places like this for thrill," he pointed out accusingly, "But if I have your word. What can I do for you guys?"

"I'll start with a cola," David told him calmly, and then pointed to each of us so we could order. When we all shook our heads, he shrugged. "When you've got a moment, I'd appreciate a minute of your time."

With a nod the bartender returned to behind the bar counter and began to pour David's drink. Even though I knew we weren't here to start any fights, I couldn't help but be anxious. Since we'd entered the bar two of the customers, the ones playing billiards, had left, and while I couldn't be sure they'd left because of the arrival of werewolves, the tension from the rest of the patrons had increased. As I looked around at each of the remaining customers I realized the lone man at the far end of the bar was staring at me.

I met his gaze, but he didn't seem to mind having been caught, he just watched on with curious intensity. It was more than the typical lusty look I received from men who were checking me out – he was staring as if he knew me. His hair was a curly dark brown, falling just below his eye line, and though I couldn't see the exact color of his eyes from my distance, I could tell they were dark too. He was sitting, but he appeared to be slightly tall, just over six foot I assumed, and through his faded and worn dark-brown leather jacket I could tell that, even though he had a thin build, he was well muscled.

After studying him for a minute as he studied me right back, I turned my attention to the bartender, who'd just returned with David's drink and squatted down at the edge of our table to talk. "What can I help you with?"

David leaned closer to the man and, to keep their conversation private, whispered, "We just need a little information, and if you don't have it perhaps you could point us in the right direction. We've been having problems with some vampires."

Out of the corner of my eye as David explained our situation to the bartender, I saw the man at the other end of the counter get up, stroll across the venue, and pass us on his way out the door. While he did I knew he was watching me. I could feel his gaze on me the entire time, and for some reason it made me feel like I should follow. Abby had said we had a vampire ally. What if this guy was him? However, there were also an unknown number of vampires out there trying to catch us, and it could be a trap. I contemplated my course of action for another second before whispering to Lacey about needing air and getting up to walk out the front door.

The cold, outside air was definitely refreshing, even though it was still tainted with the smell of vampire. That smell made it difficult to track any kind of scent to the man who had now disappeared from sight. I strode to and glanced around the sides of the building, looking for him, but he hadn't made his way around any of the corners. Or, if he had, he'd left in quite a hurry. When I returned to the entrance to look around the parking lot one last time I caught sight of something by our car. It was him, crouched near Wesley's hatchback and peering through the driver's side window.

"Hey!" I called after him, starting toward the parking lot. At my shout he stood and took off in the opposite direction. "Hey, wait!"

I wanted to follow, but every ounce of common sense in my body screamed at me not to. This area was new to me, and there could be vampires lurking around every corner. I stopped before I got too far into the dark lot and retreated until my back was pressed against the door of the bar. It couldn't be denied as I watched him disappear into the night that I was frustrated at not having followed, but I'd done the right thing. At times like this our safety had to come first.

Opening the door back into the bar I sat down beside Lacey as David continued to speak with the bartender. "You haven't heard vampires talk about kidnapping Pack members?" The bartender shook his head. "But you have heard about the increased number of missing persons? Those are vampire attacks, am I mistaken?"

"That's right," the bartended nodded and threw the towel he'd been wringing in his hands over his shoulder. If I didn't know any better, I'd say he looked tense. "The missing persons are all over the newspaper lately, but I don't let those kinds of trouble-making vamps into my bar. Only peaceful kinds here."

David nodded thoughtfully as he considered what else to ask. It hadn't seemed like he'd gotten much information while I'd been outside. "Would you mind if I asked a few of your peaceful customers if they'd be interested in helping us out?"

The bartender sighed as he stood up, and he rested his palms on the surface of the table, bending over to lean toward us. "I'm sorry, wolf. I can't have you bugging my patrons. Now unless there's something else I can get for you folks, I've got some work to do."

"I appreciate your help," David answered politely as the bartender strolled back behind the counter. He pulled out his wallet and grabbed a five-dollar bill for his drink while he glanced around the bar. "Nobody here is going to help us, let's go."

He threw the bill down on the table and stood, leading the way to the door. Lacey waited until we were outside and at the car before asking, "You think the bartender was telling the truth that he didn't know anything?"

"I know for a fact he was lying." The disdainful tinge of David's voice made my jaw clench in mirrored scorn. "I recognized one of the vampires in there from our records. He's right hand man to a vamp named Benjamin, and if there's anyone the bartender wants to keep out to avoid trouble, it's them." As we all got into the car he slammed his door with a little more force than usual, sighing as he did so. "Benjamin is notorious for pulling shit like this, and no doubt anyone who associates with him is in on it. The only problem is the good guys can never find him."

Each of us fell silent. If none of the vampires were going to help us, we were at a dead end, another waiting game. "Did any of you see the guy who walked out after we went in, he was alone?" I asked from the back seat.

Lacey and David shook their heads, but Wes nodded. "Yeah, I saw him. I didn't recognize him though."

I shrugged. I'd never seen a real vampire before coming to Oregon. I didn't even know the Pack kept track of some of them. "When I came outside he was crouching by the car and looking through the windows."

"That's weird," David muttered quietly as he unconsciously ran his thumb down the scar on his jaw. "We'll have to keep an eye out for him. What did he look like?"

"Brown eyes, dark brown hair, curly, almost long enough to cover his eyes. About six foot, a little on the skinny side," Wesley said, and then glanced back at me. "That the guy, Camille?"

"That's him," I agreed.

Thinking quietly to ourselves, everyone was silent until we reached the dorms at the school. When I got out I expected Lacy to follow, but the young girl stayed in the car. "You're not coming?"

She shook her head and leaned further over the seat so she could see me better through the open door. "No, we're going for a run tonight. You can come if you want."

I seriously considered it for a moment before deciding that, even though my strength had fully returned, my body was in need of a poison-free rest. "It's okay, I'm kind of tired. I'll see you guys tomorrow."

After they all waved bye I stood there for another second before turning and starting for the dorm building. It was a short walk, only one building away from the main office where they'd dropped me off, but now that I'd been thinking of sleep my limbs almost instinctively began to feel exhausted. Continuing forward, I grinned as I saw little flurries of snow begin to fall around me. There being so few lights between the separate buildings, the only thing that illuminated the small flakes was the moonlight, and there was something magical about how softly the delicate powder fell over my head and shoulders and onto the ground. It covered everything in a fresh blanket of cleanliness. It was something I wished I could share the magic of with Kyla.

At the thought of Kyla I let out a soft growl. It was mostly at myself for not being able to go any substantial amount of time without thinking about her, and every time I did it only brought on a fresh spurt of pain. A pain that I'd hoped time would start to heal, but that hadn't yet started to show any sign of yielding. At least all this vampire business was giving me something of a distraction. I froze, and instantly regretted being grateful for that distraction. As if on cue the wind picked up and carried to me the scent of a vampire, causing the hair on my arms and neck to rise.

Stopping and taking a deep breath through my nose, I looked around. I recognized the underlying and faint scent of body odor mixed in with the overwhelming sweet and decay. It was the same vampire I'd followed out of the bar earlier. Had he tracked us all the way here? As I glanced around I couldn't catch a glimpse of him, or even anyone for that matter. The wind was coming from east, beyond the dorm building, which meant he was probably hiding somewhere behind it. Should I follow him again? What if this was a trap? From what I'd read or heard about vampires they were rarely completely illogical. I couldn't imagine he'd ignored the direction of the wind. Surely he must have known I'd catch his scent. Was he using it to call to me?

Taking another deep breath, this time to calm my nerves, I began forward for the side of the building. I was taking a huge risk, and if it was a mistake it could be fatal, but I had to figure out who this guy was. The last thing I could handle was waiting at a dead end for something to happen. That never ended well.

Every step I took was slow and cautious, and as I reached the corner of the building I peered around it suspiciously. As I looked around the corner not only did I find the area empty, but also the scent disappeared from the air, and the tension around me seemed to dissipate as swiftly as it had come. It didn't appear this guy wanted to be found. With a sigh I turned to walk back to the front of the building. Almost immediately after I did I felt a hand on my shoulder, and with the hand the scent returned.

The suddenness of it startled me, but I'd been trained my whole life to react to an attack, and I instantly grabbed the hand and ducked sideways, making a move to pull my attacker's arm behind him. Only, as I did the vampire wrenched his hand free of my grasp. He turned around to face me and brought his outside leg behind both of mine, kicking them out from under me and sending me straight on my ass. Before I could even react to having fallen he grabbed one of my shoulders and flipped me onto my stomach, and not a second later I felt a knee dig into my back, holding me in place on the ground.

I didn't know what to do. I was in perhaps the most compromising position of my life and a guy who was obviously well trained had put me there in less than a second. It was infuriating and terrifying, but there was nothing I could do about it. Squirming and wriggling under his knee, I tried to throw him off balance, tried to roll out from his lock. Every time I attempted to push myself off the ground with my hands, he pulled them out from under me. After a minute I eventually stopped struggling, wondering why he hadn't just knocked me out or killed me yet.

"I always knew werewolves were a little jumpy," the vampire chuckled, continuing to hold me down. "But you were on high alert."

"And the guy who's got me pinned is wondering why?" I asked bitterly, once again trying to push myself off the ground, only to be forced back down another time. As my frustration and more than a bit of fear began to rise again, I started to feel a tingling in my fingertips. "You better let me up, or you're going to be sitting on top of a pissed off wolf."

"You don't feel entirely threatened, or you would have already Phased," he said confidently, and I couldn't help but think that he was right. Instincts had ultimate control, and if I felt I was in more danger then I would have Changed without being able to stop myself. Only, the itching had just started. "If I let you up, will you promise not to attack me?" he asked, hesitantly beginning to shift his weight off of my back to let me know he was serious about letting me go.

While my first instinct was to use his shifting weight to my advantage to flip him off of me and get the upper hand, I refrained, and nodded with an aggravated sigh. "Fine."

He stood, and the second he did I scrambled up and away from him. When I got my footing at a comfortable six-foot distance I realized he was pulling his outstretched hand away from where I'd been situated on the ground. He'd been offering to help me up. I kept a keen eye on him as I twisted my body to work out the sore spot from his knee while he stood there, cautiously watching me back.

"What do I owe this pleasure?" I asked sarcastically as I rubbed out the last of the kink in my back with my hand.

"I'm here to help, but if you don't want it then my time could be applied somewhere else," he told me unconcernedly and turned to walk away.

"Help with what?" I asked hastily, before he could disappear around the corner.

Shoving his hands in his jacket pockets he turned to face me again, and leaned the side of his shoulder against the wall of the building. "The vampires that are trying to kidnap your kind," he told me seriously, a grave sense of importance lighting his dark eyes.

I nodded, urging him on. "Why are they doing it?"

He pulled his shoulder off the wall, causing me to tense as my body instinctively prepared for action. He could say he was here to help, but I still didn't know exactly what helping meant, and there was no way I could trust him just yet. "I have my theories, but I know the results will be catastrophic. Not just for the werewolves, for everyone."

"Well, what are your theories?" I asked, poorly hiding my curiosity.

"Some kind of summoning," he said with a shrug. "I know they're using sorcery, but I can't say until I know for sure. I just wanted you to know you had a friend among us."

"Who's behind it all?"

He ran a hand through his curly dark hair, brushing off the flakes of snow that had collected there. "A guy named Benjamin." I nodded knowingly, recalling the name David had mentioned earlier. "You've heard of him?" the vampire asked.

"Barely," I admitted, falling silent for a moment to study the man in front of me. Based on what I'd been taught, vampires weren't necessarily evil. They acted on single-minded self-interest, and often times it just happened to spell doom for anyone else – like the victims of their bloodthirst. So what was this guy's motive? "Why are you helping us?"

"Benjamin's ambitious, and ambition like he's got is dangerous." While he answered, I noticed his eyes darting every direction. It was the only betrayal to his composed exterior, and I wondered if him being here was risky. "It's pathetic, but I've grown attached to this world. I'm not about to let an overzealous asshole ruin it."

I looked him up and down. That was it? He liked the planet earth? It wasn't because Benjamin was villainous. It wasn't because he'd found it in the kindness of his heart to help us werewolves out. It *was* purely single-minded self-interest, but I'd take it. "Why'd you come to me? Why not just go to the Alpha?"

He chuckled, his first show of being completely at ease with my presence, and raised an eyebrow at me. "Seriously? Me, a vampire, just walk right up to the Pack's front door? I've been alive way too long to start making stupid mistakes like that." He stood there watching me, waiting for a response. He was right about it being stupid to try and talk to Eli, but I wasn't relaxed enough to start finding the humor in it. "I've got a good eye for character, I thought you'd be the easiest to approach. Though, you're a bit more stand-offish than I thought you'd be."

"I don't like surprises," I answered scathingly.

For some reason I was oddly irritated, maybe because of my injured pride at being so easily pinned by a vampire. Maybe because the once magical snow had started to collect around the collar of my jacket and harden, chilling my warm skin to the point I held back a shiver. More likely though it was the fact that he was acting selfishly. He didn't care about the werewolves, which meant at any time our 'ally' could turn on us. I couldn't yet find it in me to think there was something more benevolent driving him to our alliance. I didn't trust him.

"Fair enough," he said with a smirk as he stood there quietly, studying me with his careful brown eyes.

After a few moments it appeared he was waiting for me to ask any other questions, and when I didn't say anything he nodded and began to turn. I stopped him before he could walk away. "So um, when I tell the Pack about you, do I get a name to give them?"

"Rook," he responded, turning back around to face me with a small smile.

"Camille," I told him, and after a slight, considering pause I took a step forward and held out my hand.

Maybe I didn't trust him completely, but there was no reason to be hostile and drive him away. His smile grew a bit and gained a friendly glow as he took my hand in his. I really had to fight to hold back a shiver at the icy feel of it, out of a strange fear that it would be rude, but his skin was nearly the same temperature as the frozen air around us.

Dropping my hand he turned, and moments later disappeared around the side of the dorm building. I stood there for a few seconds before a snowflake landed on my nose and melted, tickling as it ran down to my lip and reminding me that the snow on my neck was starting to freeze. When I finally reached the warmth of my own room I sat down on my bed and stared at the opposite wall thoughtfully. All we really knew for sure was that the vampires wanted three werewolves and that, for now, Rook was probably the only one who would help us.

14

Rook's boots made the slightest prints in the fresh snow as he glided toward the warehouse a hundred yards ahead of him. He'd been spending a lot of his time around Benjamin's recruits, playing poker, starting and betting on fights with the others, trying to work his way into their trust. Working himself in had been easier than he thought. Most of the other vampires were young, and they admired the skill of his fists. He thought the way they conducted themselves was barbaric, and aside from gaining their trust the only other reason he engaged in fights was to judge their strength. That would be the most useful information to him when the time came to bring the werewolves into the picture.

The night before he'd been in a bar when the werewolves came in. Since Rook had decided to help them he'd been searching for the perfect moment to tell them of the danger they were in. Last night he left the bar and hid out until they left, and once they did he followed them all the way to the private high school just outside town. Aside from being quite jumpy, the blonde didn't seem all too surprised when he mentioned the vampires to her. Though she was curious of what information he had, it appeared as though she already knew what was going on. That thought was slightly comforting to him. It made him feel he wasn't as alone in this as he thought.

Rook strode past the two vampires at the warehouse's entrance with a nod, and pushed open the large metal door. Instinctively upon his entrance his eyes darted toward the manmade wall that blocked off the far corner of the warehouse. That was what he was here for, and he'd been spending every day in this godforsaken warehouse just to get a glimpse of what was inside. Every time he looked at the light that shined over the top of the wall it drained what little joy he had in a life he already considered pitiful. He couldn't imagine what effect it would have when he actually got to see what it was. Whatever it was, it could be viewed. He knew that for certain because Benjamin checked on it every single day and had a vampire guarding the door twenty four-seven, like he was worried it would escape.

"Rook!" One of the younger vampires that stayed at the warehouse stood from a poker game with a few others, and shouted when he saw Rook enter. He nodded toward the girl on his left, "Dominique doesn't think me and Kip could take you two on one. Care to wager?"

With an inward sigh, Rook glanced upwards toward Benjamin's overlooking office. It looked as though the leader already had a visitor, so he decided he could entertain the others for a few minutes. "Sure. What're the stakes?"

Once the other two vampires got up from the table they all strode toward an empty space between it and the entrance. Noticing there was about to be a fight, the others did the same, circling the area to spectate. Feeling in his pocket for what he'd come to deliver, Rook took the vile out and shrugged off his jacket.

He dropped his jacket to the floor near the edge of the circle and handed the full vile to the nearest vampire. "Hold that for me. It's for Benjamin, don't lose it." The man nodded and clenched the vile securely in his hand, and Rook turned to face Kip and Ronnie.

"We're feeling pretty hungry. If we win, you go and fetch us some dinner," Ronnie said simply, and then after a moment's thought added with a smile, "Fresh dinner."

Rook nodded, agreeing to the terms as he began to think of his demands. There was nothing he wanted from them. Money, human blood, and alcohol were the typical wagers, but all of it meant nothing to him. What could further his goal? He was so close to getting what he wanted. Benjamin trusted him, the others admired him, and soon he'd see what he and the werewolves were up against.

"Sundresses," he said, and both Kip and Ronnie furrowed their eyebrows in confusion. Rook nodded toward a female vampire in the circle around them. "I've seen Hailey wear sundresses before. You two put on some cute little dresses after the fight, go down to the liquor store, and come back with enough alcohol so everybody gets a drink." Rook couldn't help but smirk as he heard snickers from the other vampires around him.

"Hell no!" Kip hollered instantly, scoffing at how ridiculous it sounded. "I ain't putting on no pansy ass little sundress."

Rook shrugged. "I mean it's two on one, but if you guys don't think you can do it..."

Ronnie sighed 'deal' and received a glare from Kip, who looked like he knew they'd lose and be humiliated, but didn't want to back out. After another second Kip nodded in agreement, "Deal."

The excitement around them grew as the dozen vampires began to cheer and laugh. Rook stood there calmly as Kip put up his fists and began to rock on the balls of his feet, working his way to Rook's side. Ronnie also put up his clenched fists, but moved a little closer, directly in front of Rook. Rook's eyes darted skillfully between the two vampires as he watched them carefully. Kip was rocking with his right foot behind, so he'd no doubt throw a punch with his right hand. Though Ronnie was less obvious, his right shoulder was pulled slightly back, also ready to launch an attack with his right fist. *But who would throw the first punch?* Rook thought as he put up his own. Most likely it would be Ronnie. This would be easy, and Rook knew it, but not wanting to make it look that way he knew he'd have to take a couple hits.

With his hands up to his chest he watched closely, keeping his glances soft and looking for new movement. Then he saw Ronnie tense as the vampire's shoulder pulled further back, and barely a moment later the first fist came flying. It was more of a swing than a jab, and Rook easily ducked his head out of the way. As Ronnie's knuckles scraped by his face he saw Kip winding up for a throw. He waited for it, and when the hand came flying at him he dropped on one knee, the vampire's arm going right over his head.

Avoiding the hit he began to get back up, and leading with his fist he sent it right into Kip's exposed gut, hearing cheers of pleasure from the group around them. Kip bent over in pain, and Rook swung around behind him and shoved the vampire's back, sending him flying into Ronnie, who caught him with obvious annoyance. With that flare of annoyance Rook saw in Ronnie's eyes, he knew that soon his opponents would lose composure, and the fight would look more like a brawl. Especially since it was two on one.

Without warning Ronnie harnessed that aggravation and rushed in, leading with his shoulder. Rook braced himself, but let his feet rest lightly on the floor. He could take this hit, and he *would* to make the fight seem fairer, but if he resisted it then it would only hurt worse. Moments later Ronnie's shoulder met his chest, and they both went crashing to the floor. Ronnie had a slight edge by being on top. He sat over Rook's torso and locked his opponent's arms beneath him, bringing up and then down his first fist. Rook let those solid knuckles meet his face again a second time, and then a third. As the coppery taste of blood met his tongue with the fourth hit, he wrapped the hands of his locked-down arms around each of Ronnie's ankles, and with all the strength he could wrenched up, throwing Ronnie completely off him.

Ronnie landed on his back a few inches from the bottom of Rook's feet, and before he had a chance to scramble up Rook reversed their former positions, sitting on top of Ronnie's chest. He led first with his stronger left hand, then again with his right. He managed to get in three more hard punches before he felt Kip grab his shoulders and pull him with incredible force off of Ronnie. As Rook hit the ground on his back Kip's foot met his ribs. He let out a surprised wheeze as pain ripped through his side, and before Kip had the chance to kick him again he brought his arm down, meeting Kip's legs halfway and knocking the vampire face-first to the ground. Rolling over, he grabbed the back of Kip's head, slamming the vampire's face into the hard warehouse floor before darting up to meet a just-standing Ronnie.

While keeping Kip in his peripheral vision, Rook strode forward to meet Ronnie, who, without hesitation, threw a sloppy punch that just missed its target. Rook took advantage of the miss and made a jab that hit Ronnie square in the nose. A trickle of blood made its way down to his lip, but Rook knew he couldn't stop there. He jabbed again, and again, and when Ronnie's hands covered his face, he threw his fist into the vampire's stomach. He saw Kip rising from the ground behind him, and as the vampire rushed him he ducked out of the way, catching Kip's foot with his own and sending the vampire tumbling back to the floor. Rook let a slight wince crease his expression as Kip hit his already bloodied chin on the ground with such force his head ricocheted and smacked again. The vampire turned onto his back and covered his mouth with his hands, kicking his feet on the floor in pain.

Rook knew Ronnie wouldn't be finished, but he was caught off-guard when the man's arm wrapped around his neck, and less than a second later a fist caught him in the face. Ronnie held Rook in place while he brought his arm back, only to send it flying at him again. Rook raised his own arm, and with the extra force of his other hand aiding it he elbowed Ronnie in the groin. As the vampire released Rook and buckled over, Rook tensed his leg, about to bring his knee up to meet Ronnie's face. But in a show of impromptu mercy he kicked the vampire's legs out from under him.

With a smirk Rook caught the eye of one of the youngest vampires around the circle. "Hailey, how about them sundresses?"

As the other vampires burst into laughter, clapped, and patted him on the back, Rook glanced up toward Benjamin's office. Whatever visitor the leader had was just coming down the stairs, and Benjamin stood at the top. When he saw Rook looking up at him he waved his hand, motioning for Rook to meet him upstairs. Rook grabbed his jacket and the vial from the vampire he'd handed it to before the fight, and threw his jacket on as he made his way toward the stairs. When he reached the top he knocked on the door politely, and then turned the handle and made his way into the overseeing office.

"What was the bet this time?" Benjamin asked without looking up while Rook sat in the chair across the desk.

"They have to buy everyone a drink wearing dresses," he answered simply, spinning the vial in his hand.

The corner of Benjamin's mouth turned up in an amused smile. "Clever. Tell me, Rook, why do you engage them?" He handed Rook the handkerchief from his pocket, motioning for him to clean the blood off his face.

Wounds already having healed, Rook wiped roughly at his chin until the white cloth wasn't catching anymore red, and then used it to scrub off his knuckles. "I'm doing you a favor."

Benjamin raised an eyebrow curiously, and leaned forward with his elbows on the desk to rest his chin in his hands. "How's that?"

"They're like children," Rook told him, nodding his head out the window so Benjamin would know whom he meant. "If you don't keep them busy they'll start getting into trouble. From what I can tell, trouble is the last thing you need right now."

With a nod of understanding and approval, Benjamin leaned back again and outstretched an open hand. "Do you have it?"

Without delay Rook placed the fluid filled vial into the waiting hand. Benjamin studied it carefully, rocking the emerald liquid back and forth in front of his face. "Perfect," he said, and then placed it into his pocket. "I'll put it in better hands this time. The idiot who set up the traps on the werewolves' land used the whole vial for only three. I swear I could feed half those imbeciles to the wolves." Rook faked a laughing smile, but sat there silently and patiently. After a moment of waiting for him to leave, Benjamin tilted his head questioningly. "Was there something else?"

Rook took a moment to build his nerve. He knew the end was close, he could feel it. It was now or never. "I want to see it." Benjamin's eyes glistened with the slightest shock, but his face remained apathetic, and he stayed silent. "I've been getting you everything you need, quickly and easily. I've been keeping your pets out of trouble. I'm a thousand times more valuable to you than anyone down there." Rook pointed out the window. "And I'm sure every one of them knows what it is they're going to be killing for. I deserve the same."

Benjamin sat back and folded his arms behind his head. He studied Rook with an intense stare for a minute as he thought to himself. After another minute he grabbed the only book on his desk and turned it toward Rook. It was an old, thick book; the blank red cover was faded and dirty. When it rested on the desk in front of Rook, Benjamin flipped it open to a marked page near the end. There were no pictures, no break in the page. Just a single title and a solid block of text that looked like it continued onto the next few pages.

"When I first started this little mission four years ago," Benjamin began, and motioned to the solid text. "I wasn't quite sure what we were looking for. I much prefer picture books myself, but this opportunity seemed too good to turn down."

The title of the section read Phantoms of the Otherworld, and there were two things Rook didn't like about that title. The first was the word 'Phantoms,' and the second was that the word was plural. Underneath the section title was another label. "What's a Shadow Savage?"

"I'm sure you've heard of hell hounds." Benjamin stood and began pacing at the foot of his desk as he spoke. "According to this, the devil's got some other little play things. Apparently hell's got a population problem. The Shadow Savages live in another dimension, but every once in a while they get set loose on the Underworld. This is a good read," he said distractedly pointing to the book. "Anyway, these Phantoms have an insatiable appetite for souls, and so I started thinking, wouldn't it be easier to cross dimensions than to raise them from hell itself?" He stopped his pacing, turning to Rook with a grin. "Now maybe the quack who wrote this book was just some whack job warlock, but who cares where the Savages really come from? What matters is that there's truth in every story. So I started searching, and a year ago I finally found the means to summon them."

"Are you telling me that you have soul eating phantoms down there?" Rook asked, hardly able to hide the shock from his voice. Benjamin nodded vigorously. "Seems kind of dangerous."

"Why?" Benjamin asked fiercely, eyes gaining a deranged fire like Rook had offended him, and then he started chuckling. "We haven't got a soul." He motioned for Rook to follow him as he started toward the door and down the stairs. "Besides, they were meant for the spirit world, they can hardly exist here."

Rook glanced toward the manmade wall. Was he finally going to see it? Wait, what did Benjamin mean they could hardly exist here? "Is that why you need the werewolves?"

As they reached the bottom of the stairs Benjamin veered towards the sectioned off portion of the warehouse. "The man who was in my office during your fight is an incredible wizard. There's something about werewolves that he thinks will allow the Phantoms to survive in our world."

"How will it work?" As they reached the door of the manmade wall Rook clenched his jaw, suddenly nervous to see what was behind it.

"A bitten werewolf was born human, so their souls are human, but born werewolves, like most in the American Pack," Benjamin grabbed a key out of his pants pocket and stuck it into the door, "They're animals, and they've got such strong supernatural ties. He thinks the Phantoms could survive in their bodies, like a possession." Benjamin put the key back into his pocket and pushed open the door, motioning for Rook to lead the way in.

It didn't take any effort for him to make that first step. He felt as if he were being sucked in by the all-encompassing darkness. As he entered the room he expected to see loose Phantoms, floating around like apparitional ghosts. Instead there was a tall podium in the center of the room, and the incredible blackness emanated from the single orb on top of it. This orb was the sole source of the unique light. Like a black hole it devoured everything around it. Light, color, heat, even emotion were lost in it until he was left in the cold dark of the manmade room with an alarming feeling of solitude.

"It's beautiful isn't it?" Benjamin asked, and strode forward until he was close enough to the orb to bend over and bring his face within inches of it.

Rook watched him nervously, fearing that at any second a Phantom would reach out and drag Benjamin into that frightening abyss. "What are they supposed to do for us? For the vampires?"

Benjamin straightened quickly, an angry and annoyed crease forming across his eyebrows. "Do you know what happens to humans when they lose their soul?" He waited for Rook to shake his head. "Nothing! They become nothing. Blank, emotionless, thoughtless. Like pathetic zombies."

"Living blood banks," Rook said softly, urgent fear growing in his gut.

"Can you imagine? A world full of humans just walking around, keeping our blood fresh until we're hungry and then giving of it freely, without putting up a fight or screaming for help." Benjamin paused and smiled evilly, reaching toward the orb but not daring to put his hand on it. "Then, when every vampire in the world knows I did this, knows I brought them paradise, they will worship me."

Rook struggled for composure, and forced a grin to match Benjamin's. "You'll be a god in their eyes." He turned as Benjamin walked past him and to the door, pushing it open with imperative deliberation, like if they were there any longer it would spoil the orb. "Do the others know?"

Benjamin shook his head. "They know there's to be a feast, but they're too stupid to know the means. I'm too close for one of them to fuck it up."

As they exited the room and Benjamin turned to lock it, Rook saw Ronnie and Kip returning with a bag full of vodka bottles. When they noticed him they both scowled, but waved him over. Seeing that the others wanted Rook, Benjamin clapped him on the back. "Go claim your reward. I'll call on you should I need anything."

Rook nodded gratefully and hustled over to the table where the vampires were gathering. Had he not been so worried about the coming doom he would have chuckled at the sight of Ronnie and Kip in the dresses. But he couldn't laugh, couldn't smile. Benjamin might think the Phantoms would create a feast, and maybe they would, but if there was one thing Rook had learned from his years in the supernatural world, it was that things like this never went according to plan. Maybe the Phantoms would turn humans into soulless zombies. Maybe it would turn them into lifeless corpses that would rot before a single vampire knew where to find them. The one thing Rook would stake his life on was that those Phantoms wouldn't stop until there wasn't a single soul left on the planet to devour.

When Ronnie and Kip finished pouring enough shots for all the vampires there, Rook grabbed his and raised it high enough for every-one to see, and waited until all eyes were on him. He could even feel Benjamin observing him from the overseeing office. Each vampire watched as they raised their own glasses, waiting for Rook to toast. He sighed inwardly, already trying to plan how he could stop this. He just hoped he'd figured it out before it was too late. "To the feast!"

"The feast!"

15

"Hey, Camille!" Lacey waved when I looked back at her, and picked up a light jog to catch up. "Are you and Kyla going home to train today?"

Once she reached me I shoved my hands into the pockets of my jacket and continued walking through the snowy courtyard of the school. "Yeah, I'm about to meet her in the parking lot. You want to come?"

She nodded and shifted the backpack on her shoulders. "I was thinking about it, I don't have much else to do."

"Okay," I answered, and then paused thoughtfully. I hadn't told anyone yet about Rook, and I figured Lacey would want to know as soon as possible. "You know how the Council said we have a vampire on our side?" I asked, to which she nodded knowingly. "I met him last night."

"What!" she shouted, the shock clear on her face. "When? Where? Were you alone? You could have been killed!"

I chuckled at her neuroticism. Of course I really could have been killed if Rook hadn't been a friend, but everything had turned out okay. "Last night, right after you guys dropped me off. It was the guy from the bar, I think he followed us all the way back here."

Lacey raised her hands and shook them expectantly. "And? What did he say?"

We turned the corner of the building that sat adjacent to the parking lot as I was about to answer, but I stopped short before I could tell the curious brunette. Kyla was waiting by the jeep for me to arrive, which wasn't at all surprising since her class was closer, except for the fact that Abby was waiting with her. Just seeing the girl standing there with Kyla filled me with seething jealousy, and the pain of it made me look away as we continued to get closer.

"I'll tell you later," was all I managed to mumble through the mixture of fury and agony.

I heard Lacey sigh, and was pretty sure she added an eye roll, but I was too focused on the pair near the jeep to make a comment. Abby must have heard my thoughts screaming at her, because she looked up, and at seeing Lacey and I coming quickly said bye to Kyla and walked away.

"Hey guys," Kyla greeted us as we neared the car. She watched me cautiously when we reached her, as if she could either sense the discontent or see it on my face.

I gave a brusque nod of recognition and slid into the front seat without saying anything. When Lacey got into the passenger side she turned around to look at Kyla in the back. "Camille met our vampire." At that I shot her a callous look that clearly said I wasn't in the mood to talk, but she stared back defiantly. "Well, I want to know what he said."

"Our vampire?" Kyla asked in shock. "The one the Council said would help us out?"

Reluctantly, I nodded. "He didn't say much, he was mostly there just so we'd know who he is. Said his name is Rook." I paused thoughtfully, trying to think of what else to say. Then, with a shrug of finality, added, "And he's still trying to figure out what exactly the vampires are trying to do."

"That's it?" Kyla asked, sounding mildly disappointed. "He couldn't give you any information? Like how many vampires there are, or where they're camped out."

I hadn't really thought to ask any of those things, but then again, it hadn't seemed like Rook had been interested in giving too much away. "Like I said, he didn't say much." That sentence came out with more bite than I'd meant it too, and in the rearview mirror I saw Kyla's eyebrows crumple in frustration. But what could I say? Sorry I'm on edge, it just pisses me off that you've met someone else?

"Do you want me to tell my dad when we get back?" Lacey asked in a tentative attempt to cut the tension.

I just nodded and fell silent for the rest of the drive back to the house. When we got there we found Wes in the library, surrounded by the supernatural books they hadn't bothered to clean up after I was poisoned. He glanced up when we entered, and put the book he was holding in his lap back onto the pile on the table.

With his usual charming smile he stood to greet us, getting right to business as usual. "To the glass room?"

Each of us turned on our heels back toward the door, and as we left the library Lacey headed in the opposite direction. "I'm going to go talk to my dad," she called over her shoulder. "I'll be out there in a bit."

I nodded and gave a wave goodbye as I continued to follow Wes and Kyla to the back of the house. I was shocked at how the fresh snow and bright sun made the glass room glow more than usual. The trackless powder that covered the ground and even piled up against the side of the house had the same enticing effect on me it always did, and I resisted the urge to suggest a run instead of whatever Wes had planned.

"We doing more yoga today or what?" Kyla asked as Wes turned to face us, clearly already bored at just the thought.

"Not quite," he said, and sat down on the marble floor with his knees pulled up to his chest. He waited for Kyla and I to sit too before he continued. "If you guys are up for it, I want to nurture this whole blood connection thing."

I felt Kyla look at me curiously, but I refused to meet her glance. Nurturing the connection would mean being close to her. Could I handle it? Instead of answering I just sat there, staring back at Wes and hoping he would change his mind. Only, he didn't change his mind, and after a few seconds of neither Kyla nor I offering an answer, he tried to explain.

"There's nothing written about the kinds of things you could do with a connection like yours," he said to both of us. "It's always been little more than a myth, but maybe we can see how much truth there is in it." Then he added with an excited wink, "Maybe we'll discover something groundbreaking."

It took about half a minute after Wes stopped for Kyla to speak up with a shrug. "Okay, what do we do?"

He mirrored the motion, and added a sigh as though he were hoping we'd be more excited about it. "I don't really know. There isn't exactly a guide book, so we're going to have to experiment." He paused thoughtfully. "Can you guys sense each other right now? Can you feel anything different?"

I lied and shook my head, and out of the corner of my eye I saw Kyla hesitantly do the same. Not too long ago I could sense her emotions. Like back in California, before she almost bit Jeremy I could feel her stress as if it was my own. But the connection only reminded me of what I'd lost. I didn't want to do this. Ever since we'd been spending more time apart, and Kyla had met Abby, I'd been trying to tune it out. I was sure she could feel it too, but I couldn't be sure whether she was lying or whether she simply wasn't aware of it.

Tapping his chin thoughtfully, Wes studied us for a minute, and I had to wonder what he was thinking. My relationship with Kyla wasn't something anyone really talked about in the house, but he had to know about it. Was he thinking of a noninvasive way to go about it? No matter what he decided, none of it would be noninvasive. I could hardly hide the fact that I felt tormented every time I was around Kyla, how could I cope if she could actually feel it. There would be no hiding it then.

"Okay, turn and face each other," Wes instructed, finally deciding on his approach. Each sitting cross-legged, we turned toward each other, getting so close our knees were practically touching. "Camille, hold out your hands." I reluctantly held out my hands palm up, and rested the backs of them on top of my knees. "Kyla." Wes nodded toward my hands, and when Kyla held her own hands up he gently turned them over and placed them on top of mine so that our palms were touching.

Even though I knew it was coming, I still had to hold back a flinch at the pain the touch put in my stomach. *God, get a grip, Camille,* I told myself, and then took in a deep breath. Sure, Kyla broke my heart, but Wes was right, maybe we could discover something groundbreaking. Maybe there was enormous potential in the blood connection. I could already feel it in the warmth of Kyla's hands.

"Can you feel anything now?" Wes asked, leaning forward curiously.

"I don't know," Kyla said uncertainly, looking at me to see my response.

I nodded to affirm that I could feel it, and then glanced at Wes for guidance. "Maybe if she focused more?" Maybe Kyla didn't want to do this either. Maybe she'd been tuning it out more than I was. Or she just couldn't feel it because she didn't have feelings for me anymore.

Wes lowered his legs from his chest and crossed them in front of him. "Okay, both of you close your eyes. Try to relax and breathe deep, just like when we're working on body control."

I waited for Kyla to close her eyes and then did the same. As we began to focus, and Wes stayed quiet, the world around us seemed to grow calmer. Our breathing, the beating of our hearts, the bass from a muffled radio inside the house, everything was rhythmic and slow. The heat from Kyla's hands streamed freely into mine, and were it not for that energetic flow I was sure I wouldn't be able to feel her hands at all. If not for that flow, I wouldn't have been able to make a distinction between where my hands ended and where Kyla's began.

"I think I can feel it," Kyla said softly, and as if on cue the energy intensified, like it moved more rapidly between us. "It's electric."

Wes shifted, and even though my eyes were closed I could tell it was a shift of excitement. Despite his new enthusiasm he remained quiet, not ready for the first test run to be over. Even though the rest of me was relaxed, my hands were stiff with tension, and soon an ache started in the stiff muscle on the side of my left hand. With the start of the spasm I felt Kyla's thumb slide down to rest right on it, and a moment later the brunette's finger began to sporadically apply pressure in a massaging motion.

I opened my eyes in shock. It was too much of a coincidence for her not to know. "Could you feel that?"

She gradually opened her eyes as if it took her a few moments to realize I was talking to her, and then glanced from me to Wes in confusion. "Feel what?"

"My hand was cramping up and you started massaging it." I glanced down at my hand, Kyla's finger still in place.

"I must have been zoning out, I didn't even realize I was doing it," she said, and moved her thumb back to its original place on the top of my hand.

"You couldn't feel Camille's cramp at all?" Wes asked her, to which she shook her head. "Okay, close your eyes again and try to focus really hard."

We both closed our eyes. It had always been easy for me to feel the connection, but I tried harder to focus, more interested now in what the potential of this really was. About thirty seconds after we closed our eyes I felt a sharp pain sting my arm. Wes flicked me, hard. "Hey, what the?"

He smirked and insincerely mouthed sorry. "Kyla, did you feel that?"

She shook her head, and then rotated her shoulders like this kind of work was exerting. "No, I couldn't feel anything."

"Damn." A disappointed frown creased Wes's brow, and his shoulders slumped unhappily. "Maybe we could just try to get your hands farther and farther away and see if you can still feel something."

That's what we did for the next forty-five minutes until both Kyla and I were too mentally exhausted to keep trying. We figured out that if we really concentrated we could barely sense each other from a few feet away, which was remarkable according to Wes. Lacey had come in about halfway through to watch, and she thought it was as fascinating as Wes did. After that we decided to go on a run, much to my pleasure. The fresh snow had been calling to me all day, and now that dusk had set in the cold air of the gray world outside was crisp and inviting. I was the first to Phase when we left the glass room, and I dropped to my side in the icy powder while I waited for the others to finish.

Lacey Phased next. Her copper fur stood out against the snow, and that combined with her smaller size made her look more foxlike than wolfish. Before I had time to stand she pounced on me, playfully nipping at my neck and face. I squirmed underneath the small wolf, kicking my feet in the air but not trying too hard to get up. Seconds later Kyla joined in, trying to catch my wiggling paws in her mouth. Outnumbered, now I sincerely tried to get up. I rolled over, snatching Lacey between my front limbs and pinning the young wolf beneath me before turning and jumping playfully on Kyla. The honey colored canine and I went rolling through the snow until a long, deep howl cut through the air.

We both stopped short and looked to the grayish wolf standing between the trees, watching us carefully and body tensed to run. Kyla and I gradually stood, preparing ourselves to make chase, but as Lacey tore past us the waiting wolf turned and fled. I took off after my receding companions, hearing the crunch of snow under Kyla's paws close behind me. The gold wolf caught up, and when I gave a playful nudge with my shoulder she nudged me right back. In wolf form I always felt better about where I was with Kyla. It was like we were two different people who existed in a separate world where we could be happy together. I was free of the stress and heartache because all that mattered was the run and the clean forest air, which chilled my lungs and made me feel more and more alive with every breath.

Sprinting as fast as we could between thick trees it took about twenty minutes to reach the lake that stood half frozen in the middle of the forest. When we reached it I strode to the edge and brought my front paws down hard on the two-inch thick layer of ice that kept the cold water from my tongue. Once I started lapping it was hard for me to stop, not because I was that thirsty, but the water was so cold and fresh it sent a delightful shiver straight to my core. A whole minute went by as I drank up the refreshing liquid before something distracted me. It was a faint and familiar scent, though slightly different from the ones I'd smelled before, and it made the fur on the back of my neck rise.

Vampire. This close to Pack territory was no accident, and if he hadn't attacked it was because he was outnumbered. If he was outnumbered and didn't run, then it's because he was watching us. I repressed my instinctive reaction to turn and look for the source of the smell, and instead thought more carefully about it. The others hadn't seemed to notice it yet, which meant it must be coming from further down the edge of the lake, and since I was at the end of the line my body had to be blocking it from reaching them with their noses still in the water.

I huffed to get their attention and stuck my face into the air, instructing them to sniff. Each of them did, and when Kyla let out a quiet growl I nudged her to shut up. I then looked to Wes, and nodded in the direction behind me that I thought our onlooker was hiding. His gray eyes slowly scanned the dark area, shifting back and forth a couple times before he nodded. The scent was faint, but it was still there, meaning the vampire hadn't realized yet that we were aware of his presence. Kyla growled again, impatient that we weren't taking action, but Wes simply shook his head. Instead, he nudged Lacey and Kyla and nodded them back toward the house. Kyla looked somewhat confused, but followed along when Lacey turned and began heading back the way we'd come.

Why was he sending them back? I cocked my head at him, wondering if Lacey knew what to do because there was some sort of protocol for this. It was one thing that Wes had sent two of our numbers away, another that I didn't even know where the vampire was hiding. Not being able to stand blind for another second I followed Wes' eye line to a high up spot in a specific cluster of trees. Sure enough there was a male vampire perched on a thin branch about fifty feet up. I'd been hoping that when I turned the vampire would be Rook, waiting for a good time to deliver some good news, but I didn't recognize this one.

Whatever this vampire's name was, he sure recognized when he was being stared at. Noticing that both wolves were now watching him he didn't waste time in jumping down and taking off in the opposite direction. He was only halfway to the ground before Wes and I's paws were tearing through the snow after him. Wes' longer limbs carried him farther than me with every stride, but the vampire already had a head start. The trees were thick and occasionally he disappeared behind one. Luckily for Wes and I the partially frozen lake blocked off a big route of the vampire's escape.

Or at least that's what I'd thought, until he veered right to head directly for the pond. When he reached the edge he didn't stop, though he slowed considerably as he tread carefully on the delicate surface. Wes stopped at the border, not daring to follow out onto the thin ice, and desperately looked down the lake. It was about another half a mile before the lake rounded out and looped back to the other side, so he picked up sprinting to try and cut the vampire off.

When I reached the lake I didn't stop, but slowed and carefully eased my way onto the surface. I was smaller than Wes, so I had a better chance of not falling through than he did, but I was still larger and heavier than the vampire. At least with four feet instead of two my weight was spread out evenly enough to keep me from breaking the frozen glaze. The vampire looked back, and at seeing I was following picked up his pace. I don't know why I'd followed him, my size put me at a tremendous disadvantage should I catch him and we both fall through, but when he picked up his pace so did I.

As he neared the center of the lake he stopped, and as I drew closer and closer I realized why. The ice had been thinning considerably while we got nearer the middle. If the center of the lake was frozen at all, there would only be a small layer too thin to hold either of us. I was progressively getting closer, nearing thirty yards, and the vampire looked around frantically, knowing I was catching up. In a desperate attempt at escape he backed up a few feet, sprinted, and made a daring jump for the other side. His first foot came down on the other side and went crashing through the thin ice, and before the rest of his body land- ed he spread out flat, coming down onto his stomach with an audible thud.

Even though he barely made it, landing on his stomach saved him from falling through, and as pulled his leg out of the water and contin- ued on I decided I had to try the same thing. Only about ten yards from the center now, I picked up my pace to a run. The closer I got to it the more only my momentum was keeping me above the ice. About two feet from the not at all frozen middle I couldn't wait any longer, and I threw myself into the air. A few seconds later I came crashing down, landing a little further than the vampire had. Still, it wasn't thick enough for my body weight, and it shattered beneath me.

The second I hit the freezing water I drew in a painful breath. It was so much colder than I'd imagined. I saw the vampire look back at me for just a second before he continued running. Luckily for me, his inter- est in surviving was much greater than his interest in making sure I didn't, but I couldn't let him get away. I brought my front paws up onto the unbroken ice only to have it break away once I put any weight on it. It happened twice more before I started to panic. I'd been too preoccu- pied with the chase to think about what I'd do if I fell through, and now I realized I didn't have a plan. I'd seen enough television shows about animals falling through a frozen body of water to know I needed help getting out. I scanned the edge of the lake to look for Wes, but neither he nor the vampire could be seen.

As the panic rose I frantically clawed at the edge of the glassy surface, each time causing it to shatter beneath me. *Stop!* I told myself, and took in another painful breath. I didn't have time for panicking. Each time I grappled at the edge of the ice it got thicker and harder to break. All I had to do was get to a spot sturdy enough that I could pull myself out. Keeping that in mind I again put my paws on the ice, applied weight, and fell through. Again and again and again I did the same, and the fifth time I let out a frustrated snarl. *Don't give up.* I had to do it twice more before I hit a spot that could hold my weight if I was gentle enough. I eased my paws as far back as I could reach on the surface, and digging my claws in I began to lift myself out.

It held until I got my shoulders level with it, and then broke again. When I fell back into the water I began to notice the shivering. How long had I been trying to get out of the water? I didn't know much of anything about hypothermia, but if I was shivering I imagined I should get out as quick as possible. I put my shaky paws up onto the ice again and began lifting myself out. This time I got just past my shoulders before it broke.

Okay, different approach. I turned to my side and laid my head on the ice. Using every muscle I could I slowly wiggled my shoulder up, and then lay still to make sure it wasn't going to break. I inched up until the top third of my body was steady on cold glass, but I could feel myself slipping, so I had to hurry. One. Two. On three, I threw myself off the ice in a single flop-like motion like a fish out of water, and managed to somersault my entire body onto the solid surface.

Finally out of the pond, I paused for a split second to make sure the ice would hold before I took off toward the end. I didn't care if the ground broke away after every strike of my paws, I didn't have to time spare. There wasn't even enough time to shake the water out of my fur. If Wes hadn't tried to help me it was because he was chasing the vampire, and if he'd already caught up he could need my help. Reaching the end of the lake I had no trouble finding where the vampire's footprints picked back up in the snow, but I didn't need the footprints to follow the faint sound of a snarling scuffle.

The trees were thinner in this part of the forest and so the snow was deeper, and before I knew it the powder reached my stomach. Any other time I would've been able to plow through it easy enough, but almost instantly it froze in clumps to my wet fur, blanketing my lower body in a sheet of ice. Every muscle had to work overtime through the cold and weight of the water and ice, and it was even worse my body was expending precious energy on the ceaseless shivering. Maybe I shouldn't have gone out onto the lake.

Before I could reach Wes the snarling stopped, and the forest grew eerily quiet. Ignoring the pain in my frozen paws I sped up, following the white tracks and hoping the silence didn't mean Wes had lost the fight. Two minutes after struggling through the deep, half-frozen powder I finally came upon Wes, who was standing still, long teeth bared at the deep snow below him. He was so frozen I wondered if he was hurt, but when he barely turned his head to look at me, I realized what he was doing. Just as he turned a pale fist hit him hard enough in the head to send him flying sideways with a loud yelp.

The way the vampire took off unnaturally fast through the deep snow made it clear he was running for his life. But I didn't waste a second in chasing after him, nor did Wes waste a second in recovering from the blow. The vampire took off east through the trees. As we chased, I began to notice the snow was slowly getting shallower, and the trees around us denser. I let on a wolfish smirk. The vampire had gotten lucky with the lake early on in the chase, but he didn't belong in the woods. Wes and I had more practice maneuvering through trees and keeping our footing on the uneven ground, and I was sure that as soon as the snow allowed us to run full speed we'd catch him easily.

Sure enough, just a couple minutes later the powder got shallow enough for us to pick up speed. The target was barely twenty feet ahead of us, and losing ground rapidly. Fifteen. God was his stench unbearable. Ten. Wes was right by my side. I pushed my legs faster than they wanted to go, and the burst of speed put me ahead of Wes. Five. I tensed for a spring, but just as I was about to push off the ground my legs gave way beneath me. Wes was just able to dodge me as I went tumbling through the snow. *What the hell was that?* I growled at myself angrily. I never fell like that, but usually I could feel my legs. As hastily as I could, which to my distress was dangerously slowly, I pushed myself up and off the ground.

I got up just in time to see Wes leaping for the vampire, and as he hit its back it ducked, and Wes went rolling over him onto the ground. The vampire turned on his heels, now running back toward me, but before he reached me he jumped for a tree. He began to shinny up it as I picked up a run as fast as I could manage. When I got close to the base of the tree the vampire was climbing I threw myself into the air, catching his ankle just before he got out of reach and dragging him back to the ground.

I landed awkwardly on my numb legs and went stumbling backward, still holding the vampire between my teeth. When my back finally hit the ground the force caused my jaws to open, releasing my hold. Right after being let go the vampire scrambled up, and was instantly knocked back down by Wes, who then began to bite at every inch of flesh he could find. With vast difficulty I got back up to join in the fight, and rushed in, dodging flying vampire fists. Wes was too busy avoiding the vampire's assaults on his head to pin him down, so I rushed in again from the side and clamped my teeth down on the vampire's exposed throat.

Before I could tear through the unguarded flesh a panicked bark escaped Wes. Keeping my teeth in place I shifted my eyes just enough to see him shaking his head at me. He wanted the vampire alive? I was fine with that, but I wasn't letting go of his neck until Wes figured out a way to get him back to the house. I laid my body down on the ground beside the pinned vampire, keeping my teeth against his jugular with enough pressure that he wouldn't forget I was there. As I lay, Wes let out a long, ringing howl, and the sound of a motor not too far in the distance answered back.

Lacey and Kyla had gone back to get a truck? I didn't think they'd be able to make it through the trees in a vehicle, but I was too tired to think much about it. In fact, I was too tired to think much about anything. The only thing I could focus on was my accelerated, shallow breath, coming out in clouds of white smoke around the vampire's neck. And it wasn't just my legs anymore that felt weak.

Now that the adrenaline was wearing off I could feel that not only was I tired, but it also hurt to move. I could barely even keep my teeth against the vampire's skin because it was taking too much energy, but I couldn't let the vampire know that. If he knew it then he would try to escape, and I knew I couldn't hold him if he tried. The only thing that was keeping him in place now was his fear that I wouldn't hesitate to rip into him.

I hoped Lacey and Kyla would be getting here soon, but from the sounds of it they were still ten minutes away, and that's if they could even get through the trees. I shifted my eyes again to look for Wes, who I found lying in the snow at the vampire's feet, watching our captive carefully. My attention turned back to my breathing. How long had I been in the lake? Five, maybe ten minutes. What about since then? Another ten. Then at least ten until Lacey and Kyla would get here. How long did people usually last when they were freezing to death? Hell if I knew.

Feeling like I was losing grip on the vampire's neck, I instinctively clamped down. "What the fuck!" he yelled, more out of shocked pain than anger, but that was all he said before he remembered that we could kill him any second, and he resumed his defeated silence.

Startled, I released my grip a little bit, but I had already drawn blood, and I resisted the urge to completely let him go so I could spit it out. The usual metallic bite of the fluid had turned to a painful bitterness, and the otherwise neutral taste had become sickeningly putrid. Was this the source of that horrible decaying smell the vampires always had? I was starting to lose track of time. That's why I'd bitten him. Time was slipping away and it already felt like five minutes had passed since I'd done it. No, five minutes ago I was pulling him out of the tree.

Instead of a truck, two large ATVs came through the woods and stopped next to Wes and I. Lacey jumped off her motorcycle first and grabbed two, half-inch thick steel wires that were hanging off the back of it. With wires in hand she put the vampire's feet together and began wrapping the first one securely around his ankles. To remind the vampire again that I was there and not to try anything, I tightened my grip on his neck. Or at least I thought I did, but he didn't seem to flinch or even notice. Worried now that I'd lost all strength, I tightened my grip even more. Still nothing. I gripped his neck tighter and tighter, now trying to break skin again, or at least make him cringe.

"Camille," Lacey's voice picked up impatiently, as if she'd been trying to get my attention for who knows how long. "Camille, you can let go now."

With more difficultly than I'd ever experienced in my life I released my hold on the vampire's neck and stood. Every muscle in my body hurt, and I was so stiff I could barely move. As if drunk, I staggered to where Kyla was now leaning against a motorcycle and dropped to the snow. I watched Lacey turn the vampire over and pull his arms behind his back so she could tie up his hands with the other wire.

"You roll around in the snow or something?" Kyla asked playfully, but her voice sounded so quiet, like a whisper. "You have ice balls all over you."

It hurt too much to move, so all I managed was a side-glance up at her to let her know she was heard. The side-glance allowed me to see her reach down to me, and I could only imagine the girl's hand struggled through the top layer of ice that crusted my fur to get to the wet and frigid layer underneath.

"Wes," Kyla called, her voice carrying the faint but recognizable tone of worry. "Why is Camille all wet?"

The gray wolf came over to examine me. He nudged me with his nose and then ran his face along my frozen fur. Lacey dragged the tied up vampire through the snow over to the other motorcycle and, though she was small, lifted him with ease onto the back of it. He was in a terribly awkward position as his legs dangled off the side, but she didn't seem to care, and she strapped him on with bungee cords to hold him in place.

The whole time Lacey had been putting the vampire on the ATV he'd been watching me, and now he scoffed sarcastically. "I knew she was just bluffing on my neck." He shook his head disappointedly and mumbled, "Probably could have got away too." Wes bared his teeth and growled, putting the fear back into the vampire's eyes.

Lacey glared at him and pointed at me. "Why's she all wet?"

He turned his head to look at me again, and then compliantly answered, "She fell through the ice on the lake."

"Shit." Lacey pulled out her cellphone and glanced at the time. "We got to get her back. Kyla, help me lift her onto your ATV."

Though I couldn't feel it, I watched myself get hoisted off the ground and onto the back of the motorcycle, just like the vampire. When Kyla got on, instead of letting my limbs hang over the side, she pulled them forward so that my stomach was at her back. "She's already freezing me through my jacket," Kyla said, glancing back at me worriedly, and then to Lacey, "Werewolves can get hypothermia?"

Lacey jumped back onto her own vehicle. "If she wasn't a werewolf she'd probably already be dead."

I could hear the engines fire up, and the next thing I knew the wind was flying through my already frozen fur. As if I thought I couldn't get any colder. What seemed like forever later, we reached the lake I'd fallen through, and I was fighting the urge to fall asleep. Wes must have noticed because he ran alongside the motorcycle, nipping at my paws and face. I couldn't really feel it, but just the thought of him being relentless was aggravating. The last thing I could remember I was trying to let out an annoyed growl, and then, darkness.

16

I laid the blanket I was holding over the unconscious blonde in front of the fire. We'd gotten back to the house as quick as we could, but Camille had already passed out by that time. The most we could do now was wait for her to warm up. Lacey assured me that because of our fast healing it wouldn't take long for Camille to recover. In fact, I could already see some improvement from the rosy color of the ice burn all over her body to her normal, fleshy tan.

After placing the blanket over her, I weighed my options. I could either try to find the others and see if they'd started questioning the vampire yet, or I could wait for Camille to wake up. Even though she already looked a thousand times better, and I wasn't as worried as I'd been when she was poisoned, I looked over the bookshelves for something to read while I waited. *Dracula* caught my eye as I wondered if he was anything like the vampires we were up against, so I pulled it off the shelf and took it to a chair in the middle of the library.

After only reading for about fifteen minutes Camille shifted, and after a second of looking around confusedly, she groaned. "I got to stop waking up naked."

I laughed as I closed the book and set it on the table. "No, you got to stop falling into things."

"Oh yeah, that too," she agreed sarcastically as she sat up and pulled the blanket tight around her. She sat sideways to me and scooted closer to the fire so that half her body could soak up more warmth from it.

I shook my head and chuckled, glad she felt well enough to be making jokes. "How are you?"

"I can feel my toes again." She smiled and gave her toes a wiggle. "What's happening with the vampire?"

"I don't know," I shrugged. "I was waiting for you to wake up."

She nodded as she looked around, and jumped up when she saw the pile of her clothes that I'd laid next to the fire to get warm. "As curious as I am about how that's going, I think I'm going to stay here by the fire for a little longer."

When she grabbed her jeans she pressed them against her face, grinning at the heat, and then dropped the blanket so that she could get dressed. My eyes darted around awkwardly. Her bare body didn't bother me when she was unconscious, but when the girl was awake I felt like I should look anywhere but at her. It wasn't necessarily that I minded. Even with the way things had been between us lately I was still undeniably attracted to her, but anytime I got close the blonde grew uncomfortable. I could only imagine how she'd feel if she caught me staring.

As Camille slipped her jeans over her feet, I stood. "I'm going to go check it out." Some of it was curiosity. Most of it was my needing a distraction.

Without giving her time to say anything I walked out to search for everyone. When we'd arrived with the vampire Wes got help from David and William in securing him in the glass room. As I reached the back of the house I cracked the door and peeked into the glass room to find that, though the vampire was chained to a chair, he was alone. Before he knew I was there, I swiftly turned around and headed back for the entranceway. As I reached it Wes and William were coming down the stairs.

"How's Camille?" Wes asked when he reached the bottom.

"She's awake. Warming up by the fire." Instead of stopping there he veered toward the back of the house. Will was following close behind, and when I started to follow them too I eyed the two-foot weapon in his hand. I couldn't be sure whether to call it a sword or a knife, but I was sure the thin edge could cut through almost anything. "You guys didn't talk to him yet?"

"Eli wanted us to leave him alone for a little while," Wes said, heading though the wide hall with his hands in his pockets. "It's a scare tactic, makes us seem more unpredictable."

I nodded understandingly as we rounded the corner to the back of the house. "Are you going to kill him?"

Both Wes and William looked at me and, without answering, pushed open the door to the glass room. The vampire's head twisted to look at us as we entered, and while Wes moved around to his front, William and I stayed behind him. Wes pulled a lighter out of his pocket and while he stood there, staring the vampire down, he distractedly flicked it on and off.

"Here's the thing, man," he started after a minute and put the lighter back in his pocket. "I'm really not in the mood to torture you. Can we do this the easy way?" I saw the back of the vampire's head go up and down in an eager nod. "You want to tell me what you were doing in our forest?"

"He told me to watch you guys." The vampire's voice was soft and shaky, undoubtedly strained by fear, and I was glad his fear was making him cooperative. "I was supposed to learn your habits, maybe some weaknesses, so it would be easier to…" His voice trailed off, but he didn't have to finish for us to know was he was going to say. So it would be easier to kidnap us.

Wes 'mhm-ed,' and leaned his back against the glass wall behind him. "Who's 'he'?"

"A vampire, the one who owns the bar in the city," the vampire told him.

"And who's he working for?" Wes asked.

The vampire shrugged. "I don't know for sure, but we all hear talk. I heard Benjamin's the one who's running the whole thing."

"Do you know where he's operating out of?" Wes asked, and when the vampire shook his head, he growled, "Don't lie to me."

"I'm not," the vampire said desperately. "I've never even met him. I was just having a drink in the bar and the owner offered me this job."

So the vampires really weren't stupid. They were doing a good job of hiding and they weren't going to risk sacrificing anybody who knew their whereabouts. They'd even enticed a nobody to do their dirty work. I almost felt bad for the guy.

Wes shook his head in disbelief. "What in the hell could convince you to pull a job on Pack territory?"

"Free drinks," the vampire chuckled nervously. "And he said if I found out anything that could help, then every vampire would benefit." Wes remained quiet as he watched the vampire, waiting for him to continue. "He said there would be an endless supply of food, a feast. We'd all be set for life. That's all I know, I swear."

Wes watched him carefully for another ten seconds, judging if the vampire was telling the truth or not, and then looked at William. When William lifted the sword with two hands I made for the door. I ducked out just in time to miss him finish the swing he was taking at the vampire's neck.

I smiled bye to Camille as she got off on her dorm floor, and then hit the button to close the elevator doors. It was Saturday afternoon and we'd just finished training, so now I was looking forward to getting a nap. Wes had us working on the blood connection every training session, and it was more exhausting than running all day. The elevator doors opened up at the end of the hall, and I got off of it right as Abby was coming out of her dorm room.

The girl grinned when she saw me, and began to follow me down the hall. "You just get back from training?"

I nodded, chuckling when as I opened the door to my room Abby walked right in to sit on my bed. "Make yourself at home," I told her with teasing sarcasm.

"Don't mind if I do," she smirked as I took off my jacket and draped it over the chair at my desk. "What are your plans for the rest of the day?"

With a shrug I dropped into the chair. "I don't know. Eat, sleep, homework."

Abby pointed her finger down her throat and made a gagging sound. "Boring."

"Oh yeah?" I laughed and playfully kicked her foot. "What are you doing?"

"I was actually going to run an errand for the Council. They've been having me check up on certain supernaturals to see what they know about this whole vampire thing." Abby paused thoughtfully for a second before her eyes lit up with excitement. "You want to come with me?"

I couldn't hide that I was slightly shocked at the invitation. Abby's father wasn't shy about not being fond of werewolves, and no doubt he'd be mad if he found out I went along on an errand. "Is that allowed?"

She shrugged apathetically. "I always go by myself. Who's going to know the difference?"

"Uh huh," I mumbled thoughtfully, and then gave a coy smile. "What's in it for me?"

Abby laughed, watching me with a sporty glow in her eye. "Besides getting to hang out with me?" I nodded. "What if," she started, pausing to study me thoughtfully, "I buy you some fast food?"

"Alright deal," I said instantly, and got up to tug my jacket back on.

Abby got off the bed with an unsure giggle. "That was easy."

I pretended to swoon, and said in a teasing but romantic voice, "You had me at fast food."

"Yeah, yeah, let's go," she snorted with laughter and pushed me out the door.

After I closed it behind us I followed her out of the room and back down the hall toward the elevator. "I finally get to see what you do for the Council, huh?" Abby nodded like it was no big deal. "Do you ever get in fights? Or have to chase them down?"

The elevator whooshed as it began to take us down, and Abby characteristically leaned against the wall with a chuckle. "Not usually. They have more powerful supernaturals for the more dangerous jobs." I was about to ask what kind of more powerful supernaturals, but Abby must have heard because she answered before I could ask. "Like shape shifters, telekinetics, telepaths who aren't the director's daughter."

"Are you saying you want the more dangerous jobs?" I asked as we got off the elevator and I followed her out to her car, not in the least bit surprised given Abby's headstrong personality.

"It's not that I *want* them," she started thoughtfully, pulling open the driver's door and getting in. "All the jobs are important. But if I was anyone else who's been doing this for as long as I have, then I'd be getting the more dangerous jobs and I'd do them well. My dad's just hoping I'll get bored with fieldwork because he wants me on the board."

"I see." I pulled on my seatbelt and then turned to face Abby, who was looking over her shoulder to pull out of the parking spot. "You don't want to be on the board?"

"No, absolutely not." She put the car into drive and started for the main street as she vigorously shook her head. "I don't agree with any of the decisions my dad makes, and he doesn't like being told otherwise."

"Don't you think you'd have more influence if you *were* on the council?" I asked as I watched the road. I'd been expecting us to head into the city, but Abby turned onto a back road heading east.

"Not really. My dad's been the director for a long time, so most of the members respect him too much to cross him. All the ones who don't respect him as much fear him even more. I wouldn't be able to sway a single thing my way. The way I see it, I have more influence in our relations department." At 'relations department' Abby gave a wink.

"Yeah, I guess that makes sense," I agreed, and then looked around curiously. "Where are we going anyway?"

"We're going to see the owner of an occult shop in the woods backed up to the mountain. He's the most legitimate dealer around here, so we want to see if he knows anything," Abby told me and turned onto a smaller unpaved road.

"And by legitimate you mean?" I asked curiously.

"Not touristy," she said with a shrug. "Doesn't make his biggest sales off of crystal balls and love potions." A minute later she made another turn onto a narrow dirt trail. Whoever this guy was, he lived in the middle of nowhere. "And there're a couple things you should know before we go in. He's old and senile, so he's kind of unpredictable. Sometimes he couldn't be happier to help, and others he's really unpleasant." She pulled in front of a small house and put the car in park. "Also, he's a *terrible* psychic, but he thinks he's incredible. If we want him to talk at all you got to let him think he's incredible, or else he'll get really grumpy. So, no matter what he says, just agree with him. Okay?"

I laughed at the absurdity of the request, but nodded anyway. "Okay."

"Also," she added as she opened the door to get out, "Don't drink anything he offers you. You'll be higher than cloud nine before you could even say cloud nine."

I followed Abby's lead and got out of the car. "You learn that the hard way?" I asked with a chuckle, catching the bit of recollection in Abby's warning.

"That's a story for… never," she said with a scowl, and the glare I got made me laugh.

We both walked up the four steps to the front door on the porch, and Abby held it open as I walked through. The counter was on the right side as we walked in, and shelves with various bottles, herbs and ingredients covered the rest of the store.

When the old man behind it saw Abby he suspiciously shoved a book he was reading under the counter. With a glower he pointed a withered and bent finger at her, "Hey, I ay bin makin' no o' that mergic munshin, you hear?"

"Of course you haven't, Harold. The Council asked you not to," Abby said with a smile on her face, then turned her head so only I could see and rolled her eyes.

Harold scanned me, and then looked back at Abby. "Who friend der? She shunatral too?" His voice was deep and shaky, and his speech was hindered not only by the fact that he had no teeth, but also because he was slurring so bad I could barely understand a word he said. I would have thought he was drunk, especially after the mention of what I thought sounded like 'magic moonshine,' but his stance was steady and his eyes were almost too alert.

"That's right," Abby answered, calmly passing me a look that reminded me to agree with whatever he said.

To my confusion, in the blink of an eye Harold's slur disappeared. As whatever was causing him to slur wore off his eyes gained a wild, confused look. It took him a second to catch up, but when he glanced from Abby to me, as if for the first time, he seemed to recall that we were having a conversation. "Yeah, I know a succubus when I see one," he said, laying both his long, thin arms on the countertop and directing his attention to me.

I grinned excitedly and nodded, even though I could vaguely even recall what a succubus was. "How'd you know?"

Harold's scowl disappeared behind a successful grin. "I can practically feel you draining my energy from there. You keep that mojo off me. Come in back, I need a drink."

As he turned to go through the door next to the counter Abby let out a snort of laughter just loud enough for me to hear. She even took it so far as to hold her stomach and point at me in a giggling fit before following Harold into the back. Why was she laughing at me? I thought Harold's odd behavior was funnier than whatever she could be laughing at.

When we walked through the door Harold was pouring a hot, clear liquid into small teacups on a table near his couch. We both walked over to the couch and sat down, but as Abby had warned, neither of us touched the drink. I tried to get a whiff of whatever was in the cup, but instead of smelling like alcohol or any other kind of substance, it just smelled citrusy and sweet.

Harold pushed over a small wooden chair and sat across from us. "What you here for, Joann?"

I glanced over at Abby curiously, wondering if Joann was a name she'd made up as a cover, but now wasn't the time to ask. "You've got

214

quite the customer base. I was just wondering if lately that might include vampires?"

Harold's eyes were the only things that betrayed his surprise while the rest of his exterior remained unmoved. He picked up a teacup and took a couple sips before answering. "They count on me."

"I know," Abby said reassuringly, though I wasn't sure whom he was talking about. "But you see, this is really important. I need to know if you sold anything to a vampire recently that might be dangerous."

"Abby," Harold started, and I was surprised to hear him use Abby's real name. Before continuing Harold looked to his right, pointed a finger and glared as if scolding something invisible, and then turned back to us. He paused after he took in a breath, like he forgot what they were talking about, and then said, "Everything."

Abby sighed softly, but she wasn't ready to give up completely. "Harold, the Council is pretty sure that there're some vampires trying to do something really bad, and if they do then we think a lot of humans could get hurt. I just don't want anybody to get hurt, you know?"

Harold nodded, picked up one of the other cups he'd poured and sipped on it slowly. Even though he nodded his understanding, he sat there quietly, still refusing to tell us anything useful, and I was pretty sure we were already losing him to the drink.

"Could you at least tell me if you've had any vampire customers lately?" Abby asked.

Again Harold looked to the side, to whatever he thought he was seeing. "'Gonna tell her." Then his eyes met Abby's. "One." A small smile spread across his lips before he started counting in a whisper, "Two, three, four bottles." Like he'd said something he shouldn't have, he shushed his invisible companion and clasped his hands over his mouth. "One," he said again.

I wasn't sure how Abby had the patience for all this nonsense, but it made me glad that she was the one asking the questions. Knowing she wasn't going to get anything else from him, she stood, with me quickly doing the same. "And you aren't still accepting ingredients for magic moonshine as payment, right Harold?" she added, almost jokingly as the old man followed us back to the front of the store.

"No," he told her matter-of-factly and resumed his place behind the counter. He reached into his pocket and held out his clasped hand, as if he was handing her something.

She reached out for it, and when Harold put whatever he was holding into it, she opened it to examine the item. I couldn't say I was surprised that her hand was empty, but the girl thanked him anyway. "Thanks Harold." She pulled the door open for me and waved to the old man. "We'll be seeing you. Thanks for the drink."

He nodded courteously and waved. "Bye-bye, Joann."

Abby let the door close behind us and got into the car with me. "Joann is my mom's name, I know you were wondering." I made an 'oh' face and nodded understanding. "She used to be the one who dealt with Harold all the time. He always liked her better than most the others the Council would send."

"And because he's senile he calls you that sometimes?" I asked, to which Abby nodded. "What's with the magic moonshine?"

"It's this concoction he makes. Sort of like absinthe, but stronger, and it's got a magic quality that makes you hallucinate things from the future. That's why he thinks he's psychic. Naturally that kind of stuff started causing problems for the Council, so they asked him to stop making it," she told me.

"But he still makes it?" I asked, remembering his oddly suspicious and nutcase behavior.

Abby began to laugh as she nodded her head. "Poor bastard's so out of his mind that he puts it in everything. That's why I told you not to drink anything he gives you. Truth is, he probably doesn't even know if any of his customers are vampires or not."

"Couldn't you read his mind to know for sure?" I asked.

"He's so senile I can hardly catch a coherent thought. Believe it or not, this was one of his lucid periods, and it's even worse when he's on the moonshine, which is almost always." As Abby had been explaining we'd been driving down the path toward the unpaved road, but now she pulled over and into the trees.

"What are we doing?" I asked, looking around at where we'd parked. We weren't within sights of the shop, but we hadn't gone too far either.

She opened the door and started to get out of the car, leaving me no choice but to do the same. "Harold's pretty old school, he keeps written receipts upstairs in a business ledger. I want to check it out."

"So why are we going–" As Abby began to circle back to Harold's through the trees behind his house, I stopped. "Are we sneaking in?" I asked in a whisper as if Harold could hear us. "Abby wait, what if he catches us?"

With a tickled smile Abby turned and strode back to where I'd froze. "You got to live a little," she teased. I just crossed my arms over my chest. Harold seemed out of his mind, and I didn't feel like getting on his bad side. "Harold's harmless," she assured me. "Besides, he's probably so drunk off moonshine right now there's no way he'll notice." I was sure she was right, but just the thought of sneaking into someone's house made me so nervous I could barely move. After a moment of waiting, Abby grabbed my hand and began to pull me toward the house. "Come on, I promise it will be fine."

Seeing as she was practically dragging me, I followed her toward the house without another protest. I expected that once I began to follow her compliantly the girl would let go of my hand, but she was still holding on to it. A few moments later, when I realized that she had successfully made a move to hold my hand, my heart skipped nervously. I knew she liked me, but I hadn't expected her to be so fearless in her attempts, especially since we hadn't even been on a real date yet. Though, now that I thought about it, I shouldn't have been surprised at all – she was always straightforward.

"Do you break and enter a lot?" I asked so that she wouldn't just have to hear my thoughtful monologue about handholding. Though I didn't want to dwell on it, I wasn't going to pull my hand away. I was comfortable with her, and even this small amount of physical contact felt nice.

Now that she was sure I wouldn't resist her attempts, she adjusted her own hand so that our fingers were intertwined. It was cold compared to mine, and I could already feel the heat of my skin filling it with warmth. Still, to warm it faster and to show her more completely how okay with it I was, I wrapped my other hand around it too. "I wouldn't say a lot, but I have to every once in a while," she told me, glancing down at our hands and then giving me an almost timid smile.

"As long as you aren't going to get me attacked by a senile psychic." I made quotation marks with my hand when I said 'psychic,' and Abby laughed. The back of Harold's place came into view through the trees as we neared the hundred-foot mark, and I began to seriously hope he wouldn't catch us.

"You're a werewolf," she said with a playful smirk. "You're not seriously afraid of an eighty year-old man, are you?" When we reached the house we stuck close to the wall, and Abby peeked into a window to make sure Harold wasn't around. "I don't see him in the back room, he's probably at the front desk."

We both had our backs against the house, so I leaned over her to take a peek through the window. The 'back room' was actually on the side of the building, but the stairs to the upper floor were set against the true back wall of house, on the far side of the room we'd sat on the couch in. We inched past the window to a second one nearer the stairs. With a final peek in, Abby dropped my hand and used both arms to carefully push up the glass.

The bottom of the window started at her waist, and once it was open she quietly slid through headfirst. When she finally got her feet through she crouched and waited for me to come in. I'd gotten a lot of practice climbing through windows a lot higher than this when I was first Changed and had to sneak out to run. With familiar ease I turned my back to the opening and hopped up so that I was sitting on the windowsill. When I was sure I wasn't going to slip off I threw one leg after the other over and into the house and hopped down, all without making a sound.

"Are you sure you haven't done this before?" Abby whispered, gawking at me with her jaw hanging open.

"It's in my blood," I whispered back with a proud grin. "Why? Jealous?"

Before she turned to head toward the stairs her lips curled into a flirtatiously mischievous smile. "Bite me."

I held back amused laughter as we continued forward silently and worked our way up the stairs. Before we reached the top Abby looked around the open doors to make sure she couldn't see Harold, and then led me into the first of the three rooms upstairs. It appeared to be a small office, all it had was one desk littered with papers and another with a single, very thick binder in the middle.

Abby made her way to the binder while she motioned for me to stay by the door. "You got the ears, let me know if you hear him coming."

I nodded, and posted myself at the entrance with my head hanging slightly out so I was in the best position to hear. Every once in a while I'd catch a noise from downstairs. The turning of a page, slurping as Harold drank from his little teacup, slurred mumbling at his invisible companion. What couldn't have been more than a minute later Abby stood at my side, shoving a couple receipts into her jacket pocket and ready to go. I followed closely behind as she made her way back down the stairs and to the window.

"Dun do 'at!" Harold slurred loudly from the counter, successfully making my heart jump out of my chest. I looked at Abby, who was sighing with relief that he was talking to himself and not us. "Mergic munshin," he started in a singing voice. "Bitter's nothin', mergic munshin."

Abby slid out the window with me close behind her, and we were both hardly able to contain our hysterical amusement until after we closed the window. As we strode back toward the car Abby finally let it out, and hung off of my shoulder to prop herself up as she laughed.

"He sure likes his magic moonshine," I giggled.

"Better's nothing," she agreed, composing herself with deep breaths. "That wasn't so bad was it?"

I shook my head reassuringly. "Not too bad."

As she walked close beside me our shoulders bumped with every step, and my mind returned to when we'd been holding hands. Though I'd always loved all kinds of affection, I'd never been quick to initiate it like that, especially when boundaries were as unclear as they were now. Even though Camille and I had *kind of* sorted things out only recently, I hadn't felt like I'd been in a relationship for months, and I couldn't keep holding out when I couldn't even be sure what I was holding out for, when Camille told me she'd probably never get over it. I was about to grab Abby's hand when I hesitated. But what if I wasn't ready to put myself out there? I could accept it when she made the move, but could I do it myself? Or what if she'd changed her mind?

"When I make up my mind, I make up my mind," Abby said with a smile in response to my thoughts. "And you can reach for my hand any time, because the suspense is killing me."

"Sorry," I chuckled apologetically, and without any more indecision I rested my hand in hers.

"Don't be," she shrugged comfortingly. "Anticipation is half the fun." When we reached the car about two minutes later we got in and she started up the engine. "I owe you fast food. You want to drive through and we can eat at my room?"

"Yeah, sure," I agreed as I pulled on my seatbelt, then I caught the quiet sound of a song on the radio and turned it up, grinning excitedly. "I love this song!"

Abby smiled and nodded her agreement. "Speaking of songs, have you been practicing for the talent show next weekend?" At the reminder my eyes widened, and she looked at me in shock. "You haven't even picked a song yet?"

"Is that bad?" I asked, to which she nodded vigorously. "I know! I've just been so busy with training and homework. I don't even know what kind of song to do."

She nodded in understanding and 'hm-ed' thoughtfully. "From the ones I've been to the last few years, it's always ballads that people like best."

"A ballad, huh?" I said, mostly to myself as I tried to recall some of my favorite ones. "I think I can do that."

We got to the main road a few minutes later, and drove through a fast food place before making our way back to the school. I'd never been on the inside of Abby's dorm room before. It was a little bigger than my own in order to accommodate the extra bed, desk, and dresser for her roommate. When we got there we both sat on her bed, leaning our backs against the wall with our food in our laps.

"I didn't realize how hungry I was!" I exclaimed as I demolished my first of two burgers. "You sure know how to treat a girl right."

Abby chuckled and shrugged nonchalantly as she swallowed her own bite of food. "You know, I still owe you that second dinner, and you got to let me take you on a real date this time."

"Okay," I said with a smile as I took a first bite of my second burger.

"Really?" she asked, the shock clear and exaggerated in her voice. "You're not going to put up a fight or tell me it can't be a date?"

I shook my head, laughing at how genuinely surprised she was. "No, I'll let you take me on a date. Besides, you've been trying so hard. You're kind of desperate, really," I teased, receiving a playful bump from Abby's elbow.

"Well," she said seriously, but her lips curled into a smile, "If desperate gets me a date, I can live with that. How about the night after the talent show? We'll celebrate you winning first place."

"First place?" I asked with a disbelieving chuckle. "You've got high hopes." Abby nodded knowingly, and then after a thoughtful pause started to laugh to herself. "What's so funny?"

"I was just thinking about when Harold called you a succubus," she told me, giggling louder now.

"Why's that so funny?" I sternly crossed my arms over my chest, raising my eyebrows expectantly.

She stopped snickering to look at me seriously for a moment. "You do know what a succubus is right?"

"They drain people's energy?" I guessed unsurely.

She nodded, clearly holding back more laughter. "Typically male energy." She couldn't hold it back now, and started chortling again. "Through sex."

My jaw dropped, appalled at the accusation. "That old perv!" Abby was leaned over, holding her stomach because she was so entertained, which made me chuckle a little bit. "It's not funny." I shoved her playfully, trying to get her to stop giggling.

"It is kind of funny," she told me. She paused from her laughter, thought of something, and then started up again. "And you were so excited about it too!"

"That's what you told me to do!" I threw up my hands in exasperation. "You better watch yourself before I drain all your energy!"

Abby stopped giggling and raised her eyebrows at me, squinting one eye frivolously. "I mean, if that's what you want to do."

I gave a mock scowl. "You know what, I take it back, Harold's not the perv. You are." Abby shrugged, not even trying to defend herself from my accusation, so I just rolled my eyes and changed the subject. "Anyway, what receipts did you get from his place?"

"Oh," she said in remembrance as she hopped off the bed to grab the receipts out of her jacket. Having grabbed them she sat back down next to me. "There were a lot of repeat names, but only one started popping up around the same time as all this vampire activity. I don't know what any of this stuff is on here though. Except for these two things." Abby pointed to one of the receipts. "Hemlock, obviously a poisonous plant, and valerian root, which I'm pretty sure is also some kind of poisonous plant."

I reread the words carefully, thinking of what they could have been used for. "You think that's what they poisoned Camille with?"

"Probably, along with other things," she told me with a nod. "I'm sure the effects aren't as deadly on you guys as they would be on a human."

"Who bought all this stuff?" I asked, and followed Abby's finger as she pointed to the name on the receipts. Rook. "Hey, that's the vampire that's on our side. Remember, the psychic told you about him."

"I remember, but if he's on our side why is he buying stuff to poison you guys?" Abby asked, mostly to herself, and then looked up at me. "How do you know what his name is?"

"Camille met him the other day. He wanted us to know who he is," I told her, instantly feeling like I should have mentioned it sooner, or at least even thought about it.

"Why didn't you tell me?" The disappointment was clear on her face. Or was it hurt at being left out?

"I'm sorry." I smiled as apologetically as I could, and then offered innocently, "I just got so excited about the fast food?"

She studied me for a moment before a small smirk turned up a corner of her lips. "How could I get upset when you're making that face at me?"

As I gave a pleased shrug, Abby's hazel eyes locked onto my own for a split second before she looked away shyly. It made me stare back curiously, since I couldn't remember her ever being shy. A moment later they met my own once more, and then wandered along the curves of my face, down to my mouth, and back up again. It wasn't until now, in the silence between us, that I realized how close we were sitting. Our shoulders overlapped, and Abby's face was no more than six inches away from mine.

She gave a tentative smile, and when she bit her lip it drew my attention to her mouth. The pink flesh was full and smooth, and the indent left by her teeth as she quit biting her bottom lip gave me the urge to test the feeling myself, to make my own indent in that delicate skin. The urge was instantly replaced by a startled shock as the sound of keys scraping their way into the door handle scared me out of my trance.

A second later a dark skinned girl of average height and with curly brown hair walked in, and she dropped her backpack on the floor by her own desk before she even realized I was there. "Oh, hi." She smiled, the surprise on her face apparent. "I'm Grace." She stuck out her hand for me to shake, took off her jacket, and then looked at both Abby and I curiously as we remained suspiciously silent. "Am I interrupting something?"

Now, for some reason feeling rather uncomfortable, I jumped off the bed and grabbed my jacket, which had been lying next to me. "No, I should actually go anyway."

"Oh, wait, before I forget." Abby stood and pulled open one of the drawers on her desk, materializing two notecard shaped pieces of paper. "Your tickets for the talent show. They always sell out, so everyone who's performing gets two to give to whoever they want." I took the tickets Abby was handing to me, and after a moment of consideration held one out for her to take. "I don't need one," she told me with a grateful smile. "I already have mine."

"Okay, thanks." I put the tickets into my jacket pocket and turned to open the door. As I stood in the hall Abby lingered in the doorway, waiting for me to speak first. "I'll see you later, I guess."

She gave a small smile in response, but it was clear by the expression on her face that she was disappointed. "Bye."

Not knowing what else to say I turned and headed for my room, hearing Abby's door close behind me. Only now did my heart start pounding from what had almost happened. Or what I thought had almost happened. Was Abby going to kiss me? Was I really about to do the same? The idea of it scared the shit out of me. I remembered the first time Camille and I ever kissed. She'd almost lost control and Changed, and that was after years of control practice. Would I lose it if Abby kissed me? Though I was getting better, I still didn't have the kind of control I'd like. And Abby was only human, what if I hurt her?

I closed my door behind me as I entered my room, pushing away the thoughts. It didn't happen, but now that I knew where I was going with her, I could prepare myself for it. That way if she ever did kiss me, I was ready. And what about Rook? He was apparently the one getting the vampires their supplies. Abby had a point, could we really trust him if he was the one who'd been setting up the traps on Pack territory? What if, whenever the vampires chose to finally make a solid move, we'd staked all our hope on an ally that never existed?

Abby pushed open the door to the Council office and smiled at her mom, who was sitting at the front desk. Lumbering over to the coat rack she took off her jacket and hung it up, then made her way to sit on the edge of her mother's desk.

"You seem like you're in a good mood," her mom said sarcastically at the forlorn expression on Abby's face, and she finished typing an email before looking up permanently.

"I'm just exhausted. Midterms are coming up soon, and you know how it gets up here," Abby told her with a sigh as she pointed to her head. "I have some stuff for Dad to look at, is he here?"

Her mother nodded and cast a weary glance back toward her dad's closed office door. "Maybe you should let me give it to him though. Neither of you are in the best of moods."

Abby knew her mom was offering so there wouldn't be a fight between her and her dad, which was highly likely on a day they were both irritable, but she shook her head anyway. "No, it's okay, I want to hear what he thinks."

"That's a first," her mom said with a teasing smirk as Abby stood to make her way to the closed door.

Reaching her father's office, Abby knocked and waited until she heard 'come in' to enter. He motioned for her to sit down in the chair across the desk from his own and, though he was on the phone, smiled hello as she took a seat. A second later he rolled his eyes, and without saying a word put the phone back down on the receiver.

"You didn't have to hang up," she told him.

He shook his head like it was no big deal. "I was on hold. What do you got?"

She pulled the receipts and an extra piece of paper out of her pocket. "Two things. I went to see Harold and I got a hold of some of the receipts from sales he made to a vampire." Her father held out his hand, and when she gave him the receipts he put them next to him without even looking at them. "And second," she began to unfold the piece of paper on which she'd drawn a picture. "He's pretty out of his mind, and he tried to hand me something that he didn't really have, but when he did his mind flashed an image of this."

With the brief flash she'd gotten out of Harold's muddled mind and her terrible art skills, Abby had drawn the best picture she could. It was a half-inch thick silver bar, only about three inches long and two inches wide with rounded off corners. Inlayed at the center of one side of the bar was a colorful mixture of rock, like multiple stones had been heated so hot they melted and swirled together. Around the edges of the stone and engraved into the metal were symbols Abby didn't recognize as any modern language.

She could hear her father's thoughts racing at the sight of the picture, and from them she already knew what it was, but at her mother's warning that he wasn't in the best mood she let him speak, since he hated her reading his mind.

"This is exactly what he gave you?" her father asked, resting his chin in his hand thoughtfully. "Same colors and everything?"

"Yeah," Abby nodded. "What is it? Is it rare?"

"Not entirely rare," he answered. "I've seen them a few times before."

Abby was waiting for him to answer the other part of her question, but either he didn't care to explain or he knew she'd already heard and he wasn't in a talkative mood. The elements of the bar had grounding properties for things like astral projection or dimensional travel. Whenever someone took part in spiritual wandering they kept the bar near their physical body. It was supposed to make it easier to find your way back. But why did Harold show her this?

"What do you think it means?" she asked impatiently, tired of watching him stare at the piece of paper.

He shrugged, looking at the picture for another minute before setting it aside. "Vampires don't have souls, they aren't capable of spiritual travel. You're sure he gave you this in the same context?"

"Yes," Abby groaned. Why'd he send her on jobs if he didn't trust her insight? Before he could say anything else, her eyes widened. Vampires weren't the only ones involved, and the others had souls. "You think it's for the werewolves?"

He nodded side to side in unsure agreement. "That's a possibility. It's not safe to assume anything right now, but I'll get a hold of one and keep it handy." Abby stood at that, about to leave seeing as she didn't have anything else to say, when her father spoke again. "I hear you've been spending a lot of time with the wolves."

She turned, squinting at him in shock. "How did–" But she stopped. He had ways of getting information, ways of spying on her. "Just one," she told him shortly, irritation growing by the second.

Her father leaned back in his chair, folding his hands across his stomach. "Don't get attached," he said flatly.

"I'm supposed to protect them," Abby glared, doing everything in her power not to raise her voice.

"Not by making friends." He leaned forward again, and when he said 'friends' his thoughts said something more. He knew about her interest in Kyla. She didn't know how he knew, but the fact that he did irked her.

Abby set her hands on her father's desk, leaning forward angrily. "This way is more efficient. I can protect them better if I know more about them."

"You are *not* acting in the Council's best interest," he said, a familiar, furious red tinting his face.

"The Council's interest is keeping the supernatural world in order," Abby growled, her voice steadily rising. "The wolves are our greatest allies in this. I'm doing what needs to be done."

Her father rose, pointing an irate finger at her as he yelled, "I told you not to involve them! You're disobeying a direct order!"

He wasn't taking this as seriously as he needed to be. The only thing he cared about was that in all their activity the vampires had been making a stir with missing persons in the media. He didn't seem to care if the werewolves were in danger. In fact, it appeared that because the werewolves were the targets he was intent on keeping the Council's involvement to a minimum. That made Abby furious.

"Your orders are shit!" she shouted. "We need to collaborate everything with them before this turns ugly. They've already made contact with a vampire on the inside." At that her father scowled, and she knew she'd hit a chord. "Don't you get it? By shutting them out *you're* the one who's in the dark, and if all this falls apart because we didn't do everything we could, then I'm blaming you."

Abby was so angry that she turned to leave, and when she reached the door her father yelled after her. "If you leave this building, I *will* pull you off the job!" Without turning she flipped an offensive finger and then slammed the door behind her.

When she got out she could see her mother raising both eyebrows at her in shock. "I underestimated both of you today," she said, clearly trying not to chuckle.

Abby was still too livid to find it amusing, so as she stomped toward the exit of the building she waved. "Bye."

19

I lifted my arm and pointed across the room to where I could feel Kyla was standing. Even with my eyes closed, and her practically fifteen feet away, I could tell where she was. Every training session since the first time we tested the blood connection Wes had us working on it, and we'd been making significant progress. It was slow going at first, but after we'd gotten a good idea of what it felt like, we got better at it more rapidly.

"Okay, Kyla, your turn," Wes instructed from his sitting position in the corner of the room.

Covering her ears so she couldn't hear where I'd go, Kyla took position in the center of the glass room and closed her eyes while I moved around noiselessly, until I'd picked a spot behind her on the edge of the room.

"Go ahead," Wes said loudly, so Kyla would know she could take her hands off her ears and start.

I stood as imperceptible as I could, every muscle stiff and practically holding my breath so I wouldn't make a single sound. Kyla waited just as silently, concentrating as she tried to feel where I was without using any of her other senses. After about a minute she turned and pointed a finger. When she opened her eyes a smile spread across her lips, happy to see me in front of her.

"I'm so proud," Wes said, faking joyful tears as he put an arm around my shoulders and led me back to the center of the room where Kyla was. He sat us both down facing each other, and then took a seat beside us. "I want to try something kind of new," he told us, and then moved our hands so that Kyla's were resting on top of mine. A week ago just this contact made me cringe, but I was getting over the shock of it the more we did these exercises. "Camille, I want you to tell Kyla about your day yesterday."

"Okay," I started unsurely. "I went to school."

"Oh, come on," he stopped me. "I want Kyla to be able to feel how you felt doing all these things. Be specific. Relive it."

I nodded, concentrating my attention on my memories and trying to bring back the feelings. I already knew I'd be able to feel Kyla's emotions, I'd done it before, but would she be able to feel mine? "I woke up around seven yesterday, and I'll be damned if I didn't want to sleep in until at least ten. I could barely get out of bed. I grabbed my shower stuff and some clothes and went to the bathroom to get ready for school. The water was cold since everyone else showers in the morning. It woke me up, but I got pretty annoyed." I paused to glance up at Kyla, who nodded excitedly that she could feel my aggravation.

"I was moving kind of slow, so by the time I was done getting ready I had to rush to get a bagel from the cafeteria, and I ate it on my way to class." As I spoke I brought back the sensations of stress I'd had at having to rush. "I made it to class right on time, and pretty much every one was the same. I was bored and zoned out a lot." I knew even before I started talking about it that the feeling I'd be giving off wouldn't be boredom, but rather anguish. What I really meant to say was that I didn't zone out because I was bored, but because whenever I got a moment to think my mind went straight to Kyla, and the pain wasn't getting much easier.

For the sake of the exercise I forced myself to continue, despite letting Kyla in on those private emotions. "After school I was really tired, so I went back to my dorm and took a nap. I woke up around six because my stomach was growling, and then I went to the cafeteria to get some dinner. After I ate I went back to my dorm and started my homework." I'd always been one who preferred to keep to myself, but I could only imagine how Kyla felt about me being so alone, all day. And to think that's how it was every day unless Lacey was around.

"That's all," I said, pulling my hands away from Kyla's. I could feel the girl's eyes watching me carefully, and I knew she'd at least slightly picked up on the things I didn't want her to. "That's what I did yesterday."

"Okay, now you do it," Wes said to Kyla, moving our hands back together.

"Well, let's see," she began, removing her eyes from my face and staring intently at our hands. "I took a shower at night so I got up at eight. I went to the bathroom real quick to brush my teeth, and then went back to my dorm to get dressed and do my makeup. When I was done I was running late too, so I grabbed a breakfast burrito from the cafeteria and ate it on my way. I had English first period, and the book we're reading is pretty interesting so I wasn't too bored. The rest of my classes were pretty boring though, until lunch." I could tell that Kyla really did feel true boredom. It was a restless feeling, like she was always itching to be doing something.

"At lunch I met a friend in the courtyard. It was pretty fun, we just talked about random stuff." At the feeling of joy I felt from Kyla I figured the friend had to be Abby, and I hated it, especially since I could feel it. The last thing I wanted to feel when I thought about Abby was joy. "I had a tuna sandwich for lunch... I really think the cafeteria needs a health inspection. My last two classes after that were as boring as all the other ones. Once school was done I was going back to my room when I saw my friend, so we hung out a little bit." That same feeling of elation returned, and it was almost too much. While I spent my time alone and practically dead inside, Kyla was with someone that made her happy, and that someone wasn't me.

"After a while my friend had to meet with people at The Orchid, so I went with them. We listened to music and played pool for a little while, then we started danci–"

I dropped Kyla's hands and stood up. The very last thing on earth I wanted to feel was how happy she was while dancing with Abby. "I don't want to do this anymore."

Before Kyla or Wes could say anything I paced back into the house. As I finally stopped in the kitchen and sat on a stool at the bar, I wasn't quite sure how to feel. Most of me was of course devastated, but the other part? Was I angry? Yes, that was definitely anger. I didn't get time to process my thoughts or anger, because Kyla came in right after me. I expected she'd be coming in to make me feel better, or apologize like she always tried to, but when I looked up she appeared just as angry as I felt.

"What the hell is your problem?" she spat at me from the entrance, and I just stared at her in silent shock. "Do you have any idea how hard it is to be here? Away from family, in a world I'm still trying to adjust to." She paced hotly to the edge of the bar where I was sitting, her voice a near shout. "I'd like it if I could turn to you every once in a while since you're the only thing I really know out here, but that's not even true anymore. And because you can't make up your mind, I can't move on or be happy?" I tried to open my mouth, to say anything to make Kyla stop yelling at me, but I was at a loss for words. I'd seen her upset more than I could count the last few months, but this was unexpected. "You're doing this to yourself, Camille."

That was the last thing Kyla yelled before she tried to check herself. She straightened up and took a few deliberate breaths, and then pulled two pieces of paper out of her pocket and threw them onto the bar top. Her voice was quieter now, like she was tired of yelling. "Here, I kept forgetting to give these to you. You don't have to come if you don't want to." Then she held out her hand. "Give me the car keys, I'm going back to school. You can get a ride from Lacey."

As I pulled the keys out of my pocket I studied Kyla's face. She was still very clearly mad, but there was an underlying tint of grief. Did she know how much she was hurting me, and it hurt her to see it? If so, I didn't know what I could do about it. Maybe she was right, that I was doing this to myself by not really letting myself get over her, but I needed more time. I needed her to slow down with Abby, because seeing them together was killing me.

The second I put the car keys in Kyla's hand the girl turned and left the kitchen, leaving me alone in the stillness. Feeling that if I didn't move the weight of the silence would crush me, I picked up the paper she'd put in front of me to see what it was. Two tickets for the talent show tonight. I knew Kyla was performing, but assuming Abby was going to be there I hadn't been interested in trying to go.

As I set the tickets back on the countertop Lacey walked in, looking at me worriedly. "What was that all about?"

"Kyla's perfectly happy seeing somebody else," I told her, and at recollection of Kyla yelling at me, at the fact that she wasn't helping me get over her, the anger flared back up, and I shouted out the kitchen after her even though she was long gone, "And she just loves to *rub in it my face!*"

"Whoa," Lacey said, shocked by my volume. In an attempt to calm me down she moved behind me and began to massage my shoulders. "I know it's tough, but it's going to be okay."

I laid my head on the cold granite countertop, trying to let her rub the tension out of me. "Why are girls so confusing?"

Out of the corner of my eye I could see Lacey shrug. "I don't know. That's what I love about guys, they're easy to figure out," she chuckled, her lightheartedness an obvious attempt to try and cheer me up, but it wasn't enough. Seeing that it wasn't working, she stopped giving me a massage and wrapped her arms around me in a hug. I was turned around so I couldn't hug the girl back, but just the gesture was comforting. "I love you."

I couldn't help but give a small smile. "Love you too."

"And I'm sorry this is so hard on you," she continued. "It's probably not what you want to hear because I know you'll always be in love with her, but maybe it would be easier if you just tried to accept it and have some kind of relationship, even if it's just friends. You know, since she's kind of part of the family now."

"You're right," I nodded knowingly. Of course Lacey was right. How long had it been since Kyla had broken up with me? A few months. By now I should have at least come to terms with it. So why was it so hard? What godforsaken thing kept me holding on?

Lacey released me from the hug and grabbed the tickets off the counter. "Are you going to go to this? It would be a good chance to show Kyla if you're serious about trying to be friends."

"Depends," I told her, really not wanting to go alone. "Will you come with me? There're two tickets."

With a small, apologetic smile, she shook her head. "I can't. I have a huge midterm project due Monday, and I haven't even started."

"I hate procrastinators," I scowled, and then asked dejectedly, "Can we go back to the school now? I just want to lay down."

Lacey sighed sadly, feeling for me, and nodded. It was a quiet ride back to the dorms. I knew she was right about what I had to do, but that didn't mean I had to like it or ever would like it. When we got back I went straight to my room, plopped onto the bed, and in an attempt to tune out the rest of the world I put in my headphones and fell right asleep. I awoke around seven and sat up thoughtfully. My eyes wandered to the tickets I'd placed on my desk. The show was supposed to start at seven, but if I left now I might be able to make it in time to see Kyla perform. I sat there for another second as I fully woke up from my nap, then without another thought I grabbed the tickets and dashed out the door.

I was about to get on the elevator when I stopped. *Shit.* I'd given Kyla the car keys and now I didn't have a way to get there. Thankfully Lacey was on the same floor as me. I sprinted down the hall and past my own room to get to hers, and knocked with urgency.

She opened the door looking annoyed at how many times I'd pounded on it. "Jesus, what?"

"I need your car keys," I told her hurriedly, and then tried to get her moving. "Come on, the show already started."

Without leaving the doorway she reached over and grabbed the keys off her desk, and then handed them to me. The second I had them in my hands I took off back toward the elevator, hearing her call 'bye' after me. When the elevator got me to the first floor I raced out to the red sports coupe, firing up the engine with a smile.

"Let's see how fast you can really go." I threw the car in reverse and pulled out of the school at speeds that were probably dangerous for a parking lot, but now that I'd made up my mind to go I'd feel guilty if I missed Kyla's song.

When I arrived at The Orchid fifteen minutes later there was nobody waiting outside to get in, so I gave the man inside the front door my ticket and rushed to where I could see the stage. There was a band on that sounded like they'd just started, so I pushed my way through the crowd to the side of the stage. At the entrance to backstage I tried to sneak past the guy guarding it, but he stopped me.

"I'm with Kyla," I told him impatiently.

He looked me over and then poked his head through the door. "Kyla!" After a few seconds she materialized at the entrance. "She with you?" the man asked her, motioning to me.

Kyla nodded and grabbed me by the hand, hauling me inside and to a dark corner behind one of the many black curtains. I glanced curiously around the darkened area and then back at her, wondering why I'd been dragged somewhere private.

"Kyla, you're on next," someone called from the large room around us.

With that she gaped at me, eyes wide with panic. "Camille, I'm freaking out. I've never been so nervous."

"You're going to do great," I chuckled, trying to be reassuring. "I've heard you sing and play guitar, you're amazing."

She shook her head frantically and grabbed my shoulders, giving me a shake for emphasis. "No, you don't get it. I'm *freaking out*. My fingers are itching, I don't know how much longer I can control it."

Now that I understood the severity of what she was saying I peeked out of our curtained corner, starting to panic as well. There was a glowing exit sign on the opposite side of the room. "You don't have to perform. Come on, let's go." I grabbed her hand and was about to pull her to the exit, but she held fast.

"I won't make it," she told me, shaking out her hands and taking in a deep breath as her panic grew. "Oh God, I can feel it coming. Don't let me hurt anyone."

I could feel in my proximity to her how serious she was. She was on the edge, and the band on stage sounded like their song was coming to an end. My eyes darted around frantically. What could I do? I was about to slap her across the face, but stopped. That always pissed her off, making a Change more likely. Should I just attempt to drag her out of here anyway? My heart was racing, and there was nothing else I could think of. Before I could even consciously consider the idea, and how bad of an idea it was, I put my hand behind Kyla's head and pulled her into a kiss. At first I feared the worst. The second her lips touched mine her body stiffened against me, her closed fists set against my chest like she was going to push me away, and I thought I'd failed. But then she relaxed, she melted into me, and I could feel all the tension of holding back a Change vanish in the blink of an eye.

Job done, and knowing I would hate myself for this later, I was about to pull away. But Kyla's hands opened against my chest, then slid steadily up until her arms wrapped around my neck. The brunette's lips pressed harder against my own, increasingly eager, like she wanted more than what I was already giving her. So I gave in, and I gave more.

My arms snaked around the small of Kyla's back, pulling the girl's body closer to mine. I backed her into the wall behind us so I could get even closer. And when Kyla's tongue begged entrance, I gave of it freely. As hard as I fought it, I couldn't stop myself from being lost in the kiss.

It was the first kiss since Kyla had been Changed, and it was infinitely more powerful than the first ever had been. Each time her lips moved against my own her arms tightened around my neck, like she was holding me up because she knew my head was swimming. Each time I grazed her lower lip with my teeth I could feel the purr in her core. And each time I pressed her harder against the wall to get even closer, she pressed right back. Then all at once I came to the realization that this kiss would probably be our last, and I'd have to enjoy it as such. The thought hurt me, and even more it scared me, and because of that I didn't ever want it to stop.

So when the crew called Kyla's name for her to prepare to go on stage, I bit into her lip one last time. Because I didn't want this to end, because I didn't want her to leave, because I was angry at her for making me feel this way, and most of all, because after this was done I wanted her to remember it. I'd wanted to bite hard, but I still bit harder than I'd meant to. It was hard enough to break skin, and for Kyla to have to wipe away the blood that surfaced with the back of her hand. When she pulled away to stare at me in silent shock, I could do nothing but stare right back, surprised at myself for letting it go so far.

"Kyla, front and center!" the man, that annoying, annoying man, called again, this time impatiently.

I wondered why she wasn't leaving to perform, or at least saying something. Then I realized I still had her pinned against the wall, my arms still wrapped tight around her waist, my body still pressed as close as it could get. I dropped my arms and reluctantly pulled myself away, Kyla still staring at me.

"Kyla!" the man called again, this time getting closer, and then mumbling to himself he pulled back the curtain we were behind. "Are

238

you Kyla?" Slowly, as if dazed, Kyla looked at him and nodded. "Well, let's go," he motioned for her to follow him. "You got about ten seconds before you're on."

As Kyla began to follow him she walked backward, still focused on me. I tried hard to decipher what it was I saw there, in those bright green eyes that watched me, but I couldn't tell. Before she turned around to take her place backstage her tongue flicked to the blood that had resurfaced on her lip, and then her eyes were gone. The second I knew I was no longer being watched I collapsed to the floor, where I stayed for less than a second before I stood.

I couldn't wait here. If I had to see her again I might lose it, might break down. I had to hold it together, at least until I got back to my dorm. The green glow of the backstage exit sign caught my eye, and I darted for it, sprinting to the car the second the door closed behind me. If it was at all possible for me to get back to the school in less time than I'd gotten to The Orchid, I did. As I got off the elevator I made to sprint for my room, almost knocking down someone on my way there.

"Hey, Camille?" I had my door open and was halfway inside my room by the time the guy caught up with me. It was the other werewolf, the one I hardly ever saw. Nathan. William had a room on this floor, they must have been hanging out. "Hey, are you okay?"

I'd been moving so fast up until this point that my emotions hadn't been able to catch up with me. Now that I stopped and turned to face him, it hit me like a ton of bricks. The pain, the shock, the frustration. I'd gone to the show to finally be just friends with Kyla, and what did I do? The complete opposite – I kissed her and didn't pull away when I should have. What about her kissing me back? No. She was a freshly bitten werewolf who, as far as I knew, hadn't gotten laid. She reacted the way I assumed any wolf in her situation would have, and there was no way I could let myself accept any other explanation. Not if I wanted to keep my sanity.

As Nathan stood there waiting for an answer I looked him up and down. I could seduce him if I wanted to. Isn't that what most people did after a breakup? They had a rebound? As far as I knew it was supposed to make you feel better. Maybe that's what I needed. At least I imagined it would help me forget about the pain for a while. I grew disgusted with myself before I let the idea go any further. I didn't even like guys. I'd never been with anyone sexually. How could I even consider the thought? I was desperate, desperate to forget what I wanted so badly for Kyla to remember.

"No, I'm okay, thanks." I knew Nathan was about to say something else, but I closed the door anyway.

After I shut it I leaned my back against it, sliding to floor as I once again collapsed. Then I let them go. The tears I'd been holding back now flowed freely down my cheeks. Every once in a while my shoulders shook, rocked by a profound sob. I sat there for about an hour until my body was sore and the salty tears had made my skin raw. Then I stood, looking around for my mp3 player, and when I found it I put my headphones in my ears, turned it all the way up, and lay on my bed. If anyone came to the door I didn't want to hear them. I especially didn't want to hear if Kyla came looking for me. I just couldn't look the girl in the eyes. Not yet. The tears still ran until my pillow was soaked, but eventually I fell asleep.

I couldn't hear anything, so I don't know what it was that woke me up in the middle of the night. Maybe it was the cold breeze that came through the window, which had been closed when I'd lain down. Or maybe it was the hands I could feel coming toward me, even with my eyes closed. Without having time to think about it my instincts kicked in, and I flew at my attacker. We both crashed to the ground beside my bed, and I had my hands around my assailant's head, ready to break his or her neck, when the familiar scent wafted to my nose.

I dropped my target and angrily pulled the headphones out of my ears. "Jesus Christ, Luna." I sat there catching my breath, my heart still beating what felt like a million times a second. "Dumbass, I almost killed you just now." Luna stood, chuckling, and made her way over to the light switch to flip it on. I glared, still furious at my twin for scaring me, and kicked at the bed in frustration. "I'm serious. You of all people should know better than to sneak up on a sleeping werewolf." I reached up and tugged closed the window that she'd sneaked through.

She ignored me and sat down on the bed, studying me for a second. "Dude, you look like shit." She glanced around curiously, and no doubt noticed the mascara stains on the pillow, because then she looked back at me, finally getting serious. "Have you been crying?" I just nodded, holding back a fresh flow of tears that had been replenished by a few hours of sleep. If there was anything I hated, it was being vulnerable, but I'd been holding back the pain as best I could for months, and I couldn't do it any longer. "What happened?"

I stared hard at the floor, unable to look my sister in the eye. "Me and Kyla. We kissed."

Confusion spread across Luna's face. "Shouldn't that be a good thing?"

"She's kind of been seeing someone else. I don't know how serious they are." I shook my head, reminding myself of the point. "She was supposed to perform in a talent show tonight, and she got so nervous that she was about to Change. I didn't know what else to do, so I kissed her." It was clear on Luna's face that she was sad at seeing me in this state, but she didn't say anything, so I continued. "And it worked. I was just going to pull away and forget about the whole thing, but then she kissed me. I mean *really* kissed me, and I couldn't help it, I just kissed her back." A tear made its way down my cheek and I quickly wiped it away, refusing to let myself cry again.

"But, she kissed you too," Luna said, clearly in hopes that it would make me feel better.

"You know how the urges get, I mean, you're the biggest horndog out there." Even in my emotional state I couldn't resist teasing my sister, and the jab made me smile just a little. "Of course she kissed me back, and remember, the somebody else."

She nodded understandingly and sat there in silence, unsure of what to say.

"Whatever. I can't keep doing this to myself. I got to let it go. That's what everyone's been telling me to do anyway," I said and straightened up, attempting to change the subject so I could push it out of my mind. "When did you get here?"

"A few hours ago," she said, and received a curious glance from me. "I was with Will for a little bit."

"See." I couldn't help but giggle. "Horndog." Luna just shrugged, unable to defend herself. "And didn't I tell you that you'd miss me enough to run here eventually. You did run here, right?"

She just smirked. "Yeah, but who said I ran here for you?"

"Don't lie, I know you did." I glared at my sister, and now that I was beginning to make myself forget about earlier that night, I was starting to realize how much I'd missed her. "How're Mom and Dad, and everyone?"

"They're good," she told me with a smile. "We all miss you. Sky was going to come with me, but Eli called her and Michael with a job at the last minute."

I nodded understandingly. I would've loved to see my older sister, but when Eli sent Sky and Michael on jobs for the Pack, I knew it was important. "Did Will tell you what's been going on here? You shouldn't have even come by yourself."

"Yeah, he told me," Luna said, laughing. William must have been frantic that she'd come by herself judging by how amusing she found it. "And I already told him I'll let you guys run me back to the Oregon border if you want to."

I sat there thoughtfully for a moment before I stood. "Are you too tired from your escapades, or are you up for a run?"

She jumped up excitedly and followed me to the door. "I'm always up for a run."

I grinned and led my sister out the building. A run was the perfect thing for me to do to spend time with Luna while also providing an escape. And run I would, until I could barely breathe and all I could think about is how tired my legs are.

"Camille." I knocked on the blonde's dorm room door, harder this time than I had before, and the hundred times before that. "Camille, if you're there, please let me in."

A boy in the room next to hers opened his door and squinted in the bright light of the halls. "Hey, can you like, shut up or something?" I glared at him, a look that must have appeared fiercer than I thought, because without saying anything else he went back inside.

I knew it was six a.m. on a Sunday morning and that everyone else probably wanted to sleep in, but I didn't care. Now Camille was probably avoiding me, avoiding having to explain why she'd kissed me. I mean, I knew why she'd kissed me in the first place, and I was lucky that it actually did stop the Change. Then I found how much I'd missed her lips, or the feel of her body, and even though I knew she just wanted to be friends, I couldn't help but want more. The confusing part to me was when she kissed me back, and it wasn't just a kiss. There was more passion in that small moment than there had ever been when we were together.

After my performance I'd gone back to look for her, but she was gone, nowhere at The Orchid. As soon as I could leave I'd went to her dorm, but if she was there she wasn't answering. Now she was avoiding me, maybe because she felt bad for leading me on. Or maybe because she knew I'd want some kind of explanation.

"Camille!" I raised my voice a little louder and knocked again, but still, nothing.

A door cracked open a bit further down the hall, and a sleep-bogged Will stuck his head into the hallway. "What are you doing?" he asked me, his voice deep and groggy.

"I'm looking for Camille," I told him, making my way toward his room. "Have you seen her?"

He stepped out in just pajama pants, every strand of his long hair going a different direction. "Uh," he rubbed the sleep out of his eyes as he tried to wake up enough to form another sentence. "Luna came last night, they probably went out."

"Oh." My eyes dropped in disappointment. Not just because Camille really wasn't there and probably wouldn't be back for a long time, but also because I would've liked to see Luna. The small, quirky blonde had been one of my best friends, especially after the Change, and I missed her quite a bit. "How long is Luna going to be here?"

"I think she's leaving tonight, probably around seven," Will said, putting his hands in the pockets of his pants and leaning his head against the doorframe.

"Thanks." I gave him an apologetic smile. "Sorry I woke you up."

He nodded and slipped back into his room, leaving me alone in the empty hall. Usually Camille and I went together to training on Sunday mornings, and normally we didn't leave until at least seven-thirty. As I sauntered back to the elevator I figured I might as well go to the house now and see if anyone was around. Since I was already dressed and ready to go, I went straight down to the first floor and out to the jeep. When I got on the main road to the house I pulled out my cellphone. I'd already called Camille a few times and, since I'd probably already come off as desperate, figured it wouldn't matter if I called again. However, just like every other time, it rang until voicemail picked up, and just like every other time I didn't bother leaving a message. She knew what I was calling about.

I wistfully pushed open the front door of the Pack house and listened intently, but I couldn't hear anyone talking. Everyone must still be sleeping. Then I inhaled through my nose, catching what I'd hoped I would, Luna's scent. So she'd been here sometime, and hopefully that meant Camille had been there too. Along with the many scents there was the faint aroma of coffee, and I followed my nose to the kitchen, where I found Wes sitting at the bar.

"You're here early," he mused when he saw me come in, and took a sip from his mug.

I plopped down in a stool across from him and shrugged. "I've been looking for Camille. Have you seen her?"

"I heard her and her sister come in for a few minutes last night, around three I think," he told me with a thoughtful nod. "It sounded like they left out the back."

"To run?" I asked thoughtfully, to which Wes gave a half nod, half shrug.

"What happened to your lip?" he asked, and when I looked up he was studying my bottom lip carefully.

I touched the small cut with my fingertips. It had been bruised the night before, but because of our accelerated healing it was now just a blood red nick. There was one on the inside of my lip too, which I mindlessly ran my tongue over. "Camille." Even more confusing than the fact that she'd kissed me back was that she bit me hard enough to draw blood. It was out of character for her, and I hadn't the slightest clue why she'd done it, but now, every time my tongue touched the inside of my lip I got a vivid reminder of the kiss.

"She hit you?" Wes asked, an eyebrow raised in shock. "That doesn't seem like her."

"No, she didn't hit me." I shook my head and then stood, not wanting to talk about it. "I'll be right back."

I could feel him staring after me curiously as I made my way out of the kitchen and headed for the glass room. When I reached it I walked through the glass doors to the outside and to the waterproof box we always put our clothes in when we ran. Sure enough, when I opened it there were two sets of clothing inside. One I knew was Camille's, and the other was drenched in Luna's scent. I rummaged through it for a moment and then pulled out the cellphone I also recognized as Camille's. *That explains her not answering my calls.* Even though there was that excuse, I knew if she wanted to talk to me then she would have. She wouldn't have disappeared from the show, and wouldn't have taken off into the woods with Luna.

Even though I told Wes I'd be right back, I lay on my back on the cold, white marble of the glass room and stayed there. The sky had been slowly turning gray since I'd left the dorms, and now the first tints of orange were beginning to color the morning. I could hear the wind cutting around the corner of the house outside, whistling to me. Telling me in its ominous song that I was truly losing Camille. That the only chance I would get, my chance last night at the show, was gone. I shouldn't have performed. I should have left with her, done anything other than let her get away, but now she was gone.

After I'd been lying there for a while I heard a quiet, familiar gait nearing the door, and a second later Wes stepped in, looking down as he stood above me. "Comfy?" I just shrugged. "Is Camille not coming to train?"

"I guess not," I told him, still looking up at him from the same spot on the floor, refusing to move. "It's not like she talks to me about anything."

"What's the deal with you two?" he asked me, and his eyes scanned mine carefully, genuine worry dulling their stony gray color.

I sighed, and blinked away a single tear so he wouldn't see it. "Doesn't matter. Whatever it is, it's over."

Wes mirrored my sigh, but his was deeper. "I think I know what you need." I just stared up at him, waiting for him to complete his thought or leave me alone. "You need a drink."

I pushed myself up onto my elbows, not believing I could have heard him right. "Like, a drink, drink?" He shrugged, and his lack of response informed me that I'd heard correctly. "It's only seven in the morning." Despite the fact that I was unsure about the offer, I was interested in why he would even offer in the first place. He just shrugged again, and held out a hand to help me off the floor. "I thought we weren't supposed to drink?"

As I finally stood Wes turned back toward the kitchen, me following close behind. "That's what we tell all you young ones so you don't get into trouble. What we don't tell you guys is that our metabolisms are so fast it would take a hell of a lot of alcohol to make Changes hard to control." After that he paused and looked back at me thoughtfully. "Well, I don't know about you, since you're new to it. But seriously kid, I have never seen a more depressed werewolf in my entire life." He smirked teasingly even though it was true, and I couldn't help but feel bad that I was starting to affect his mood as well.

In an attempt to lighten up just a little bit I glared at him. "This isn't some creepy attempt to hit on me is it?"

He looked at me for a split second in shock, obviously because he hadn't expected me to make that kind of comment, but he didn't try to hold back a laugh. "How old are you?"

"Seventeen."

"Sorry to disappoint, you're a little young for me." He laughed again to himself as he turned into the kitchen. "Besides, I'm not really your type."

"Yeah, I guess not," I chuckled as I sat on a stool.

Wes set two small shot glasses out and reached into the highest cabinet above the refrigerator, pulling out a glass bottle of dark brown fluid. After he pulled the cap off the bottle he filled each of the two shots and then set it aside. I picked up my drink and sniffed it, scowling at the smell.

"What is it?" I asked, setting it back down with disgust.

"Come on," he said in disbelief. "You're a southern girl, I thought you'd know your whiskey when you saw it." I shook my head, causing him to eye me suspiciously. "Is this your first drink?"

I gave a bashful nod. "I had a beer once, don't know if that counts."

"Wow," he said to himself, and then he threw a drink down his throat and filled the glass again. "When I was your age I was stealing liquor and bumming cigarettes."

"You?" I scoffed in disbelief as I watched him knock back another shot. "But, you teach us how to do yoga." This time my scoff turned to a laugh.

"Everyone's got a wild side," Wes grinned.

Curious, I picked up my own glass and copied him, taking it down with a single gulp. The second I swallowed it I coughed. It burned at my tongue and throat and all the way down to my stomach, and the underlying sweetness did nothing to sedate it. After the cough I covered my mouth with my hand as I gagged, and my eyes watered at the pain. "That's disgusting!"

Wes chuckled as he filled both of our drinks again, and I raised an eyebrow at him. I used to have friends that would get a little more than buzzed after three drinks, and they did it all the time. I'd never drunk before, and wasn't it supposed to be stronger if you weren't used to it? Wes seemed to be able to read my mind though, and he shook his head. "You won't even feel it, I promise." I shrugged and took his word for it as I gulped down the second one. "So," he started, and knocked back his own. "You want to talk about it?"

The reaction to the second drink was the same as the first, and it took me a few moments to recover. "No, not really." I pushed the glass away from me, not wanting to experience the awful burn again. "You weren't the best kid, huh? What changed?"

"I met Eli, grew up," he answered, moving to sit down across from me. "Finally had somewhere to belong."

I'd heard him talk about his life before, how he was bitten and Eli had saved him. "What about girls, I never hear about you guys bringing anybody around. Have you ever been in love before?"

"We aren't allowed to bring girls back to the house. It's too risky," he told me, playing mindlessly with the cap on the whiskey bottle. "I thought I was in love once. She was feisty." His lips turned up in a reminiscent smile. "After I was bitten I tried to tell her the truth because, you know, I loved her, and she just thought it was a really bad excuse to break up with her. Man was she pissed. Even threw a glass lamp at me." He lifted up the long brown hair that covered his forehead and showed me an old, faded scar, and then laughed. "She was always such a bitch. I mean, the sex wa–" he stopped and looked at me, a slight chagrin turning his cheeks a faded pink. "You get the point."

"Yeah, I get the point," I laughed at his minor embarrassment, though I really did like this side of Wes. It was a lot more entertaining than yoga-Wes. "If you really thought you were in love with her, then how'd you get over it?"

"I slept around a lot," he told me honestly, and then cast me a scolding glance. "Which I'm not saying is the right way to do it, but it was the only option I saw." Then he looked at me sadly and propped his head in his hand. "Look, I don't know what exactly happened between you and Camille, but it's obvious you're trying to get your mind off it. If you don't want to train today, I got a project you can help me with."

"Okay, I guess," I said unsurely, and when Wes got up to leave the kitchen I followed him. He led me back to the glass room and then out the door, to where on the far side of the house there were a few shovels and part of the ground was marked off with little orange flags. "What is this?"

He tossed me a shovel and made his way to the center of the large oval shape the flags made. "Before all this vampire stuff started happening, me and the others got bored pretty easy. So we started bugging Eli about putting in a pool."

"Seriously?" I asked in disbelief. It was so cold right now that I couldn't imagine swimming, though I was sure it was warmer during the summer.

"Yeah," he laughed and stabbed his shovel into the dirt. "He agreed, but said he wasn't paying any contractors to come and do it. You know, he's the private type. He said it was fine if we did all the work ourselves. We're going to dig the hole for it, then Richard, you know Will's dad, he's in construction so he's going to do the cement work."

"You got it all figured out, don't you?" I chuckled as I shrugged off my white jacket, not wanting to get it dirty as we dug, and set it back in the glass room on the floor. "Alright, I don't mind helping."

So I did. I helped Wes dig near the side of the house until about five, when I had to leave because I'd made plans with Abby. When I got back to the school I changed and washed away all the dirt I could find. As I sat there on my bed, with about ten minutes to spare before she would knock on the door, I pulled out my cellphone, wondering if I should try to call Camille one last time. But I put it away with resolve. There was nothing left I could do, and it was time for me to move on. Not wanting to sit there in silence, I got up and decided to go to Abby's room early.

When I knocked on the door her roommate opened it and smiled at me. "Hey, Kyla right?" I nodded with a friendly grin. "Come on in."

I walked through the door as Abby was putting on her shoes, and her hazel eyes brightened excitedly at the sight of me. "I was just about to come get you." She finished slipping on her last shoe and then tugged on her sweater. "Ready?"

With a nod, I followed her to the door, and before it closed behind us I waved to her roommate. "It was nice to see you again." The girl smiled and said 'goodbye,' and then I walked with Abby toward the elevator. "Does she know you can read minds?"

Abby shook her head. "No, I don't really tell anyone who isn't different, and she's just a normal human." She leaned against the side of the elevator as it took us down, and like she usually did she studied me. "Hey, what happened to your lip?"

"Ah, no, no, no, no, no, get out." I frantically waved my hands by the side of my head as if that would keep her from hearing my thoughts. Luckily, desperately thinking only of kicking her out of my head kept me from thinking about kissing Camille.

"Whoa, I'm sorry," she said, and hastily tried to change the subject. "You studying for midterms yet?"

The doors opened up to the first floor, and while we stepped off I tried to calm down a little bit. "I'm sorry. It's just, tonight, could you try to stay out of my head?" I felt bad for asking since I knew she couldn't control it, so I added softly, "Please."

She nodded thoughtfully, watching me with a curious worry in her eyes. "Are you okay? We could go out another night."

"No, it's fine," I told her with a smile, and in an attempt to calm both of us down I placed my hand in hers. "I want to go."

She grinned, and as we got to the car we both jumped in. "You're going to like where we're going. It's nice and loud, so I won't be able to hear your thoughts." She still looked a little bit worried, but she kept on the comforting smile.

"Okay," I said, and was going to ask where she was taking me, but I knew she liked surprises, so instead I answered her earlier question. "No, I haven't even cracked a book for midterms yet. You?"

"I studied a little bit, but I still have a lot to do," she told me. "How'd the talent show go last night?"

"Third place," I blurted in another attempt to keep from thinking about the kiss. Now I focused on that, and wouldn't let myself think about anything else. "I won third place. A comedian got second and then some band took first. They were last to go and they were really good."

"I think I know who you're talking about," Abby said with a knowing nod. "They always save that band for last because they always end up winning first. If it wasn't for them I'm sure you would've come in second. By the way, I'm sorry I missed it."

"It's okay." I tried to keep from thinking about how good it was that she didn't go. I wasn't sure why I was trying so hard to keep her from knowing about the kiss, but it was hard work. Feeling my mind slipping, I asked quickly, "Where were you anyway?"

"I had to run another errand for the council." Abby looked at me with another inquisitive glance. It had to be obvious to her that I was trying extremely hard not to think about something. "It was a little farther away though, so I didn't make it back in time."

I nodded understandingly. "Did you find out anything important?"

"No," Abby shook her head. "Harold was the only one we got anything even worth looking at from. The vampires are doing a good job laying low."

"Yeah, no kidding," I said sarcastically. "I got to ask, where are we going?"

Abby laughed and pointed out the window to a large, brightly lit building as she turned down the street it was on. "Well, we're here."

We pulled into the full parking lot and I curiously tried to look into the building, but while the outside was bright, the inside was dark. Even from the parking lot I could hear loud music, and my first thought was that it was a club.

Abby reached for my hand as we got out and began to lead me toward the building. "It's not a club. Even though I know dancing with me is just your favorite thing."

I laughed and rolled my eyes teasingly. When we walked through the front door I couldn't deny I was a little surprised at what I saw inside. It was dark because there were only a few normal lights, and the rest were black lights. Through the loud music I could hear the rhythmic pings and pongs of the arcade games we passed on our way toward the back of the building.

"An arcade, huh?" I asked, loud enough so Abby would be able to hear me.

"I wasn't planning on playing games. I was actually hoping you'd be more interested in this." She led us through to the second part of the building, and the music wasn't quite as loud as the roar of the small speeding engines in this brightly lit area. I grinned as I watched go-karts zoom around the winding track in front of me. "Have you ever been?"

"No, but it looks awesome!" I shouted as my hand tightened excitedly around Abby's.

"Okay come on, I got to put our names in and then we'll get something to eat." She started toward a counter and then gave the guy behind it our names. After that, while we were waiting for our turn, we went to the small pizza place that was attached to the arcade. It was still loud enough in the pizzeria from the music that I was sure Abby couldn't hear my thoughts, and the less I tried to control them, the easier it got not to have to.

When we sat down at a small table with our slices of pizza I smiled down at the greasy blob of bread and cheese, and then grinned at Abby. "You even got me junk food."

"I do what I can." She shrugged and waved the comment away with exaggerated nonchalance.

"I never would have known this place was here," I told her, looking around the arcade and through to the racetrack. "Everything hides behind all the trees."

"Gems like this are rare, but there are *some* fun things to do out here." She followed my eyes as we took everything in. "I'm glad it's a school night though, it's not as crowded as it usually is."

I nodded and took an enormous bite of my pizza, making sure to swallow before I spoke. "How many times have you raced?"

"Quite a few," she answered, and then cracked her knuckles confidently. "I'm pretty damn good, if I do say so myself."

"Oh, is that right?" I laughed, raising a disbelieving eyebrow at her. "I think you're a little too cocky. I bet I could kick your ass out there."

"Care to make a wager?" Abby crossed her arms over her chest in defiance.

"Okay," I said, mimicking her challenging position by crossing my own arms over my chest. "What'll be?"

She stared blankly at me for a second, and then squinted in thought. "I don't know. I want an 'I owe you', for anything I want."

"Within reason," I said as I tentatively stuck out my hand to shake on it, and Abby nodded. "And I want the same."

"Deal." She took my hand, and as she shook it with an already victorious grin our names were called over the loudspeaker. "You're in trouble now."

We excitedly made our way over to where we were going to get into the go-karts and put on our helmets. There were a couple other people that were going to be on the track at the same time as us, but as we started out Abby and I were side by side. I gripped my steering wheel, staring over at her with a competitive glare. The lights ahead of us flashed red. Then yellow.

On green I hit the gas, and the go-kart wrenched forward as it threw me into the lead. I only held my position ahead of Abby for half a lap before the girl cut inside as we made our way around a turn. I didn't let up though throughout each of the fourteen laps, and I stayed right behind her, occasionally bumping into her and receiving a scowl from the attendant overseeing the race. At the end of the last lap around the track Abby threw her fist in the air, passing a gloating grin back at me.

"I want a rematch!" I hollered at her through the muffle of my helmet.

I heard her say 'okay,' and we waited patiently at the starting line for the next few people to take the empty go-karts. This time around I took off just as I had before, only now I kept glancing behind me as we made our way around the track, cutting Abby off and stopping her from taking the lead. I finished that race ahead of her, and so naturally we had to break the tie. We went through one more race, of which Abby came out the victor, and she jumped happily as we made our way back to the front desk.

"Alright, alright. You're the champ," I admitted, giggling as I tried to push her shoulders down to get her to stop jumping.

"Damn straight," she beamed as she handed the man behind the desk her credit card to pay for our races. He swiped it quickly and had her sign the receipt, and then we headed back to the parking lot.

"Okay Earnhardt, do you know what you want yet?" I asked as I followed Abby outside.

"Earnhardt?" She raised an eyebrow at me as we both got in the car.

My jaw dropped in shock. "Oh come on, you don't got to be country to know who Dale Earnhardt is." Abby just shrugged. "NASCAR?"

"Sorry, doesn't ring a bell," she said, and catching my next thought added, "And no, I'm not kidding." She chuckled as I buried my face in my hands in pretend disappointment. "I don't know what I want yet, I'm going to claim my prize when you least expect it."

"Oh geez." I rolled my eyes sarcastically. "Remind me never to make a bet with you again."

She gave a coy grin. "If there's one thing I've learned in my old age, little one, it's never to make a bet you don't know you can win."

"Want to arm wrestle?" I teased, to which Abby, knowing she would lose, instantly shook her head.

We arrived at the dorms just a few minutes later, and Abby shivered as she got out of the car. "I swear it just got ten degrees colder."

"I don't know why you're only wearing this jacket." I grabbed the thin material between my fingers and laughed. Even my coat was thicker than that. "You don't have to compete with me, I'm too hot."

"And I'm the cocky one?" she scoffed, and quit rubbing her arms as we entered the warmth of the building.

When we reached our floor we stepped off and started for my room. "When are you going on another errand for the Council?" I asked as I unlocked my door and pushed it open.

Abby shrugged with a smug look on her face. "Why, want to break into another house?"

"Maybe," I told her dubiously as I took off my jacket and set it over the chair at my desk. "I got a taste for the life of a criminal."

She chuckled and plopped down onto my bed. "What kind of fantasy world are you living in?"

"I don't know," I admitted with a laugh and sat down next to her. "Thanks for tonight though, I had a lot of fun."

"Don't worry about it. I'm glad you had fun." She smiled at me, and I smiled back as I sat there patiently, waiting for her to say something else.

Only, instead of saying anything she nervously leaned forward so that our lips met in a soft peck, and when I didn't protest or pull away, they met again. At first I didn't know what I was thinking or feeling, Abby's lips were velvet soft and her touch delicate, but after a few moments something came over me. All at once the emotions from the day, the last few months, they came barreling back, and they worked their way into this kiss.

I kissed harder, deeper. I put my hand on Abby's chest and pushed her down so I was on top. I wrapped one arm around her waist and pulled her so close I felt a huff of breath against my lips, squeezed out of her by the strength of my embrace. My other hand pulled her knee up so her leg would hug my curves, then it slid up her thigh and to her backside, where I grabbed to bring her hips more intimate with mine.

I welcomed the affection, but this wasn't a passionate, romantic kiss. It was an outlet, a desperate try at an escape. Like I was living it again, a graphic flash of my kiss with Camille danced across my mind. The way her arms curled around my body. The way she pressed herself so hard against me. The way she bit into my lip. With that memory came every frustration, every bit of confusion, and every hurt. With this kiss I was taking it out on a poor girl that had never been anything but sweet to me. I was letting loose everything that caused me distress through the storm of desire I threw on Abby. And though there was something inside screaming at me to stop, it wasn't until I felt Abby pushing against my shoulders to interrupt me that I started snapping out of it.

"Kyla, stop," she pleaded gently, still delicately pushing against my shoulders and finally getting me to pull away.

Shocked and embarrassed, I backed up until I was sitting at the far edge of the bed. "I'm so sorry." My mouth was hanging open. "You shouldn't have had to hear any of that." I wasn't only shocked at myself. I was appalled. "I shouldn't have kissed you like that."

"No," she shook her head as she sat up. "I needed to hear that. Is that what you've been trying to keep from me all night? About you and Camille." Then she rubbed her neck like she was stressed out, and spoke to herself, "God that was strong, I could practically feel her."

I couldn't hold still any longer, so I got up and paced at the side of the bed. "I've been trying so hard to let her go, but I can't. I'm so sorry." I stopped to look at Abby for a second and then, still ashamed, stared down at the floor. I'd never felt as guilty as I did now for leading her on this whole time, but now I had to tell the truth. Not just to her, but to myself. And it hurt just to say it. "I can't stop loving her."

"Don't be sorry," Abby told me, and then, slowly and thoughtfully, inched to sit on the edge of the bed. "I have a confession to make, and I really hope you can forgive me." I looked up at her curiously to find that the fear was clear in her bright hazel eyes. "Camille's still in love with you," she admitted. "She doesn't know he made you break up with her."

"What?" I said mindlessly as I tried to process what Abby was saying. How could Camille not know? "What do you mean? How do you know that?"

She couldn't even look me in the eyes anymore. "It's all she ever thinks about, and your stories don't match up. You think she just couldn't forgive you for hurting her, but she thinks you really meant to break up with her. She thinks you don't love her."

"Oh my God." I was too shocked to hold myself up, and to keep my legs from failing I fell into the chair beside me. "This whole time, and with you, I just kept breaking her heart over and over again." I stood, and then, finding myself still weak, sat back down. "I'm such a bitch."

"No, Kyla." Abby got off the bed and knelt on the floor in front of me, taking my hands in hers. "Please don't blame yourself. If you're going to blame anyone, blame me. I knew you still loved her, I could just tell, and I kept it from you anyway."

"But why?" I glanced up, and for the first time I could see that even though she was trying to make things right, she was hurt I hadn't chosen her, and for that I could never be angry with her.

"When I knew you'd never love me?" she asked, finally pulling her eyes off the floor and locking onto mine. I nodded, and she gave a sad shrug. "You were worth the risk anyway."

"I'm so sorry," was all I could say. I could hardly think, didn't know what to think even if I could.

"Please, don't be sorry. I knew what I was doing." Abby stood as she spoke, and still holding onto my hands she tried to pull me out of the chair. "Come on, go see her. It's not fair of me to keep you any longer."

Finally stirred to action, I got an exciting spark of hope in my chest. I grabbed my cellphone from off the desk and yanked open the door. Once I had it open I stopped and turned back to Abby, who'd been following me out. "Thank you. You know you deserve so much more than I could ever give you, right?" She gave a disbelieving smile, but nodded anyway. I gave her a gentle peck on the cheek. "Thank you."

Then I was off. As I raced to the elevator I dialed Camille's number. It rang and rang, and as I got off the elevator it switched over to voicemail. I continued down the hall as I dialed again, banging on her door at the same time the phone was ringing. A sound caused me to stop knocking and press my ear to the door. I was able to hear the ringing of her phone coming from inside. Thinking she was sleeping, I hung up and pounded louder, calling her name. When she didn't stir from inside or come to the door I paused, wondering if maybe she'd gone out and forgot her phone.

I jogged the few doors to Will's room and knocked, hoping he was there, and sighed with relief when he opened the door. "Hey, did Camille get back yet?"

"Yeah, she got back about an hour ago," he nodded and glanced down the hall toward the blonde's room. "I don't think she was planning on leaving, she should be there."

For the first time the excitement faded, and a small pit began to form in my stomach. I made my way nervously back to Camille's room, hearing Will follow curiously behind me. "Camille!" I yelled this time and knocked loudly enough on the door that if she was sleeping there was no way she wouldn't be able to hear. Still, there was no answer.

Now, growing too worried for comfort, I grabbed the handle and gave it a hard twist, not caring if it broke. The metallic crunch freed the door, and it swung slowly open. As I strode in the cold night breeze blowing in from the wide-open window gave me the chills. I reached sideways and flipped on the light, and the scene inside sent a shiver down my spine. Camille's phone was on the desk right next to the jacket she always wore when she went out. The sheets had been pulled off the bed, and in some struggle thrown to the floor. The chair from the desk had been kicked over and the standing lamp lay broken on the ground. I put my hands to my head – all I could do to hold back sheer panic. This wasn't right. Something happened to Camille. Somebody took her.

"Holy shit," Will mumbled as he picked up a large syringe-like needle with black feathers coming out the end.

I strode over and looked at it as he held it between his fingers. "Is that a tranquilizer dart?" Before he could answer I brought my foot back, sending it flailing at the fallen chair as hard as I could. "Goddammit!" The pain in my toes screamed at me, but I didn't care. I was about to pick the chair up, and in my anger planned on throwing it out the open window, but the buzzing of Camille's cellphone stopped me. I grabbed it to see who it was, but the caller ID read an unfamiliar number. "Hello?"

"Camille?" the voice asked, recognizing that it wasn't Camille who'd answered. The male voice sounded as panicky as I felt, and he spoke fast. "Camille, it's Rook."

"Camille's gone," I told him, ready to give up and crawl under the desk. This couldn't be happening again. "They took her."

Through the phone I could hear the screeching of tires as the car Rook was in came to an abrupt stop. "Okay look, I just got to Camille's dorm building, are you nearby?" I choked 'yes' in a quiet whisper. "Get every werewolf you can down here now. We'll call the others on the way. And hurry."

Will pulled his head away from being close to mine since he'd been listening to the phone conversation. As he bolted out of the room to Lacey's I followed, dialing Abby's number in my own phone. "Lacey!" Will knocked on the young girl's door once, and when there was no answer he kicked it open.

"Kyla? What's wrong?" Abby answered her phone with the question, knowing that if I was calling her now there had to be something wrong.

The scene in this room was similar to Camille's. The window was wide open, an empty dart on the floor. "They took Camille and Lacey. Meet us downstairs right now."

She didn't even waste time with a response, just hung up. When Will and I got to the first floor she was already waiting for us, and each of us ran outside to where there was a guy with dark, curly brown hair practically pulled onto the sidewalk in a sporty white sedan. When he saw us he waved, hurrying us to get inside, which we wasted no time doing. Rook sped away from the school, pushing his small car to its limits.

Both Will and Abby pulled out their cell phones at the same time, and Rook looked back at them in the rearview mirror. "It's a warehouse. Two-eleven on Carver." Then he passed a glance over at me in the passenger seat. I was shaking my legs and tapping my hands on my knees in a frantic attempt to keep from losing my mind, and he said softly to all of us, "We may already be too late."

Abby was the first to get an answer on her phone. "Dad, the vampires made a move. We need everyone." She paused to listen. "Yes, as fast as you can. A warehouse near the office, two-eleven on Carver." Another pause. "See you in five."

As Will called Eli, Abby leaned forward to talk to Rook. "Hey, you got any weapons or something?"

Rook turned and pointed to a fold down part of the seat between Abby and Will. "It opens to the trunk."

She pulled down the center of the seat and felt around in the back, a second later pulling out a sword that she laid across her lap. At the sight of it I leaned forward, resting my woozy head on the dashboard. All of this was starting to make me feel sick. Why did it have to happen now? What if we really were too late?

I felt a hand rub my back, and I turned to see Abby trying to give a reassuring smile. "We'll get to her on time."

When I sat up I could see the warehouse coming into view, already two more cars outside of it. A group of older people that I assumed were from the council had two vampires on their knees outside.

"If we aren't too late," Rook started, slamming on his breaks and bringing the car to a stop right behind the other two, "Don't let them finish the spell." We all got out of the vehicle in a hurry and Rook popped open the trunk, pulling out a sword of his own before he rushed over to the other vampires.

"You know, I actually liked you, Rook," one of the vampires said, looking up at Rook with anger in his dark eyes.

"Who are you?" one of the older men, who looked like the leader and possibly Abby's father, asked Rook.

Rook ignored him and walked straight to the kneeling vampires. "Is that right?" he asked, acknowledging the vampire's statement. He scanned the area around him to make sure no one was too close, and then he swung the sword, bringing it clean through the vampire's neck. "I always thought you were a prick." He pointed the sword at the other vampire, who flinched at the movement. "Did they start yet?" The vampire just nodded, and without a moment's hesitation Rook dealt another deadly blow with the blade.

At the sound of another car behind us I turned to see a familiar SUV pulling up with all the other Pack members inside of it. They were bringing the vehicle to a stop when I heard a loud thud as Rook knocked open the doors with the sheer force of his palms, exposing the way inside. That was exactly where I wanted to be, inside, where I could find Camille. Everyone seemed to want the same thing, because they rushed into the warehouse at once behind Rook.

Even as chaos broke loose, and once-startled vampires came alive to assault the group that moved into the warehouse, I pushed my way through to the front. I moved carefully behind my allies, avoiding attacks from vampires so I could find who I was looking for. Then I saw them. The three large cages, circled around a podium with a glowing black orb on top of it. I scanned the wolves inside the cages, wondering why they weren't fighting to break out, but they were all unconscious. No doubt put to sleep with the same poison that had been in that trap. My eyes darted around frantically, locking onto a vampire standing on the far side of the warehouse. There were two others at his sides, guarding him, protecting him, and a third with a thick book in his hands.

When the vampire saw me watching him he glared at the one who held the book, and I heard him yell 'finish it.' I broke away from the chaotic tangle of my allies and vampires, starting for the leader at a sprint. Seeing me coming, the two that were guarding him ran forward to meet me. Nothing but fury guided me now, and when I got close enough I targeted one of the vampires. I leaned into my shoulder, and with force that surprised even me I knocked both of us to the ground. I didn't wait to scramble up. I wanted the one with the book, and I'd get him no matter the cost.

I made it to my feet, but as I stood the other vampire skillfully grabbed my arms and locked them behind my back. I struggled savagely, managing to get one of my arms free right as the man I'd knocked to the ground sent his fist flying at my face. It caught me in the cheekbone, and my head whipped to the side with the force of it. After the blow I let out an instinctive roar, and a large gold wolf burst out of my skin. In staggering shock the vampire let go of me, and I turned on my hind legs, catching his neck between my jaws and bringing my razor sharp teeth straight through with a violent crunch.

Before the other vampire had a chance to make a move I turned, baring my teeth at him with a furious snarl. He stared at me, feet frozen but still holding his ground. I had to charge him. I had to get to the one with the book before he finished. But as I shot a brief glance over the man holding the book was already closing it. My eyes darted back to the vampire in front of me, whose lips turned up in a sickening grin, and then to the orb in the middle of the cages.

The glass of the orb shattered with a resonant pop, and an incredible, dark light filled the entire warehouse. The light was most blinding in the center, just above the podium, as three flashes of it burst into the air and then formed a dazzling ball near the ceiling. Even though it burned my eyes to watch, I stared. What was that thing? There was only one reason now that the vampires could have needed three werewolves. There had been three streaks in that single ball that hovered, that sucked all the white light away and filled the warehouse with an ominous, black light.

I had to do something, and my only instinct was to try and catch it in my teeth, just as I'd done with the vampire. I crouched, preparing to launch myself toward the light, but as I did the ball separated. In the blink of an eye each streak shot into one of the unconscious wolves, and the black light was gone. In the same instant the streaks disappeared and the light was restored, I hit the floor.

For me, everything went black.

As soon as those frightening streams of energy were released, Abby's heart sank. Everyone stopped to watch, whether in terror or triumph, as the entire warehouse went film-negative dark. She wasn't even sure yet what they were, but whatever it was couldn't be good. Then, before she or anyone else could even make a move to do something, anything, the streams disappeared into the caged wolves. Out of the corner of her eye as she watched, she saw the gold wolf that Kyla had transformed into collapse to the floor. At first she feared the worst, but though there a vampire nearby, it hadn't touched her. Kyla had gone unconscious when that thing went inside Camille.

As the light returned to normal everyone picked up the slaughtering like it had never even stopped. Abby watched as the vampire near Kyla eyed the unconscious wolf suspiciously, then grinned and began moving forward to finish what he'd started earlier. *Oh, hell no,* Abby thought as she rushed over, kicking him away as he kneeled and took Kyla's wolfish head in his hands, preparing to snap her neck. He went rolling away with an angry snarl, but was on his feet quicker than Abby could blink. She held the sword Rook had given her in both hands, pointed defensively at the vampire that now turned on her.

There was one thing Abby really hated about vampires, especially in situations like this, and it was that she couldn't hear their thoughts. For some reason, maybe it was their undead-ness, their thoughts just didn't exist outside themselves. Which made it impossible to mentally predict this vampire's next move as he stood there, carefully watching Abby and the sword she was holding. He feigned to the left to see how closely she was paying attention, and when that put him just close enough to strike she nicked him in the arm with the weapon. Even though she'd taken out a vampire already, she was still shocked at how humanly delicate their flesh was, albeit the wound closed and disappeared almost instantly. But they weren't invincible, and that gave her confidence.

Again the vampire faked left, and once again Abby nicked him, in almost the exact same spot as the last time. Before the second wound disappeared he feigned right, and she smirked as she got him in the other arm. The smirk instantly disappeared though as she wondered why he hadn't attacked yet. Was he judging her speed? Gauging her skill? They both knew that without the sword she didn't stand a chance. He was faster, stronger, fiercer. As she watched, her body tense for action, he rushed her head on, pushing the sword out of the way with his palm so it wouldn't pierce straight through his torso.

His hands were so busy keeping the sword away that when he finally made a reach for Abby's head with his arms she ducked out of the way, swinging the blade as he continued past her. She heard a crunch as the weapon caught the back of his neck, severing the spinal chord as he fell to the ground with a thud. She'd seen how quickly they healed. So for good measure she strode to where he'd fallen and sent the sword clean through with a single swing. It still shocked her that they bled. Before this she'd never fought with a vampire, and she hadn't quite expected them to bleed. It almost made them seem too human for her comfort.

Abby made her way back to Kyla, picking up the large wolf's head and then setting it gently back down as she examined it for injuries. She carefully opened the wolf's eyes with her fingers, and the normally bright green iris was nearly invisible around the severely dilated pupil. She was still breathing, which was always a good sign, except that it was more like panting, every breath fast and shallow. Abby ran her fingers sadly through the golden fur. She didn't really understand why Kyla, who was usually a brunette, had blonde fur, but somehow it suited her.

A shrill, deafening metallic grating pulled Abby out of her thoughts, and her attention was torn to the cages. Two of the wolves, the black one and a smaller copper colored one, had ripped the solid steel doors clean off with just their teeth, and they now stood outside the cages, watching everything before them. Their stares were eerily blank and lifeless, glazed over in a stale white film. Tearing through the cages must have caused some kind of damage, because blood was dripping down each of their bared fangs. Not only were their blood stained teeth and menacing snarls enough to freeze Abby to the core, but every bit of long fur from the back of their massive heads to the tip of their tails was sticking straight up. Now Abby realized what this was, and why Rook had told them not to let the vampires finish the spell. It was possession.

Abby's eyes were forced off the wolves when she was grabbed from behind and thrown to the ground. A second later a female vampire was sitting on top of her, hands locked around her throat. She tried desperately to buck and throw the woman off, and then tried to pry the cold hands from her throat. When that didn't work she frantically searched the ground around her, eyeing the sword that lay too far for her to reach. She stretched for it anyway, and the vampire took a single hand off her throat just long enough to hit her in the face. The closed fist caught her in the nose, and she wasted precious air choking on the blood that flowed back into her throat. She desperately threw her fists now any way she could in an attempt to free herself, but her lungs were starting to burn too much to bear.

Then, as the tunnel vision started closing in on her, she felt herself freed. An enormous multicolored wolf grabbed hold of the vampire with its teeth, its jaw so massive that it covered the girl's entire neck and the lower part of her jaw. Then he ripped her off of Abby, violently tossing the lifeless body aside.

Abby bolted up into a sitting position. "Thanks," she choked to the wolf as she struggled to spit up blood and gasp for air at the same time.

In her stupor she glanced back toward the cages, but the wolves were gone, and there were two large holes in the side of the warehouse where she could see out into the dark night. She looked all around her, noticing the world had suddenly grown quiet. It appeared most of the vampires had bolted instead of fighting, which left the ones who'd remained terribly outnumbered by everyone who'd barged into the warehouse. They were lucky in that respect, because as Abby took everything in, it didn't appear they'd suffered any fatalities. Just like that and as quickly as it had begun, this part was over. But they weren't done yet. The two wolves had gotten away, and whatever they'd been possessed by did *not* look friendly. Then there was Kyla, and the dark brown wolf had to be Camille, both still unconscious, and for some reason the energy hadn't yet claimed her.

Abby scrambled up and rapidly made her way to the unopened cage. Her and Camille had never been on the best terms, but seeing her trapped, inanimate, it was too much. So she wrenched back the heavy bar that held it closed, and when she got the door open she grabbed the motionless wolf's front paws, struggling against its weight to pull it out.

"Abby, close that damn door! She could still wake up," her father shouted angrily, storming over when he noticed she was trying to pull Camille out.

She scoffed at him bitterly and continued to throw her weight back, gradually tugging the wolf out of the cage. She blamed him for this. When he finally came over and grabbed her shirt collar to pull her away she turned on him, fuming. "You think that cage is going to hold if she *does* wake up?" she yelled, pointing at the dented, tossed aside doors from the other two. "We have to save her before that thing possesses her."

She was about to continue pulling Camille out of the cage, but stopped when she realized everyone was watching her, even the five other werewolves. All except for Kyla, of course, who was still unconscious, just like Camille.

"No," her father said, picking up the sword she'd dropped on the ground not far away. "We have to kill her before it has the chance."

"Like hell you are!" Abby put her hands on his chest and shoved him back away from the wolf, and her protests were backed by five menacing snarls.

Her father turned on the werewolves, fury creasing his intimidating brow. "Would you rather we have to hunt her down like an animal?"

Each of the wolves inched forward, deepening their growls, their position on the matter perfectly clear. It made Abby start to panic. She had no doubt the Pack wouldn't hesitate to attack if it meant saving one of their own, and as much as she knew her dad was an asshole, she didn't want him to die.

"Lahni!" she shouted desperately at the psychic, who had been kneeling over Kyla for the last few minutes.

With a deep sigh, Lahni stood and made her way over, all eyes watching her. She then knelt over Camille, running her hands along the side of the wolf's face and through its thick brown fur. "It's the connection," she said softly, and then turning to Abby's father she spoke loud enough for him and the wolves to hear. "There may still be hope."

I was plummeting through a black abyss. I tried to scream, but I was falling too fast to get it out. Falling too fast to even breathe. There was a swirl of gold about me as I dropped through the incredible darkness, and I reached for it desperately. Then we landed, the gold thing and I. We hit the ground.

I awoke with a gasp, struggling for air as if I'd been under water for too long. But it felt like I was breathing in fire. This strange, foreign air stuck to the insides of my nose and throat and it burned, searing away at my lungs. I coughed, trying to rid it from inside of me, but every time I took in a breath to cough again it filled me even more.

"It'll fade," a familiar voice echoed to me through the darkness. I opened my eyes, finding that it was actually blindingly bright. "Doesn't get any easier to breathe, but it won't hurt so bad in a minute."

"Camille?" I squinted toward her and sat up. The blonde was about six feet away on the ground, knees pulled up to her chest as she watched me. "Where are we?" I heard my question quietly repeated to me through the continuing echo.

I looked around, it was painfully bright and white, but not the kind of white that produces colors. It was just blank light. I looked for the sun, or a moon, to tell me if it was night or day. Only there wasn't either one. The entire sky seemed illuminated by an invisible source, if I could even call it a sky. It was more of a vacant nothingness that surrounded everything, that *was* everything, except the ground we sat on. Everything else, the icy, dusty ground, the expanse of rocks and boulders that formed barren hills and immediately surrounded us on three sides, even Camille and I, everything else was shades of gray. Camille's blonde hair and her normally brilliant brown eyes were depressingly lacking in color.

There truly was nothing but rock, which must have been why our voices seemed to reverberate off of everything around us. Though there was no wind, and even the lack of any sign of weather, it was cold. It was like it was the nothingness that caused the temperature. I imagined just as it would be in space, where the only thing that made it freezing was the absence of heat. I shivered and pulled my own knees up to my chest. As I moved it caused a flurry around me, drawing my attention to the tiny particles that floated up from the ground – like dust, but more the shape of short, microscopic threads – and hung in the air. I took in a breath and watched some of the particles rush into me. They had to be the source of the incredible burning in my throat and lungs, which was finally starting to subside.

"I don't know," Camille answered softly. "The last thing I remember the vampires shot me with something, and I passed out as they were trying to drag me out the window. Then I woke up here."

"When did you wake up?" I asked, lazily scooting across the ground and closer to Camille. The second I started toward her she flinched and began backing away. "Why are you backing away from me?"

She looked me up and down, suspicion and worry in her now gray eyes. "Are you real?"

I furrowed my eyebrows, shocked at the question. *I feel real...* "What are you talking about? Of course I am." I began crawling forward again, and while Camille was stiff with tension, she remained in place. Now I began to worry. "What's wrong?"

"I woke up, and I was coughing from the burn," she told me, and I followed the girl's eyes to the small rocky hills across from us. "I heard a yell, and then a man came sprinting from over there. He was so thin, and dirty, and all he had on were these faded shorts, and even those were so thin I'm surprised they didn't fall apart. It was like he'd been here for so long he'd just gone crazy. He was furious, mad, and he attacked me. I think he was going to kill me. Then I heard a thud from somewhere. And you, I mean, the wolf you, it started tearing into him, and then he just... kind of... evaporated into the air. And you, the wolf, saved me, then it looked at me and it just ran off."

I simply stared at her, entirely unsure of what to make of anything she said. It sounded crazy. "What the hell," I mumbled to myself, and then glanced back up at Camille. "Do you think we're dreaming or something?" It sure felt like some kind of a nightmare to me.

She shrugged, and her body relaxed when she was sure I was real, or maybe that I wasn't going to attack her. After another moment of thought she shook her head. "It feels too real. When that guy attacked me, he hit me in the mouth, and I could taste the blood." She pulled down her bottom lip to show me where he'd hit her, and sure enough there was a small cut on the inside. "What's the last thing you remember?"

I had to try hard to think of what happened before I woke up here, it all seemed so distant now. "Rook brought us to the warehouse to try and save you. I was trying to get to this guy, he was holding some kind of spell book – Rook said we couldn't let him finish it. I was almost there but I didn't make it, and these three things, like lights, they just blasted into you guys, they went inside-"

"You guys?" Camille interrupted. "What do you mean you guys? Who else got taken?"

"You, and Nathan, and," I hesitated, knowing she wouldn't like what I had to say.

"Who else, Kyla?" she pressed, almost forcefully.

I looked at the ground and whispered quietly, "Lacey."

"Fuck!" Camille shouted, though I couldn't quite tell if she was angry, or scared, or worried. "Are they okay?" she demanded instantly.

"I don't know," I shrugged instantly and honestly. "The second that thing went into you I must have passed out or something, and then I woke up here with you."

She was quiet for a minute as she took everything in, her arms still wrapped around her knees. "You think the lights brought us here?"

I gave a combination of a nod and a shrug. "I guess, but I don't know why I'm here. It only went into you, I wasn't even close to you." We both thought about it for another minute as we stared at the particles in the air, and then my head shot up. "You don't think..."

Camille's gaze wandered up and into my eyes, staring as if she could read my mind. "The blood connection?" I nodded, and she thought about it quietly. "I guess it's possible."

"Possible?" I asked, and then scooted closer to her excitedly. "Think about it. If we can feel each other from twenty feet away, if you can feel my emotions like they're your own, who's to say when that thing dragged you here it didn't somehow bring me with you?"

Camille rubbed her temples harshly, giving a haggard sigh. "Then where do you think we are?"

At that I looked around. The sky, or lack thereof, the floating particles, the eerie echo, the lack of any other form of life, the complete lack of any kind of sign of Camille's attacker, if there was one, all of it was weird. "In your head? Maybe another planet? Or dimension? I don't know," I guessed, and Camille instantly chuckled at the absurdity of those ideas, but her laugh immediately subsided and her face grew grimly serious, like she was really considering it. "Right? Look around. This sure as hell isn't like any other place I've ever seen, and it's definitely not... Earth. It feels like the twilight zone out here. And it's not every day I can be a wolf and a human at the same time."

Before Camille could answer there was a loud yowl that cut through the cold air in a deafening screech, and echoed at us for a while after it ended. My eyes grew wide with fear, and Camille mirrored my look as she glanced around, body tensing again. "What the hell was that?" she asked. Whatever made the noise wailed again, and this time it sounded closer. "Should we hide?"

"Don't have to tell me twice," I said, and at the same time Camille and I both scrambled up, sprinting for the outcropping of rocks ahead of us.

The collection of large and poorly fitted together boulders formed extensive and inconsistent hills with big crevices in between each rock. As we reached it we dove into the least obvious space that was big enough to fit both of us, and slunk down as far as we could into the darkness. From starting up so quickly my heart was pounding and I was out of breath, but as much as it hurt to keep myself from getting the oxygen I needed, I slowed my breathing so I wasn't panting too loudly.

The screeching howl echoed again, and at the sound of it both of us crammed closer against the stone at our backs. The opening of the crevice we'd dove into had been just large enough for us to get through, and it dropped off inside like a pocket so that we had to stand in order to see out of our hiding place. I began to stand now, hesitantly at first, keeping to the shadows so that whatever light shone through the opening didn't give me away. Then I felt a tapping on my arm, and turned to face Camille, who was pointing at a hole in the top of the rocks behind us. Before I could give a silent protest she wormed her way through, gone a moment later in the shadow above.

I was about to risk calling out for her, afraid of being alone here for even a second, when her arms appeared from the darkness, waving me in. As I followed her through another wail sounded in the air. It was more muffled this time, now that we were deeper in the rocks, but it was definitely close. I explored the darkness around our new hiding place, finding it was a little bigger than our last, though not quite as deep since the most I could lift myself was into a crouching position. There was a small strip of light seeping through on the bottom of the rocks on the far right side of our cave, so I crawled to it and lay down on my stomach so I could see out.

Camille slunk over and lay by my side, peering out into the light as well. The strip appeared to cut through a thick boulder, because the light seeped in from an opening about four feet away. Through it we could see the ground on which we'd first awoken, and a small area around it almost to the hole we'd first entered the rocks through. The screeching sounded again, cut off by an exploding thud as something hit the ground like a meteor, causing a flurry of particles and chunks of dirt to go flying into the air.

I watched the fresh crater carefully, and almost scrambled back as the creature that made it came crawling out. The first thing I saw was the head. Its skin was pitch black and smoother than glass, like fine polished obsidian. Every accentuated line of that massive feline-like head looked razor sharp – from the steep edges and furious creases on the bridge of its nose, and the foot-long, flattened out ears that ended in a needlepoint, to the four perfectly white, hand-length fangs that protruded forward out of its mouth because they were just too long. Even though this monster of a thing had the structure for a nose, the bridge ended in a small horn as sharp looking as those fangs and that pointed straight up.

The creature's lack of a nose caused me to inhale quietly through my own, for the first time realizing why having one wasn't necessary. There were no smells. Not the musty aroma I expected in this frigidly dank place between the rocks. Not the stale dusty smell I'd have expected from the particles outside. Even Camille's scent, which was normally so fragrant and intoxicating, was nonexistent. *At least that could work to our advantage,* I thought as I continued to watch the thing, my heart pounding in terror.

It had a disproportionately long body, like some kind of weasel, though the shape of it was entirely feline, just like its frightening head. If it had any resemblance of a fur, it was that its glassy black skin grew out in long, porcupine-like spikes that at this moment laid flat against it, and like a mane stemmed all the way down the top of its back and down the backs of its legs. Near the bottom of every one of its four limbs, on the back above its half-claw, half-paw feet, it had a sort of dewclaw. Only, these were three inches long, and looked about as deadly as everything else on its body. The last thing to emerge was its tail. A thin, glassy whip the same length as its entire body, with those same narrow spikes along the underside of it, spread out into a lethal fan.

As soon as it was done climbing out of the crater it created the thing stretched its legs, and then crouched so low to the ground its belly nearly dragged. Despite the position, however, it moved at lightning speed. I watched as in less than a second it had dashed nearly ten feet. Then it moved again, and stopped. Like a lizard, its gestures were executed in a sporadic flash, and every time it stopped it looked around intensely, its eyes nothing but empty black pits in its massive skull. It made its way to the boulders, checking the crevices it could fit its head into, and peering into the ones it couldn't. The fourth cave it looked into had been the one Camille and I dove in, and I silently sighed with relief that Camille had found the opening to hide deeper, because if not we'd probably be dead.

As it searched, I noticed something happening not far away, near where we'd woken up. The tiny particles stirred, zipping through the air to a common spot. Soon, enough of the particles had collected there to make a solid wall that glowed at the presence of the monstrous thing. It had to be some kind of a gateway, and possibly the only way out of this place. Regardless, the creature continued on, gliding up the boulders and checking a couple more crevices before it slithered down and toward the door.

Its tail whipped through the air with a curious flick as it neared the portal in a cautiously crouched stalk. It studied the glow for a minute, looking hesitant at the sight of it, and then extended its muzzle toward it, gradually until it came into contact. The very moment the tip of the monster's snout met the portal there was a thunderous crack, and the thing's entire body lit up with an electric spark. It must have been painful, because the creature stumbled back in frantic convulsions. Once the electricity faded it faced the glow, digging its claws into the solid ground so furiously its long nails disappeared into the dirt, and then it let out a demented and violently deafening roar.

The wretched sound came to an abrupt stop as the creature suddenly looked off into the barren distance. It turned, slithered to the end of our dead-end gorge of boulders and stopped again, still staring off toward whatever it had heard or seen that we couldn't. Then, as quickly as it moved it rolled into a ball and exploded into the air, transformed into that same energetic light that I'd seen enter Camille, and disappeared into the luminescence of this strange world.

I lay there silently, too scared to even move, and Camille seemed to be feeling the same way. There was something more menacing in this world than the man who'd attacked Camille, and I'd never dreamed of anything more heinous looking in my most horrifying nightmares. Even though the creature was gone, I could still see the portal glowing bright, and it didn't look like it was going to fade. It also didn't look like we were going to be able to get through it, seeing as the creature couldn't either. What appeared to be our only way out might electrocute us if we even touched it.

We must have stayed quiet and still for another ten minutes before Camille whispered in a quivering voice, "Was that the thing that went inside me?"

"I don't know. I think." I got off my stomach now and sat against the wall beside us. "I never saw *that* thing though. When I saw it, it was just the light." I shuddered at picturing that beast crawling about, looking for us. It was evil, and it was terrifying.

Camille sat up without saying anything in return, and scooted back to sit at my side. When she backed up out of the tiny light that seeped through the rocks she disappeared into the darkness, and even though I could feel the girl next to me, I couldn't see her. After another minute I started to panic. "Can we get out of here? It's too freaky in the dark."

I heard her shift in the gloom, and got the feeling like she was watching me. "Can you not see anything?"

I felt something brush my nose, as she must have been waving a hand in front of my face. The way she asked the question made me feel like something was wrong. "No, can you?"

"Yeah." Her voice was strangely thoughtful, and a second later she shifted again. "Arm wrestle with me."

"What?" I asked in shocked protest.

She pulled on my arm, trying to get me to lie down. "Come on, just real quick."

With a sigh I lay down where she was directing me and stuck out my hand just to humor her. As she grabbed it and said 'go' I pushed, trying to pin her arm down.

"Are you really trying?" she asked, though her curiosity sounded mildly accusing.

"Yes," I grunted as I tried to throw some of my weight into it. "I'm really trying."

With that she easily shoved my hand down and let go. "I think it's because your other half ran off."

"The wolf?" I asked, sitting back up and leaning against the rock.

Camille moved, and a second later I felt the girl's shoulder as she sat next to me. "Yeah. When I was growing up we learned a little bit about different theories on being a werewolf. For a bitten werewolf like you the theory was that Changing caused a sort of split, like in your soul or something, whereas for born werewolves like me, the split doesn't exist."

"You think wherever we are it split up normal me and werewolf me?" I asked, and in the dinge I heard Camille 'mhm.' "Then I'm just a human again." Since being Changed, I'd never considered the 'what ifs' of if I could be human again or had never been Changed, but now that it was happening, I didn't like it. Then a thought hit me, and I started to panic. "Camille, I'm still out there." It was strange referring to the wolf as myself, but I didn't know what else to call it. "What if that thing kills me? What's going to happen to human me, if the wolf me dies?"

"Shit, I don't know." Camille sounded just as worried as I felt, and I heard her shifting toward the exit. "Come on, let's see if we can find you."

I followed her down into the first cave we'd been in, and then back up to the outside world. The monster that had clearly been searching for us earlier was nowhere in sight, and as we strode to the entrance of our inlet and scanned the flatlands around us, neither was the wolf. I looked back over my shoulder to the boulders, and then began climbing up to the very top. When I finally reached it I could see forever away, and I squinted into the brightness of everything around me, doing a three-sixty as I searched for myself.

"See anything?" Camille called from the ground below.

I could see everything, but none of what I was looking for. It was like looking over an ocean of barren nothingness, with scattered boulder formations like the one I was standing on now. Except, unlike peering out over the ocean, where the horizon cuts off how far you can see before your actual eyesight does, there was no horizon here. The world I could see was limitless, never-ending. It went so far that what I assumed were more hills of rocks looked like tiny specks, like shady stars in this vast, bright galaxy.

I started climbing back down as I answered, "No."

"I can't decide if that's good news or bad news." Camille offered a hand as I hopped to the ground from the last big boulder.

"Me either." I plopped down dejectedly and rested my back against the rocks. "But from up there you can see for thousands of miles, and I didn't see that beast anywhere. I think it's long gone." I'd been staring up at Camille as I spoke, and now, thinking of an idea, I stood up to meet her eye to eye. "I wonder if you can Phase." She just shrugged, not really getting that I was suggesting she do it. "Well, try it," I told her more obviously. She just stared at me unwillingly for a few seconds, and I figured she was being shy since it was just the two of us. "I won't look."

"It's not you," she told me, putting her hands on her hips and looking around suspiciously. "I don't want to be caught naked if that thing comes back."

"That thing's gone," I tried to reassure her, but she squinted at me disapprovingly. "What if there are other madmen out here, and we get attacked again? I'm just a human now. We need to know if you can protect us." She scowled at me for a minute, but it succeeded in getting her to cooperate.

"Fine," she whined, and then made a swirling motion with her finger. "Turn around."

I did as I was told and spun around so I had my back to her, waiting patiently for her to Phase, or not. A second after I turned, Camille's jacket draped over my shoulder, and I looked back at her with a raised eyebrow.

"Can you hold my stuff?" she asked with an innocent smile. "If we need to run I don't want my clothes left behind."

I nodded and pulled the jacket off my shoulder so I could drape it over my arms. A second later her socks fell over my shoulder and onto the jacket. Then another moment later her jeans, followed by her shirt. I'd just been holding everything absentmindedly until her bra dropped onto the pile of clothes in my arms. That's when my heart jumped, and when I was holding her underwear a second later the blood rushed to my cheeks at the varied feelings I was getting, particularly in between my legs.

Sure, I'd seen Camille naked plenty of times when we ran together, and I'd even admit to myself that I'd sneaked a not-so-innocent peek or two. Or three. But there was something about the way each article of clothing had successively fallen over my shoulder that was tantalizing. It caused me to scold myself for getting distracted. I didn't mind the inappropriate thoughts. In fact I rather liked them, even though I couldn't blame the lustful stirring on the animal, but now was the worst possible time to be thinking about anything other than getting out of this place.

A nudging on my elbow pulled me from my daydreaming, and I grinned when I turned and saw a dark wolf. "This is good news."

The wolf nodded, and then nudged me back around so that I had my back turned once again. "Thanks," Camille said a second later, reaching around me to grab her first item of clothing.

Christ, Kyla, hold it together, I cursed to myself as Camille reaching over my shoulder caused me to rouse again. I could only imagine how close to me her bare body had to be in order for her to be able to reach her clothes, and I got the sudden urge to hold them farther away, in hopes she'd brush against me. I couldn't do it though, and all too soon I was turning around to give back the jacket.

"What now?" she asked, and after she'd pulled her jacket back on she sat with her back against the rocks. I was about to answer when, as if somebody flipped a switch, the world around us went dark. The white sky turned black, and now the ground and the boulders glowed a pale gray – the only source of a small amount of light. Was this supposed to be night? "What, no sunset?" Camille asked sarcastically, as if in response to my thoughts.

"It's so weird," I whispered as I sat down beside her.

"Yeah," she nodded in agreement. "It would be pretty cool if it wasn't so fucking creepy here. What should we do now?"

With a shiver at the chill, I shrugged and pulled my knees up. "All we can do is wait."

Abby and the others had managed to pull both the blonde and brown wolves onto two of the cots they'd found lying around the warehouse. Now she stood there silently, glancing from the wolves to her father, and then back to the wolves.

"Can you get that thing out of her?" Abby asked her dad and pointed to Camille. He was the best warlock she knew. If anyone could save them, it was him.

He nodded, though it was clear on his face and by the way he was ranting profanities in his head that he didn't like it. "Maybe, but I need to know exactly what I'm dealing with." He cast a furious eye at the one and only prisoner they'd managed to keep alive, the vampire with the spell book. Before he began to question him though, he turned to Abby's mom. "Joann, take everyone back with you and start a search for the other two. Call me when you've found them. I'll stay here with Lahni and the wolves."

Abby glanced at her father curiously when she noticed she'd been left out of the instructions, and from his mind she gathered he knew he couldn't force her to leave. She watched as her mother simply nodded, and every one of the Council members followed her out in grave silence. As they left, Abby's eyes flicked over to Rook and the werewolves. Three of the wolves had remained that way, and now lay on the hard floor with their heads resting on their paws, watching with eyes full of worry. The other two, one Abby knew was Lacey's father, and a man with black hair, blue eyes, and a fierce looking scar on his face, had Changed back, and now sat nearby on the edge of another cot waiting, for something to happen.

The vampire had been placed in the metal cage out of which Abby had pulled Camille, and knowing trying to escape would be a death wish, he sat in it shivering and clinging to his book. Now Abby's father turned on him, glaring as he growled through his teeth, "Tell me everything. What did you summon?"

The vampire flinched under the warlock's hard stare. "Phantoms," he confessed instantly, and when he received a still cold, unsatisfied stare back he continued. "Soul-eating phantoms called Shadow Savages. They couldn't survive on our plane so we needed the werewolves for possession."

"Why hasn't this one woken up?" Abby's father asked sharply, pointing to Camille.

"I-I don't know," he admitted, and his voice quavered with fear. "When they entered the wolves they were supposed to take their souls somewhere – th-th-they have their own plane of existence – to kill them, that way the wolf's body would be empty. They could just take over. It must not have killed her yet."

Abby's heart sank at this information. What did that mean for the other two?

"And this other one?" Her father pointed to Kyla.

The vampire shrugged his still shaking shoulders. "I don't know, I swear. I've never seen anything like that."

"The other two, they're out there now, feeding?" Abby's father asked, and sighed angrily when the vampire nodded. "This shouldn't be the Council's priority," he mumbled to himself, thinking about all the humans the Phantoms could feed off of as he glanced down at the two wolves.

The comment was met with a deep growl from one of the Pack members, but he ignored it. Instead, he held his hand out to the vampire. "Give me the book, we're done with you." As the vampire handed the book through the bars of the cage there was the scraping sound of metal, and the dark-haired man with Lacey's father picked up a sword off the ground. "You're not killing him," Abby's father told him as he took a step toward the cage. "The Council is not an executioner."

"We're not a part of the Council," the man muttered with an angry stare.

"Sit down, wolf," Abby's father warned, his voice sharp and his tone purposeful, and she heard him mentally prepare an incantation in case he needed to counter an attack.

With a sad, dim look in his eyes, Eli reached up from his seat and grabbed the man's arm. "For Nathan," the man protested quietly. "And Lacey."

"Sit down, David," Eli whispered.

It was clear David didn't want to obey as his mouth set into an angry scowl, but he dropped the sword, which fell to the ground with a metallic clatter, and sat back down.

When Abby's father was certain David wasn't going to get up again he turned back to the vampire. "If the council hears about you *ever* going near a spell book again, you won't be this lucky." Then he turned toward the warehouse entrance to get things he needed from the car, calling back to Abby over his shoulder. "Abby, set him free."

She waited until he disappeared out the door, and then made her way over to the sword that David had dropped. She could feel everyone's eyes on her as she picked it up. They thought she was going to kill the vampire herself.

As she made her way over to the cage she reassured them, at the same time casting a warning to their prisoner, "It's just in case he tries anything." She undid the bar that kept the cage door shut, and followed the vampire with the tip of the blade as he began to crawl out. "The other wolves, they're gone?"

The vampire stood before her, and it was clear by the look on his face that he knew what she meant. They were gone. Dead. His nod filled Abby with a biting fury. Lacey, the fun, playful girl she'd known since Lacey first got into high school was gone, and this asshole killed her. Abby took a deep breath, clenching the fist of her free hand, and then hit him as hard as she could in the face. The vampire barely even flinched, though he was clearly surprised. It still made her feel a little better, and she would have hit him again if it hadn't felt like she'd punched a brick wall.

"You're lucky he's got rules. Now leave." She glared at him, and as he instantly took off toward one of the holes the Phantoms had made in the wall she shook out her hand. "Goddammit that hurt so good."

"Vampire," Eli called as the prisoner neared his exit. The vampire stopped at the hole and turned to look at him. "The warlock might have rules to follow, but we don't. And we never forget a face."

Without looking back the vampire bolted out into the dark night, and Abby sat down on the floor in between the two cots that held Kyla and Camille. When a disbelieving tear rolled down her cheek she instantly wiped it away. Everyone else was holding it together. She couldn't be the first to buckle. Though the fact that Lacey was gone had sunk in, she still didn't want to believe it. Even in her line of work, she'd never lost a friend before. She didn't know how to handle it, and she wished her father had let the werewolves get justice.

Abby looked up at the gold wolf, trying hard to hear some kind of thought. Usually if someone was sleeping she could still hear them and their dreams. Only, with Camille and Kyla, she got nothing but silence. Wherever their minds were was too far for her to find them.

One of the gold wolf's paws was dangling over the side of the cot, and she gave it a sad but playful swat. "I promise we'll get you both out."

I grabbed another small pebble from the ground and tossed it as far as I could. Then I watched as Camille did the same, only she threw it about three times as far. We'd been sitting near our boulder-hill for too long to count. If we went by the sky's changes from light to dark, which we considered day and night, we'd been sitting here for two days, not counting the first time we woke up. It certainly felt like two days, maybe even longer. Everything had been quiet since the first time we saw the monster. No sign of it, no sign of any madmen, and still no sign of getting out.

We repeated the process of throwing rocks, Camille's again going much farther than mine. "This isn't fair," I whined at my poor arm. "I like being a werewolf."

We'd been lucky enough to find my other half. Or, more accurately, it had found us. During my shift to sleep it came back, and when I woke I found it snuggling against Camille, who had her arm draped over it as she was keeping watch. She'd removed her arm rapidly when she realized I was awake, and I couldn't help but smirk at that, even as I thought about it now. In *both* of our waking hours the light gray wolf hovered close to Camille. Guess it really was me, though I have to admit it made me slightly jealous.

Camille just chuckled at my complaining, and pointed to a far off outcropping of boulders. "Bet I could hit that one way out there."

"Yeah right," I scoffed in disbelief. They were at least three football fields away.

She stood up with a pebble in hand, and after winding up she sent it flying. It sailed through the air for a while before it landed right on the collection of rocks she'd been aiming for. "Woo!" She jumped excitedly, and her shout echoed back at us.

"Your target was too big," I teased as she sat back down.

"Oh, whatever. Jealous much?" She laughed and instinctively draped her arm over the wolf that slept on the ground near her seat, but she instantly pulled it away when she remembered I could see her.

I watched her as she stared across our cold wasteland, absentmindedly tossing a pebble from hand to hand. Since things had quieted down and we'd been comfortable enough to even get bored, I'd been thinking about what Abby told me. I wanted nothing more than to tell Camille and set things straight. At first I held back because of our situation. Somehow it didn't seem like the right time. Now the time felt right, but I just didn't know what to say or how to begin.

"Camille?" I started hesitantly. If I kept dwelling on it I didn't know if I'd ever get it out. I waited patiently for her gaze to meet mine. "Why'd you kiss me? That night at the show."

She went completely frigid, and deliberately looked away. "Is now the best time?"

"When would be better? When we're dead?" I asked, intentionally glancing around at where we were.

"We're going to get out of here," she said quietly, still refusing to look at me.

I turned my body so I was facing her, letting her know that I really wanted to talk about it. "Don't avoid the question."

"To stop the Change," she offered with a shrug, blankly staring at the pebble in her hand.

I knew that much was true. I also knew Abby wouldn't lie to me about the whole thing being a misunderstanding, but I needed to hear the truth from Camille first. I needed to know she really still wanted me. "After that."

It took a minute for her to say something as she sat there thoughtfully, now distractedly playing with the wolf's fur. "It doesn't matter," she eventually answered with biting displeasure, "You have Abby."

I winced, but I knew I deserved it. I'd all but flaunted Abby in her face. She shifted under my gaze, and a second later, not being able to take it anymore, stood and leaned against the rock. Still I pressed, part of me needing to hear it from her before I put myself out there. "You're still not answering the question."

"I don't want to talk about it, Kyla," she said pointedly, finally looking at me with a decided spark in her eyes.

Again I flinched, but this time I grew mildly irritated. Why couldn't she say it? I was giving her the perfect opportunity. I felt like I was practically begging for her to admit it, but she wouldn't. "Jonathan made me break up with you."

Shocked, Camille blinked a few times, then licked her lips, and then stared for another minute. "What?"

"God, Camille, are you serious?" I threw my hands up, frustrated now that she really hadn't realized it. That I'd spent the last few months thinking the first and only girl I'd ever loved truly didn't want me anymore. "I never wanted to break up with you. He threatened to kill my family if I didn't make that call."

"You mean-" she stopped short, still in shock.

I waited for her to finish her sentence, but she didn't, so I finished it for her, "I still wanted you."

"Wanted," she repeated quietly to herself, and then looked at me. "Past tense?"

What did she mean past tense? Why would I even be bringing this up if I didn't still want her? My eyebrows furrowed in aggravation.

"No, not past tense." I wished I'd spoken a little softer, because I could see Camille cringe at how sharply I'd answered.

"Well, why didn't you say anything?" she asked defensively. Why wasn't this going the way I wanted it to?

"Why didn't I say anything? I thought it was obvious," I told her and stood, my own frustration building. "I thought you knew and you were just using the pain as an excuse not to be with me."

"If I didn't want to be with you I'd say it to your face," she growled, clearly offended. Then she paused, taking in a breath to calm herself. It didn't work, and when I didn't say anything she continued, "And why in the hell would you think it was obvious?"

"Couldn't you tell how I felt about you?" I raised my voice for the first time out of pure desperation, and now the wolf, which had been watching us from the ground, gave a soft growl. I pointed a finger at it and glared. "You're supposed to be with me on this."

Camille ignored the exchange and raised her voice a little now too, getting increasingly disgruntled. "Yeah, sure, I could tell, for a whole *month*," she said sarcastically. "What was I supposed to think after so little time? That you wanted to be with me forever? I mean, I wished, but I was a fucking werewolf for Christ's sake! It was obvious I was going to get you hurt, and I did. I almost got you killed! I thought you'd learned what was good for you. And I'm a girl! You practically said it on the phone that night that you weren't gay. You could have been experimenting for all I knew!"

My jaw dropped. "Is that really what you think?" I said bitterly. "That I'd use you to experiment?" Even though my anger was growing, I told myself this was good. It certainly felt good, in a tortured, painful sort of way. We'd both been through hell the last few months. We had to get our frustration out. Right?

Camille looked around like she was taken aback, like she'd just been ranting and hadn't really meant to say that. She pinched the bridge of her nose, sighed, and then spoke softly. "No, I don't really think you'd do that." She was thoughtful for a second before speaking again.

"But I told you I loved you," she said accusingly, "And you looked terrified."

"I *was* terrified!" I hollered in exasperation. "Jesus, Camille. What do you want me to say? That I was afraid of getting attached to you? That I couldn't say it back because you came home from a fight that day wounded and hurt, and I was scared of losing you? I was terrified of my feelings being real!" I took a few shallow breaths, trying to calm my temper, trying to keep from yelling. "Is that what you need to hear?"

We were both silent for a minute while I stared at the ground, not really knowing now what to say. Then Camille reached out for my hand, and taking it she pulled me to her. "Come here. I'm sorry."

I let her pull me close, and even though her arms felt good wrapped around me, I was still upset, still angry. It took a moment of wracking my brain to figure out the cause. "No. Why?" Pushing away from her, I couldn't stop a tear from falling down my cheek. "How could you just stand there this whole time and watch me be with someone else? Why didn't you fight for me?"

"Fight for you?" Camille practically huffed, and now her brows furrowed with outrage. "Fight for you!" she shouted louder this time. "Kyla, I gave up everything for you!" she pushed off the rock to yell, pointing an irate finger at me. "I tried to help you control your Changes, even though every time I looked at you it felt like you were ripping my heart out all over again. When that didn't work I left my home, my family to go to Oregon with you! Even in Oregon I trained with you, every time, but you still didn't act like you wanted me. When you found Abby I was pissed, because nothing I did was enough for you and I had nothing else to sacrifice." She paused and finally took a breath so she could continue. "I've always been subtle and you know that! When have I ever tried to push you into anything? I was willing to let you go because I thought it would make you happy. But don't you dare say I just stood by, I wouldn't have given this much for anyone but you!"

I stood there with more tears flowing down my cheeks now as Camille leaned against the rock behind her, chest heaving from shouting. I wasn't crying because she yelled at me, I could handle that. I was crying because I was ashamed, because the more Camille and I got off our chests, the more I felt like this was my fault. She offered a hand, but I couldn't even look her in the eyes, let alone allow her to hold me again. I didn't deserve it.

"Kyla," she started as she dropped her hand, "I still don't know how you really feel about me. Do you even still want me?" I looked up into her eyes and nodded. "Tell me exactly how you feel."

I just stood there staring at her, but I still felt so ashamed it was hard to even do that.

"I need to hear the words," she told me, her voice slightly tainted by worry.

I opened my mouth, but after a second I shut it again. I could admit it to Abby. I could even admit it to myself. Why was it so hard for me to say it to Camille?

"You can't even say it." Her gaze lowered sadly. "Goddammit, Kyla, please."

Why was I so afraid? Maybe I couldn't handle her yelling at me as well as I thought. No, that wasn't it. It was because I was terrified again, and because in all Camille's yelling, her rants, her infuriation, she hadn't said it either.

"I need you to say it." Her voice was rising again as she pulled her back off the boulder, but not out of anger. Out of desperation. "Kyla, say it!" she finally yelled.

I flinched, and out of instinct I shouted right back, "You say it first!"

"I still love you!" she hollered without hesitating, and now she leaned back again, watching me, waiting to hear the same words.

Kyla, just say it. I was frozen. None of this was happening the way it was supposed to. This wasn't supposed to happen through a fight. I wasn't supposed to force the words out of Camille, and it shouldn't have to be forced out of me. This wasn't the passionate, heroic moment I thought it was going to be. Plus there was that fear again. That fear that if I said it then one of us wouldn't make it out of here, and *that* I would never be able to live with. After all this, I was still afraid of losing her. So I froze.

"You still can't even say it." Giving up, Camille peeled herself off the boulder and pushed past me toward the cave, and sensing a change, the wolf got up to follow.

Now I started to panic. We couldn't end it like this. Not after months of agony. Not after we'd been so close to finding each other again. "Kiss me," I begged frantically before she could disappear into the crevice.

She stopped walking and turned around to face me, but she still looked so angry that I was scared she wouldn't do it. Instead of waiting I shot forward, catching her lips with mine before she could back away. But it was as if she was ready for it, because I immediately felt her hand cup the side of my face with reception.

When her lips first touched mine they'd been hard and furious, but it only lasted a second before she gave in, just like she had at the show. I felt her free hand rest on my hip, while the one on my face slid down my chest and lightly across my stomach to settle on the other one. In response I wrapped my arms gently around her neck, pulling her even closer, and a moment later hers snaked completely around my waist. This was what I wanted. The moment I needed to be able to finally tell Camille the truth. I could feel it in the way she held me, in the way she kissed me, that she wanted me all along. This was how things were supposed to be between us.

I pulled away from her lips to nuzzle my face into the warmth of her neck, planting a soft peck on that smooth, bare skin before finally looking her in the eyes. "I love you. I always did love you, and I'll never stop." At the confession Camille's lips grazed my forehead, and after all the yelling and frustration the tenderness of it was too much. I buried my head back in the crook of her neck so she wouldn't see more tears. "I'm so sorry I hurt you."

"Please, don't cry," she begged as she wrapped her arms tight around me. "This was as much my fault as it was yours. Besides, I'd go through it again if I still get you in the end."

"I don't ever want to be without you again," I said, wiping away what I knew would be the final tear. "We both have to get out of here, okay?"

She nodded, and after wiping the dampness off my cheeks she dropped her hands. "I promise."

I was about to kiss her again, to start filling my insatiable longing with those wonderful lips, but then the monster's fierce yowling sounded in the distance. My eyes shot to the wolf, which was already scrambling up the rocks to its own hiding place, and I took that as my cue to hide as well. Grabbing Camille's hand I darted for the crevice, and when we got into it we crawled up deeper into the rocks. Laying down where we could see out into the light we both watched silently, hearts pounding in terror. We were so intent on waiting to catch a glimpse of the monster that we didn't notice the gateway glowing brighter and brighter until something came rolling out of it with a thud. It was a man, who now lay unconscious on the ground.

I looked from him to the billions of particles that formed the portal, and then over at Camille. "This could be our chance, we should run for it."

I assumed she'd agree, and began to scramble up, thinking of desperately making a break for the gateway, but she forcefully pulled me back down. "We don't even know if we can get through it," she said in a hurried whisper.

Before I could try and convince her it was worth a shot the earthy explosion as the monster hit the ground echoed through our hiding spot. Resuming my place beside her, I looked for it, but it must have landed behind the patch of rocks about a hundred yards from the entrance of our inlet, because I couldn't see it anywhere. Then the man started coughing, just like Camille and I had when we'd first woken up. He sat up, hacking so hard I heard him gag, and then a few seconds later he stopped to take in a series of calming breaths. We watched him stand up and glance around with a wild, terrified look in his eyes.

Panicked for the man, I took in a deep breath to yell and tell him to hide, but Camille's hand clamped down over my mouth. "Don't you dare," she murmured as commandingly as she could. "We're both getting out of here alive, remember?"

She waited for me to nod before removing her hand, and we both went back to watching helplessly. The man was stumbling forward, still looking around, dazed.

"Hello!" he yelled, and I practically smacked my forehead. *Shut up, you dumbass. Hide!* "Hello?" he yelled again.

Then I saw it. It glided from behind the rocks, watching the man silently. In its lizard-like movements it crept forward and stopped. It was out there in the open with nothing to hide behind, but its motions were so swift and precise that the man hadn't yet seen it. It was so smooth it practically slithered forward again, and again, and the third time the man finally saw it.

Shock and horror riddled his face, but he didn't waste a second in turning and making a break for the rocks that Camille and I were hiding in. Like lightning the thing was after him, and this time it didn't stop. Its limbs moved so fast it seemed to be gliding over the ground, never touching a single toe to it. The man slid under a crevice somewhere nearby not a second too soon, and I now watched with extreme curiosity, wondering what the creature, which was too big to fit into any of these holes, would do. The thing howled at him furiously, stood on its back legs to stretch its long body into the air, and then brought its front legs down on the rock with so much force that it pulverized the man's shelter.

Shattered pieces of rock and dust went flying everywhere, and in a single swipe of its paw the thing caught the man in the arm with its claws and threw him over its shoulder. The man landed with an 'oomph' on the ground near where he'd first woken up, and the thing turned on him before he could even catch his breath. It stood above him now, front feet planted on and claws buried in his chest. That spiked, whip-like tail twitched almost happily through the air. Now the man screamed, flailing his arms against the thing that pinned him to the ground. I watched in fright, expecting the monster to use those massive fangs to take a chunk out of the man's flesh.

Instead it just stood there, eyes locked onto him as he wailed. I stared in shock as moments later the man started to disintegrate, as if into thin air. *Maybe Camille really did see a madman.* His feet started to disappear first, dissolving from bottom to top into tiny particles like the ones in the air. Only, these particles didn't float away. They flowed into the monster's eyes, causing a dim glow. The more of the man that thing absorbed the brighter and brighter the holes in its skull got, until the man was completely gone. Then, as quickly as they'd brightened, the glow disappeared, and the thing gave a satisfied and sinister stretch of its neck.

Now the monster did the same thing as the first time we saw it. It made for the portal. This time, however, it didn't lumber over curiously. It dashed toward the thing, sprinting so hurriedly that it reached it in less than a second. The result was the same. That electric spark shot through it, and it stumbled back in writhing agony. Once it recovered it hollered irately, turning toward the nearest boulders and furiously smashing a handful of them to dust.

Taking its rage out on the rocks seemed to calm the creature down, but despite my hopes that it would now roll itself into a ball of energy and leave, the thing turned back to the hill and began to peer into each of the crevices. It was still looking for us. When it came to our hole Camille's grip tightened on my hand, causing me to realize for the first time that it was even being held. The thing lingered at our other hiding place, even stretching one of its long front limbs in it to feel for us. Then it moved on to the other ones, searching each one hastily. When it got to the last crevice at the end of the rock formation and hadn't found us in any of the places it looked, it angrily swiped at a boulder, its claws making four deep gashes in the rock. Then, just like that, it took off.

It was now that I finally started to put the pieces together and understand what was going on. Each time the portal opened it alerted the monster, that's how it'd known to come looking for Camille and I. Whatever the vampires had done, I was pretty sure they'd made Camille the link for it. It had to devour her just like it did that man, and then it'd be able to get out. That's why it kept looking for us.

When I was calmed enough to even speak I still kept my voice at a whisper. "Camille," I said, staring out into the light. "We are so screwed."

"I know," she agreed, pushing herself up and disappearing into the darkness.

Hearing her scoot to the entrance, I followed until we reached the outside, glad that once again the monster was long gone. My other half was already there, back from wherever it had found to hide and sitting outside our crevice, waiting. Camille made her way to the wolf and set her hand casually on top of its head, though I couldn't be sure whether she was trying to comfort it or herself. My eyes scanned the smashed up boulders, taking in the damage the creature was capable of. Once my gaze landed on the portal curiosity got the best of me, and I strode over.

From a distance the particles almost looked like a solid door-shaped wall with a slightly energetic glow. Up close, however, there was enough empty space throughout that I thought I might be able to stick my hand clear out the other side. That curious part of me wondered if it was only the monster that wasn't able to get through, and I wanted to test it for myself. Without considering the risks I lifted my arm, slowly extending my hand toward the portal.

"Don't touch it!" Camille shouted as my hand came within millimeters of the portal.

It startled me enough that I jumped back, and then I turned to give her a glare for scaring me. But once I turned I caught sight of a man crouched in the boulders behind her, looking like he was preparing to lunge at her. "Hey!" I yelled frantically, but it was too late.

The man let out a furious holler as he leapt from the rocks. He came crashing down on Camille's shoulders, sending them both tumbling across the dusty earth. I'd already sprung into action by the time they came to a stop, but so had the wolf. It reached them before I even got close, and it clamped down on the man's arm with its jaws, giving him a hard tug and tossing him easily off of Camille. Once the man landed on his back the wolf pounced, pinning him to the ground with its muzzle only inches from his face, snarling ferociously enough to frighten even me. The assailant let out a muttered cry that sounded like 'woah,' and defensively covering his face with his arms he mumbled other incoherencies so rapidly it sounded like another language.

Camille scrambled up from her spot on the ground and stormed over to the pair, with me close behind her. "Who are you?" she asked angrily, scowling down at the man under the wolf's massive paws.

"E-English," he stuttered in relief as he recognized our words. Then he stumbled over a few words of his own before he found the ones he was looking for. "Don't let it eat me!"

In response to his pleas the wolf growled again, and the man whimpered in terror. "Then answer the question," I commanded from my spot at Camille's side, reluctant to call off the wolf yet because we didn't know if this guy would try to attack again. "Who are you?"

His frightfully wide eyes locked onto me, and behind the paleness in them I could tell he was struggling again to find the words. "My name is... Greg."

I glanced over at Camille to see if I could tell whether or not she wanted to let him go. So far it didn't appear that she did. "Is this the guy that attacked you the other day?" I asked her. I knew she said he'd disappeared, but if disappearing didn't mean you were gone forever, that was important information.

She shook her head, but before she could say anything the man spoke again. "Please," he begged. "I heard yelling before. I mistook you for the insane ones."

"Are there a lot of other people here?" Camille said, furrowing her eyebrows curiously.

Greg gave the smallest shrug he could so he wouldn't upset the wolf. "A few. We hide in the rocks. Most of them have been here so long they've gone mad."

Camille and I both looked at each other while we considered his claims. He looked borderline insane himself, but he also looked terrified of the wolf, and I doubted he'd try anything as long as it was here defending us. Camille simply shrugged, and so I tapped the wolf's ribs with the back of my hand and motioned for it to get off of him. It sauntered to my side, still watching the man suspiciously, its lip curling every few seconds to show its long white fangs as a warning reminder. The man didn't try to get off the ground once we'd set him free; he just sat up and brushed himself off, visibly making an effort not to make eye contact with the wolf. Eventually his gaze wandered up to Camille and I, and I wasn't sure exactly where to go from here.

"Who are you?" he asked after a minute of us staring at him. We both told him our names, and he smiled amicably, growing more comfortable as he decided we weren't an immediate threat to him. "Pleasure to meet someone sane that hasn't been devoured by those dreadful creatures." His speaking seemed to be improving the more he said. Judging by the tattered look of his clothing it must have been a long time since he'd had to speak to anyone, maybe it took an effort to recall language.

I was a little surprised to hear him say 'creatures' in the plural, but it made sense seeing as there'd been three streams of light that came out of the orb. "Three of them, right?" I clarified.

Greg nodded, glancing wearily toward the entrance of our caved inlet. "Although I haven't seen two of them recently."

From that I thought I was putting it all together. Why the vampires took three werewolves, and what happened to Lacey and Nathan. They'd been brought here too, and if that sinking feeling in my gut was accurate, they'd been devoured and the other two creatures had escaped through a portal. All the last one needed to do was find Camille, and it

would be able to get out too. I just didn't know what the vampires wanted these horrifying beasts for.

Camille shoved her hands into the pockets of her jacket. She had a
worried look on her face like she was figuring it all out too. "How'd you
get here? And when?"

"Well, I can't say when I got here," Greg started as he finally
pushed himself off the ground. He brushed the dust off his pants and
then set his hands against his thighs, staring blankly around like it was
difficult for him to recall what happened. "I'm pretty sure I was walking
home one night. Yeah, and there were a man and a woman. They were
creepy looking, and they knocked me out and took me somewhere."

"The vampire kidnappings," Camille whispered to me, and I nodded
in agreement.

Greg's eyes widened at that. "Vampires?" After a thoughtful pause
he looked away. "Vampires," he repeated to himself, as if it made more
sense. "When I woke up they were saying some weird stuff. Before I
ended up here I'd think I was crazy, but I'm pretty sure it was magic."

Trying to piece together Greg's story, I furrowed my eyebrows and
glanced over at Camille. "You think they were testing the spell on humans first?"

"Maybe," she shrugged, and then looked at Greg. "Can you tell us
anything else you remember?"

"Feels like it's been decades since I got here," he said, tensing his
bottom lip apologetically, "I don't remember much at all, I'm sorry."
He was friendlier now that he was more at ease, and in a show of curiosity he extended a hand toward the wolf, studying it with awe. His fingers got within inches before the wolf snapped at him, and he pulled
away with a gasp. "What breed is this canine? It's the largest animal
I've ever seen." At his question he bent over to get eye level with the
wolf, and it growled at him, clearly irritated by his examination.

"Werewolf," I told him, waiting for him to lose a couple fingers as
he extended his hand toward it again.

At my answer his eyes widened and he stumbled back, mumbling franticly, "Are you crazy! Get it away from me!"

"It's perfectly safe," I said defensively, somewhat offended at his reaction to my other half.

He took a couple more panicked breaths before calming down a little, and then he glanced back and forth between the wolf and I. "Are you sure?"

"It won't hurt you," Camille told him with a chuckle. "I'm a werewolf too."

Despite his somewhat amusing reaction, I couldn't get it out of my mind that he said he'd felt like he'd been here for decades. "Greg, what year were you born?" I asked.

"Uh," he mumbled thoughtfully, "Seventy something," he answered, eyeing the wolf like he wanted to try touching it again.

"Nineteen seventy something?" I clarified, wondering how he couldn't remember a simple detail like the year he was born when he couldn't have been here that long. He nodded. "Something doesn't add up," I told Camille, quietly enough that Greg wouldn't hear.

She passed a stealthily suspicious glance toward him. "What?"

"I don't know," I answered, feeling a shiver travel up my spine. Though I couldn't quite put my finger on it I knew something wasn't right about this place. It made me uneasy, and all I could think was, *someone please get us out.*

25

Abby watched as her father hastily worked over Kyla, occasionally glancing into one of his own spell books and then back at the werewolf. His thoughts were racing so rapidly it was hard for her to figure out exactly what he was doing and what his reasoning was, but at least she knew he was really trying. It had only been about forty-five minutes since the Phantoms had entered the werewolves, but for Abby that was forty-five minutes too long. She just hoped the amount of time they were unconscious didn't make it harder to pull them out.

With a warlock as a father, she'd learned some of the basics of magic. One of the important things she'd learned about any kind of out of body experience was how crucial it was for the subject to be grounded, or spiritually attached to his or her physical body. According to her father, he had no way of knowing whether Kyla was grounded or not, so he was working to get her back first so there was no chance of her being stuck once he pulled Camille out.

Reaching into the black duffel bag he'd gotten from the car, her father pulled out the small silver bar with the different colored stones in it. The one that Harold had imagined giving to her. The golden wolf was lying on its side on the cot, and as her father set the bar on the side of Kyla's chest just below her front limb, Abby heard Eli give a mental protest. It wasn't just that the silver was touching Kyla, but it was also close to her heart, and he especially wasn't comfortable with that.

Eli went back and forth with it in his head for a minute before he finally said something. "Does that really need to be there?"

"Yes," Abby's father said without looking up as he buried his nose in his book once more. "And it needs to be as close to her heart as possible." Then he turned to face Eli with a serious expression, and about the most sympathetic one Abby had ever seen him give. "A little silver poisoning is worth it if we can get them out alive. I need it to help guide her back."

Abby heard Eli wish that her father would explain things as he was going along to help ease the werewolves' minds, but she knew her father far too well to think it would happen. When he was as focused as he was now, Eli was lucky to even get a response. She could understand the wolves' concerns. Her father had never been too friendly with them or willing to help, but now there were lives on the line, and she knew that nobody could be better or more trusted for the job. Even with all her worry about getting them out, she had tremendous faith in her father's abilities.

Another five minutes passed as Abby's father poured over his book, then he walked over to the center of the warehouse where the Phantoms had first been released. After searching for a minute he picked up a large chunk of the glass orb that had shattered. Stretching the piece of glass as high as he could get it above his body he closed his eyes and began to mutter under his breath. It was always times like these, when her father was working magic, that Abby was fascinated to hear his thoughts. It was such a flow of vision and emotion and language that she could never quite understand what he was actually saying, but his thoughts were so rhythmic, so tranquil that she wondered how her father, who was such an uptight and often angry man, managed such serenity.

As he held the piece of glass in his hands all the little shards that had scattered everywhere began to float silently into the air. It took a few minutes to gather what seemed to be the hundreds of tiny fragments that fit into the small orb, and each one hovered there until every single piece had been identified. Then each small bit of glass whizzed through the air to the one he was holding, and like a puzzle took its place until the whole orb had been put back together.

He examined it closely after he was done, and then walked back to the cots and handed Abby the now perfect sphere. "Hold this for me."

She took it from him and turned it over in her hands. It was so smooth and flawless it was as if it had never been broken. There wasn't a single scratch on it. Now her father moved back to Kyla, placing one hand over the silver bar on her chest and another on her head. Then he turned to the five werewolves, who had been standing anxiously nearby this whole time.

"You're not going to like this," he started in the calmest voice he could, "I need you guys to leave. I don't think the Phantom is connected to this one, but with the kind of connection these two have there's no knowing for sure. I fixed the orb, but if the Phantom comes back with her, I want to make sure it has nowhere but the orb to go."

Hesitantly Eli and David stood, followed by the three wolves that hadn't moved from their spots on the floor since all of this began.

As they made their way to the door, David stopped. "Hold on just a second." He jogged out the warehouse door, leaving the others behind to look after him curiously. A minute later he returned with a few articles of clothing in his hands and tossed them to Abby. "They might want those when they wake up."

With that the werewolves made their way out into the cold night. The way he'd said 'when' and not 'if' was mildly comforting – at least Abby wasn't the only one who was still hopeful. She set the clothes and the orb into a pile on the floor and stood across from her dad, whose mind was already starting to focus on the spell he'd need.

"You ready?" he asked her, giving the most reassuring smile he could.

She nodded. "Are you?"

With a sigh, he nodded as well. "Let's get them out of there."

I leaned my head against Camille's shoulder as we sat propped against the boulders, and watched as the girl fondly stroked the hand I'd placed in her lap. "Wouldn't it be nice if we could watch the sun rise?" I asked and looked out over the dark sky and glowing ground. The longer we spent in this strange world the harder it had been getting for us to sleep.

Camille nodded. "Any minute now." A few more seconds passed and then the wasteland brightened, as if in the blink of an eye. Startled by the sudden light the wolf, which had been sleeping on the opposite side of Camille, picked its head up and looked around suspiciously. When it realized that it wasn't in danger it dropped its head over Camille's thigh and drifted back to sleep.

Reminding myself that the wolf *was* me, I resisted the urge to give its head a jealous shove off of her, and instead poked it in the cheek. It gave a tired growl, but other than that it refused to even open an eye at me. When Camille chuckled at the exchange I pulled my head off of her shoulder to glare at her. "What are you laughing at?"

"It's so weird, you being jealous of yourself," she told me, still laughing. "It's like you have multiple personalities or something."

I just rolled my eyes at her, looking toward the open land to see if Greg was coming back yet. He'd walked off not long before this, just like he had plenty of times before, mumbling about needing to tend to his mother or some nonsense like that. I was practically one hundred percent sure there was nobody else here with him, but if he truly believed he'd been here for decades, then whatever insane thing he'd come up with for companionship had kept him sane enough that he hadn't turned into a madman. The more we talked to him the more excited he seemed to get that there were people around that hadn't been devoured yet. All he could talk about was how great it was that two of the creatures were gone, and all I could think about was where they were now and what kind of chaos we'd left behind.

Camille and I sat there for a few minutes, staring at the various collections of rocks and the lack of anything else besides that. This was the start of our fourth day here. Anytime that monster wasn't around it was so quiet, and if it weren't for Greg's occasional, half-crazy ramblings and a looming fear that the monster might come back, I'd be tempted to call it peaceful. We'd talked about what our options were. The first option we could see was waiting for someone back home to pull us out. The second was bringing the monster back and seeing if all three of us could get through the portal at the same time. If it *was* possible, we'd probably still have to fight the thing when we got wherever the gateway took us. Neither of those options sounded entirely appealing, but seeing as we'd promised that we were both going to get out of here alive, the first was slightly better.

"Do you feel hungry?" Camille asked, but she didn't wait for a response as she continued to think out loud. "I only feel hungry if I think about food. We've been here for four days. We should be starving... And really, really dehydrated."

"I don't know." I shrugged. "Maybe we don't need food or anything here. Greg's never mentioned eating." We sat there for another minute in dull silence, Camille still gently stroking my hand. "If it wasn't so creepy, and that thing wasn't trying to kill us, I wouldn't mind too much staying here. Just me and you."

Camille exhaled a huff of breath in a smiled agreement, and I mentally added if it wasn't so boring. More time passed as we just sat there, and starting to grow restless with lack of exercise, I stood. I paced in front of Camille and the wolf, back and forth with my hands in my pockets, kicking at pebbles on the ground. A nice, long, werewolf run sounded real nice right now. As I paced, stretching my legs with every stride, I noticed Camille's head following my movements. In a teasing manner my hips gained a sporty sway, and out of the corner of my eye I saw her lips turn up in a coy smile.

Without giving her a chance to glance away I shot her a look, raising an eyebrow curiously to let her know she'd been caught watching me. "Are you checking me out?"

She gave the most innocent smile I'd ever seen and shrugged. "I'm bored, what else am I supposed to do?" Her eyes followed me while I moved closer, still playfully swinging my hips. "Besides, your just so-" Then her breath caught in her throat when I seductively lowered myself to sit back in her lap. "Beautiful."

I cupped her face in my hands, kissing her in a long, soft peck and then pulling away to give a flirtatious smile as her hands slid roughly up my thighs. "Do I even want to know what's running through your head right now?" I could already see the thoughts in her eyes, and I could feel it in the unconscious grip she maintained over my jeans.

"Depends." She smirked, and straightened herself up to whisper suggestively in my ear, "Could you handle it?"

The way the warmth of her breath felt against my skin, the way her lips skimmed my ear, it made me shudder, but she didn't pull away to see my reaction after she whispered. Instead she kissed down from my ear, planting open-mouthed pecks along my neck and only stopping to suck on the muscle above my collarbone. The feel of those delicate lips and soft tongue against my skin caused me to flush with heat, and I wrapped my fingers through that long blonde hair, leaning in to the feel of her mouth so that I might get more. With my hands tangled in Camille's hair I led her head away from my shoulder and down along the edge of my low cut tank top.

She continued to caress my chest with her lips, every once in a while grazing the soft skin with her teeth, until it was too much for me. Call it unimaginable boredom, call it months of building tension, but whatever it was made every touch bewitching. She was beckoning me with each graceful kiss. So I pulled myself back just long enough for her to tilt her head up, and then I caught those stimulating lips with my own. I threw myself into it, and lost myself completely while her hands slid further up my thighs to my hips, then under my shirt and up to my waist. There was something about the way her hands felt on my bare skin that made the plaguing fears and stresses of the last few days melt away, until all I was left with was the underlying desire that had been torturing me for far too long. It commanded me to leave Camille's lips and kiss down her jaw line, and when I finally got to her neck I bit into the sensitive muscle, feeling the vibrations as she let out a satisfied moan.

As I sucked on that same spot where I'd bitten I felt nails drag gently down my back, leaving goose bumps in their trail and causing me to deepen my mouth's hold on Camille's neck. She titled her head back to encourage it, and my unruly lips began to lead me back up to her ear so I could kiss and nibble at her earlobe. One of the hands she'd settled on the small of my back moved around to the front, carefully sliding up my stomach and between my breasts before moving back down. I smirked against the flesh of her jaw, amused by the innocence of the fumble when I felt her hand hesitate as it brushed against the button of my jeans, but slowly, timidly, her other hand followed, and they set to work undoing it.

"I thought you didn't want to get caught naked if the monster came back," I teased, a tempting whisper in Camille's ear. "And what about Greg?"

"He won't be back for hours." Her hands never faltered again as they undid the button and moved to the zipper, but I could hear her give a quiet, amused chuckle. "And I'm not the one getting naked."

"That's no fun." I playfully pecked her on the cheek and rolled off, standing up to saunter tauntingly away. "You got to butter me up better than that."

I didn't get far, because Camille stood instantly, catching my hand and pulling me back into a kiss. Once my lips touched hers again she turned us around, and pushed me back against the rock so I was comfortably sitting at the rounded edge. While she maneuvered a single thigh between my legs one of her hands worked its way around the back of my neck, and the other barely grazed the skin of my chest, falling slowly down to my stomach and then once more working its way under my shirt. In the back of my mind, through the haze of desire for the way Camille felt and tasted, I vaguely remembered that she'd never done this before, and that this wasn't the time or the place. But I wasn't positive we'd ever get out of here, so I stood there pressed between the rock and her toned body, telling myself it was here and now, now or never. It wasn't hard to forget with the way she was kissing me. The way her finger was running delicately under my pant line. The way her thigh pressed even harder between my legs.

She broke away from the kiss, and all I could do was lean into her as she brought her mouth to my ear. "Buttered up now?" While she spoke, the hand she'd been playing underneath my pant line with slipped all the in, caressing low on my bare hip.

My only answer was to let out a needy whimper, and in response I could feel her hand move in the direction I wanted. But for every tiny bit it moved she stopped to suck at my neck, and the closer she got the more painfully aware I became of the aching desire. It got so strong, and Camille was going so agonizingly slow that I placed a hand on her elbow, willing her to close the distance.

The more I tried to get what I needed, the more she seemed to enjoy teasing me. Eventually I grabbed hold of her ear in my teeth, biting desperately hard as I begged, "Please."

In reply her hand slipped down, and I was in the process of letting out a gasp of surprise, and relief, and pleasure when a vicious gag rocked me from the inside out.

Shocked and frightened, Camille pulled back, looking at me worriedly as she tried in her playful way to make light of it. "Well, that wasn't the reaction I was hoping for."

I waved a hand in the air, trying to reassure her through the sudden sickness in my stomach. "No, it wasn't you. God, I want you so ba-" I was cut off by another dry heave, and I threw my hand over my mouth as if that would stop it from happening.

"What's wrong?" She took a concerned step forward but stopped, unsure of what to do.

"I don't know." A choking sound from nearby caught our attention, and we looked over to see the wolf suffering from the same sickness. It was standing on all fours with its head angled toward the ground, retching with nausea. "I don't feel right."

That moment all the tiny particles of the portal began to vibrate frenziedly, and a pale glow shone through as if from the very heart of it. Both Camille and I stared at it curiously, wondering what could be causing the change in behavior. I'd just started to wonder if somebody else was coming through when I doubled over with another straining heave. I'd barely straightened up when, without warning, I felt myself violently ripped off the ground. I was pulled through the air and toward the portal at such an alarming force and speed I didn't even have time to scream.

In the split second it took for me to feel settled I still wasn't over the shock, and I woke up in my wolf body, struggling to stand on my unexpected four limbs and falling over the side of a cot to the floor. The instant I hit the ground I sprang back up, looking around wide-eyed. I was back in the warehouse. Nobody was fighting anymore. In fact there was hardly anyone around at all. Abby was holding her hands out with the palms toward me, and she kept saying my name over and over again soothingly.

"Kyla, it's okay. We got you out. You're safe," she told me, and then reached down on the opposite side of the cot, pulling up a pair of clothes for me. "Here."

I Phased without thinking twice, and grabbed the clothes that Abby was handing me. "Are you getting Camille out?"

Her face colored red at the sight of my naked body, and she turned away shyly to face her father, who'd also looked away. "My dad's going to pull her out right now."

Mentally apologizing so I knew Abby could hear, I began to pull on the clothes. "What the hell?" I'd lifted my arm to put on the shirt only to experience a searing pain below my armpit. I craned my neck to search for the source – a rectangular shaped, severely blistered burn in my skin. At the sight of it I heaved again, and this time I had to run a few feet away as something actually came up.

"Silver poisoning." Abby's father watched me carefully as I came back over, and gestured to the cot I'd fallen out of. "You should sit down."

"You opened the portal," I told him as I sat, ignoring anything but what would help to get Camille out faster. "She's probably got between five and fifteen minutes before the monster shows up."

Abby's father nodded and instantly began to prepare. He picked up the glass orb that the streams of energy had broken out of and placed it on the cot under Camille's chin. Then he picked up the silver bar that must have made the mark on my skin, and placed it in the same spot on Camille's wolfish body. I eyed the dark brown wolf, still unconscious in the cot next to mine. In the four days we'd been stuck in that godforsaken wasteland, they'd had to pull me out just as we'd found a way to entertain ourselves. Out of the corner of my eye I saw Abby's head shoot in my direction, and my cheeks colored as I remembered she could hear my thoughts.

But something else from it had caught her attention. "What are you talking about four days?" she asked, eyebrows furrowing in confusion. "You've only been unconscious for an hour."

Now her father's head shot up, and his wide eyes stared at me thoughtfully. "Time rift."

"You mean an hour here, is four days there?" It took a minute to sink it, but when it did I started to panic. I stood, running my hands stressfully through my hair. "You have to get her out of there! Now! That thing is going to be looking for her, she might not even make it a day by herself!" When Abby's father didn't start moving as rapidly as I'd have liked I was about to yell again, but I felt suddenly weak.

Maybe it was the fact that Camille was stuck in there, alone and in danger. Maybe it was the fact that I had silver poisoning. Either way, I lay down on the cot next to Camille's and threw an arm over my eyes, shielding them from the bright light of the warehouse. I heard Abby's father shuffling around hurriedly and knew he was going to get her out as fast as he could. I just hoped with everything in me that it was fast enough.

A weight pressed the side of the cot as Abby sat down on the edge of it, and a moment later her hand landed gently on my stomach. "Hey, we'll get her out, okay?" I nodded as I pulled my arm away from my face, the light making me queasy again. "Are you okay? You look pale."

"I'm going to puke." I hastily pushed myself off the cot and ran to the same spot I'd relieved myself earlier to do it once more. Gripping my pained stomach I trudged back over, dropping myself onto the cot. "I hate silver."

Without saying anything Abby got up and walked off somewhere, but unwilling to pick up my head I couldn't tell where to. As I lay there I heard the warlock start mumbling, and for that I forced myself to sit up and watch. He had one hand over the silver bar and the other on the wolf's head. His own head was slumped over, and he was muttering too quietly and too rapidly for even me to hear.

"He's working as fast as he can," Abby reassured me as she sat down at my side with a first aid kit in her hands. "I don't know what will help with the queasiness, but there's some ointment for the burn."

I nodded and lifted my arm, allowing her to push the side of my shirt up to the wound. I held the garment in place with my other hand while she pulled some burn ointment out of the first aid kit. It was just a small foil package, but when she ripped it open and poured it onto my skin I grimaced at how cold it was.

"Sorry," she laughed apologetically. I tried to force a smile to let her know it was okay, but I could hardly take my eyes off the wolf. "I know it's tough, but tension only makes it harder for him to focus," Abby said as she spread the cream with her fingers and then tugged my shirt back down, trying to get my mind off of how little we could do. I nodded again and took a deep breath to calm myself. Knowing my attempt had been futile Abby took a different approach. "Four days, huh?" Another nod. "Did you get to work things out with Camille?"

"Yeah." Now I looked her in the eyes to give a grateful smile. "You were right. Thanks for telling me."

"The dynamic duo is back together again," she grinned, giving me a playful nudge.

"Dynamic duo?" I repeated with a chuckle. "Are you sure you want to talk about this?"

"Sure," she shrugged, though she didn't seem entirely positive. "It helped seeing both of you unconscious. I never really stood a chance." I raised an eyebrow at that, not sure I understood what she meant. "You guys are so destined to be together that your souls are connected," she explained. "How could I compete with that?" She stopped at hearing my thoughts, and spoke before I could express it. "Don't say you're sorry again. Forget about it. We can just be friends, okay?"

Before I could respond a vicious snarl and kick sent Abby's father flying backward, and the dark brown wolf sprung up, snapping its jaws wildly in every direction. My first thought was to get Abby out of the way so she wouldn't get bit, so I shoved her as far as I could. Next my eyes scanned Abby's father to make sure he wasn't injured – he appeared fine. Then I caught a glimpse of the orb. It was filled with that energy again, but it was teetering on the edge of the cot, about to fall off and shatter against the cement floor. Camille was still snapping ferociously, panicked and disoriented, catching everything she could in her teeth and sending it flying. I dove for the now-falling orb anyway, and right as I hit the ground I felt the wolf's teeth slash through the back of my shoulder.

More worried about the glass than I was about myself, I curled up in the fetal position to protect it against damage, and as I did I saw Abby take a step forward to come to my aid. "Don't move!" I warned her. Camille was still panicking, but when another tear against my skin never came I turned to look directly at her. "Camille! Calm down, it's me!"

The wolf snarled angrily at my shout and its ferocious gaze locked onto me. It took a few seconds before she seemed to recognize me, but when she did she hesitantly stopped growling. Her eyes darted from me, to Abby, to Abby's father, and then to the deep gash in my shoulder. She inched forward, nudged me apologetically with her nose and then buried her face against my neck. I ran my fingers tenderly through the fur up the wolf's chest and ended with my hand behind its head, the best I could manage in the way of embrace with the animal.

I let the wolf stay buried against me for a minute before gently pushing her away. "You're safe now. We have some clothes for you."

I hoisted myself off the ground and carefully handed the orb to Abby's father, who eyed the wolf suspiciously as if she'd attack again. Then I grabbed the extra pair of clothes off the floor and set them on the cot beside Camille so she could Phase and get dressed. By now the shock had worn off, and the gash on the back of my shoulder was beginning to sting dreadfully. I craned my neck to see behind me and get a look at it. The lacerations were deep, and blood had already soaked the side of my shirt.

"I don't suppose you have any spares?" I asked as I turned to show Abby my bloodstained top.

She winced at the sight of it and shrugged. "I don't know. David gave me the clothes. I can patch it up so it stops bleeding, and then you could ask him."

I nodded and pulled the shirt up my back and over my head, leaving it on my arms so I could cover my chest with it. Camille had Phased back now and was getting dressed, and I could see her eying us, especially Abby, suspiciously.

"Jesus, Kyla," Abby mumbled while she wiped the blood off my back with gauze, causing me to recoil as she neared the wound. "It stopped bleeding already, but you might need stitches. I most definitely cannot do stitches."

I eyed the first aid kit that she'd set on the floor beside us. "Is there any tape in there?" She nodded. "Could you just tape it closed and I'll get it taken care of later."

"Okay," she agreed unsurely, reaching into the box despite the concern on her face.

"Did you guys get everyone?" I asked, grimacing in pain as she pulled my wound closed. "All the vampires?"

"No," she answered, pressing the first piece of tape against my shoulder. "Most ran away, including the leader. We were too distracted to go after any of them."

I didn't get to respond because Camille finished getting dressed and came over, standing in front of me and awkwardly surveying the way Abby was touching me. "I'm really sorry. I didn't mean to hurt you."

I shrugged it off, but the way guilt riddled Camille's face I wished Abby would hurry so I could pull the girl into a hug. "It's alright. Why were you so freaked out?"

At my question Camille's eyes welled with tears. "It had me, Kyla. When you got out the portal opened and it came back. I hid, but it was so sick of looking for us that it just started smashing all the boulders. It found me. It had me, but Greg came back and tried to fight it off." She sniffled and wiped away a defiant tear. "It got him, and it had me too. If you guys didn't pull me out when you did..." Her voice broke off as tears started streaming down her face. They were fearful tears, relieved tears.

I checked behind me as I felt Abby stop touching my back, and when she nodded that she was done I pulled my shirt back on and rushed forward, pulling Camille into a hug. Her arms wrapped tight around my waist and I rubbed her back as comfortingly as I could, trying to make her feel at ease. It was over, and we'd *both* made it out, just like we promised.

Feeling Abby's presence depart, I glanced over my shoulder to see that she was making her way to the entrance of the warehouse. Even her father was swiftly packing up his occult supplies, and I could tell by their restlessness that this night wasn't over. I gave Camille's back another rub before pulling away. "It's okay, you're safe now." I tenderly wiped the tears off her cheeks, waiting for her to say something.

She raised her own hands to her face to removed the final drips of moisture and finish what I'd started, and then she looked at me, wonderfully brown eyes still watery. "Everything that happened in there was real, right?"

At first I wasn't sure exactly what she meant, then I realized that she wasn't asking about the length of time, or the desolation, or the monster. She was asking about us, and with the frightened, worried way she asked me, I couldn't help but giggle. "It was real," I assured her, resisting the powerful urge to tease, and when I pecked her on the cheek she grinned.

The warehouse door opened and Abby came back in, followed by Eli, David, Wes, Richard, and Will, all of who smiled happily when they saw that Camille and I were awake. For the first time, as the werewolves entered, I noticed there were two other people in the building. Rook had been leaning in a corner the whole time, and the psychic stood a few feet away from him. Both of them had been quiet and still, but now they made their way over to where everyone else was collecting.

"I'm so glad you're okay." Eli grabbed Camille in a sad hug, and in an odd show of affection he hugged me as well. "You too, Kyla."

The warlock waited just long enough for Eli to let me go, and then cleared his throat impatiently. "We still have two phantom-possessed werewolves on the loose."

Out of the corner of my eye I caught Abby glare at his insensitivity, but Eli nodded in agreement. "We'd appreciate it if the Council let us handle it. They *were* our own."

We all looked to the Council's director, who considered it for a moment before giving a half-nod. "You'll have to take myself and Lahni with you. You can't just kill a phantom."

At the semi-approval, Eli wasted no time in delegating. "Wes and Richard, you go with Camille and Kyla to get Nathan. David, Will, we'll go after," and he almost choked on the word, "Lacey."

"Wait," I stopped him, my tone careful so as not to disrespect his authority, and I made my way to Rook, whispering in the vampire's ear that way nobody else could hear. When I was done talking he nodded, and so I turned back to the rest of them. "I'd like Camille and I to go with Rook."

"Okay..." Eli said uncertainly, mirroring the confusion I could see on Camille's face. "Why?"

I took in a deep breath and met Camille's eyes with my own. "We're going after the son-of-a-bitch who started this whole thing."

27

I watched as half the Pack members and the psychic drove away from the warehouse to finish the nightmare that had began earlier tonight. A few of the Council members had worked some kind of locator spell and discovered the phantoms were heading for Portland, the nearest major city with an abundant supply of souls to feed on. When the car disappeared my eyes fell to the snow beneath my feet, and I tightened my grip on Kyla's hand. I couldn't have been more grateful for her volunteering us to go after the vampire who'd started this. If I'd had to go after one of my own kind I knew I wouldn't have been able to finish the job.

"You sure you guys don't want any help?" Abby asked, coming up to stand beside us.

"It's safer without you," I told her, my statement coming out harsher than I'd meant it to as I tried to adjust to a different dynamic than the jealousy of a strained acquaintance, but I gave the girl a grateful smile, and my thoughts were much gentler. The way I saw it, even though I'd never particularly liked Abby in the past, I owed her. Not only for helping come to my rescue, but also for getting Kyla back to me. It wasn't just that we'd be able to focus more if she wasn't around, but she really would be safer if she went with the others.

She nodded her understanding, gave Kyla a hug, and then, much to my surprise, gave me a hug too. "Be safe," she said, and then her lips set in a hard line as she clenched her jaw. "And uh, kill that no good vamp, will you?"

Both Kyla and I nodded readily. After that Abby left with her father and the rest of the Pack, leaving me behind with Kyla and Rook. Rook had agreed to help us find the vampire he identified as Benjamin and to see our task through to the end. I didn't quite understand it when I considered his motives for even siding with us in the first place. If anything I'd have thought he'd want to go after the Phantoms. Maybe he just felt like he owed it to us.

The first place he wanted us to look was the bar that the other werewolves and I had gone to find information. He said Benjamin was too arrogant to go into full-blown hiding, but he'd be paranoid enough to surround himself with other vampires.

A sudden burning heat at my back caused me to turn. Rook had materialized a can of lighter fluid, and apparently after squirting it throughout the warehouse he'd just touched a lighter to it.

"We should probably go now," he told us, calmly putting the lighter back into his pocket and making his way to his car.

We followed, and when I got into the passenger seat I turned to him curiously. "Won't there still be evidence?"

I was talking about bodies, vampire bodies. I hadn't paid much attention to whether or not there were any lying around when we left, and from what little I knew, flames didn't do the trick with normal corpses. But Rook shook his head. "They're already dust. Fire's for the rest of the evidence."

"What's the plan?" Kyla asked, leaning forward from the back seat.

"I'm almost positive Benjamin is at this bar in town. On any given night there're roughly five or six vampires in there, plus the owner. I don't know about you guys, but I'm not looking to make this any harder than it needs to be." He paused while both Kyla and I nodded our agreement. "I'll go in alone and see if I can draw him out. Hopefully it's as simple as that, and we can just take care of him right then and there. You guys should Change though. We're fast, and if he gets away I don't think you could keep up like this." As he finished he eyed me up and down so I'd know by 'this' he meant human.

"You sure we won't draw attention?" I asked thoughtfully as I tried to picture what was around the bar. All I could remember was that it was dark.

"Yeah," he answered, and looked back at Kyla through the rearview mirror. "It's pretty dead around there. Lots of buildings, but they're all businesses and it's a Sunday night. Stick to the shadows just in case and I'm sure you'll be fine."

We drove the rest of the way to the bar in silence. The more I sat there, tensely waiting to arrive, the more and more the anticipation grew. I'd have liked to say that this wasn't about revenge. That Benjamin was dangerous, and we had to get rid of him because eventually he'd hurt more people. It was true, but even truer was that he'd almost killed Kyla and I, and he killed Nathan and Lacey. That alone was enough.

Finally we arrived at the bar, and Rook parked in the street to the side of it instead of the parking lot so no one would see us coming. We got out and he leaned against the hood, waiting to make sure Kyla and I were ready before he tried to lure Benjamin out.

"After you guys Change, sneak around back and wait in that alley on the side so no one sees you." He peered toward the blacked-out windows of the building, trying to see in. "Don't worry about me if anything comes up, you just get Benjamin."

We both nodded, and before we began to pull off our clothing in preparation for the Change I turned to Kyla, placing my hands on the girl's shoulders and looking her seriously in the eye. "Are you sure you're ready for this? I've had training and years of play fighting. Are you sure you can handle it?"

She gave a bold, confident smile. "Yeah, I'm sure, and you'll be right here with me."

"I will," I agreed reassuringly, even though it was more to reassure myself. "Just promise me you won't bite off more than you can chew. He's not worth you getting hurt."

"I promise," she told me, leaning forward and kissing me to seal the vow.

I grinned that irrepressible grin I got every time she kissed me. After not having her for what felt like much too long, even though I knew it was really a short time, I was sure I'd never get over the feel of her lips. I tried to wipe the smile off my face and nodded, then took off the men's basketball shorts I was wearing and threw them into the back seat.

It took less than a minute for both of us to strip and Phase, and when we were done Rook glanced from us to the bar. "You guys ready?"

I huffed the affirmative, and when he began to stride toward the bar Kyla and I made our way around the back. I crouched on the side of the bar with my head out just enough that I could see when anyone came through the door. Kyla was right beside me, in the same position so she could see too. We heard Rook open the front door, and the second it closed behind him all chatter and what little clink of glasses there had been inside stopped. The interior of the bar fell dead silent, and if every vampire in there knew about Benjamin's plans, I could only assume Rook was highly unwelcome.

"Benjamin," I heard Rook say in greeting, and every muscle in my body tensed at just knowing he was inside.

"You shouldn't be here, friend." A familiar voice – the bartender? – said in response to Rook's greeting.

"That's fine, I'll leave," Rook told him calmly. "I'm just here to settle a little score with Benjamin. But you don't look so happy to see me, Benny." The sarcastic and teasing tone of Rook's voice was like music to my ears. I didn't know who Benjamin was, but I could only imagine the anger that kind of sarcasm could muster.

"Boys." At the sound of the unfamiliar voice there was the scraping of chairs, and three pairs of heavy footsteps sounded against the wood floor of the bar.

Then the front door opened, and I peeked around to see Rook being carried out by three men. "Come on, guys," Rook laughed fearlessly. "You know I don't want to have to hurt you."

I wasn't sure if he was just talking shit or if he really was that confident, but as I was about to lunge forward to come to his rescue a door opened and closed at the back of the bar. Then a light pair of footsteps picked up speed as they retreated from the scene. Turning on all fours I nipped Kyla in the neck to get her attention, and then took off toward the footsteps, hearing the other wolf right behind me. I barely saw our prey as he turned a corner to head down a different alley, but not before I caught a glimpse of his face. Based on what Rook had described earlier, that was definitely Benjamin.

I rounded the corner of the alley, nearly sliding out in the slippery snow as I did, and continued forward. As we sprinted after him he knocked over every trashcan he could, trying to create obstacles for us. He looked back, eyes wide with fear as we easily dodged or hurled over each hindrance, and then his face brightened up as he thought of an idea. When he turned down another alley he tried the first door he could, and when that didn't open with a single twist he moved to the next one. I came around the corner just in time to see him disappear into a building, slamming the door shut behind him.

So he thought we couldn't open doors? I skidded to a halt in front of the entrance and felt Kyla almost barrel into me from behind. I stood in front of it, backing up as far as I could in the fifteen-foot wide alley. Once I had my back against the building on the opposite side I used it to push off of, and with all the speed I could muster in that short distance sent myself vaulting toward the door. When I got close I jumped sideways into the air, crashing into the door with my shoulder, breaking it from its hinges and sending it flying open.

It slammed to the ground with a thunderous boom, and then everything went quiet. The way what little moonlight there was shone into the building and onto the white walls created a ghostly glow, and the soft wind whistled smoothly through the now empty doorway. It had opened up to large cubicle-filled office, with stairs directly to our right leading to the second floor. Impatient to catch him, Kyla began to tread upstairs, evoking an instant growl from me that let her know she wasn't going anywhere alone. She stopped, and with a displeased huff waited patiently for me to decide what to do.

I cropped my ears forward, listening closely for any type of sound. When none came I lifted my nose to the still air. There was definitely the faint scent that let me know a vampire had been here, but for some reason their scent never stuck to anything they touched. It just hovered, floating and migrating through the air like dust so you could never pinpoint a location. I crept carefully forward, leaning back on the pads of my feet so my nails wouldn't clip the hard ground as I walked, and kept my ears alert for any sound. Still, all I could hear was Kyla's quiet breathing, following close behind me.

We padded silently past the first set of opposite cubicles, peering under the computer desks as we went. It was a row of five on each side, and we searched every one, finding nothing. At the end we veered right to go down another identical stretch. There was only this and one more, and if we didn't find Benjamin here then he had to be upstairs. Kyla walked close to my side, our shoulders pressed together as we each checked the small offices. There was nothing in this row either. We turned down the next row, checking the first set, then the second and the third. Even the fourth set of cubicles was clear, but as I came perpendicular with the fifth cubicle there was a swift movement.

I turned my head at the flash of action and just in time for a computer keyboard to shatter across the side of my face instead of my nose, and I reared up, tumbling backwards from shock more than pain. I was scrambling to get up, but Kyla recovered from the surprise faster and let out a roaring growl as she took off to chase Benjamin, who'd disappeared through the cubicles. As she vanished there was a crash from the farthest corner of offices that sounded like a computer had been knocked to the floor. I forced myself off the ground and took off after Kyla, shaking away the bright spots in my eyes. As I rounded the corner I saw her, nose in a cubicle and unable to see Benjamin sneaking up behind her.

I let out a warning bark just a second too late, and watched Benjamin's foot connect hard with her ribs. He kicked hard enough to send her flying into the edge of the cubicle wall, and she fell to the floor with a winded yelp. Then he took off back through the cubicles. I galloped over, worriedly nudging the fallen wolf with my nose, and Kyla instantly pushed herself off the ground with an angry snarl. It took a few breaths and an impatient stretch for her to recover from the pain, and then we started forward, once again in search of the vampire.

It was only a few more seconds before we heard the light sound of footsteps running across the floor above us. At the noise we took off toward the stairs, only slowing when we came to the top. It was much like the lower floor – open space filled with cubicles. This time we tried a different approach, and sticking to the walls of the building we maneuvered around the outside of the room. As we crept through the narrow hall I could smell the stench of vanilla and decay getting stronger, though I couldn't tell exactly where it was coming from. We were nearing the last row of cubicles, and because of the strength of the smell I assumed that Benjamin was down this last row.

I passed the fourth section and was making my way past a metal storage cabinet, about to turn down the final row, when I felt Kyla collide with me, knocking me forward and out of the way just as the heavy metal cabinet at my side came crashing down. We rolled ahead, and the instant Benjamin started his escape from the scene I saw Kyla make a reach for his ankle, catching it between her teeth. She clamped down, bringing him to the ground with us as we all tumbled. She maintained her toothy hold on him as long as she could while she waited for me to scramble up, until his other foot connected hard with her chest, and the force of it made her let go.

Fearing for his life, Benjamin was up and running in the blink of eye, leaving a battered Kyla gasping for air. Determined as she was it only took her a second to recover, and then she impatiently nudged me forward because I'd waited for her instead of pursuing the vampire. As we started to chase after him yet again we heard the shattering of a window, and Benjamin jumped out the second story pane at the end of the hall. We tore through the office toward the sound, and without stopping I hurled myself out of it, hitting the ground on all fours as I continued running. I heard Kyla land with a thud behind me, followed by the quick patter of the golden wolf close behind.

Benjamin tried turning sharp corners and backtracking through certain alleys in attempts to lose us, but nothing worked. He had a good lead, but we were too determined for him to shake us. Beginning to get desperate, he started circling around through the back roads and alleys of the businesses for a main street. We followed him, unable to catch up for a good five minutes before he burst out of an alley and onto a lighted road in front of a high-end restaurant. I stopped at the edge of the darkness, where I was still shrouded in shadow, and snuck a look through the windows that wrapped all the way around to the sides of the restaurant. Benjamin went crashing through the front door, knocking waiters and customers out of the way as he worked his way to the kitchen in the rear.

I slouched back, turning around to make my way through the alley behind the restaurant where the kitchen opened up. We stood with our heads poking around the corner, watching the door with muscles wound tight in anticipation. About thirty seconds later Benjamin shot out and turned to make his way back to the main street. Not wanting to risk losing him I was about to lunge, but a slight glimmer in his hand caught my eye. It was a knife. I wasn't sure restaurants these days really used silver utensils, but judging by how nice the restaurant was I wasn't willing to risk it. I nudged Kyla and nodded toward his hand so she wouldn't make the same mistake I was about to, and when she nodded I crawled forward.

We stalked Benjamin all the way to the edge of the street, following him so silently he wasn't once aware we were behind him. We stayed in the alleys as he started backtracking along the road, staying in the light and close to the few restaurants and stores that were still open. Every once in a while we'd have to go around the back of a building in order to get to the other side where we could continue following him. After about three minutes of watching him from the dark he seemed to relax, like he thought he'd lost us.

Then his safety net came to an end. Across the next intersection he reached there were no more restaurants, bars, small shops, or even people. When he got to the curb he stared out into the darkness that may or may not be hiding the wolves from him, and then he took off running. Instantly we burst out of the dark behind him, in hot pursuit once again. The sound of our strides against the snow-covered street and our soft growls with each intake of breath alerted him to our presence. I was sure Benjamin would never tire of being chased, but he was going slower than he had before, daring us to catch up as the silver weapon he still held in his hand gave him confidence.

Eventually daring reached its peak, and Benjamin skidded to a halt, pivoting on his heels to face us. Startled, both Kyla and I came to an abrupt stop in front of him. Our ears lay flat against our heads, and we bared our teeth in menacing snarls as we stared him down, watching his every move. He held his weapon at the ready, waiting for one of us to attack so he could take a swipe. Each of us stayed frozen in the standoff for a full minute before Benjamin's lips curled up in a smile, as though he thought he'd won. He knew neither of us would risk a wound from that knife, and I hated the grin it allotted for.

My ears twitched at the distant sound of running footsteps, but I kept my focus on the vampire ahead of me. "I think we've reached a stalemate," Benjamin snickered. The smug twinkle in his eye made Kyla and I seethe, and our snarls grew in volume.

The running footsteps coming from an alley nearby continued to get closer until they slowed, and finally Rook appeared. "Give it up, Benjamin."

The sound of Rook's voice and him coming to stand beside us allowed me to relax, if only a little. However, his appearance had the opposite effect on our target. "You're a disgrace to our kind," Benjamin hissed, face twisting in hatred. "An alliance with mutts. And when I offered you the only thing we really need."

"There are other ways, you know that," Rook told him, calmly inching forward.

At Rook's movement Benjamin took a quick step back and glared. "We weren't created higher on the food chain to feed on beasts." When he could see that he wasn't successfully appealing to Rook's appetite, he tried appealing to his conscience. "It's more humane anyway. Feeding when they aren't aware of it, can't feel it."

I bristled at that, letting out a nasty snarl. Killing three werewolves to set loose insatiable phantoms isn't humane. Being trapped in a phantom's world until it eats your soul. Humane? The way that man got attacked by the Phantom, while Kyla and I were trapped, the fear in his eyes. That wasn't humane either.

"Benjamin," Rook sighed. "We can chase you all night until the sun comes up. Then what? We both know you can't stay in the light all day running."

Benjamin looked puzzled now, a sense of defeat clear in his eyes. He glanced to Kyla and I, both of us watching him more curiously than ever. Finally he nodded, and held the knife out for Rook to take. As I watched Rook take the silver weapon my heart started racing. Benjamin was no longer putting up a fight, and he wasn't armed. Sure, he wasn't innocent, but could I kill him now, in cold blood? I wanted justice more than anything, but I wanted it through a fight, not through murder.

Nudging Kyla, I motioned with my muzzle to an alley not far away, and as she began to lead Rook and Benjamin into it to finish the job I followed close behind, eyes more watchful than ever even though Benjamin seemed to be complying. With Rook's hand on his shoulder he followed Kyla to the alley, to his death. But as soon as they passed the opening his foot went up, and it came crashing down on the side of Kyla's back, sending her flying into the wall of an enclosing building. In a flash another knife fell from his jacket sleeve and he brought his arm up, preparing to send the point straight through the fallen wolf. Before my body had time to react Rook grabbed the arm that held the knife, and Benjamin turned with as much force as he could and sent his free hand straight into Rook's chest.

In order to shake loose Rook's grip as the vampire went tumbling backward, Benjamin had to let go of the knife, which fell to the cold ground with a deafening clatter. Finally free of Rook's hold Benjamin took off down the alley and around the corner of the building, and with a furious roar I began another pursuit. Only, this time Benjamin had pushed his luck, and he'd pushed me too far over the edge. He'd killed one of my best friends. He'd almost killed me. And now he'd tried to kill the one person I couldn't live without. He'd just filled me with the fury I needed to end him.

I took off so fast after the retreating vampire that as he rounded the corner I almost had the end of his coat. As I came around the corner myself I did so with such speed that I nearly crashed into the opposite wall. But as my speed sent me into the wall I hit it with my feet, and I used the momentum to spring forward and close the final distance between Benjamin and I. I ricocheted off the wall and flew at him. Landing on his back sent him straight to the ground, and though I knew I had to get my teeth around his neck to finish the job, having him pinned filled me with a drive to devastate.

The gut wrenching taste of that rotten, bitter vampire blood saturated my tongue as I began to rip and tear at the flesh of his back. I'd been angry and defensive before, but now I was filled with a fury like I'd never known. Benjamin yowled in pain, but I just kept tearing at him, for Nathan, for Lacey, for Kyla, and for turning me into this violent creature that needed to see him in ribbons. When he tried to raise an arm behind him, in desperation trying to get some hold on me, he had to pull his arm away as my fangs snapped at it fiercely.

Finally, when the horrid taste became enough to cut through my rage, and when there was almost nothing left of Benjamin's back to tear at, I wrapped my teeth around the back of his neck. With a single clench of my jaws I sent every one of my sharp teeth clean through, and a twist of my head severed Benjamin from his last glimpse of life and put him out of his misery. Then, blinking away the life that meant nothing to me, I released my hold on what semblance of a neck Benjamin had left. Not only was the blood soaked snow filled with an unbearable stench, but the taste was so foul now that before I could go and check on a battered Kyla I scooped mouthfuls of clean snow and crunched it between my teeth, desperately trying to rid my tongue of it. While I did that I noticed Benjamin's body shriveling up, until a few seconds later all that remained except for a putrid smelling dust was his clothing. After four spit out chunks of snow the taste had dissipated enough for me not to feel the need to gag, and I made my way back around the corner.

Kyla was standing, at full height the top of her head reached Rook's shoulder, and Rook was gently examining her, poking at the ribs Benjamin's foot had come down on. His fingers pressed one of the bones, causing Kyla to let out a pained whine, and he swiftly pulled away. I trudged over and stood in front of her to watch Rook. As I watched him continue his examination, her head stretched forward, and her wolfish tongue ran twice along the side of my head, just above my eyes where there was no vampire blood.

It was a strange feeling, such a canine display, since the most I'd ever shown affection while in wolf form was play fighting. Even in wolf form we acted almost human, communicating with our eyes and not-so-animalistic nods and huffs. I figured Kyla must have been acting on instinct alone, because the gold wolf looked away shyly afterwards, embarrassed that she'd executed it so candidly. With a toothy smirk I strolled forward, affectionately rubbing my head into the side of the wolf's neck, assaulting myself with the sweet scent that made me quick-ly forget about the horrid taste that still invaded my senses.

The smell of a purer blood wafted to my nose through Kyla's fur, and I followed it to find that the gash I'd made myself in her shoulder had reopened, and blood was now streaming down the side of her leg, staining her golden fur a dirty, burnt orange.

"I'm no doctor," Rook started as he took a step away from Kyla. "But I don't think he broke anything. Your friend was right though, you should probably get that shoulder stitched." Kyla nodded her under-standing, and Rook unconsciously mimicked the nod in thought. "The car's right down the street, I was driving it looking for you. Stay here and I'll be right back."

With that he took off jogging out the alley and around the corner, leaving Kyla and I alone in the quiet night. The sight of her seeping wound caused a flurry of guilt in the pit of my stomach. I let out an apologetic whine as I rubbed my head into her neck again, and then pressed my muzzle tenderly to the bloodstained limb. Once I touched her leg a fresh flow of blood ran down and over my nose, and I pulled away shamefully. At seeing the guilt in my eyes she playfully nipped at my jaw, then ran her long tongue along the side of my head again. When the only response the action received was the hint of a smile in my eyes, the honey colored wolf bowed enthusiastically, tail wagging in unison with the rest of its body.

I could tell even through the joyful movements that each one was strained and painful. While I appreciated the effort, I didn't want Kyla to be in any more agony, and fortunately Rook pulled up at the end of the alley a second later. He jumped out of the car with a familiar red box in his hands, and as we trotted over he place it on top of the trunk.

"Here, when you guys wanted to come I grabbed the first aid kit out of the warehouse." He eyed Kyla's shoulder and with a teasing smirk nodded toward it. "I don't want any blood in the car."

With that he grabbed his can of lighter fluid and made his way to the back alley, and a few seconds later a fiery light from that direction confirmed his actions. I was the first to Phase, and I opened the car door to grab the baggy men's clothes we'd put in the back seat. Before getting dressed I searched the first aid kit for alcohol pads, and went through four of them wiping away at the putrid blood that had spattered across my neck, chest, and arms. Since Kyla was trying to pull her clothes on with only her unbloodied arm, I still finished as the brunette had just pulled on her shorts.

Once she'd tugged on the lower garment, she used her clean hand to press the shirt over her chest and held her bloodstained limb out to me. "Can you help me? I don't want to get my clothes any dirtier."

I nodded and searched the first aid kit again, pulling out the last of the alcohol pads. "Are you cold?" I asked, eyeing Kyla's half-naked body as I used the pad to wipe away the blood that ran the length of her arm.

"No." She shook her head and then craned her neck behind her as much as possible so she could see me. "Please stop feeling guilty," she begged when she saw the look on my face. "It was an accident." My expression twisted and I was about to scoff, so she quickly added, "And it doesn't hurt even half as bad as it looks."

Not knowing how to respond, I just sighed. "It stopped bleeding." I copied what I'd seen Abby do earlier that night and draped tape over the wound after I pinched it shut with my fingers. For extra protection, I taped some gauze over it too. "Are you sore?"

"I will be tomorrow," she chuckled, probably just to ease the tension, even though I still wasn't particularly happy that *she* had taken most of the night's beating.

I dug through the first aid kit one more time and grabbed a two-pack of painkillers. "Take these." I handed the pills to Kyla, who downed them immediately regardless of how we both knew the medicine would burn off before she even felt the affects.

Rook had been leaning against the hood of his car, and when I finally felt that he was watching me, I looked up to confirm it. "You really did a number on him," he stated, talking about Benjamin. I just shrugged. "I didn't peg you as the bloodthirsty type."

"Desperate times," I defended, and though he watched me for another second with a knowing look in his eyes, he dropped it.

I didn't like that he was pointing it out. What I'd done to Benjamin was not only unmerited and cruel, but it wasn't like me. I'd killed before, but never did I enjoy it as much as I enjoyed making Benjamin suffer, and never so brutally. I shook the thoughts away. I didn't want to think about how this had changed me. Not yet at least.

Without another word all three of us got in the car, and after a relatively silent drive Rook dropped Kyla and I off at the dorms. We'd considered going to the Pack house, but neither of us were sure we were ready for the reality of tonight to fully sink in, and the mood at the house was sure to be dark and desolate. I could hardly shake the feeling myself, mostly because though I'd told Kyla to take it easy and she'd done her best to listen, she still got hurt the most. No matter what I did, no matter how hard I tried, Kyla was always in danger. *We* were always in danger.

As Kyla and I got into the elevator of the dorm building she gave an annoyed sigh. "Are you still upset because I got hurt?" she asked, and I'd almost forgotten she could feel my emotions again. When I nodded she turned and gently cupped my face. "Well, stop, okay? If anything you should be happy. You got Benjamin and I didn't get myself killed." She paused, and a second later a smirk brought out the dimple in her cheek. "And you weren't your normal clumsy self."

The elevator opened up to her floor, and as we got off I simply gave a smile of acknowledgement. I wasn't ready quite yet for joking. "I just want to shower and lay down." Even though I'd wiped it off, I could still smell vampire blood on myself, and then there was the smell of the blood that seeped through Kyla's bandages.

She sighed again, but this time it was more sympathetic, and she nodded in agreement. We both rinsed off in the dorm showers – grateful it was late enough there was nobody else around – and by the time we got back to her room I was weighed down by exhaustion. I barely managed to pull on clean clothes before I fell into bed, and I was already half asleep when Kyla slid in next to me. I felt the girl's head on my shoulder, and when I wrapped an arm around her she laid her own across my stomach. The only thing that brought me any comfort now was the warm body beside mine.

"Kyla," I said softly, and heard her hum in response. "I love you."

"I love you too." I felt her lips press delicately against the bottom of my jaw, and the gentle touch filled me with enough warmth that I was able to drift to sleep.

28

I tugged uncomfortably at the black skirt I was wearing and looked around at the sullen faces. Even though it was a bright day, and the sun reflected off the pure snow around us, it was so dark. Everyone's clothes, their faces, their moods – it was all so gloomy. Even the two caskets that were surrounded by all these despairing people were a shiny black wood. Normally when the Pack held a funeral it was just Pack members, and there was no ceremony, no speeches, and definitely no preacher. But Lacey had always been so outgoing that everyone loved her, and Nathan had his own friends too. For their sakes Eli had wanted to have a traditional human funeral.

Despite wanting it to be traditional, the whole thing had been skipped straight to the burial. There was no viewing. The human parts of Lacey and Nathan had been destroyed in that phantom world. When the possessed bodies were found and the phantoms taken out, there was nothing left but the wolf. It was entirely unnatural for a dead werewolf to remain canine, but I found it kind of poetic. In wolf form had always been when I felt the freest. Without the wolf, I wouldn't be who I was. Wouldn't be Camille. If I had the choice, I'd wish to remain in wolf form at death too, and to be buried as such to pay tribute to *that* part of my spirit, the part that always made me feel most alive.

My eyes drifted to the smaller of the two caskets. Lacey's casket. Never again would I look on that smiling face, or hear the laugh that had been such a large part of my childhood. Lacey was gone, and as I glanced up at my Alpha I could see that with Lacey had gone that last bit of Eli's soul. He'd recover and carry on for the sake of the Pack, but I would always see the loss and the emptiness in his eyes.

The pain on Eli's face and the pain I felt in my own chest caused a tear to break loose. When I lifted a hand to wipe it away I felt Kyla's arm slide around my waist and pull me close in a loving embrace. At the same time another person's hand fell on my shoulder, rubbed comfortingly across the top of my back, and then fell away. Another escaped tear ran down my cheek at the gentleness of my companions, and desperate for any kind of comfort I wrapped an arm around Kyla's waist to pull the girl closer, while my other hand reached for the one Abby had touched me with.

We stood like that while the preacher finished his speech, and then while the caskets were lowered into the ground. The whole time I fought, without success, the tears that stung my eyes, and I didn't let go of my companions until it was time to follow tradition and throw a handful of dirt over the caskets. Then, after saying his or her final good-byes, everyone left, everyone except me. When the area around me was empty I made my way to one of the chairs that had been set up, and sat while I watched two men begin to refill the ground with dirt.

A minute after I'd been sitting there, watching silently and fighting more tears, Kyla returned and sat at my side, putting an arm around my shoulders while the other hand went to my thigh.

"You say bye to Abby?" I asked, leaning my head against her shoulder. She just nodded and squeezed me a little tighter. After almost a minute of silence I felt I had to explain why I was still sitting there. "I'm scared they'll be lonely, if we leave just yet." I knew it was crazy, but sounding crazy was better than feeling guilty about leaving.

Kyla nodded again while her fingers ran mindlessly through my long blonde hair. "We can stay as long as you want to." Another few minutes of silence passed by. "You know they won't be lonely though. · They have each other."

Now I nodded, and we sat there for another twenty minutes in silence. Finally, when I felt we'd been there long enough, I stood and grabbed Kyla's hand. "Come here, I want to show you something."

I led her to a gravestone adjacent to where we'd just lay Lacey, and when I got there I pulled up my knee-length skirt a little and got on my knees in front of it. I could feel a slight dampness soaking the bare skin of my knees, but I didn't care. Neither did Kyla, who knelt down beside me.

I gave her a moment to read the name on the gravestone. Katie Might. "Lacey's mother?"

"Yeah," I confirmed, and ran my fingers through the grass in front of the polished stone. "I don't know about the afterlife, but I like to think they're together again." More tears stung in my eyes, but I took a deep breath to calm myself. "I know they're happy."

Kyla let me stay there for a few minutes until I was satisfied. I put my fingertips to my lips and then pressed them against the stone to say goodbye. When I stood, Kyla stood with me, and I felt the girl's strong arm wrap around my waist again as we started our walk to the jeep.

"I bet you're just dying to get out of Oregon," I said in an attempt at lightheartedness, ready to rid the feeling of despair. Ready now for this whole thing to be behind us.

Kyla was silent for a few moments, and I could tell she was contemplating something. "I've been doing a lot of thinking," she said eventually. "I think I want to stay."

"Okay," I shrugged. "We can stay until you feel like you have enough control."

"No," she said and stopped, turning and taking my hands in her own. "I mean I want to stay here, with the Pack." My eyebrows furrowed as I took in her words, and she must have worried I was getting upset, because the brunette added, "I know you hate fighting, but this whole thing with stopping the vampires and taking out Benjamin... I felt like I was actually making a difference. I felt like... I don't know, like this is what I'm meant to do." I could feel my expression shift to show the shock that I felt, but Kyla ignored it to continue explaining. "It's like, we've been given all this strength and power, and I want to use it for something other than running a few times a week."

I still didn't know what to say, but there was a stirring inside of me, and it was more than the passion that the blood connection allowed me to feel from Kyla. She added finally, "And I know you don't like it, and I know it'll be dangerous. So if you say 'no' I'll drop it, and I'll go back to California with you or wherever you want and we'll live our lives safe, and I'll never bring it up again."

I stood there with Kyla still holding my hands, looking up at me with those bright green eyes and waiting for an answer. This is what Benjamin changed inside of me. My perspective. Though I couldn't give *all* the credit to Benjamin. It had been changing in me for a while. Ever since the first time our lives had been threatened by the mutts in California. I'd always hated the violence that came with being a were-wolf. I never understood why the Pack was so black and white when it came to dealing with someone's life. But now I understood that it wasn't because brutality was our nature.

The violence was necessary. In our supernatural world, the law was survival of the fittest. I still wouldn't say I liked it, but now I understood it. The ferocity, the bloodshed, it was survival. It was protecting the ones I loved. And through protecting the ones I loved maybe I could save other lives too. Just like we'd prevented the Phantoms from feed-ing off of and killing unsuspecting humans.

"Okay," I answered with a consenting sigh.

Kyla's eyes widened in shock, like she wasn't sure she'd heard right. "Okay? Okay you'll think about it, or okay we'll stay?"

I sighed again, and despite the fact that I agreed with her, I just hoped this didn't turn out to be a bad decision. Though I knew as long as I had her, I could get through anything. "Okay, we'll stay."

Can't Get Enough?

Keep reading for a special preview of Zoe's highly anticipated romantic novel *Interference,* and don't forget to 'Like' Zoe's Facebook page @ www.facebook.com/Author.ZoeReed

Interference

In the small but competitive world of women's inline hockey, I'm a rising star. But Taylor Becks is still the best, even though she doesn't talk to anyone. She especially doesn't talk to me. We're rivals, and with our teams there's a history of rink-bound violence. So... how is it I'm falling in love with her?

Interference

Another glance at the tied up scoreboard told me there were only nine minutes left in the last period of the game. The other team had called timeout, and now everyone was just standing around the bench, waiting for the referees to blow the whistle and signal that the game was ready to start again. As I leaned with my elbows over the boards and stared down at the tiled rink below my borrowed skates, a movement on the left caught my eye, and a second later my best friend, Victoria, bumped me with her hip. Through the steel cage of her helmet she gave me a knowing smile, and then turned around to lean her back against the boards.

"So, J, what do you think?" she asked me as she pulled at her jersey, which read Cyclones on the front, and because of the sweat had begun to stick to her stomach.

I turned to mirror her position, and glanced out over the rink before answering, "I wish you'd told me this was a tournament."

Victoria and I had been friends since grade school. Normally her and some of the other girls that were hovering around the boards played scrimmage games at an ice rink nearby. She was the one who'd taught me to skate, and since she'd always played hockey, I'd always hung around and more often than not joined in on the pickup games. Even though they usually practiced at an ice rink, roller hockey was the first love for each of them. When Victoria had called me that morning telling me her team needed an extra player, I thought she'd meant for a scrimmage. Little did I know that her and the other players had rallied together a bunch of extra inline gear for me to sub in at this tournament.

"It's just a small tourney," she justified, blue eyes betraying her internal laughter as she absentmindedly slid the blade of her hockey stick across the floor.

I scoffed and rolled my eyes as both of our gazes drifted to the world outside the boards. There were three rinks at this outdoor facility, each one occupied by a tournament game. After already playing five games throughout the day, we'd made it to the championships, and this was the last women's game of the weekend. Still, the stands of each rink were filled, with more people standing along the outside to watch through the glass. Loud music could be heard filtering over the boards from the booth of a radio station that had showed up just for the occasion, and plenty more booths lined the walkways between rinks to occupy the hoards of people who weren't watching a game. It may have been a small tournament by Victoria's standards, but for the first real game I'd ever played, it was pretty damn big.

"Hey, Jordan." The coach tapped me on the shoulder, so I turned to look at him, eagerly awaiting any advice he could offer. "Don't look so nervous," he laughed. "You're doing good, I just need you to do one thing for me." I nodded, patiently waiting for the tip. "You're fast and you've got good hands, use it to get goals instead of penalties, okay?"

My cheeks colored red, but I laughed anyway. That was his advice? Sure, I'd played more than enough scrimmage games with the team to be able to hold my own in a high level tournament, but I didn't have the experience to know what kind of hits were considered dirty or not, especially since you couldn't check in roller hockey like you could in ice hockey. For that, I'd earned two penalties. One more and I'd get kicked out. So... maybe his advice *was* pretty sage.

One of the refs blew his whistle and made his way down the rink to the right faceoff circle near our goal. Along with the other players, I pushed myself off the boards and coasted to the circle, taking my place on the hash mark just outside it. One of the other team's forwards took position directly in front of me, practically placing the blade of her stick on top of mine. Before leaning over into position I scanned each of the players on the rink. Even after only two periods, I'd learned which players on the other team to look out for. Which ones were the goal scorers and which ones were most likely to take my head off and get away with it.

Another thing I'd had to adjust to after playing so many ice games with Victoria was the number of players on the rink in roller hockey. I'd always assumed five and a goalie was standard, but in these inline games I learned the number was reduced to four and a goalie. It came as a bit of a shock at first, but I couldn't say I minded. Less players on the rink meant less people to watch out for. It also meant there was more room to skate and pull off stunts that were harder to do during an ice game.

The referee pointed at the other team's goalie at the far end of the rink and, receiving a nod, looked to our goalie. When she nodded too he held the black puck over the faceoff circle, and a second later dropped it. The two players' sticks clashed in the center for only a moment before the puck went flying to one of the other team's defenders, who was waiting near the boards in the middle of the rink. The second she felt it hit her stick she received it and sent it across to the defender on the opposite side. I was already on my way to the second player that received the puck, and by the time she got it I was nearly three quarters of the way there.

She held the puck on her blade, cradling it near the boards with her eyes darting from me to the other players on her team, waiting either for someone to open up for a pass or for me to get there so she could try to skate around me. It was clear by the speed I'd already picked up that I was going to get to her first. *Goals, not penalties,* I reminded myself as I neared striking distance. The look on her face said she thought I was going to hit her, and her body tensed as I drew near. Instead, I stretched my stick across her body to hers, and hit the puck backwards as I flew by her.

I'd hit the puck hard enough to knock it over her stick, and I picked it up as I continued with it, alone, toward the other team's goalie. The goalie coasted forward, squaring up and making herself large in the net. I was at the top of the circles in front of the net now, so I brought my stick back with the puck and cruised left. The goalie followed my every move, shifting to the side with me. Finally, with a flick of my wrist I released the puck, but instead of sending it to the left side of the net like I'd been lined up to do, I angled my stick to shoot at the top right corner. My breath nearly caught in my throat as it sailed through the air, and then I sighed with disappointment as it hit the post with a loud ding, which deflected it up into the safety net above the boards.

With the puck hitting the net the referees had to blow the whistle, and when I heard the coach shout 'switch' each of us made our way back to the bench. Upon sitting, Victoria grabbed her water bottle and squirted it through the cage of her helmet and into her mouth before handing it over to me. I did the same, squirting it toward my face and not-so-accidently spilling some of it down the front of my jersey. At first the icy fluid stung as it hit my chest, but after I got over the initial shock I grinned at how cooling it was.

"That girl is pissing me off." One of the players I was familiar with, Holly, fell onto the bench next to me and pulled off her helmet, wiping her short black hair away from her forehead before sticking it back on.

"Which one?" I asked, leaning forward and glancing onto the other team's bench. Then I pulled a hand out of my glove and grabbed the ponytail of my long, straight blonde hair to throw it over my shoulder.

"The forward." She nodded discreetly toward the other team's offensive side of the bench. "Number eighteen."

Victoria leaned over from the other side of me and glared at Holly. "Holly, you get in a fight with her every other game. I swear to God if we lose because you get a penalty, I'll kick your ass."

I couldn't help but smirk. Between Victoria and I, she was definitely the hot head, but she was nothing compared to some of the other girls on the team. I'd never gone to watch any of their inline games before, but all too often Victoria would complain about how many fights would break out, especially between them and the team we were playing now, the Misconducts. And if I was counting correctly, Holly also had two penalties. One more and she was done.

"I'm going to kick *her* ass if I feel her stick clip my wheels again," Holly grumbled. "No joke, she's just waiting until the ref can't see so she can trip me."

It was obvious Victoria had something else lined up to say, but the whistle cut her off, and yelling 'switch,' the coach pushed us off the bench. This time I took the faceoff, which once again started down near our goal. I'd have been more comfortable if the puck ended up in the other team's zone more often, but all rivalry aside, they were good, and they controlled the play a majority of the time. The Misconducts forward took place directly in front of me, and as the ref skated over we lined up for the faceoff.

The ref threw the puck down between us, and instead of going in and battling with her for it, the second it hit the ground I knocked her stick out of the way with my own, leaving the target open for less than a second, which was more than enough for me to go back in and get it. With the puck on my blade I whizzed past her, skating up the boards while my other forward went up with me near the center of the rink. She had someone right behind her, but her stick was open so I shot her a pass. When it hit her tape she came to an abrupt stop, and unprepared for it the defender who'd been following skated right past her. Now open she sent the puck back to me, and I was getting close enough to the net that I had to start thinking about my shot.

There was just one more obstacle, a defender who'd been skating backwards ahead of me, just waiting for me to get closer so she could take a jab at the puck. Knowing I had to pull some kind of move to go around her, I did the one that I'd practiced tons of times during scrimmage games. As I neared her, I led with the puck and faked going around her to the right, but at the last second I brought the puck in between her stick and body over to the left, and pushed it forward with my backhand while my body continued right. The normal reaction to the move was for the defender to become momentarily flustered, giving me a chance to get by and score a goal. Only this defender didn't seem fazed. She followed my body, and when I tried to skate around her to the right, she stepped right in front of me, putting a glove on my chest so she could block my path.

I was going to try and backtrack to see if I could skate around her before the other team's second defender had a chance to pick up the puck, but I paused at the sound of a thunderous thud against the boards, followed by a familiar voice shouting, 'fucking bitch!' At the sound of a few whistles I turned to catch sight of the refs trying to separate a very angry Holly from number eighteen, and I instantly rushed over to lend a hand. I put my arm in front of Holly, who was still charging an equally pissed off forward, and tried to lead her away, while the girl who'd just stopped me from scoring tried to get her own teammate away from the fight.

When Holly realized she wasn't getting anywhere near the girl, she turned her rage to the referees. "Hey asshole, you didn't see her trip me? What fucking game are *you* watching?"

My head shot up at the sound of her talking back, and I wished she wasn't wearing a face cage so I could shove a hand over her mouth. The Misconducts' defender looked just as shocked, because her brown eyes met mine, and they shot me a hard look as if to say 'keep her in line'.

I tugged the side of my mouth into an apologetic half-smile at the defender, and pulled Holly harder toward the bench. "Dude, calm the hell down."

"Hey, hey, hey," the ref called after us, and I stopped to see what he wanted. He was pointing toward the exit of the rink. "She's out."

"Son-of-a-bitch," Holly growled loudly as she pulled away from my grasp and made her way to the exit. When she reached it she turned around to shout more parting words to the ref. "Get your goddamn eyes checked will you?"

Curious how the other team's defender had gotten her player to settle down so quickly I glanced over as I made my way back to my own bench, where everyone else had gathered. I wasn't able to catch her trick though, because the girl, whose jersey read 'Becks' with the number sixty-four on the back, was already leaned over the boards listening to her coach talk.

The second I got back to my own bench the same ref skated to the scorekeeper's box, which separated the benches of the two teams. "Number three," he called over the glass to the scorekeeper, "Two minutes, roughing. Two minutes, unsportsmanlike." Then he made his way to our coach. "I need someone to serve the penalty."

Every girl on my team groaned. Holly had earned a four-minute penalty, and by now there were less than four minutes left in the game. Seeing as I was the newest player, and no one else wanted to do it, I started for the penalty box. "I'll serve it."

The boxes sat next to each team's bench and were separated by glass, and when the game picked back up Victoria came over and pressed her mouth to the corner so she could talk to me. "They're going to score now. I'm going to have to kick Holly's ass."

"I'm not serving *your* penalty too," I teased, and then to make conversation I looked out into the bleachers. "Is Austin here now?" I scanned the full area outside the rink for Victoria's boyfriend, but I couldn't see him amid the crowd of people.

She nodded and followed my gaze to the area where she, too, had to search. "He got off work right before this game. He should be out there somewhere."

Another whistle accompanied by uproarious cheers from the crowd caused both Victoria and I's heads to turn, and then slump when we saw that the other team had scored, breaking the tie with only two minutes left in the game, and making the score four to three.

"Told you," Victoria said with a shake of her head. Her spirits picked up quickly though as she looked at me with a grin on her face. "So, coach says he wouldn't mind you playing for us from now on."

"Vic," I whined. It wasn't that I didn't like playing, it was actually even more fun than the scrimmage games, but almost every bit of gear I was wearing at the moment was borrowed, which meant in order to play I'd have to buy new stuff.

"J," she copied sternly, raising her eyebrows and challenging me to complain.

"I can't afford to buy all this gear."

"We're like… halfway sponsored." That earned a laugh on my part, and she glared. "No seriously, you'll get pants, jerseys, and gloves for free. I have some shin guards that I don't use anymore, and nobody really wears elbow pads. You already have a stick. All you need to get is skates and a helmet." Then she batted those big blue eyes at me and gave an innocent smile. "Please."

I was about to protest, knowing that skates were extremely expensive, but then I remembered the hockey rink Victoria worked at had a pro shop. "Only," I started with a sigh, "If you can get me a discount on gear."

The grin on her face grew bigger than I thought it possibly could, and as the buzzer for the end of the game went off I nearly thought she was going to come over the penalty box wall and hug me. Luckily she saved me the embarrassment, and we all made our way to the center of the rink to go down the line and shake hands with the players on the other team. We waited around on the rink while the announcer called all of our names and gave us all our second place, fake silver medals, and then had to wait a little more while he gave the gold medals to the other team. Then we were released to the locker room.

"Second place bitches!" one of the girls shouted excitedly as she ripped off her jersey and plopped onto one of the benches that lined the walls of the locker room.

Everyone laughed while another girl, Charlie, pulled a case of beer out of her hockey bag, not at all to my surprise since I'd already adjusted to their habit of drinking after scrimmage games. She held up a can and made shushing noises until she had everyone's attention. "First beer goes to Holly." She tossed the can across the room to Holly, who had been sitting in the locker room waiting since she'd gotten kicked out of the game. "For hit of the night, girl, that shit was epic!"

Charlie then proceeded to throw cans of beer to every player in the room, but stopped a throw short when she came to the last, and youngest, player. "Hey wait, you're not twenty-one. More for me."

I couldn't help but chuckle at Charlie's teasing. The youngest player on the team was only nineteen, but I'd seen the girl drink after scrimmage games plenty of times, and none of the other players, especially Charlie, seemed to mind. So the teen dropped her jaw, offended, and held out a hand for the beer. "Give me the beer, Charlie." Charlie held the can in front of her, eyes locked on the younger girl and smirk growing wider by the second as she slowly inched her finger toward the tab to open it. "Charlie!" the girl yelled, shout interrupted by a laugh.

The tip of Charlie's finger slid under the tab, but before she had a chance to pop it up the girl pounced on her, wrapping her arms around Charlie's neck and taking them both to the ground. As they wrestled over the beer that Charlie still held tight, the coach walked in, smacking his forehead with the palm of his hand as he took in the scene before him.

"If you guys practiced half as much as you partied," he started, a smile breaking his scowl, "We might actually take gold."

As if to deliberately ignore his comment, another girl named Linda pulled out her mp3 player and put on dance music as loud as the volume would go. At the sound, a few other girls, who by this time had their skates and jerseys off, got up and started dancing. The coach just rolled his eyes and leaned against the door of the locker room, patiently waiting to see if anyone would listen to him.

"Come on, coach." One of the girls grinned, trying to get him to dance with them.

He shook his head, so another girl chimed in. "Yeah, Nick, come on. You won silver too, you know. You should celebrate."

Again he rolled his eyes. "I'm too old for this." And with that he pushed open the door, laughing as he left us in the locker room.

The girl who'd started the music, Linda, shrugged indifferently as he left, and sitting back down she lowered the volume. "It's lady's night at The L. Who's down?"

Cheers went up from a majority of the girls in the room, and only two shook their heads. "It's twenty-one and up, jerk." The youngest player sipped on the beer she'd wrestled from Charlie and gave our teammate a playful glare.

The other girl who shook her head gave a shrug when Linda looked at her questioningly. "I've got church in the morning."

"Wow," Linda mumbled disappointedly, and then glanced over at Victoria and I. "Vic? Jordan? How about you?"

By this time I'd finished taking off all my gear, and was in the process of putting my short shorts back on when Linda invited us. I beamed as I finished tugging them and then my flannel shirt on, and gave an excited nod. "I'm in." Then as I pulled my hair back into a messy ponytail I gave Victoria a look that told her she had better say 'yes.'

Even though I shot her the look, I knew she liked dancing as much as I did, so it didn't take long for her to nod in agreement. "Yeah, sure, I'll go."

Victoria was ready to leave as I pulled on my tennis shoes, so I chugged the rest of the beer Charlie had given me and tossed it in the trash. Austin was outside the locker room waiting for us when we left, and he came over to give Victoria a kiss hello.

"What, no hug?" she joked as we continued to walk out to the parking lot.

He grabbed her hand to show her he loves her, but winced at the thought of a hug. "You're all sweaty."

"Wimp," Victoria chuckled. "Hey, we're going to The L."

"Okay." Austin shrugged, and then tossed his head to get his long brown hair out of his matching brown eyes. "You going too, Jordan?"

I adjusted the straps of the enormous hockey bag I had draped over my back as I nodded. The rest of the walk to the parking lot, I let Victoria and Austin have their moments. When we finally got there I opened the trunk of my little black sedan and threw the bag into it, then put my stick into the back seat. I was about to get in when Victoria, who had parked right in front of me, waved to get my attention.

"Hey," she called, already halfway in her car. "We'll follow you to your sister's and then all drive together in my car."

I raised an eyebrow, even though she probably couldn't see it under the dim of the streetlamp. "Okay, but why don't we just go straight to the club?"

"Because anytime you get drunk you end up going home with some random girl," she said, mouth turning up in a smirk. "At least this way, tomorrow I don't have to drive to pick you up *and* take you all the way back there to your car. I can just pick you up and take you home."

I was about to protest the change in pattern, but then I realized she was right. Instead, I gave a playfully flattered grin. "You're such a good friend."

"Yeah, yeah." She waved me off and finished getting into her car.

Following the plan, I drove the eight minutes to my sister's apartment and parked in my usual spot on the street. Part of me wished there was time to go upstairs for a quick shower, but I couldn't keep Victoria and Austin waiting, so giving up that wish I jumped into the back seat of her car. The ride was quiet for a few minutes, all except for the radio, which played quite loudly from the front seat, until Austin turned around to face me.

"Let me ask you something," he started, pulling at his seatbelt so he could turn all the way around. "What's your secret?" I chuckled at the glare Victoria shot him, but my dark blue eyes must have shown my confusion. "Pimp much?"

I laughed even harder now as Victoria's glare turned into a full-blown grimace, but Austin pretended not to notice. "I don't know." I shrugged. "Everybody loves a cute lesbian?"

"Yeah, that's true," Austin agreed dazedly, eyes glazing as if he was daydreaming. He smirked when Victoria caught his tone and pretended she was going to punch him in the arm. "Just kidding, babe. But seriously, I was just wondering, because you're single and you get laid more than I do." This time Victoria did hit him, and he mouthed the word 'ow' as he rubbed out his arm.

My mouth dropped, and my voice gained a teasingly surprised tone. "Vic, are you one of those girls that uses sex as leverage?"

"No," she growled quietly, though in the glare of the dashboard's lights I could see her cheeks tint to almost the same color as her auburn-red hair. I almost snorted with laughter as Austin turned just enough to nod his head at me, earning another glare from the girl beside him.

"Sorry bud, not everyone's as charming as me." I patted Austin comfortingly on the shoulder. Then I leaned forward as if to whisper in his ear, but spoke loud enough so Victoria could still hear. "But, here's a little tip. Vic's the back rub loving type. Quickest way into her pants," I told him with a wink. Now Victoria turned to scowl at me, but I was having too much fun embarrassing her to stop. "Seriously, she could hardly keep 'em on for me, and you know how straight she is."

He was laughing hard now, and he grinned excitedly as he pounded his fist against mine. "Thanks for the advice."

"Oh my God." Victoria covered her face with one of her hands, shaking her head in exasperation. "How about I just drop you two off at the club so you can pick up chicks together?"

Teasing even further, I shrugged and nodded, but Austin leaned over and pulled her head to roughly plant a kiss on her cheek. "You know I love you." Victoria grinned happily now that Austin wasn't picking on her, but she had grinned too soon. "Besides, what luck would I have at a gay club?"

I tried to stop a snicker, which only ended up coming out in a snort, and Victoria gave a defeated sigh. Deciding maybe it was time to lighten up I changed the subject. "You know what I want know?" Both her and Austin 'hm-ed' curiously. "How is it that at least half the girls on our team are gay?"

Victoria giggled and looked back at me through the rearview mirror. "That surprised you?" I nodded. "That's how it is for almost every team. Hockey attracts gaybos like you," she said sarcastically and stretched her arm back to poke me in the forehead.

With a giggle I shoved her hand away. We arrived at the club a few minutes later, and after waiting in line outside for about twenty minutes made it in. Since Austin agreed to be the designated driver, the first place Victoria and I hit was the bar. Then after finding a few of the girls from our team we danced for a couple hours. Going back to the bar every once in a while for another shot, it didn't take long until I had quite a bit more than a pleasant buzz going on. Eventually we split from the rest of the group, and after a little while longer I split from Victoria and Austin, but that didn't stop me from dancing and making the occasional trip back to the bar.

***

I woke the next morning feeling like I hadn't just woken up on my own, but was unable to figure out what exactly had caused me to stir. It wasn't the unfamiliar ceiling I was staring at now, or the silky green sheets that felt pleasantly and surprisingly cooling against my naked body. It could have been the mild hangover that materialized in the form of a pounding against my temples. I lay there for a minute, trying to figure out what it was. The feel of the sheets was inconsistent across my hips, and thinking that might have been it, I slid my hand beneath the covers until I reached skin, not mine. I carefully peeled back the covers to reveal a slender leg, draped delicately over me.

I remembered enough from the night before not to be shocked at finding myself with company, or in somebody else's house for that matter. It wasn't the leg that had woken me either, but it did catch my attention now. With my eyes I followed the smooth skin up to a feminine pair of hips, then a waist, a shoulder, to a gentle face half-covered by light brown hair. *She's cute*, I thought to myself, and almost jumped out of my skin at a vibrating beneath my back. *That's* what had woken me up! Trying not to wake the girl beside me, I reached my arm underneath me and pulled out my phone.

"**Wakey, wakey**." The text from Victoria flashed across the screen, and I unlocked the touch screen to find that she'd texted me three more times before I'd woken up.

I checked the time before texting her back. 8:30, a little too early if you ask me. "**Morning**," I responded, and then as smoothly as possible eased the leg off of me.

A light groan made me pause, but when the girl shifted herself away I sighed with relief and silently pushed myself off the bed. It took a minute to find my clothes amongst the scattered articles on the floor, but eventually I managed, and I was just pulling on my shorts when the phone vibrated in my hand.

"**Where you at? I'll come get you.**"

Tiptoeing out of the room I strolled down the short hall of the one-bedroom apartment to the kitchen and living room. Hoping to find what I was looking for, I made my way to the kitchen, eyes scanning every inch of the counter. A smile creased my lips when I glanced the pile of mail sitting neatly in the corner, and I hopped up to sit on the countertop as I picked up the first envelope. *So, your name is Kristen.* Below the brunette's name was the information I was looking for.

I unlocked my phone and pulled up my text messages. "**136 Shady Street. Huntington Beach.**"

After hitting send I hopped off the counter and patted myself down in order to check my pockets, and was happy to find that my wallet was still in my shorts and I didn't have to risk going back into the bedroom to get it. I was on my way out the door when my bare foot his a sneaker. *Oh shit, shoes.* That's what I was forgetting. The one I had stepped on was mine, so where was the other one? Knowing me I'd kicked them wildly any which direction the second I made it through the door. Under the coffee table? No. Back in the kitchen? No. Under the couch? Nope. Ah-hah! On *top* of the couch. I grabbed my shoe from off the back of the couch, vaguely wondering how I'd managed to get it up there in the first place, and sat down to pull it on.

As I hit the cushion my phone vibrated in my pocket, so I pulled it out to read Victoria's text. **"Thanks for picking somewhere close this time :P. GPS says be there in 5."**

Before getting up to leave I took a brief look around. The small apartment was nice enough. A flat screen TV hung on the wall opposite me, and directly below it was a small bookshelf with various pictures on it instead of books. The coffee table at my knees caught my attention. That had a book on it. I turned the book so that the title was facing me and read it. *Ethics of Medicine. So Kristin's pre med, not bad.* I pushed the book away from me with my index finger, scolding myself for even taking a curious peek. I wished I had the guts to stay for a cup of coffee, especially on those mornings I woke up with a pounding head, but I could never get over that I thought it would be awkward to stick around. Usually a name was the most I wanted to know, and I didn't want any obligation beyond that. Not a second meeting. Not a phone call. Not even a text. What did Victoria call it? Emotionally unavailable.

The door quietly clicked shut behind me, and I strolled down the stairs to the first floor. The second I left the indoor building I had to shield my eyes with a groan, since the brightness of the sun caused my head to throb, but after a few moments I got used to it, and squinting was enough to ease the pain. I had to pause at the exit and look around, my eyes scanning the area around me for the likely place Victoria would drive to. The apartment complex was two buildings set perpendicular to each other, and I'd left through an exit that put me smack dab in the middle of the two. The complex's only parking lot stretched wide in front of the two buildings, so I made my way to the edge and sat down on the curb.

A few minutes later the glimmer of a light blue car making its way through the lot made me stand, and when Victoria pulled up I jumped into the front seat. "Morning sunshine!" she beamed at me, speaking purposefully loud. My ears were ringing for seconds after she finished her greeting, and whining from the annoyance I waved her off. "Have a good night?" she asked, her tone sympathetically lower as she pulled the car away from the curb.

"Mhm." I pulled the seatbelt across my chest and buckled it with a click. "Thanks for picking me up."

"Drive-through coffee?" she suggested, to which I nodded as vigorously as my aching head would allow, letting her see my lips turn up into a wide grin. "Really, how was your night?"

"It was good," I told her, and then knowing the look I was getting, laughed at her raised eyebrow. "No, I'm not giving you any details."

"Fine," she sighed, and after a moment glanced at me carefully. "You know, you should get a girlfriend."

With that I shrugged. "What do I need a girlfriend for?"

Victoria mirrored my shrug as she took a moment to think. I could tell by the look on her face she was being careful what to say, but I also knew I didn't like this conversation. Not now, and not the other hundred times we'd had it. But patient as I was, I was going to let her say her piece. "So you didn't do this to yourself anymore."

Okay, that line was new. The sincerity in her voice actually made my heart drop. I gulped. "What do you mean?"

"You know what I mean," she said softly, timidly, as she shot me a side-glance, hoping I wouldn't be mad. I wasn't mad. I was thrown, and I'd admit it a little bit offended. I could have easily guessed she didn't entirely approve of my methods of seduction, but she'd never actually said it before. "Your parents were wrong-"

Now I waved my hands in the air, stopping her midsentence. "Please, Vic, don't practice any of your psychology stuff on me right now. I'm hung-over, I'm tired, and I'm really not in the mood to talk about my mommy and daddy issues." Even though my waving was frantic, my voice was verging on pleading.

"It's not practicing when I know what I'm talking about," she tried to jest, but I refused to give her the satisfaction of seeing the slight smirk that tugged at the corner of my mouth. "I know." She finally nodded, and out of the corner of my eye I could see her chest rise and fall in another sigh. "I just worry about you sometimes. You're so," she paused for a thoughtful breath, "Emotionally unavailable."

That phrase was grating. It hit my ears like nails on a chalkboard, and they just kept biting that chalkboard over and over again. Anger was rarely a choice emotion for me, but I came damn close. Victoria must have been able to tell, because she gave the cutest, most sheepish smile she could. "I'm sorry. I love you." Then she batted her eyes at me, just like she always did when she wanted something. "Don't kill me."

"I'm not emotionally unavailable," I grumbled, crossing my arms over my chest defensively.

I wasn't planning on giving a response other than that, since I *really* didn't want to talk about it, and luckily I didn't have to, because Victoria pulled into the coffee shop drive-through. When she got to the intercom she rolled down her window and waited for the employee's voice to come through.

"Hi, could I get two small coffees, and," she paused and looked over at me, trying to judge if I could stomach food.

"Carbs," I told her as I eyed the menu. "Lots of carbs."

She laughed and turned back toward the intercom. "And two bagels with cream cheese."

As she pulled around to the window I grabbed my wallet out of my back pocket and handed her my debit card to pay. She looked like she was going to protest, so I shoved it into her hand. "For picking me up." At that she shrugged and took the card, handed it the cashier, and then received our items. "How was *your* night?" She handed me the food and my coffee, and I took out her bagel to begin spreading cream cheese on it.

"It was fine," she answered, eyes growing increasingly hungry as she watched me prepare her food. Finally I handed it to her and she took a big bite.

"What time did you guys leave?" Now it was time to spread cream cheese on my bagel, and I scraped out every last bit possible.

Victoria gulped down what must've been half of her food as I took my first bite. "Right around the time you left with..."

"Kristen," I supplied through a full mouth, and then washed down the bite with some coffee, wincing as it scalded my tongue. "When are you going to get me some cheap hockey gear?"

"I like how the only time I can get you to come to the rink I work at is so you can get discounted stuff." She laughed when I shrugged, unable to come up with a good excuse. "How about Friday?"

A familiar apartment track came into view as Victoria rounded the corner and pulled up to the sidewalk near the closest building. When she stopped, I jumped out of the car and turned around to lean against the doorframe. "Okay, Friday. Thanks for the ride."

She nodded and waved. "See you on campus tomorrow."

I trudged to my sister's apartment, which was on the first floor of this building, and dug through my pocket for my keys. The front door opened up to the living room, which was only half-separated from the kitchen by a tall, long counter. On the left side of the main room a TV sat on an entertainment center against the wall, and a coffee table and black leather sofa rested in front of it. At the right side of the living room was the hallway that led to the bathroom and two bedrooms.

When I walked in, my twenty-six year old sister's light head of dirty-blonde hair popped up from looking at something in the kitchen, and her blue eyes locked onto me as I strolled to the dining table. "Where have you been?" she asked shortly. "You could text me if you're spending the night out so I don't worry."

"Sorry," I mumbled, plopping into a chair and sipping my still hot coffee.

"I don't care if you are twenty-one-"

"Two, Jamie," I interrupted with a chuckle. "I'm twenty-two."

She sighed like that was beside the point. Which to her, it really was. "I don't care if you're twenty-two-"

"Honey?" a deep, sleep-bogged voice filtered from the hall, interrupting her again. "Where'd you go?"

"I'm in the kitchen," she called, glancing at me as her face turned crimson.

I raised my eyebrows at her, gawking in offense. "Don't act like you missed me last night," I teased, laughing now as the shade of her cheeks darkened.

The male voice, belonging to Cameron, was more than familiar. Jamie and him had dated for three years before he finally popped the question a couple months ago. I was a little bit surprised to find he'd spent the night, since sleepovers were usually held at his apartment. That was because despite the fact that I wasn't a kid anymore, it seemed Jamie still felt the need to protect me, even from knowing that her and her fiancé did the dirty, hence the blush.

Jamie ignored my comment and looked me up and down. "Did you play hockey yesterday?" I nodded, and her mouth pursed in disgust. "Did you even shower yet?" A mischievous grin spread across my face, and shaking my head I widened my arms, preparing for a hug. "Don't even think about it," she warned, slowly starting to back away. I stood up from my seat, arms still stretched wide, and inched closer. "Jordan, don't you dare." Luckily, I was blocking the only way out of the kitchen and she was trapped. I rushed forward to wrap my arms around her and, even though she's a couple inches taller than me, picked her up and squeezed her. "Jordan!" she shrieked, desperately fighting against me and trying to wriggle out of my grasp.

"What is going on out here?" Cameron staggered out of the hall-way, short brown hair going every direction and rubbing his half-closed gray eyes. All he had on was a pair of sweatpants and socks, and he rested his bare arms on the kitchen counter, smiling when he saw the assault on Jamie. "Oh, hey, Jordan."

I grinned at him and, deciding that my sister had had enough tor-ture, released her from the hug. "You smell like sweat and booze," she grumbled angrily, straightening up and flattening out her t-shirt and pants with a disgusted look on her face, before turning her gaze on Cameron. "Babe, go put a shirt on."

He sighed and slowly pulled his arms off the counter. "I don't mind!" I told Jamie, laughing as her face once again turned red, this time because of her half-naked beau. "Cameron's my inspiration to stay in shape."

"Hey, thanks, J." He grinned his appreciation but turned back toward the bedroom anyway, flexing as he made his way down the hall. Cameron had been a swimmer in high school, but loved it so much he continued to swim every morning, which gave him his lean, muscular figure. I'd decided years ago that if I were a guy, I'd want to look like him.

When Cameron disappeared, Jamie turned her eyes back on me, waiting for me to do something. I knew she was watching me, but instead of making eye contact I glanced around the room. My gaze hit the coffee table in front of the couch, and curious, I made my way over. It was littered with pictures, ninety-five percent being of a small blond toddler, with enormous blue eyes and barely a full set of teeth, smiling happily at the camera. As I sunk into the couch I grabbed one of the pictures, running my fingers lightly over the child's face while Jamie sat down next to me.

"I'm sorry," she apologized, hand resting gently on my back. "I was going to clean up last night, but-"

"No," I stopped her and set the picture down to pick up another one. "I want to see them. Please, don't ever hide them from me." I stared at the new picture I held in my hands, fighting the sting of a tear in my eye. "His hair is getting so long."

The toddler in the pictures I only knew from photographs, usually just tiny ones in Jamie's phone. I had come out to my parents the day after I turned eighteen, and had waited so long to do it because I could have predicted their reactions. I knew they'd be disappointed, and definitely angry, but I hadn't prepared myself for being kicked out. Not even legal adulthood could have prepared me for the pain of being disowned by the only people life guarantees should always love you. Fortunately for me, Jamie had known about it for a long time, and since she was older she was already moved out, and welcomed me with open arms.

At the time I was kicked out, my mother was two months pregnant. It was hard hearing Jamie talk all the time about how round she was getting and about all the possible baby names. Just like Jamie would get to, I wanted nothing more than to see him, to watch him grow up and spoil him with toys and hugs. So when our little brother, Justin, was born, I assumed seven months of no contact had been long enough for my parents to get over the fact that I was gay. Only, I was wrong. When I'd tried to visit soon after his birth, they closed the door in my face, angrily telling me they didn't want their son anywhere near a pervert. All I'd ever seen of Justin was photographs and the occasional home video. For the last four years I'd had to watch him grow through pictures.

"He's starting preschool tomorrow." Jamie smiled, picking up another picture and studying it fondly. "He's so excited."

I laughed, having to cover my mouth with my hand as it nearly came out a sob, and quickly wiped away the tear that had forced its way out. "He doesn't even know I exist."

"Now, that's not true," Jamie said, and grinned proudly when I cast her a curious, watery-eyed look. "I make sure I mention you. Mom *hates* it when I do," she paused to wrap her arm around my shoulders and pull me into a hug, "But I want him to know about his other big sister."

I leaned into Jamie as another tear fell. "You're the best."

"When Mom cuts the chord enough to let me babysit," Jamie started, rubbing my arm and then releasing me from the hug. "I'll bring him around here so he can finally meet you."

I nodded, albeit hesitantly. We both knew the only reason our mother didn't let Jamie babysit was because she was aware I still lived with Jamie. Until she was sure that I wouldn't be around, I could be pretty sure she'd never let Jamie take him for the day. With a deep, calming breath, I set the picture back on the table and stood. That was enough emotion for me for the day. "I guess I'll go shower now."

When I finally got in, the hot water on my body and the steam that filled the bathroom worked wonders on my head, and by the time I was done showering I felt completely rejuvenated. Though physically I felt better, emotionally, I couldn't get Justin out of my head. When I stepped out of the shower and had wrapped the towel around me, I used my hand to wipe the condensation from the mirror. A full head of soaking blonde hair and dark blue eyes stared sadly back at me. *Maybe Victoria was right...* At the thought I shook my head. Even if it was true, I couldn't agree. Acknowledging it meant admitting it, and admitting it meant having to do something about it.

I was just finishing up brushing my teeth when Jamie knocked on the door. "Hey, me and Cameron are leaving for church. We'll be back later."

Church? I flung the door open, startling Jamie and causing her to jump back. "Is it Sunday?" She nodded, not even able to finish the action before I flew past her, desperately holding the towel around me so the wind of my speed wouldn't knock it off. "I was supposed to be at work at nine!"

I wasn't even paying attention to if they had left or not as I rummaged through the dresser in my room, looking for my work uniform. I pulled out my purple bookstore shirt and threw it on, frantically getting ready as fast as I could. Of all the days I could have picked to be late for work, I had to pick a day that I didn't even have a good excuse. It wasn't just that my boss loved to make an example out of me whenever I messed up, but today my mood was not solid enough to deal with getting yelled at. Again.

65334523R00224

Made in the USA
San Bernardino, CA
30 December 2017